LANDING
ON CLOUDS

'Right,' said Helen, I'm going to close my eyes, and put out my hands, and if the present isn't there before I count to ten, I shall send you away, and I won't allow you to make love to me this afternoon.'

Well, Helen was asking for it, wasn't she? Robert opened the bag, took out the bottle, and poured his blood over those expectant hands. There was a second, yes, I think it might have been as long as a second, when Robert reached a height of ecstasy entirely unknown to the majority of men, when, as they say in Latin love poetry, he reached the very stars. He had given himself over; he had put his soul in a vessel and he had given it to the woman he loved.

Olivia Fane was born in 1960. She studied Classics at Trinity Hall, Cambridge, and trained as a probation officer in Leicester. She went on to work as a psychiatric social worker with young offenders in Cambridge. She has been married twice and has three sons. She lives in Cambridge.

LANDING
ON CLOUDS

Olivia Fane

Mandarin

A Mandarin Paperback
LANDING ON CLOUDS

First published in Great Britain 1994
by Mandarin Paperbacks
an imprint of Reed Consumer Books Ltd
Michelin House, 81 Fulham Road, London SW3 6RB
and Auckland, Melbourne, Singapore and Toronto

A CIP catalogue record for this title
is available from the British Library
ISBN 0 7493 1831 7

Printed and bound in Great Britain
by Cox & Wyman Ltd, Reading, Berks

ASTOPOVO

The Countess Sophia Tolstoy Remembers Her Husband

Lyovochka, as you waited in the station-master's shack
And all those cameras hovered round your bed to watch you go
Through the brimstone smoke and clatter of the railway track,
Eager for your shrivelled body, sheathed in linen, clean as snow,
Did you feel as if your family were huddled there around you
And curse their wretched babble, distracting you so,
As you did when you retreated with your writing to the orchard
When the children caught the measles? I was with you. Did you know?

Well, sometimes on a midnight when I heard you breathing by me
In the dark, after our wedding – is it fifty years since then? –
I would stroke your back and smell your sleeping body warm beside
    me,
Agonising how to make you let me know you, let me in.
A spelk in your finger, a sickness in your head,
I crippled you year by year; locked you up with shrieking children
Till you knew that you were going mad, slammed doors, and wished
    me dead.
Thus we grew slowly grey together, side by side, in bed.

When you left me in October as the orchard leaves were burning
I knew that all was over. Though I surely did undo you,
Lyovochka, just as surely as the trees will keep on turning
The salt earth into apples, I sustained you too; and truly
As you cursed the lust and dirt in us, hungry to be chastened,
Free in your work, as you bade me then goodbye,
You severed the thick roots that for fifty years have fastened
Deep into my heart and sucked it dry.

KATRINA PORTEOUS

Heard melodies are sweet, but those unheard
Are sweeter; therefore, ye soft pipes, play on;
Not to the sensual ear, but, more endear'd,
Pipe to the spirit ditties of no tone.

John Keats *Ode on a Grecian Urn*

For Katrina

PART

1

ONE

The first time I met Robert Standing was in my bed. A row with his wife, locked doors, a cold night, an address at last with an open back door. Upstairs, there was warmth in the bed. No bright lights, no explanations. He was friendly, innocent. I trusted him. He introduced himself in the morning.

Robert's wife wouldn't take him back, and he stayed with us for three months. I knew at once that I would write about him. It seems to me now that I understand him better, even, than my own husband. It was as though there were a weight of himself pushing forward everything he told me. He made no speeches, no practised justifications. It's flattering to be the object of anything like a confession. Perhaps it made me admire him more than I should. Even when he told me about Sophia, I was aware of myself thinking, 'Here's integrity for you', as if he had an over-riding quality in him which made the things he did somehow forgivable. But when I told him that I wanted to write about his life, he said to me,

'You must meet the women. You only know half of what happened.' So it was *his* suggestion. I'd intended to write something about purity, the unfortunate consequences of a pure life, but the women I met confused me.

The pattern of a life is clear so long as there is a single description of it, but when I met the women I only saw damage, and I realised I was writing the book as much on their behalf as his, or indeed mine. Nor is it only the women I've sought out; I've managed to trace old pupils of his, teachers, schoolfriends and others under his influence; I've spent time at his family home in Oxford, where his brother gave me access to letters, diaries and photograph albums: all in the effort to be a neutral observer of a life, and all of it swaying me to one side or the other. I remember saying to him once, 'Robert, I've never met a man more true to himself than you', and he said to me, 'But is that a virtue if there's no good in me to be true to, and if I'm simply feeding the bad?'. 'You're not bad,' I said. 'I was born bad,' he said, 'haven't you read my mother's diaries? I was doomed from the start.'

Robert's mother was Russian. I have seen a photograph of her. Princess Olga Kozlovsky, direct descendant of Catherine the Great, and sixteen years old. She has a strong face, with dark serious eyes, and her lips are thick and full. She is sitting in the sun on some white steps, a colonnade behind her. The family country house; it could have been anywhere in Europe. What is always so poignant about these photographs is how very *ordinary* Russian aristocrats look amongst their wealth, innocent, easy, straightforward. You look very hard at their faces to see if you can see even a hint of some sort of foreknowledge, and there never is.

Two years later, Olga was sharing an apartment in Paris with her former governess, Mademoiselle Lafaurie. She earned money by teaching Russian to French Communists. Her parents were dead. Her natural openness, trust, optimism – also dead. She retreated into herself, or, more accurately, away from herself, passively enduring criticisms from her students, who considered her a traitor to the cause. 'Why did you desert your country?' they would ask her. 'Did you fear equality with your countrymen?' 'My parents are dead,' she would say, blindly. 'Is that a defence,' they mocked, 'You should respect the architect, Miss Kozlovsky, who clears away the rubble before he starts to build.'

Mademoiselle Lafaurie began to call herself 'Madame'. There had been a brief moment – the sixth of June 1919, while crossing the Russian–Finnish border at two in the morning – when roles had ceased to matter, when Olga's deference towards her governess was temporarily suspended in favour of solidarity. But later the solidarity turned to gratitude, and the gratitude to indebtedness, and their mutual and unstated belief that there was nothing Olga could ever do to repay that debt. So when Madame Lafaurie accused her of being spoilt, there was always more than a hint of reproach, the unspoken 'You'd be dead if it weren't for me' before the 'How can you even suggest giving up teaching? What would you do instead? Clean floors? We need the money, my dear Olga.'

After four years of this half-existence, Olga met her husband, William Standing. He was an Oxford philosophy don who had come to Paris to hear Jules Lequyer discuss his *Analyse de l'Acte Libre*, and happened to be staying in the apartment opposite. One night, in the middle of January 1925, Olga's hands were so numb with cold that she dropped her keys outside her door. Dr Standing picked them up for her. So unaccustomed was Olga to a spontaneous act of kindness, that she gave Dr Standing a look of such warmth and trust he could never forget her, and many months after his return to England Dr Standing addressed a letter to the '*jeune femme*' at 'appartement 16, 78 rue de Verneille'. Madame Lafaurie momentarily regretted being a 'Madame', considered throwing the letter away as being in bad taste, but eventually had the good grace to give it to Olga. Olga and William wrote to each other for five years; and after that time Olga decided to leave everything she knew, for the man in whom she had confided everything she was. In 1930 they were married.

And then Oxford. Olga was thrown into a life of which she simply didn't know the rules. There were huge, empty days to be filled, and William for an hour at the end of them. It occurred to her that marriages were perhaps easier where there was a slow process of the discovery of the other: of course, William would ask her how she had spent her day, whom she had seen, where she had walked; but he never referred to the hundreds of letters she had written to him or their contents. And when Olga mentioned his own letters, he would seem embarrassed and awkward, as though what he had written in his solitary passion could be discounted now that they were living real lives.

Nor did Olga make friends easily. It was not so much the language which proved a barrier (after a mere six months Olga's English was almost as good as her French), as the fact that the bulk of her experience had been so entirely different from anyone else's. Nobody ever said to her: 'Ah yes, I know *exactly* what you mean', because they never did; she offered up no handles on to which her acquaintances could hold; she presented no landmarks which were recognisable. William's friends (who once or twice a week would come back with him from the faculty and worm themselves into Olga's precious hour) admired her and thought her beautiful, but their questions to her were polite rather than curious (their curiosity having previously been satiated by asking William how she had managed to escape from Russia), and Olga answered them in the colourless tones that matched their own.

The feeling of being unknown can be as desperate as that of being unloved. William, who held the very key to Olga, rarely used it, but loved her as he might have loved a perfect essence. When she strayed from that essence he did not understand her, so she remained in a sort of capsule, in which no process was allowed to take place. She wanted a child, because she imagined she could teach that child how to love fluidly, and with his body, lying on her and feeding from her, how important bodies are to love with, she thought.

Olga looked up and saw the bodies of Charlotte and Rosemary Hoare, the sisters of a colleague of William's. And, for William's sake, she had been visiting them for a year in their drawing-room in North Oxford. In fact, thought Olga, their bodies were barely distinguishable from their furniture, spindly and stiff.

'How simply delightful that you are going to have a baby,' said Rosemary, and her shoulders hunched back.

'Yes, simply delightful,' said Charlotte, and she looked in the mirror above the cold, marble fireplace and began rearranging the pins in her greying hair.

There was a pause, and pauses are never permitted in polite circles, so Olga said, 'I can feel the baby kicking'.

The sisters looked at each other. It was now up to them to break the silence which was steadily establishing itself.

7

'And this kicking,' said Charlotte bravely, 'what does it *feel* like?'

'It feels like a very extreme sort of love,' said Olga.

'Love?' they asked together.

'Yes, love,' repeated Olga.

'But how can you love something that hasn't even been born?' asked Rosemary.

'In some ways it is easier to love someone you've never met. You create your own perfection, and you love your creation.'

'But that's not love, of course that's not love,' they said, and their bodies loosened in enthusiasm.

But Olga insisted: 'In a way it is the purest form of love. You love what you feel you need to be whole. I love this child in me now, and in a way I loved it even before it was conceived.'

'That's simply ridiculous,' the Hoares exclaimed.

'You can't argue with me,' said Olga victoriously. 'If I said I was in pain, you wouldn't argue with me. Give me, please, the credit for recognising a feeling I've felt before. I love this child. You cannot know how I feel.'

When Olga left, Rosemary said about her, 'I never realised how terribly *affected* that woman is.'

'No', said Charlotte, 'nor did I.'

Robert Standing was born in September 1933 after a long labour. The radiant Olga took him from the nurse and held him close to her breast. Then she put her hand, so lovingly, over his small, damp head. But Robert arched his back, refused to feed from her; he didn't seem able to relax, but was all taut in her arms. Already he was somebody else.

As the days went by, his separateness increased. He fidgeted. Perhaps what upset Olga most was that he didn't seem to *need* her. He looked at her with as intent a look as his unfocusing eyes could muster; or, to be more precise, he stared at her, as he stared at everything, desperate to see what sort of world he had been born into. For Robert, everything was equal, including his mother.

Even when he was no longer a baby, Robert never seemed able to engage with anything; he simply watched, and watched hard. The Hoare sisters enjoyed their observation that Olga was obviously having so little satisfaction in her 'perfection'. Rosemary said, in private: 'Poor little thing, having Olga as a mother. She simply has no *fun* in her, don't you think? Have you ever *seen* such a serious-looking three year old?'

Then Olga had another baby, David. Even in the hospital, he would lie on her, perfectly still, curled up like a pet mouse; and when William was working late, Olga used to take him into her bed and nestle up with him, a self-contained unit of love and dependence. Sometimes, when Robert came to her bedroom after a nightmare, wanting comfort, Olga used to push David away from her, as though she had been caught in an act of adultery. And revenge would always be taken. If Robert's face betrayed no love, neither did it hatred; he was cool and rigorous in his brotherly tortures. He would loom up behind David several times a day: 'Eat the shampoo,' he would command, or 'Prick your finger with this pin. I want to see it bleed.' But as far as Olga was aware, Robert never used violence, only his irresistible authority. There were times, however, when it crossed her mind that this was what murderers were like when they were young.

But it would be a mistake to give you the impression that Olga was unappreciative of her elder son, that she could find nothing in him to love. Several times in these

9

early years she refers to Robert as being 'like a child today'. 'Robert was cold in the house but like a child in the wood,' she wrote on 9 May 1939, 'he gave me a bunch of spring flowers and remembered the names of all of them. The light from a single candle can be more precious than a hundred days.'

Also I should mention that during these years of early motherhood Olga's prose style in her diaries distinctly warms up. She writes without the intensity or introspection which coloured everything during her time in Paris, or the childless years of her marriage. It was an extraordinary thing about Olga that despite the damage done to her own heart, she was able to love well. Robert taught her that love had to be unconditional, and David taught her how to express that love. Again and again Olga refers to 'the strength of a love which is difficult' and 'the importance of learning to love what is other from oneself'. A year after David's birth, she wrote, 'It is strange how the one son has given me the strength to love the other better'.

Olga's entry in her diary on the 17 September 1939, the day after Robert's sixth birthday, and shortly before David's fourth, gives us a very clear idea of the sort of mother she was:

'I notice my hand still shaking as I write this. This day should have happened many months ago. The trip was Rosemary Hoare's idea. How could I have consented? She said, "Olga, why don't we make an excursion today?" How I hate the word "excursion". There is no joy in such an ugly word. "Where do you want to go?" I asked her. "We should take a train to the country. We don't see anything like enough of our beloved Cotswolds. Darling Olga, we want to see pink in your cheeks, and not just yours, but those of your delightful sons." "Well," I said, "suggest a day." That's how I was trapped.

'The dear boys were certainly happier than I, they even cheered me. Even Robert's fidgeting endeared him to me, and when the train came into the station, all steam and noise, he came close to me and held my hand, his eyes wide and frightened. How I loved the fearless Robert for his fear. When we got into our carriage, we gave the boys the seats by the window. Perhaps the Hoares were right. When they stood up on them to get a good view, I should have told them to get down. But how happy they were, like puppies, and it was supposed to be a fun day, wasn't it?

' "Do you always let your sons jump on the seats?" said Charlotte Hoare. Of course I knew it was coming. "They're not causing anyone any harm," I said. What muse got into me today, and inspired me to fight?

' "I was on a train the other day," said Rosemary, "and there was this boy, a wild young thing, and he was leaving dusty footmarks all over the seat. I said, 'Excuse me, I don't think anyone's going to enjoy sitting there when he's done.' And do you know what, she ignored me. I thought she must have been foreign. But then, I wish you could have seen her face, the ticket collector came by, and told the mother to keep the boy under better control. Anyway, she was so humiliated, that she took her boy and went to sit in another carriage. Of course, I've noticed, *your* boys' shoes are quite clean. But you never know, there might be a rule about it."

'So I said, "Boys, perhaps you should sit down for the rest of the journey. I'm sure you'll be able to see just as well."

' "I won't," said Robert, simply.

' "Sweets," said Charlotte. "Of course, I've brought the boys some sweets."

'David is too free with his kisses. I noticed him kissing the Hoares on the platform, and now he was kissing them again. Robert said "thank you" and sat down. I was proud of him. He opened up the little tin of boiled sweets, and one by one he put them into his mouth and slowly sucked them until the last sharp edge of sugar had melted. I used to eat sweets like that. I watched David. Before he had even tasted one, he began offering them to the Hoares. "Have one," he said to each in turn, smiling generously. Then he put a sweet in his own mouth and crunched it up as fast as he could, before beginning the round again. "What a delightful boy he is," said Rosemary. "Let me give you a kiss, David." "Do you know, I've never known that boy cry," said Charlotte. "An utterly adorable boy," they might have said in unison. "Another kiss . . . another kiss . . . another kiss." These Hoares.

'I was waiting for the denouement. Within minutes David's tin was empty. I watched David watching Robert's mouth – was I cruel? I wanted him to know regret. "Could I have a sweet, Robert?" he asked.

' "Of course not," said Robert.

'I delighted in the Hoares' incredulity.

' "Robert won't give me a sweet," sobbed David.

' "Now come on, Robert," said Charlotte, assuming an air of maternal wisdom, "David's given all his sweets away to the grown-ups, and that's why he doesn't have any left. David is a very generous little boy, and I would say, wouldn't you, Rosemary, that he's well on the way to heaven."

' "Yes," said Rosemary, "David will definitely be going to heaven."

' "Now," said Charlotte, "if you want to go to heaven too, you've got to learn how to give. How many sweets do you think he ought to give David, Rosemary? Six?"

' "Yes, or perhaps eight. Just think how many he gave us."

' "All right, Robert. Take that first step to heaven. Give David eight of those sweets."

' "No," said Robert. Robert, I could have hugged you.

'Then, of course, it was my turn. They only looked at me, and I'm afraid I was weak.

' "Robert, you know you really ought to be a bit more generous." Robert did nothing.

' "Olga," said Charlotte wisely, "what that child needs is a good smack."

' "Don't smack me, Mummy," said Robert.

' "You simply mustn't let him get away with that sort of behaviour. He's got to learn right from wrong."

' "But he hasn't done anything wrong," I said. "He just hasn't done anything particularly right."

' "Olga, I must be serious with you. He has defied us. Defiance is a sin."

' "Charlotte, defiance is not so bad when one has a true belief."

' "And you're suggesting that Robert, a six-year-old boy, has, what was your little phrase, a true belief? My dear Olga, I'm afraid you have a very mistaken attitude about children. Children, Olga, and you can ask any Englishwoman, have to be taught what is true. Isn't that right, Rosemary?"

' "Absolutely right."

' "Robert," I said, and I think I said it in a way that let him know I was with him, "why don't you want to give David any sweets?"

' "David gave all his sweets away and he's going to heaven. It's sweets or heaven, isn't that right? Why should he get both?" And he said it in such a reasonable way. How I loved him for it.

' "That seems sensible enough to me," I said.

'I pretended to be looking out of the window, preferring to draw out my victory. A mere glimpse at these women's appalled faces afforded me a delicious ease.

' "Look," I said, "how pretty your English cottages are."

'They couldn't speak to me, and I thought, what a relief this silence is, what a relief to the masquerades we play. Truly, today marked the end of them.'

From what I can gather (and I have to admit that the evidence lies rather in the *omission* from Olga's diaries of contrary evidence) William was a distant father over these first years. Before Olga had children, she complained of his long absences from her, of his sad inability to confide in her, and of the paramountcy of his work. But when she understood the limits of her marriage, she stopped trying to push against them, and began counting the blessings she knew she had. William, in a gentlemanly sort of way, looked after her, and she was grateful to him. And if the whole is set in its historical context, it is not surprising that William left the supervision of his children almost exclusively to his wife. What is perhaps more surprising, is that early in 1940, when Robert was still only six years old, William decided, quite suddenly, that he should take his son in hand.

William wanted to talk about war, and war, as William had long since decided, was about fathers and sons. Women might weep in the chorus, might beat their breasts, but they stood at the back of the stage and could not know the weight of action. His older brother had died at the Somme. He remembered the day his brother enlisted, and how his father had held his hands and hugged him. He was fourteen then, and tall. He'd gone upstairs and dressed up in his brother's uniform. The waist was loose but the leather belt had kept the trousers up, and the heavy wool had made his skinny shoulders broad and like a man's. 'Well Dad, Jim, how do I look?' He stood before them, enjoying the prospect of their mock congratulations. But they'd both been angry with him. The mood had already shifted, and he'd been excluded from it. When he was upstairs again, folding the uniform and returning it to its box, he found a postage stamp on his brother's desk, signed his name on the back, and stuck it to the inside of an inside pocket. And while his mother was laying her contorted head on the kitchen table, crying over the news of her son's death, he could only think of the stamp. Perhaps it was still usable. Or was it disintegrating, even at that very moment, drenched in his brother's blood? He had signed his name, 'William Standing', and in his dreams, for a long time afterwards, he saw blood encroaching on the 'W'.

There is, of course, a feeling of wanting to set things right for one's children. The child brought up in poverty will, if he has the means to do so, be too generous to his own; the child who feels stifled in a large town will move his own family, if he can, to the country; and the child who is bored in the country will bring up his own children in a town. William Standing considered his childhood flawed in one respect: he had approached life too lightly, and his parents hadn't checked him. In June 1918 he told them he'd been selected for aircrew training. His mother cried, and his father remained impassive. He was glad to get out of the airless house and be flying at last. Even the one or two sorties he'd made had thrilled him, adrenalin and speed drowning fear. Men he knew had died, of course, but none had been close to him. He'd survived his two months of war. It had perhaps taken him another two years before fully understanding what he had been part of, two years before discovering the degree to which he missed his brother. His parents had stood by watching him, but they had said nothing. And he wanted to make sure that Robert never experienced that same pervasive guilt of weightlessness.

So, when war broke out again, William took it upon himself to teach his son about the tragedy and the inevitability of what was going on around him. He read him all the war poets, he took him to Sedgemoor and Naseby, he took him to war graves. And William fed off his son's sensitivity: there seemed to be no nuance that Robert did not immediately grasp, no reference that he did not understand. At night, Robert would wait for his father to come to his bedroom. He would kneel down next to him and say, 'Robert, dear boy, where are the soldiers tonight?' 'They're in the trenches, Daddy, and they're cold. They're too frightened to sleep, Daddy. They're thinking of their homes, and one of them is remembering being a boy.' 'What can he remember, Robert?' 'Daddy, he suddenly can't remember because the man next to him is dead.' And the boy's only seven, thought William proudly, as he said good-night.

On Robert's eighth birthday, William asked a friend of his to paint, in italic writing, a poem on the walls of Robert's bedroom. I've seen it: the present inhabitants of Roxberry House (as the Standings' house is still called, in

Melbourne Street, Oxford) can bear neither to remove it nor live with it, so they use it as a large boxroom. The ink has faded a little after fifty years, but otherwise it remains exactly as it was. There are four lines painted near the top of each wall, like a frieze:

> I know that I shall meet my fate
> Somewhere among the clouds above;
> Those that I fight I do not hate,
> Those that I guard I do not love;
>
> My country is Kiltartan Cross,
> My countrymen Kiltartan's poor,
> No likely end could bring them loss
> Or leave them happier than before.
>
> Nor law, nor duty bade me fight,
> Nor public men, nor cheering crowds,
> A lonely impulse of delight
> Drove to this tumult in the clouds;
>
> I balanced all, brought all to mind,
> The years to come seemed waste of
>   breath,
> A waste of breath the years behind
> In balance with this life, this death.

And this last verse was painted on the wall which faced Robert's bed. He didn't understand a word of it, but because his father had caused it to be there, it fulfilled his father's purpose: it took hold in him like a root.

So the war years came as a blessing: life became real and urgent. William joined the Air Transport Auxiliary, and throughout the war delivered new fighters and bombers from the factories to the Squadrons; Olga worked in a factory, which manufactured brass connectors for aircraft hydraulic systems; David went to kindergarten; and Robert began school in earnest, and he thrived. It was a small day-school – the 'Mayfield' – near his house, and his teachers had never taught a child so receptive, so imaginative, so willing. Here Robert learnt to play the violin, and at the end of his first term his music master wrote in his school report: 'I have never, in twenty years of teaching, taught a boy who played the violin as though he knew the very soul of it. It is almost uncanny: he is a child, and yet he does not play like a child.'

It may have been the fact that he didn't talk very much, but he gave off an aura of wisdom, which made pupils and teachers rather in awe of him. He had the habit of looking at the face he was talking to for far longer than is socially permissible, with the effect that people were under the impression that he could see right through them. But his eyes would rest with innocence, they did not stare, they did not penetrate, no teacher could accuse him of impertinence. It never occurred to Robert even to distinguish enemies from friends, with the result that he had neither. There was his father, and after his father came the rest: home, school and war. And these nourished him equally.

When Robert was twelve, and the peace began, there was a large surplus of aeroplanes, and William bought a Tiger Moth for one hundred pounds. At last he could teach his son to fly; 'I'll teach you to land on clouds,' he said, 'I'll teach you all I know.' And an even greater solidarity, if that were possible, arose between the two of them.

———

There was no part of Robert that remained untouched by his experience of flying: its contradictory nature exactly matched what was beginning to be his own. He liked the power of it, and the powerlessness; he liked the freedom of it, and the feeling of being at the mercy of the wind; he liked the glorious edge between mattering so much and mattering so little. At nights, especially: father and son one behind the other, the extraordinary sensation of hovering in space, flying through the clouds and then seeing them lit up by moon and stars, the cold wind on his face, the body snug in the leather cockpit, the feeling of suspension on the edge of the world, of belonging to the whole universe more than to any part of it, and then the feeling of belonging to a part of it, recognising the landmarks beneath him, the lights of Oxford, the reassuring noise of the engine, and his father's hand on his shoulder.

In the same year as he began to fly, in the same year as the peace began, Robert won a scholarship to a public school, Winston House, in Sussex.

'They lost forty boys during the war, Olga.'

'Is that a reason to choose a school?'

'They held a memorial service in their chapel last month, beautiful chapel, sixteenth century with the original pews, angels on the rafters. The headmaster told me that the congregation spilt out into the courtyard, must have been a thousand of them at least.'

'I'm sorry you missed it.'

'Olga, it's a good school.'

'Persuade me, then.'

'Olga, Prime Ministers have been to Winston. Some of our greatest diplomats have been to Winston. And there's a boy I supervise, Herring, I was talking to him only this afternoon. Charming boy, father's a brigadier in the Green Jackets. . . .

'And you're not, William. You can't send Robert there. Anyway, I've talked to him. He doesn't want to board.'

'Don't you dare talk to him behind my back.'

'William, he's not the right type.'

'What do you mean he's not the right type? For God's sake, Olga, pull yourself together. I know you weren't given much of an education yourself, but give me the credit for knowing the value of a decent one. Robert simply can't turn down an opportunity like this. Olga, look at me. I won't let him.'

How strange it was, thought Olga, when her husband spoke like this. 'It is as though a metal plate has fixed in his head, making him deaf and blind all at once,' she wrote in her diary. 'When I comply with him, he is himself again, everything is forgotten. It means I cannot resist him. Do I resist him? For years he has been so close to Robert. I used to thank God for it. They are so good for each other. And now what is he doing to him?'

Olga didn't resist him. She dutifully laid aside any further thought on the subject and concentrated her energies into making that summer of 1946 as perfect as it could be. Her diary is filled with descriptions of successful expeditions, picnics, and an account of a family holiday in North Devon. But when September came into view, when the clothes lists were inspected and the uniform bought, her diary entries change their tone, and the hanging on to the present seems more urgent.

On 25 August she wrote: 'Today I watched Robert play his violin under the cedar trees. There are two weeks left before he goes up to Winston House – two weeks left of him as he is. I find myself mentally photographing him so as to keep records of expressions which are bound to be lost. *Qu'il joue comme un ange, quelle beatitude.* I'm writing this at six in the evening. It's still warm from a hot day and Robert is sleeping on the grass. His arms are outstretched, mouth open, breathing gently. *Il est bien dans ses rêves.* Two books are open beside him. William gave them to him this afternoon – "going-to-school presents" he called them – a book of Auden's poetry and *Jane's Military Aircraft.* Robert was so happy with them. But still I can't help feeling, how much compensation will they be?'

Olga was right. Winston House was not a suitable school for Robert. That very same aura which had won him friends and admiration at his prep school, lost him friends here. They found him arrogant, far too clever, sadly lacking in the team spirit. In this alien world, Robert simply cut himself off from everything he saw. He found the boys' ignorance irritating and he had no interest in being initiated into the Winston House slang. The trouble was, that he did not *care* what the nicknames of the teachers were, so that he neither knew them nor used them. He would go off for walks by himself – even on his first day there he went off for an hour before the 'bounds' talk given by the headmaster, and found himself in trouble for going beyond a particular wood. It was the Winston House way that if a gang of them had gone they would have returned as heroes, but only one . . . From the first, then, he was an outsider.

The bullying began before the first week was out. To begin with, Robert did not even notice. He found the dead rat in his desk one morning and simply put it in the bin. An initiation rite, perhaps. He was contemptuous. A boy called Johnson, skinny and red-haired, had put the rat there: he watched the scene and swore vengeance.

Boys were for ever messing up Robert's desk, or hiding textbooks, scribbling over his prep; but again Robert barely took any notice. It didn't bother him whether his desk was tidy or not and there was no point messing up what was already messy. When his work was scribbled over, he wrote at the end of it, 'I trust this can still be read'. So the teachers knew what was going on, but there was a policy at Winston House of non-interference – boys will be boys, it was better that they sorted out their differences amongst themselves.

And then, about a fortnight after the term began, Johnson's loathing of Robert Standing lent reins to his otherwise rather paltry imagination. It was after a biology lesson. They were studying the earthworm, and Dr Rogers, the master, had distributed to each of the twenty boys two worms, taken from a large sweet jar filled with alcohol. Then Dr Rogers handed out wax-bottomed dishes, small dissecting knives and pins, and gave instructions to the boys on how to hold the worm, and slit the body wall up its mid-dorsal line. He told them to pin the sides out flat and to cut out the alimentary canal, explaining, as he did so, how the creature digested its food. Then he took them through the nervous system and the reproductive organs. 'There's no need to snigger, Johnson,' he said, 'the worm is sexless, a hermaphrodite.' But few of the boys could distinguish much. This was their first dissection. They felt squeamish. Even pretty Standing looks unhappy, thought Johnson.

At the end of the lesson, the dishes, the knives and the debris of the worms were collected into three piles. 'Who'll help me take this lot to the sluice room, then?' asked Dr Rogers, 'Johnson, you've obviously been enjoying yourself this morning. Show a little spirit, boy, up you get. Hurry up.' When Johnson began pouring the worm debris into a plastic bag provided by Dr Rogers, he thought, 'I would have volunteered anyway. This is delightful stuff. Perfect, absolutely perfect.' And when he took the bag into the sluice room, he found two syringes already in the sink. 'Too good to be true,' he thought, and he put them in his pocket. How happy he was in his journeys to and from the sluice room that morning, how happy he was when Dr Rogers dismissed the class and he felt the bag of worms under his jumper. It was now break.

Johnson immediately summoned his friends. 'Marshall, you take the second syringe. Go on, the rest of you, find him and hold him down. Here Marshall, have some worms. Take the stopper out, you fool. That's it, squash it down a bit. Let's get him then.'

They found him on a grassy bank, set aside from the courtyard where 'play' officially took place, so no masters were nearby. He was reading the book his father had given him, his one retreat from this new world, and even now Robert remembers the verses he was reading when they found him, from Auden's 'In Time of War':

Wandering lost upon the mountains of our choice,
Again and again we sigh for an ancient South,
For the warm nude ages of instinctive poise,
For the taste of joy in the innocent mouth.

They held him down hard. Johnson did the talking.
'First of all, Standing, we don't like you because your hair's far too dirty. You're at Winston now, Standing, and we have clean hair at Winston, don't we boys? So

we thought, because we're terribly considerate, that you might care to try a little worm shampoo, which we've made especially on your behalf. It's quite the rage among the lower echelons, I've heard,' and he squeezed a little of the mixture over Robert's hair, 'and perhaps a little here wouldn't go amiss,' he said, as he squeezed the stuff in diagonals across Robert's forehead. 'And have you ever heard of worm bogies? I think we'd better put a little of this in your nose, so that you know what they feel like. Marshall, this syringe is finished, give me yours.' Marshall obeyed, fascinated. 'We put a little here, in your ears,' he continued, 'and now, for the *pièce de résistance*, if you know what that means, I think you need a little worm lipstick. What lovely lips you have, Standing. I can't say that I've noticed them before, and how pleased, how very pleased I am to have the opportunity. But Standing, your lips are simply crying out for a little worm lipstick, aren't they, boys?'

Robert automatically pursed his lips. He had made no other resistance. How could he? Anyway, they were not hurting him, so he was transporting himself into another world. The taste of joy in the innocent mouth, can you taste joy? Of course you can, you taste it in the air when you fly. And suddenly there was no air: they'd blocked his nose so he had to open his mouth to breathe.

'So, you don't think you want worm lipstick, do you?' Johnson delighted in meeting resistance. 'Well, there are five of us here, and we all think how pretty you'd look with it, don't we?'

Their fingers prised open his mouth as though it were a shell, and suddenly Johnson forgot about lips, mouth was more interesting. He pushed the remaining worm mixture deep into Robert's gullet, and triumphed as Robert gagged.

The bell went. They let him go, and went back to the classroom. Robert missed that lesson. Later he apologised to the master and told him he wasn't feeling well. He spat the raw salty stuff out of his mouth, and walked towards the lake beyond the games fields. He took his clothes off and swam, naked in the water. He dived deep and took the water in his mouth, drinking it, washing in it. Then he lay on the water looking up at the sky. That was where he belonged, up there with his father. It was the only time he cried during his six years at Winston.

The bullying continued, but there's a limit to the amount one can abide reading about. Robert was tied to the bed with a bag of ice attached to his genitalia, had his head shoved down the lavatory, had the insides of his legs burned by steam from a kettle (he was tied to a chair first) and the list goes on, and if I sound flippant it's because Robert himself related these episodes so lightly, with the tone of what-more-can-you-expect-of-such-a-place and a shrug of the shoulders. 'But it wasn't all bad,' he insisted. 'One adventure I remember with particular affection.' 'Adventure?' I said, 'how can you call torture "adventure"?' 'I shall have as much pleasure in telling you as I've had in my clear memory of it,' said Robert, and this was what he told me.

'Would you say, Olivia, that it's possible to be wise and innocent at the same time? Because, when I look back, I'm quite certain I was both. I was innocent, in that for those months at least I was incorruptible, cut off from Winstonian attitudes, not even knowing those attitudes but preferring my own, and I was wise in that I understood that I was morally correct in doing so; I was, if you like, smug in my innocence. So I said on one beautiful November afternoon, "Would anyone like to go for a walk with me?" Nobody said that sort of thing at Winston, as unbelievable as that might sound. Or at least, my tone was wrong. I spoke sweetly. I knew it had come out all wrong the moment I said it, but it was only two months after my arrival there, and I still had the strength in me to enjoy the fact that my innocence was as provocative as it was appropriate. Olivia, that autumn day was radiant.

'The boys laughed, of course. "Pick us some flowers, will you, Standing?" I can hear them now. But there was one brave boy who was more innocent even than I . . . No, you can't be brave and innocent, so which was Quentin Castor? I'm afraid he was simply innocent. Anyway, he said, in a voice that matched even mine for sweetness, "Yes, I'll go for a walk with you". Suddenly the laughing stopped, and all eyes were on us. Us. The first time I had been part of an "us". He was blond, I was dark, we were both terribly pretty. And we *were* innocent, surely that adds to it, we honestly were.

'Quentin and I hadn't even heard, at that stage of our career, of one of the more celebrated Winstonian activities, "stalking". I once heard a master describe it to a prospective parent as "an ingenious version of the game 'tag' ". Ingenious, perhaps, because those who are being "stalked" are actually ignorant of the fact – it was a true bloodsport. They gave us ten minutes to get a head start, though we, of course, were utterly unaware of such generosity. In fact, those ten minutes were rather pleasant, I remember. It was warm, and we took our jumpers off. I don't think we talked much. We had never properly met before, and were feeling a bit shy.

'When I realised we were being followed, I was reluctant to mention it for a couple of minutes. Isn't that a curious thing, that there was a time when thoughts of survival came second, when the pleasure of the warmth of the sun on us was greater than any foreseeable pain. And in retrospect, of course, I was right.

' " Can you run?" I asked Quentin. But running was no good – the trees were silver birches, too tall and thin to hide behind and any bushes there were had lost their leaves. Then we heard voices. "They can't escape now," they said. And then Johnson took command, sent everyone off in different directions and we knew we were done for. "Well," I said to Quentin, "this is it. We might as well sit down now." The dear boy instinctively took my hand, as though I was his mother. He was shaking and I said, "They won't kill us, you know. Let's sit down."

'Olivia, miracles can happen without prayers, or perhaps that's just what Quentin was doing – praying. Right in front of us was a hole in the ground. We had no idea how big it was, or what we would find at the end of it, but we pushed our bodies through the earth without a thought, and emerged, after a few feet, into a badger's set. How comforting, how cool was that damp, black, mother earth. We huddled together, listening out for the boys, and we knew we were safe.

' "I tell you, I saw them."

' "Where are they, then?"

' "They can't have disappeared into thin air."

' "Where exactly did you see them?"

'All of this was music to our ears, and then one word, "Look", and the fear slipped back.

' "Look, there's a hole, they must have gone down there."

'They nearly left us in peace, after it was decided that it was humanly impossible to get down it, and then they saw the handmark. Even then, nobody felt tempted to follow us. They talked about smoking us out. That would have been fairly gruesome, but thank God none of them had any matches. They tried prodding us with sticks, but when at last they had found one long enough to reach us, I managed to get hold of the end of it and break it. Then they all tried peeing down the hole, but nothing got past the initial angle at the entrance, and they were foiled again. Then one of them, on Johnson's instructions, of course, set off back to school to get a torch. "We can at least take a look at those little love-birds," he said, and the moment he said it, it occurred to me that that's exactly what we were. We were holding hands in our hole, or at least Quentin was holding mine, and I noticed we were squeezed even more tightly together than our confined space gave us excuse for. When the light came in, we automatically separated, ah, there was the true grief. One by one an upside-down head appeared at the entrance of our hole, with a torch in front of it. Then a head actually spoke, "Come on," it said, "kiss each other," and suddenly the head was pulled out and Johnson's replaced it. "Yes, kiss, go on, kiss. If you don't, we're going to bury you alive, we'll start shoving earth down."

'As far as I was concerned, no threat was necessary. Or at the beginning, I suppose, our kisses were a little automatic, self-preserving more than selfless, conscious of an audience. But they finally left us in peace. Olivia, we took our clothes off, and lay down with our legs squeezed up the tunnel. I had my first orgasm. That, Olivia, is surely a relevant piece of information for a biography. I had my first, full-blown orgasm. Was it Quentin's first? I don't think he told me.'

They never repeated it. They never even talked about it. Perhaps if the school condoned that sort of thing, their friendship might have flourished more than it did, but Quentin was not an articulate boy, and apart from the fact that neither of them entered into mainstream school life, they had little in common.

However, there is no doubt that Quentin fell in love with him. Robert was in the year above, and seemed endlessly brilliant. When he spoke, it was as though a prophet had spoken, and he dutifully recorded Robert's infinite wisdom in a notebook. In fact I've seen it – Quentin returned the book to Robert a year ago. It's written in a rather irritating epigrammatical style. This is the sort of thing:

'*Said while eating an orange*: "If you had to locate truth in an orange, do you think it's more likely to be found in the *rind* of it, which, if you remember contains the *zest*, or the *pith*, or the *flesh*, or could it possibly be (my dear Quentin) that truth is in the *pips*?"

Elsewhere in the notebook is a long list of books that Robert had recommended. It was evidently Quentin's intention to get through the whole lot of them: there's a column for the titles, a column for the author, and finally a column headed 'comment', and where there is a comment it's invariably 'jolly interesting'. But Robert liked him, and, during these years, this was the closest to friendship that he ever came.

But whereas Quentin confided in Robert, as he might to a confessor, and bravely told him what he thought about (in the vain hope that Robert would some day remark, 'Well, that's an interesting idea', which he never did), Robert confided in no one. He respected no teacher there; indeed, he felt contempt for the majority of them. As a result, he put no energy into his work: he wrote to placate, not to please. His love of poetry, which during his first year had been his one oasis of privacy, he later began to think was so untrue to life it was absurd and a waste of time. Likewise, after the first year, he gave up playing the violin, mainly so that he could avoid the school orchestra, which was a greater torture than most.

Of course, his parents noticed the change in him. Olga had prepared herself for it, and on the whole, dealt better with it than William, who felt as though part of himself had died. He could not understand Robert's withdrawal, Robert's coldness towards things which had previously been so dear to him. But he went on giving him poetry books, hoping to win him back, only to find them later, unopened, on his desk. What saddened him most was that he had been on the verge of introducing Robert to philosophy. He felt that Robert had it in him to be an extremely able philosopher, but now, when he talked to him, there was rarely more than a flicker of responsiveness, and as the months went by it became apparent that the only interest they still had in common, or could still *talk about*, was flying. But flying, thought William, even when you fly with someone else, is an essentially solitary activity.

There was a further change in Robert over his last two years at Winston, and in some ways this was even more alarming than the first. At least Robert's detachment was a recognisable part of himself and was even lovable. But when the bullying stopped, and perhaps, in some odd way, because Robert at last began to enjoy his work and entered a little more into school life, he adopted some of the mannerisms and ways of speaking of those very people whom he had previously so condemned.

At the time Robert considered himself the stronger for the change in him. After four years of living at the edges, he was happy to be appreciated for his wit, and finally respected for his intelligence. But the sensitivity, for which his father had so loved him, seemed utterly alien to this 'Winstonian' who arrived home in the holidays. William at last recognised that the education he had willed on his son had been a disaster; and the wit of Winston House from his son's mouth grated on him.

All of this was the public Robert, the Robert who appeared to the world, and it is simply the mark of a solitary man when the world includes your parents. For William could no longer see those parts of Robert which had remained the same. But the energy one has by nature doesn't suddenly disappear, it simply goes underground, and Robert's energy, stored up for so long, was like a geyser, bubbling under the earth, waiting to send up a spring of hot water. But William, sadly, was never to see this happen.

The telegrams came on 17 December 1951. Breakfast had just been cleared away. The one addressed to Robert told him that he had won a scholarship to Trinity College, Cambridge. The one addressed to Olga told her that her husband, during a reunion weekend in Wales with others who had served in the ATA, had died in a plane crash. The weather was fine and the cause unknown.

TWO

Felicity Lipton was a doctor's daughter, a gentle, slight, pretty girl who wore flowery dresses and a scarf in her hair. It was her first term at Girton and, like Robert, she was reading Natural Sciences. In 1952, there were approximately ten male undergraduates to every female and in the Natural Sciences Department perhaps as many as thirty to a female. In addition to this extraordinary statistic, Felicity, as I have said, was pretty and there wasn't a single Natural Scientist who didn't automatically desire her. Robert, however, was simply unaware of the competition.

Varsity magazine had called him 'the most beautiful man ever to have matriculated into the University of Cambridge', and when Felicity first saw Robert at a lecture on the uses of the cloud chamber in nuclear physics, she wanted, though she might not have put it in so many words, to put her arms about his neck and touch his chin with her nose. When Robert first saw Felicity, he thought 'female', and vaguely wondered if she was pretty under her glasses.

Then, one afternoon, Robert decided he would win her. It was after a lesson in practical chemistry. There was a small queue to use the washbasin. Felicity had her hands under the tap. Robert, directly behind her, had poured some liquid detergent on to his own. In a moment of inspiration he joined Felicity under the water, taking hold of her hands and sliding his own all over them, Felicity's stomach churned.

'Hello,' he said to her, 'would you like to come flying with me?'

Felicity replied sweetly, 'But you don't even know my name.'

'I may not know your name, but I know you, and I'll know you better too, if you'll let me.'

Her stomach churned again. 'Well, I will come flying with you. I may be crazy, but I suppose you only live once. I've never been flying before, and it must feel amazing.'

'It does feel amazing. You'll see. I've already booked a Tiger Moth for Saturday afternoon, two o'clock, for an hour. Do you have any suitable clothes? Two or three pairs of trousers, lots of jumpers – it can get pretty cold up there, but we can borrow leather jackets and helmets from the aerodrome – do you have any warm gloves?'

'I'm sure I'll be able to borrow some.'

'I'm afraid we'll have to bike there – it's about three miles away – will that be all right? I could meet you at about midday at the Round Church; we could take a picnic and make a day of it. What do you think?'

'It sounds splendid, perfectly splendid.'

Dear Felicity, wondering how she could stay pretty in two pairs of trousers and two jumpers, whose main anxiety was that wouldn't she look awfully fat, who was worried because she was short-sighted and she didn't know whether she'd be able to wear her glasses under the flying goggles. What should she bring with her on the picnic? Would Robert think she was being too keen if she cooked some cheese scones? She longed to make a treacle tart. She even bought the ingredients for it, but then she just didn't dare. She blushed at the thought of him saying, 'Did you make this for me?'. In the end she brought some cheese sandwiches with her.

'I'm sorry about the cheese sandwiches,' she said, 'I would have brought something more interesting, but I ran out of time.'

'Don't worry about that,' said Robert. 'We'd feel sick if we gorged ourselves before flying. I've only brought some fruit and biscuits. Would you like a banana?'

They had stopped on a grass verge about half-way to the aerodrome. The sky was overcast. Felicity longed to walk a little way further from the road, the cars bothered her, and it would have been so easy to get out of earshot. Why didn't Robert suggest it? He barely talked or looked at her. 'He thinks I look frumpy in these stupid clothes,' she thought. She sighed and felt awkward, she didn't know what to talk to him about. He was so beautiful. Why was she so gauche? This was all her fault, the picnic going so badly. She wasn't interesting enough, she had nothing to offer him, she felt awful.

Then, quite suddenly, Robert leaned over towards her and took off her glasses: 'I've always wanted to see you without those,' he said. Then he kissed her forehead lightly and told her she was beautiful. But, and this is the extraordinary thing, he then put the glasses on the grass beside him and immediately resumed looking into space, as if kissing this poor girl and telling her she was beautiful had been a mere aside, while for Felicity, of course, the real-life event of what had been going on in her imagination for days left her weak.

But when the beat of her heart was beginning to return to normal, there were other preoccupations, the main one being, should she or should she not put her glasses back on? Had Robert had his fill of looking at her? Or, if she left them off for a while longer, might he kiss her again? She looked at him to try and gauge by his expression what his intentions were, but couldn't see his face clearly enough, so, reluctantly, she put her glasses back on.

Her stomach hit a new low. He wasn't thinking about her at all. She ached to be let into his private world, or more, to have a place there. She suddenly felt unbearably hot in all those clothes. She couldn't think why she hadn't simply brought the extra jumpers in a bag with her. Neither of them even tasted the cheese sandwiches. They got on their bikes and went on their way.

Robert hadn't flown for more than a year. This was his first time at the Cambridge aerodrome. He felt disorientated. While he was wandering between the hangars, uncertain where he was heading, Felicity hung on his tail, feeling nervous and bulky and plain, and hating herself. Then the headquarters were found, the proper officials approached, pilot's licence shown, everything in order, and they were suddenly there on the runway, beside the little silver Tiger Moth, which seemed to poor Felicity more like a fragile model than something which could actually take off. 'It looks so old-fashioned,' she said. 'Doesn't it have a roof on it?'

'You don't need a roof. What do you want a roof for? You look warm enough.'

And when Felicity suddenly looked even warmer, he saw that he hadn't been treating her well and wanted to begin again. He kissed her on the cheek and told her that he was an expert pilot and she needn't worry, she'd be safe in his hands. He asked her whether the leather jacket wasn't a little big for her, and told her yes, of course she could keep her glasses on under the goggles. Then he settled her into the seat in front, and said that it was a strange thing about Tiger Moths, the pilot sat in the back. He told her not to touch anything, because there was dual control, but if she wanted to say something, this was the intercom. Above all, he said, enjoy it, give yourself to the sky, there was no feeling like it.

Felicity peered over the leather bumper in front of her. A man began turning the propeller. He saw her and smiled at her. Suddenly she was extraordinarily happy, and everything was going for her. The man shouted something, Robert turned on the ignition, the man gave another hard push of the propeller and stood back. It worked: the propeller spun round of its own volition, and now they were gaining speed down the runway. Suddenly Felicity felt herself being carried up into the air, two, three, four hundred feet, she was flying. The whole world took on a new depth, as though she had only ever known it in two dimensions. She saw a flock of wild geese – never had she seen anything quite so magical. She saw them land, white in the black earth, and felt she was being lifted up to heaven.

Robert's eyes were blurred. He couldn't see properly. He didn't know where he was, he recognised nothing. He kept looking out for a yellow sea of barley, but there was none there; he remembered hills and trees full with life, but there were none there; he remembered villages in the valleys – but where were they? Where was he? Who for God's sake lived in this barren landscape?

What sort of people were they who thought of this as home?

He kept the plane climbing, higher, higher they went, till they broke into the cloud above them, and for a few moments they were lost in a turbulent fog. 'Don't worry,' said Robert, on the intercom, 'we'll be through this in a minute.' They were; Felicity now knew what ecstasy was: the sun, hidden for so long, was now brilliant; the clouds beneath her looked as though you could drop into them, that they would somehow soothe you and look after you for ever – was this what heaven was like, in fact?

Robert took a glove off and felt the nape of Felicity's neck in front of him, burying his fingers deep below the leather and the wool. 'Are you there?' he said on the intercom. 'Yes, of course,' said the intercom back to him. 'Then I'll tell you something. Did you know that you can land on clouds? The conditions have to be absolutely right, of course, the clouds have to be exactly as they are.'

'Are you sure that's right?' asked Felicity.

'Of course I'm sure. The conditions couldn't be more perfect. Surely you can see the energy in those clouds below us and we're weightless up here. We have no weight at all, to speak of.'

'I had no idea,' said Felicity.

'We'll try it, shall we? I'll show you today, and next time we come out you can have a go.'

Felicity might have been on her father's lap, for the trust she had in him.

'What we do is this, we put the throttle back, like so, then the flaps down – do you see how we're losing height? God, it's lovely up here, isn't it? Now, I'm aiming for that cloud over there, do you see the one I mean? The one that looks rather like a conch. Trim the tail back, it's so easy. You know, don't you, that I'm going to teach you how to fly? Right, we're coming into land . . . now.'

Robert, teaching her how to fly, Felicity's last happy thought. They hovered momentarily on top of the cloud, then Robert switched off the ignition. The silence of it, and then, whoosh. One wing dropped, down the plane fell, spinning dizzily through the clouds. Seconds like hours came and went. Smothered, disorientated, and then out again into the air, the world seen from a bird's eye, three hundred and sixty degrees round, and the solid ground getting closer.

Death, it's the first thing you think of. They both thought of it; they thought they were going to die. Robert felt tired and happy, as though he'd spent the day walking in the snow numb with cold, and now at last he could see the lights of a warm house. All he had to do was knock.

'God help me.' A little voice on the intercom. He remembered that the voice had a warm neck, and he switched on the ignition. Expert he was: he righted the plane, a mere two hundred feet above the ground, and soared up again into the sky. He flew fast under the clouds, feeling the energy flood in as it always used to. Then, after a few minutes, when the adrenalin subsided, he brought the plane in to land.

Felicity was holding her head in her hands. She did not move. Robert lifted her out of the plane. He tenderly removed her helmet and goggles and those wretched glasses, but she did not even look at him. Her face was yellow, waxed with fear. He laid her down on the grass and began talking to her.

'You might think you're dead, but you're not,' and he stroked her sticky hair. But she said nothing, and it was as though she registered nothing. Then he hugged her hard, and went on, 'I'll find the life in you, don't you worry, I know where it is'. He hugged her and laid his head on her chest.

'Don't you worry,' he said, 'I'll get it back for you.' Then he shook her. Then he hugged her again. For the first time since his father's death he cried.

Four officials from the aerodrome surrounded them. 'What the hell were you playing at?' said one of them.

'Is she all right?' said another. 'Are you a mental case or what?'

'You understand, young man, that you won't be flying here again.'

'You should go and see someone, mate. I think you'd better get out of here.'

Robert carried Felicity all the way back to Cambridge. He was not anxious about her: if anything, he felt that he had saved the girl's life rather than almost taken it. He rested once, at the picnic spot, lay on the grass with Felicity beside him and he looked up at the grey sky. He thought about what lay on the other side of those clouds, that brilliant light, those same clouds, menacing on this side, cushioning on the other. Landing on clouds. No, you couldn't do it.

He walked on. Felicity's body was still limp, but her mind was stirring. She found herself wanting to say, 'You can't possibly carry me all the way back to Girton. I'm much too heavy. And what about the bikes?' There was nothing more momentous in her mind than that, but she couldn't say it. It was as though two parts of her brain had disengaged themselves; her words were in the back of her head and she couldn't move them to the front of it. So she stayed silent, and tried to express herself with her eyes, but even *they* didn't seem to be able to function properly; she felt herself trying to put life into them, trying to show that she was aware of what was happening, but the muscles in her face did not respond to what she was feeling, and she could only look, knowing that her look was dead.

But Robert saw only life, and rejoiced in it. He looked down at her, so still in his arms. Her fair hair was matted; her face yellow and shiny. And he wondered at his ability to love so much.

He carried her all the way to Girton. The heavier she became, the happier he was; when his arms ached, the pleasure of remembering the cause was a hundred times greater than any physical discomfort. Then he carried her upstairs to her bedroom and laid her down on the bed, next to a teddy bear in a hand-knitted jumper. He took off her shoes and went to the washbasin to get her a glass of water.

'I love you,' he said to her, 'you have taught me how to love. Now drink this, my dearest.'

Felicity stared at him uncomprehendingly. Again the words stayed at the back of her head. She took the glass and held it, but she didn't drink. Her mouth was dry, but she couldn't get herself into a position in which she could drink without the water dribbling down her. After a few minutes she gave the glass back to him and then lay down with her eyes closed. Within seconds she was fast asleep.

She slept until dawn, and Robert moved the teddy on to a chair and lay next to her. Sometimes he would lay his head on her chest to hear her heart; sometimes he would hold his hand an inch or so above her mouth so that he could feel her warm breath. When she woke up and looked at him, he felt joy at the memory of her having eyes that could actually see him, and ears that could hear him. 'I love you, my dearest,' he said.

But the ears that heard him were numb. And the words at the back of her head were jumbled.

Robert drew up two chairs to the bedroom window. The curtains had stayed open all night, and he took her by the hand and led her to the armchair, propping her up with pillows. Then together they watched the sunrise. For Robert, what he saw had meaning for him only so far as Felicity was seeing it too; but Felicity barely noticed what she saw. She told Robert, without so much as looking at him, and with her eyes focused on the glass in front of her, that she wanted to be left alone. She said she wanted to have a bath, clean herself up, change her clothes. Robert couldn't understand at all, when the two of them, in his eyes, had practically become one. His desperation gave way to anger and contempt at her lack of feeling – the sunrise was supremely beautiful that morning, glowing with expectancy and benevolence – and she . . . what was it that she wanted to do? Change her clothes? Put on a little lipstick perhaps, pretend that nothing had ever happened between them? Who was this *other*? Nobody that he knew, for sure. What a vain, shallow woman she was, even detestable.

'I'll go,' he said.

They saw each other in lectures, of course. They even smiled at each other, from time to time, but the smile was polite: there was no body behind it; it hid, rather than revealed. Meanwhile, Felicity found herself endlessly courted by many tens of scientists, and even married one a few years later. But it has to be said, and she herself has confided this to me, that her experience with Robert Standing was the most significant of her life, and that the

41

Felicity before and the Felicity after were qualitatively different.

I went to visit her in her three-storey house in Islington. Her four grown-up children have left home. Her husband is now a consultant rheumatologist. The house feels empty and tidy. When I mentioned Robert Standing to her she laughed.

'Do you ever think of him?' I asked her.

'Not now,' she said, and then she paused. 'Well, occasionally perhaps.'

'Then why do you laugh?'

'Let me show you something,' she said.

She opened a drawer in her desk and took out a key. She was calm and efficient. Then she unlocked another. It was crammed with typescript.

'Six novels,' she said, 'or six versions of the same one.'

'Can I have a look?' I said.

'By all means. I have to apologise for them. You see, they were all written while the children were still young, all within about twelve years of the incident.'

'Have you shown them to anyone?'

'No,' said Felicity.

'Did you have a title?' I asked her.

'Oh, yes, I always knew the title. It was ready-made: *Landing on Clouds*.'

'I like it,' I said. And then I read out the first line: ' "To be rejected by someone you love is like stalling in mid-air." That's sad. I hope the endings are happier.'

'Sometimes they are,' she said. She walked over to the window and drew the outline of a child's smiling face on the glass. But when she turned round, the rims of her eyes were red.

* * *

On 30 November 1952, Olga received her first communication from Robert: a postcard of Trinity. 'My college,' wrote Robert on the back of it. And then, 'You'll be pleased to know I've been flying. I hope you're well, and the garden is healthy. Love to David, if you see him.' Olga was so happy that she even went to church. The postcard was so *normal*, Robert must be so *well*. So she wrote back immediately and told Robert she was coming up to visit him.

Robert met his mother off the train. 'You shouldn't have bothered to come,' he said. 'I know,' thought Olga when she saw his face, 'I know.'

It was an icy December morning, and they walked from the station. Olga's shoes kept slipping on the pavement, and Robert kept saying, 'Are you all right, are you all right?' but he offered her no arm. 'I'm afraid Cambridge is awfully cold at this time of year. You really should have waited till the summer to visit.'

'I wanted to see you, Robert, and you wrote me such a nice card.'

'I suppose you'd like to see my rooms while you're here. I'm afraid they're not much to look at. They're in the corner of the building, and frankly, they're a bit dark. Here we are. Whewell's Court. Trinity proper is over there.'

'I'd love to have a quick look,' said Olga.

'I'll wait for you,' said Robert, and Olga crossed the road and put her head round the Trinity gates.

'You certainly chose a very beautiful college. What a shame they didn't give you a room in that lovely court.'

'The first years get rooms here. Come on, I'll show you.'

Robert had warned Olga that they would be dark, but why didn't he bother to turn on the light when they went in?

The day and the room vied in their lack of hospitality. No attempt had been made to make it comfortable; there were no pictures on the walls, the tatty leather armchairs had no cushions, there were barely any books on the shelves, just a few science textbooks – why hadn't he brought any of his poetry with him? There were no pictures of his family, no hint of any past, no hint, even, of any person living there.

'Would you like some tea?' said Robert.

'That would be very nice, dear.'

'I can't remember how you have it.'

'Milk, no sugar.'

'The gyp room's on another floor. I won't be long.'

Olga sat in the leather armchair and looked into the ugly, empty fireplace. Was this what Robert looked into, night after night? What went on in his head, sitting here?

Robert, meanwhile, was looking for matches. The box by the gas-ring had run out. If he felt anything at all, it was a sort of boredom. He didn't want to go downstairs to talk to his mother. The only thing they'd ever had in common was dead, and how he loathed pleasantries.

He came down ten minutes later with no tea. 'I'm sorry,' he said, 'I couldn't find any matches.'

'Well, let's go out to tea.' said Olga, 'It's so gloomy here. It's a shame you got a room facing north.'

'Well, I'm sorry you don't like it. I suppose it isn't anything special. Let's go to the Whim, then. The true centre of university life, if that's what you're looking for. How's my little brother liking the army, then?'

'I think he's quite enjoying it. But he's thinking of joining the RAF.'

'Another flier, hey, good luck to him. I've given it up.'

'But you said in your card . . .'

'Why did I ever send you that card?'

They drank their tea. Neither tasted the teacakes. 'How are you enjoying Natural Sciences, then? Isn't it rather dull, all facts and figures? I never did understand why you didn't do English. You always seemed just the type to read English Literature.'

'Books are for children, mother. Books are for children, to warn them of the ghastliness of getting any older. And books, I suppose, are for the very old, so they rejoice in the fact that they're nearly dead. But who in the world could bear to read a book when he's in the prime of life? When he's actually in the thick of it? Who could prefer reading to living? Perhaps a dull man living a vacuous life. Which is worse, do you think, vacuity or tragedy?'

'I read', said Olga, 'so that I find out about how other people live. And those lives don't have to be either vacuous or tragic.'

'Give me an account of a life that is neither.'

'I was reading a book only the other day, now, what was it called, and the hero inherited a factory from his father . . .'

'Ah, so he was a socialist.'

'Well guessed,' said Olga, forcing a laugh.

'He discovers the factory was badly run and decides to change it. And a sub-plot might be that he begins to lose faith in the father that he had loved and respected while he lived.'

'You should be a novelist.'

'It's a tragedy, mother. A person is built out of his own past. If he discovers that the past is false, he loses part of himself.'

'Here, at last, Robert, you're wrong. The hero leaves his past behind, and is the stronger for it.'

———

'No one is stronger for leaving one's past behind.'

'Well, in this book, now what was it called . . .?'

'For God's sake, you're talking about fiction. Don't you know any real people?'

'Of course I know real people. But in fiction there is a far broader range . . . and they give us understanding . . .'

'I suppose there might be a broader ranger in your case. How is old Mrs Pringle and her cabbages? Still growing them, is she?'

'Mrs Pringle died about four months ago.'

'Oh, another one gone. Well, then, Mr Percy, how's he? Arthritis any better? See that, mother, I remembered he had arthritis. You did go on about it so. But on a merrier note, how are his cucumbers? Or do you think I'm being snobbish? Perhaps we should talk about Dr Hunt's new book. See, mother, I listen when you talk to me, though often I wish you wouldn't. Was he pleased with the reviews? They thought it was good, I see. He should be feeling pretty smug, wouldn't you think? How am I doing? Not bad, am I? I understand that Mr Percy is a happy man because of his cucumbers. I understand that Dr Hunt is a happy man because of his reviews. Don't you think I have understanding now, mother? And I haven't read a book for five years.'

'I hate you when you're like this.'

'I wouldn't be surprised if you hate me all the time. What sort of a son have I been to you? I would say I was fairly unmotherable.'

'Of course I love you, but I can't talk to you when you're like this.'

'When I'm "like this"? How can I persuade you that you're seeing your son as he really is?'

'Oh darling Robert, please.'

The waitress began to hover around the table waiting to be paid. Olga put four shillings on the table and they left the Whim for the open air. They both felt too sad to speak any more. Olga took a taxi to the station. Robert went straight back to his rooms.

At the end of this day, 10 December, 1952, Olga wrote the only Russian entry in her diary: *Moi syn ne tronyl menya*. My son did not touch me.

THREE

Robert was happiest when he had power, and the area where he found he had categorical power was women. He knew that, whatever he wanted, he could simply pluck it and it would be his. The objects of his desire were normally slight: the way a bow was tied in some hair, the angle of a nose, a fleck in the eye, shoulders of an exact breadth and deportment: any of these were enough for him to wish for possession.

Robert saw himself as the gatherer of the beautiful. 'There is beauty in everyone,' he would say diplomatically, but when he had extracted the beauty, the remainder, to his eyes, was pulp, and held no meaning for him. Nor did these pulped women ever blame Robert. They simply acknowledged that the beauty of Robert's soul had found the squalor and mundanity in their own, so why should he continue to have time for them? So they went on their way, uncomplainingly, hating themselves, and continuing to love Robert with their remaindered hearts.

But there was a girl in her final year who did not conform to the view of women which Robert held. The girl who broke the rule was Helen Wakehurst, for however hard Robert tried, he could not separate her from her nose, or her shoulders, or the thick black hair that hung on them. He wanted every sublime part of her.

It was at the beginning of the summer term, and Robert was in the Reading Room of the University Library. He was working on nuclear reactions in the sun. As he turned to page 300, he found a little note tucked inside. It read: 'I don't know your name, but you're more beautiful than the Monteverdi *Vespers*. I've always wanted to kiss somebody before speaking to them. Could I kiss you now? I'm sitting near the main door, on the left as you come towards it. I'm reading *Wagner, the Man and his Work*.'

Robert knew her immediately. She looked up at him with eyes impervious to modesty and got up from her chair. Without so much as a gesture, she walked through the Reading Room door, on through the Catalogue Room, left towards the North Wing, and up three flights of stairs. She was like Orpheus with his lute, but she did not look round. She took him to a hidden dead end of the stacks, and once she was there, once she was three quarters surrounded by books, she turned round to face him and held his cheeks in her hands. Then she felt his lips with her finger and her eyes smiled at him. Robert gave himself to his fate: he held her head back and began kissing her, and his only desire was that it should never stop, and his only regret was that it would. In fact, it went on for about half an hour.

There is something about kissing somebody you do not know, when you have never heard their voice, when you do not know their values and their virtues, because the recipient represents, for the duration of the kiss, the sum of all their sex. There is no anxiety, because you are not kissing a person, who might think this or that of you, you are kissing an idea, and where the woman happens to be beautiful as well, an ideal. The kiss isolated is therefore the kiss perfected. This was what Robert was thinking of as he kissed her.

Still they had not said a word. When the kiss was over, Helen flung back her thick black hair and barely looked at him. Then she walked on, through the stacks, down the stairs again, never looking behind her, Robert on her tail. In the entrance hall of the library she said to him, 'So what's your name?'.

'Robert Standing.'

'College?'

'Trinity.'

'Well, I may come and visit you one day,' she said 'You never know.'

Three days later she did. It was 9.30 p.m. Robert was working. He had barely slept or eaten or read a word since the kiss; he was trying to catch up. There was not even a knock at the door. She came in behind him and put her hands on his shoulders, at the precise moment Robert was imagining her breathing on his neck. Robert stood up and immediately attempted to kiss her, but she said 'no' and sat down in an armchair. 'It's cold,' she said. 'Could you put your gas-fire on?' So he lit his gas-fire, and the blue glow filled the room. 'Turn off your reading light,' she said. He turned it off and waited for the next command. 'Right,' she said, 'I'm going to take my clothes off, but you mustn't touch me, you mustn't lay a finger on me: if you do, I'm going to leave.'

Then, standing by the gas-fire, luxuriating in the warmth of it, she unzipped her dress and let it fall to her ankles. Then she stepped out of it, and finally, quite straightforwardly, without a hint of provocation, and with as little self-consciousness as though she had been completely alone and about to get into a bath, she took off her plain white pants and let him look at her, naked, in front of the blue fire.

Every other woman that Robert had made love to, of whom, at this stage of his life, there may have been about six, had offered up her body to him as though it were a sacrifice and as though it were nothing more than a clumsy appendage of the soul, with the result that her heart was there, but her body absent. The trouble was that Robert didn't very much want their hearts and they were giving him more than he bargained for. There was no heart here, thank God, no excess baggage at all. Every part of her firm flesh was moulded to perfection and he hungered for it.

She came up to him, knelt down at his feet and began undoing the buttons of his shirt. Then she dug two of her fingers into the base of his neck, running them firmly down in a line towards his stomach. It was unbearable. She knew it was. His mind and strength were lost, and he held her head and tried to kiss her. She immediately got up, the triumphant goddess, and swung her hair back in victory. Her dress zipped back up, and gone: Eurydice.

Robert tortured himself for three days. He couldn't work, he didn't sleep, he thought he would never see her again. He thought he had lost her for good. He went to the library, but she wasn't there; he went to Girton, to Newnham, he did not even know who to ask for. But the vision of her body never left him.

Then, on the third afternoon, she came into his room. 'What are you doing mooning around inside on such a lovely afternoon? Come for a walk.'

'They went for a walk. Conversation seemed to be totally out of place. Robert did not know where to begin. Did she realise that he didn't know her name? Wouldn't she be appalled if he asked her? So he didn't. Three miles out of Cambridge and barely a word had passed between them. 'Look. A proper wood,' said Helen. 'God knows how anyone lives in this part of the world. It's so ugly, don't you think? I hate places without hills, don't you?'

Robert longed for something clever or witty to say, but nothing came. He felt too full to choose anything in particular, so he said, 'Yes, I do'.

Then she said to him, 'Do you know what I've always found particularly erotic? I've always liked the idea of all those courtiers of Henry VIII taking a lady-in-waiting into a wood, hitching up her dress, and doing her, just like that. No messing about, no excuses, no pants, no barriers. Just, enter here.'

Then, when they had walked a little further, and a little nearer the wood, she said to him, 'You know, I'm not wearing any pants under this dress. Do you like this dress, by the way? I like them when they're full like this, and I like them tight around my bosoms and my waist. It's restricted here, it's restricted here, but then it's free. Come into the wood now, come and do me, just like that.'

He took her into the wood, and lifted up her dress. Waist down, at least, was all his. At last he could take his time to feel and kiss her sublime legs, he thought, and began running his fingers between her thighs. 'Come on, Henry,' she said suddenly, 'remember who you are. Enter here. That was the condition.' And so, uncomplainingly, he did.

When they were walking back to Cambridge, she said to him, 'My name's Helen Wakehurst, and I'm at Newnham. I read music. Tell me about you. What do I know so far? Robert Standing. Trinity. G6. It's Natural Sciences, isn't it? You don't *look* like a scientist, thank goodness. Why did you do it?'

'I don't know,' said Robert. 'Perhaps it's because it attempts to make what is complicated clear, rather than the other way round. Science tries to tell us what actually *is*, not beguile us with appearances.'

'You're not an intellectual, are you? Oh dear, I feel certain that you are.'

'Oh no, I'm honestly not at all, I promise you.'

'Thank God for that. There are simply too many of those around Cambridge.'

For the next five minutes there was a pause. Robert tried to think of something amusing to say, which would prove once and for all that he wasn't the slightest bit intellectual. But he couldn't.

'What sort of meals do you get in Newnham?' he asked.

'For God's sake,' she said, looking at him hard, 'what I want to know is whether you enjoyed having me in the wood?'

'Oh yes, that's real. Making love to you, Helen, that's the bones of reality. What a purity you have about you.'

'Goodness, you're the first man to think I have a purity about me.'

'Well, what I mean is that there is no fluff about you, you look at me directly, you don't try to hide anything, you are completely yourself, which is more than you could say for any other person on this goddam earth. It's very odd – I feel I know you completely. I feel I've been searching for you, and now I've found you – it's pathetic, isn't it.

I loathe sentimentality, but I've been feeling ludicrously sentimental. I've been listening to the hit parade, can you imagine, I've even been doing that. I was hanging round Girton yesterday, and there was a window open. The radio was on. It was playing "Love, don't eat my heart out" – I can't remember who was singing it – it was a bad song, of course it was bad, but I can't get it out of my head. It just seemed exactly true. But why did you do all that for *me*, Helen?'

'Because you wear such baggy shirts and I feel like untucking them for you, and because you are extraordinarily beautiful.'

Robert's cheeks burned with pleasure. 'What did you say you were reading?'

'Music.'

'Music. I didn't know you could do music here. I used to live by music when I was a boy. I played the violin. I can't remember exactly why I gave it up.'

'Well, you should take it up again. I play the violin. And the piano. I could teach you if you like.'

'Of course you must teach me.'

They were half-way back to Cambridge. The idea of Helen teaching him the violin removed any urge in him for conversation. When she felt his fingers on the strings, would she stand behind him and encircle him? Would she congratulate him when she saw how well he played? Here at last was a way he could show her the feeling he had in him. Now she would know what he was like, really like. There was no point in telling her, in words, when he could make her feel it by playing to her. So for the rest of the walk each returned to their private worlds: Helen was congratulating herself on her three-pronged seduction, and the fact that the great Robert Standing was now hers (in addition to which, she'd won a pound from a friend for the dare); Robert was thinking of music, and how he couldn't understand how he had neglected what had once been his lifeblood for so long.

Robert left Helen at the gates of Newnham. He was happy to say goodbye to her, even eager to return to his privacy, so that he could let his imagination run, and relish the pleasures in store for him. After he was back in his rooms, he immediately wrote a short note to his mother asking her to look out his old violin for him: he thought he'd take it up again, and he'd be coming up on the Saturday to pick it up. Then he walked back and forth from his bedroom to his sitting-room. He'd lie on the bed, writhing in a five-minute ecstasy, and then he'd be up again, looking out of the window, or again, in the sitting-room, at his desk, looking towards the gas-fire, and then he turned the fire on, not because it was cold, but so he'd be able to remember more exactly what happened that night. Then he changed into the shirt he was wearing when she unbuttoned his buttons, and smelt it all over, because it hadn't been washed since, and he was sure that he could smell his own desire in it; and then he lay on the floor beside the gas-fire, and felt the warmth of it; he closed his eyes and thought, as feelings go, this must surely be the best.

When he had had his fill of his imagination, Robert got up, put on a blazer ('Ablaze in a blazer' he laughed) and went out to post his letter. It was nine o'clock, almost dark, but there was beauty in the 'almost', and he walked for a while on the Backs, watching the purple in the water becoming ever deeper, the great shadows of the colleges behind him, and he rejoiced in civilisation, in order, in the cosmos, in the beauty of movement from A to B, in process, in design, in perfection. There was an end in this life, and he thought that he had found it. He felt that he was himself, as he really was, and that he wanted to give all of himself to this woman Helen. He wanted to feel enveloped in her shroud of truth and loveliness, and feel protected by her from everything which was polite and banal and untrue.

You have to remember that at this stage it never crossed Robert's mind whether Helen loved him in return; apart from the business with Felicity, which now seemed to Robert no more than an aberration, he was used to female love. What had always concerned him was whether his exacting standards could be met; he had never considered himself on the receiving end of other people's requirements. He was always the subject of affairs, never the object of them. Therefore, when Helen didn't visit him for a few days after the walk to the wood, he simply thought that she was waiting for him to visit her, and he'd do that the moment he had his violin.

When Robert went home to Oxford that Saturday, everything he saw was more beautiful than he'd ever remembered it: the fields were full with spring, luxurious with new growth, and promising even more. As he sat on the bus, trying to recognise the flowers on the verges before they had sped past his window – the cowslips, the oxslips, the violets and wood anemones, the lady's slippers, the early campions – he thought, there must surely be a God to oversee all this, and he said to the old lady at his side, 'God has given us so much. How can we thank Him?' and when the lady patted him on the knee and smiled with pleasure, he suddenly felt that he loved her too, and he loved everything and everyone.

When the bus arrived in Oxford, and one by one the passengers cautiously negotiated the steps to arrive gingerly on to terra firma, he jumped straight off it, with one joyful leap, and in fact he looked quite ridiculous, but his mother didn't think so, and when she saw him she felt a surge of happiness run through her, because her dear son had thawed at last.

They hugged, perhaps the first maternal hug since Robert was twelve; then they talked, about easy things, like the differences between Oxford and Cambridge, and gardening. When they were home, Robert admired Olga's flowers, and asked her whether she'd ever thought of growing vegetables, and did she remember how they used to plant radishes and carrots together? And how he used to pull them out of the ground before they were fully grown, because he couldn't bear not to know what they looked like under the ground? They had lunch in the garden, sitting on the grass, and they talked about David, and how he'd decided not to join the RAF after all, because he was doing so well in his regiment; and they talked about the neighbours, and about Olga's voluntary work. Then after lunch, while Olga was in the kitchen clearing up and making coffee, Robert lay under the cedar tree, and thought what a marvellous mechanism branches were, a place where beauty and function strode arm in arm. He looked up through the leaves to see if he could find the topmost branch, and then tried to imagine what he would see if he were looking down from the sky, and when he had found the tree, in his mind's eye, he began to look for himself lying underneath it, but the branches were too thick.

Olga came out with the coffee, and sat down on the grass beside him.

'Did you manage to find my violin,' asked Robert, without getting up.

'Well, I found it, yes,' replied Olga, 'but you know, it's the wrong size, it's child-size, three quarters, or whatever you call it. But I've got good news for you, while I was looking for yours, I found your father's.'

'What am I supposed to say to that?'

Olga continued, nervously now, trying to ignore the change in tone.

'It looks a really nice one, really old – aren't they supposed to be old? I've no idea. Do you know, I never heard him play – I often asked him to, but he said he'd forgotten how, and he couldn't bear the thought of making a hideous noise – you remember what he was like. But he did tell me once that he'd played in an orchestra when he was an undergraduate here, so he can't have been that bad.'

'I'm afraid he was, mother. I heard him once when I was about eight. I was terrified he was going to suggest we played together.'

'Surely you could have forgiven your own father for not playing as well as you. I'm sure you weren't *that* precocious.'

'Music's never been particularly important to you, has it mother?'

'Robert, I'd have thought you would have liked to own something that was your father's.'

Robert went on lying under the tree and said nothing. Olga said she was feeling cold and went inside to find a cardigan. She didn't put it on, but sat shivering in an armchair with it on her knee. Had she been tactless? Could she have predicted that reaction? It wasn't that she hadn't thought about it. Don't they say it *helps* to own something that used to belong to a person you loved?

Robert, it never helped me either. I'm surrounded by his stuff, and it's never been a comfort. I should have known. I blame myself.

Robert went on looking at the sky, and watched the clouds build up. 'If I were there now,' he thought, 'I wouldn't even see this tree, let alone myself.' So he closed his eyes, and imagined that he was flying at night; hearing the noise of the engine, feeling the cold on his face, watching the light of the moon on the clouds moving fast beneath him, and suddenly he is hearing his father shouting at him, down the old-fashioned Gosport tube, 'One day, Robert, we'll land on those clouds down there.' An involuntary 'no' comes out of his mouth.

He got up, and went into the house. On his way upstairs, Olga called after him, 'I'm sorry if you had a wasted journey.'

'No, no, it wasn't wasted.'

'Are you staying the night?'

'No, no, no. I was never going to stay the night.'

Robert went on up to his bedroom and shut the door. He tried to recognise the person who had lived there and looked for clues. There was a picture of a boy praying on a mountainside. No, he thought. A drawing of some Indians in a cave, with painted, staring faces. Nothing to do with me, he thought. He sat down at the desk in there – surely it was too small even for a boy – and he remembered when it was first put in his room, a surprise to find after school. He looked in the drawers – old exam papers, letters, his father's handwriting – 'I thought you'd like these' his father had written, and he frantically began searching for something it might have referred to, but he found nothing. He gave up, and banged the drawers of the desk shut with his knee.

He lay down on his bed, wanting to sleep, but when he looked up he saw the inevitable poem on the wall above him:

> I balanced all, brought all to mind,
> The years to come seemed waste of breath,
> A waste of breath the years behind
> In balance with this life, this death.

'Father, how could you do that to a seven year old, for Christ's sake? How could you be so wrong, and yet make him believe it? Life is a gift; it isn't a compulsory sentence. It's a gift because I can give it back, I can choose to die; but I've chosen *life*, and I must use it, and fill it, and find out how to live it well. It's like a film, a biography. I can walk out at any time, but I'll miss the shape of it, and the reason for it. And it's the most extraordinary kind of film, because I'm a participant in it, with lines to say, and I can choose those lines, and what I say and do affects what happens in it. Father, it's even better than a film, because it's real, and the people I touch have warm blood in them, just like mine. I have this over you, father: I can go out in the streets with a pin, anywhere in the world, and prick the arm of any person I meet, and there'll be blood in them. I am part of a great, bloody whole.'

Olga knocked and came in. 'Tea?' she asked. 'Would you like some tea before you go back?'

Robert started and sat upright on the bed 'Yes, that would be brilliant,' and he smiled at her. 'I'm sorry I got in such a bad mood,' he said. 'Of course I'll take the violin with me. It was just a surprise, I suppose. But you're absolutely right to have thought of it. Thank you, mother.'

There was tea, the fetching and the admiring of the violin, the kisses goodbye, the journey back to Cambridge. It was raining now, thunder, four hours in the bus, but Robert's optimism was only tempered, not cauterised; and he was thinking of Helen as the darkness fell, not his father.

When he was back in his rooms, he noticed them for the first time. 'God, these rooms are sterile,' he thought. 'Think how mány feelings must have been felt in this room, and not a trace of them left.' Then he tried to work out whether more of the previous occupants of the room were still living, or whether more of them were dead. Probably dead, he decided. And each of those dead undergraduates had probably thought, 'What an excellent thing it is to live', but they were dead anyway. 'Well I'm not,' he thought, 'I'm not,' and he took the violin out of its case and longed for his future.

At this particular stage in the affair, Robert felt under no compulsion to visit Helen: simply the idea of her was enough to sustain him. It was almost as though he was preparing to meet his maker: he was getting the violin tuned, he was even catching up with his work, in which he'd fallen badly behind. He felt calm, clear, intelligent. He visited the Sidgwick Museum in Downing Street to look at the fossils and the dinosaurs. He saw an exhibition of Dutch landscape painting at the Fitzwilliam. He felt, quite simply, on top of things, as though there were a muscle running through his life.

Two weeks had passed since the day in the wood. Helen

couldn't understand it. She had been expecting visits by the hour. She had boasted to her friends that the matter was sewn up: he was badly in love with her. 'What men want', she had said to them, 'is to be kept waiting. It's ridiculous, such a small thing, such large results. Pathetic, really.' But then he didn't turn up. Why the hell not?

Then one day, on 3 May, he did. Helen was working for her finals. She was marginally anxious she would fail them outright. So she was working. He knocked, and came into her room. Helen was surprised at how pleased she was to see him, and said that she had missed him and why hadn't he come before. 'Ah, well, I've been getting my violin fixed, remember? I want lessons from you.'

'Well, of course you must have lessons,' she said, and immediately untucked the back of his shirt and spread her hands over his silky back, 'I'll give you any lessons you like.' Robert kissed her, and they cleared the bed of revision notes and lay down on it together. But Robert had not come for sex. He simply wished to renew his idea of Helen, and be reacquainted with his own desire. And when his body was fully awake with it, he left her. Helen sat on the edge of her bed and swore at the empty room. She wanted Robert to come back, and hated the feeling of wanting him. 'This won't happen again,' she determined.

Robert practised hard for his first violin lesson. He found he had forgotten nothing; if anything, he played better than he did as a child. The instrument, he found, was an extension of himself, his own gut akin to the gut of the strings. He practised passages from the Monteverdi *Vespers* (remembering the note Helen had left him in the library) and when he felt that he had perfected them, he left a message in her pigeon hole: 'Come and teach me what you know.' Helen came, ready for the game, ready for a further seduction, ready to show him where to put his fingers; but she wasn't ready for what she heard. How could she ever have thought she was central to this man's life? For a moment, she loathed her own arrogance and felt trivial. Then she felt deceived and was petulant. Then again, she lost herself in the music. For he could play a hundred times better than she could. She could teach him nothing; she was surplus.

Every chord he played was for Helen; in every phrase could be heard, 'Here I am, have me', and when he had finished the piece he kissed her and told her that he loved her, that he was all hers, that she could do what she liked with him and that he had never loved like this before. If he played well, it was she who had been his inspiration, who had taught him everything that he needed to know.

For Helen, the speech came as a relief, because there was no doubt it was sincere, and she felt much more comfortable being the beloved (as she was accustomed to being) than anything else more demanding, and which might even have begun to distract her from her work (and she was determined to pass those finals). And she was further relieved when she had made the mental decision never to play with him. So Helen resumed her authority and said, 'You play beautifully. You know you do. I couldn't possibly teach you anything, and you know that too. But please don't love me so much. I promise you that I'm not worth it. You make me feel trivial by playing like you do.'

'Darling Helen, you are the least trivial person alive. You are my idol, and you put everything in perspective for me. I feel I see everything so clearly now, I feel I understand everything. It's like an arrival, a recognition that I've arrived.'

'Robert, I don't deserve any of this. I think you're an amazing man. I've never heard anyone play like you in my life. But I've got to be on my way, I'm afraid. These finals are looming up and I'm getting behind with my revision.'

'But you can't go now. I'm going to tell you about my father.'

'I'm really sorry, Robert. I'll hear about your father another day. I've got to be strict with myself on this.'

'But I wanted to take you out to supper.'

'Look, I'm sorry, but supper's going to have to be after the exams. They're only three weeks away, you know. Haven't you got any?'

'But surely this is important.'

'Well, at the moment I have to say that the most important thing on my mind are these blessed exams. I want some sort of job in music, you see, and there's a lot of competition.'

'But all you have to do is pick up your violin and play. Who could turn you down? You could have any job you wanted. You could be in any orchestra you chose. Within weeks you'd be playing solos for them.'

'Well, I can't take that chance, I'm afraid. Look, I've got to be going. I'll be seeing you though. Take care.'

The next day Robert went to visit her. She was working. He said, 'Why did you leave so soon yesterday?'

My God, did Robert understand nothing? 'Finals,' she said impatiently. 'Don't you have exams?'

'I do, but what's an exam? What's an exam, for God's sake? Irrelevant, completely irrelevant.'

'They are not irrelevant.'

'So you want me to go?'

'Yes. No. I don't know. Look, I like you Robert, and I love having sex with you. But I've got to work; you don't seem to understand. Listen, why don't you go now, and come back after lunch? In fact, come to think of it, we could well do this on a regular basis. "Regular basis" sounds a bit clinical, but I know myself after lunch. I'm sleepy, I can't work and I'm bored. So why don't you come then, every afternoon? You could come, we could have sex, and then you could just, well, leave again. The whole thing shouldn't take more than about twenty minutes. That should be all right. But I want no chat, I don't want to know anything except about composers, right? In fact, it might even help me to work. What do you think?'

All Robert could think of was how beautiful she was when she swung her hair back like that. She could ask for anything and he would give it to her. What was she asking for? He barely heard her.

'I don't understand,' he said.

'I want you to come and have sex with me in the afternoons,' said Helen.

'Is that what you want, Helen? Oh, Helen, of course. When, when shall I come?'

'What's the time now? Nine thirty. God, you were keen. Lucky I was up. Come back about half past one. Look, is this all right? I'm sorry to sound so clinical about it, but it's the only way I can fit you in, and I like you, honestly I do.'

The arrangement went smoothly for a week. At half past one every afternoon, Robert went to Newnham, upstairs, down the shiny grey corridor, and into Helen's bedroom, F16. Then he locked the door behind him and kissed her, unbuttoning her shirt as he did so; Helen simultaneously taking off her pants, beautifully naked on the bed; Robert, urgently undressing, at last, inside her again, the *raison d'être* of the previous twenty-four hours, his daily visit to the Sublime.

But by the end of that first week, the twenty-three hours and forty minute gap between visits was becoming intolerable. A minute of this waiting seemed more like ten thousand years. In fact, it seemed to Robert that the moment the waiting began all over again, namely at ten to two every afternoon, was the same moment that life began to emerge six hundred million years ago, and he himself would have to complete the cycle of evolution before he could visit Helen again as Modern Man. What happened was that he spent till about 8 p.m., or in other words, a hundred and seventy million years, as a pre-mollusc, vulnerable to everything, a spineless sponge; then he spent the night as a gastropod (a further hundred and seventy million years), the most important part of the gastropod being the stomach; at dawn, however, he emerged victorious as Tyrannosaurus Rex, the most noble of dinosaurs, sinking, alas, twenty-eight million years later into that evil-looking fish, the manta ray. By nine in the morning he was more himself, a black-headed gull, and had made further progress by midday, as a great Arabian oryx. Finally, forty-three million years later, he was a primate walking down the shiny corridor of Newnham; he was Homo Erectus turning the door handle; and finally, he fell into his lover's arms as Man, Robert Standing himself, recognisable once more, right on cue.

It has to be said that Helen didn't notice that anything odd was happening to Robert; of course, she knew that he was in love with her, this was all par for the course, but her sympathies did not extend beyond the twenty-minute allotment, and by ten to two her mind and body belonged to dead composers, and Robert might as well have been, well, a spineless sponge. Whenever Robert tried to tell her anything, or begin some paean to her, she would say to him, 'No, I'm sorry, this is not the time for all of that, I don't want to know – remember our agreement?', and so Robert's entire being became concentrated into an ever more dangerous essence. There was no place into which it could flow, and there was simply no possibility, if the situation remained as it was, of there being any dilution of it. Something was going to have to give.

One week after this arrangement began, he went, at two in the afternoon, to the University Library. He had to pull himself together. He had to put her out of his mind, because she was eating it away. So he tried to work. He opened a book on Newton's Law of Gravitation. He read:

According to Newton's law, every particle of matter in the Universe attracts every other particle with a force which is proportional to the mass of each particle concerned and inversely proportional to the square of their distance apart. In symbols the law may be written:

$$F = \frac{Gm_1m_2}{d^2}$$

where F is the force of attraction between the particles, m_1 and m_2 are their masses, and d is their distance apart.

Oh God, is this true? What hope is there? Is it inevitable? But then he thought he hadn't understood it properly, and he read it again. He decided he didn't understand it at all. He got up and went to South Front 4, where all the science books were. Perhaps he should look up some exam papers. But then he started picking out the books one by one, *The Mechanics of Particles and Rigid Bodies*, *Electron Diffraction*, *The Theory of Metals*, *Diffusion*. He opened them at random pages and spread them out on the table. Diffusion in Liquids: 'The diffusion or wandering of the molecules or ions of a solute in a solution from a region of high concentration to one of low concentration is a process resembling the conduction of heat in a metal from a point of high temperature to one of low temperature.' How perfectly precise. Then again, in another book: 'The subject of mechanics is motion and the causes of motion. Sometimes we are concerned with motion alone, and sometimes with the causes alone. The cause of motion is force.'

'Force, yes, force,' he said out loud. 'That's it.' But a minute later he couldn't decide why he had thought, 'that's it'; it suddenly became incomprehensible again; what had he been thinking about that it could have made sense to him? But then it occurred to him that he knew it all already, and he ought to find something he didn't know. So more books came out of the shelves, more books spread out on tables, until all the empty tables were full of them, and a few people who had come there to work looked at him curiously, and thought that perhaps he was just having a bad time. But nobody said anything to him, they just left him to it, wandering from table to table, snatching sentences here and there, gases, vectors, rigid bodies.

. All of a sudden he felt incredibly tired. He remembered that he had barely slept for about ten days – how many hours was that? Two hundred and forty. 'I think I must go to sleep', he said out loud. There was a snigger somewhere, and he felt embarrassed and awake again and he left the room quickly, leaving all the books on the tables, hoping that it all seemed normal enough and that they'd all be put away somehow.

He walked down the main corridor of the Library, and he tried to look purposeful, as though he knew where he was going. Then something, God knows what, made him say to a librarian he met, in an efficient and scholarly voice, 'Could you remind me where the English poetry section is, please?'

'Let me see,' said the librarian 'North Wing 5, I believe. Yes, North Wing 5.'

Wasn't that the place where he had first kissed her? Why hadn't he realised that the love of twenty generations had been squeezed into the space that surrounded them? Helen must have realised that for sure, but he hadn't known what was happening to him. She had taken him there. She knew.

As he walked on down the corridor and up the stairs, walking, the self-control of it, assuming an air of normality, even of boredom and world-weariness, pretending he was an undergraduate like the rest of them, with exams ahead, he knew that he was on the right track, that this was the section of the library in which truth lay, where the answers were. He felt a gush of clarity come into his head, and when he was there, when he was three quarters surrounded by books, he ran his fingers across the spines of them, and occasionally he would pause, when it was a book he knew, as though he was somehow receiving the energy from inside it. Then he arrived at the *Collected Poems of Isaac Rosenberg*; he hadn't read them. But when he was sixteen his father had given him a copy and told him that if he wanted to know what was what,

Rosenberg could tell him. But he hadn't even bothered to open it then. Now he did.

It is odd how lovers believe in fate. If they meet, or don't meet, it is fate. When one discovers that the birthplace of the other is within ten miles of one's own, it is fate. If the birthsigns are the same, if they've read the same books, if they both happened to be living in Namibia when they were two, all these are signs that they were destined for each other. When Robert took the *Collected Poems of Isaac Rosenberg* from the shelf, the book fell open on page 63. Fate, *in perfecto*.

He read:

> I am the blood
> Streaming the veins of sweet-
>   ness; sharp and sweet,
> Beauty has pricked the live
>   veins of my soul
> And sucked all being in.

Suddenly Robert knew the causes of the universe, knew the nature of being, and *he knew where the soul was*. Oh God, how could he have been blind to it for so long? It was obvious, there was no alternative, everyone in history knew the answer, the whole Bible was about it, *the soul is in the blood*. Of course, everything slotted into place.

Jesus Christ was giving his soul at the last supper. That's why Jews have to bleed their animals before eating them, that's what kosher meat is, it's meat without the soul in, it's meat without the blood in. And Jews are right. And Jehovah's Witnesses too, weren't they the people who didn't believe in blood transfusions? Of course, it was

70

obvious. And if he wanted to give his soul to Helen, he had to give her his blood.

He felt he was Einstein. Perhaps this was how Einstein felt after he had discovered his theory of relativity. This is what it feels like when you arrive at Truth. And he read the Truth again, so that every word was ingrained in him; and then he left the Library and went to Jarrolds to buy six large sheets of blotting paper, and he went to Eaden Lilley next door and he bought himself some needles, and he took the neatly packed parcels back to his rooms.

Then he opened up the roll of blotting paper, and laid out the sheets one by one on his desk, two rows of three. He was hungry to get at the needles, to rip open the packet and stick them in his fingers. He longed to feel the pain of it. Now he was going to give her part of himself. The first jab through the tough skin of his index finger, tough first, but then sliding in, sharp and sweet, and the red oozing out of him. Blood, brilliant red, the common element in all of us, something which is yours to give, something private and common. On each of the six sheets he wrote a line of the poem with his finger-pen, and whenever the blood of a particular prick dried up, he felt a surge of adrenalin at the prospect of jabbing himself again, and each fresh jab was delivered with a greater sense of urgency, as if he wanted to make sure that the message got through.

When his work was complete, he was calm. He thought he'd even managed to made it look like his hand-writing, despite having pricked the fingers of his left hand. How odd it was that his right hand had been so insistent on doing the jabbing. He went up to the gyp room and made himself a cup of tea. There was an undergraduate already there, and he said to him: 'Hello. How's the revision going? When do your exams begin? Frightful business, all of this, isn't it? Any hot water left in that kettle?' and the undergraduate said, 'Yes, here, have some. No, the revisions's not going too well. How are you doing?' 'A bit erratic, at the moment. Never mind. We'll see how things go. Thanks for the water. Good luck.'

Back in his room he drank his tea and found some old biscuits. He thought he'd go to Hall that night and make sure he had a good supper. But he didn't go, because he fell fast asleep in the chair, and he didn't dream, and he slept until dawn.

It was about four thirty in the morning. He turned his chair towards the window and watched the light come. His body felt tired but his mind was still clear. He knew that he wouldn't be turned away today. When she saw him, just as he was, when she recognised the power in him, and how much he could give to her, would she just say, 'No, not today'? So he felt a quiet confidence as he went over to the table to look at his red manuscript.

But blood is disappointing: it does not stay red. When Robert saw what he had written, it was suddenly as soulless as if it had been written in brown ink. He did not hesitate. Destruction requires an empty mind and a singular purpose, and he had both. He tore up the blotting paper into tiny pieces, then put them into his empty fireplace and went upstairs in search of matches, but he couldn't find them, he was in too much of a hurry to look, and he ran down the stairs again and back into his room. He tore each of the tiny pieces in half again, carefully and methodically, and then he put them into a paper bag, and went out for a walk.

He was going to put them in the Cam. What cannot be destroyed by fire can be destroyed by water. But then blood is thicker than water, and can something destroy something else which is more substantial than itself? Because surely the water would know it was blood, even if it was brown, the water could tell. Water was the great sifter and could tell true from false. Water was the great judge, and he didn't dare to throw the paper into it.

It was 7.30 in the morning. He thought he would have breakfast in Hall, he needed a good breakfast. So he sat, his bag tucked close beside him, in the great dining-hall of Trinity, and he chatted to the young men sitting near him, one of whom was the president of the May Ball, so they all talked about dancing. In fact, it was quite an animated conversation for breakfast time, and Robert made them laugh, and when he left them they said to each other: 'Well, at least someone seems to be relaxed round here,' and someone said, 'It's all right for him, he'll get a first standing on his head.'

Then at 8.30 a.m. he realised that God was speaking to him. God came in the shape of a large red cross, painted on a lorry which was parked outside the Guildhall in the market square. A hand-made poster was stuck on to it: 'Give blood. One hundred donors, please, today, 8 a.m.-6 p.m. First Floor, Guildhall.'

Could any other donor on that day, 15 May 1953, have run up those stairs so fast? No air of normality now: if anyone had seen him, he might have held him back, suspicious of his motives. And how would Robert have explained himself? 'Enthusiasm. Literally. The Greek. En . . . thu . . . siasm. God is in me.' Because as he ran up the stairs, he thought God was in him, and he said to himself: 'Now that he definitely exists, I must think about my life again, as soon as this is all over.'

But the receptionist, a Mr Pinker, about fifty years old and a perfect combination of efficiency and goodwill, brought him back down to earth. 'Hello, please have a chair,' he said brightly. 'Thank you for coming. Have you been a donor before?'

'No, I haven't,' said Robert.

'We're always happy to welcome new donors,' said Mr Pinker, 'and we would like to know, for our records, what exactly persuaded you to come this morning?'

'Though I say so myself,' replied Robert modestly, 'it was God. Jesus gave his blood, didn't he, and he set quite an example. And he gave his blood because he loved us, he did it for love.'

'You're right, young man,' said Mr Pinker, 'and that's a very fine way of looking at it.'

'It's the only way, sir,' said Robert, radiantly.

Mr Pinker smiled at him but decided not to pursue it. 'If I could just take down a few details, then,' he said. 'Your name?'

'Robert Standing.'

'Age?'

'Nineteen.'

'Are you an undergraduate, by any chance?'

'Yes, I am.'

'Ah, yes, I thought you might be,' and Mr Pinker smiled broadly at him, as though clearing his mind of a niggling doubt. 'Well, it's a straightforward business, Mr Standing, nothing to worry about. You'll give your blood just behind that screen there, and then you'll wait in the room next door, just for fifteen minutes or so, and you'll be given a cup of tea. Does that seem all right to you?'

'That seems fine.'

'Mr Standing, thank you in advance for your time. I'll take you to the bleeding room.'

So Mr Pinker introduced Robert to the plump, rosy nurse behind the screen, and told her it was his first time, and that he was an undergraduate at the university. They both looked benevolently at him, 'It's a good habit to get into', said the nurse, 'this giving blood. Not enough young people do, it seems to me. Now, let's have a look at that arm of yours. Thank you, lovely, he's certainly keen, isn't he, Mr Pinker? We could do with more of your sort. Yes, look at that vein there, that's just the ticket, no problem at all.' Mr Pinker beamed with good humour. 'Well, Mr Standing, I'll be leaving you in Nurse Goodison's capable hands. Good luck.' And he went back to sit behind the desk on the other side of the screen.

Nurse Goodison took Robert to a couch, and told him to lie down, then she carefully rolled up his sleeve and attached a sphygmomanometer to his arm. 'Well, love,'she said, 'and what made you decide you wanted to give blood? Cor, there's a blush. Did your girlfriend tell you to come along? That's what usually happens, you know. The girl says, "Well, what about saving some lives, then?" and off he goes.' As she examined the sharpness of the needle, and attached it to the syringe, she went on, 'What you're doing now might be thought of as, well, an act of heroism, if you like. And do you think men would bother becoming heroes if it wasn't to impress their women? I used to work in the London Blood Transfusion Service, you know, and we used to hand out medals there. Every ten times you gave blood you got a medal. That's how it should be, I think. You deserve medals, you do.'

Then Nurse Goodison swabbed the inside of his arm with spirit, and an equally plump, rosy doctor came through with more smiles, more thanks, as though it really was an act of heroism. 'Robert Standing,' said the nurse. 'It's his first time.'

'So, Robert,' said the doctor, 'and how can I encourage you to make a habit of this? Now, let's have a look at your arm. Look at that vein, nurse, perfect, not too near the surface, not too invisible. You were obviously made to give blood, Robert. Raise the pressure to 80mms, nurse.'

'Yes, doctor,' said Nurse Goodison.

'Needle, please.'

'Here, Doctor.'

'Thanks.'

And the needle went in. The luxury of it. That fierce jabbing at his fingers seemed petty, hysterical. This was deep. This needle had entered the wall of a vein, a pathway of his blood, it was genuinely inside him. Robert wanted to watch his blood leave him, but the tube was rubber, so he had to be satisfied with watching it drop into a glass bottle, the size of a pint, and watching the red fill up, his red, his blood, stuff which came from inside *him*.

Then, when the bottle was full, the doctor took the needle from his arm, and Nurse Goodison put a generous swab of cotton wool on the puncture, and said, in a bright voice, 'Now then, bend your arm, right up, that's right'; and the doctor said, 'Well, that was painless enough, wasn't it? I hope we'll be seeing you again, and try and get a few of your friends to come along, we don't see enough of you undergraduates. Persuade them, won't you?'

'I'll certainly try,' said Robert.

'Then I'll be going. Take good care of him, won't you, nurse?'

'Of course I'll take care of him,' she said.

While Nurse Goodison was removing the rubber tubing from the bottle, and sticking labels on to everything, Robert asked her, 'Nurse, what happens if I change my mind?'

'Change your mind, love? Change your mind about what?'

'Change my mind about giving the blood. I mean, I don't know where it's going to or anything. I mean, is it still mine, at this moment, or is it yours? I mean, according to you, have I already given it?'

'Well, I must say, no one's ever asked me that before. But come to think of it, I think I know what you're getting at. When I was working in London, and I suppose that's a while back now, but when I was working there,' (and her eyes brightened as she remembered), 'all the blood we used in transfusions was fresh. When there was an accident, we'd simply call up a donor, and he'd be over in a jiffy. He'd give his blood, and oh yes, he'd know exactly where it was going to, exactly whose life he was saving. Most likely he'd even meet him. There, that was a good system. What I'd call personal. It's not surprising we were able to get more donors in those days. I mean, what happens now, you might ask. Where's all this blood going, you might ask. Well, I'll tell you. It's going to be stored up in fridges in some blood bank somewhere, and it just doesn't seem right.'

'Nurse, how clever you are, and there was I simply unable to express myself. You see, nurse, you're right, I just don't like the idea of my blood going to some anonymous bank, just being given a label and stored up in some bottle crate. I want to give it in person,' said Robert, enthusiastically.

'But how can you give it in person, when there hasn't been an accident?'

'Perhaps I could take it straight to Addenbrookes Hospital on the off-chance that there's been an accident. I mean, there are always accidents, all the time, and in fact, that's why I thought I would give blood in the first place, I actually wanted to *give* it, and if I'd known it was going to be stored up in some fridge somewhere, well, the truth is, I wouldn't have gone through with it.'

Robert looked at the poor nurse with as much earnestness as he could muster, and the truth was that the nurse, who was nearing sixty, was as taken in by him as if she had been nearing sixteen.

'Well, I understand you and I don't understand you. What would I tell the team if I simply let you walk out of here carrying that bottle of blood?'

'The truth is, dear nurse, it is you who have helped me to see reason. I have to admit, I was anxious when I came here. I wasn't sure what I was letting myself in for. But you, nurse, have helped me understand my fears, and I'm grateful to you.'

'But I can't let you do it. I mean, what would I say?'

'How would you like to have *your* blood put in a fridge somewhere? I can see, nurse, that you're a sensitive woman. It wouldn't be an easy matter for you either.'

'Mr Standing, I really must draw a line. It's only blood, after all.'

Robert suddenly understood the course he had to take. He leapt off the couch and theatrically picked up the bottle of his blood. 'Dear Nurse Goodison,' he began, 'this is not just blood, like you say, this is *from inside me*, and I am sorry, I am terribly sorry, for all the trouble I've caused you, and you've all been terribly good to me, and I think you're wonderful, nurse; in fact, you're as good as a nurse could be, but you have to understand that the sacrifice was infinitely greater than I had anticipated and I simply cannot bear the idea of this bottle of my blood ending up in a fridge.'

On being told that she was wonderful, and by a man such as Robert, Nurse Goodison's heart made its first leap in thirty years. The cogs of her spiritual anatomy creaked into motion, and Robert, sensing progress, kissed her cheek and repeated the praise; then he picked up his blood, hid it under his jumper, almost ran through the reception area, shouted goodbye to the astonished Mr Pinker, a further goodbye to the glimpse of the astonished Nurse Goodison, and went down those stairs, two at a time, out into the street, out into the open air. Then he walked as far as Parker's Piece, and finally, at half past nine in the morning, lay down somewhere in the middle of it, with the glass bottle of his blood safely in his hands, resting on his chest, close to his heart. He felt he had caught his own genie and it satisfied him for a long time.

When at last he went back to his rooms, there were only two hours to go. Then it occurred to him that Helen might not understand immediately what he was offering to her, so to make it clear he wrote out the Poem 'I am the blood' on an envelope, and stuck it with sellotape to the bottle. Then he practised giving it to her, he practised little speeches of devotion. He pretended that his room was Helen's, and he practised entering it. He said to her: 'Helen, from the moment I met you I have loved you, and I have wanted to give you everything I own. But what are physical objects compared to the soul? Or, to put it another way, doesn't it seem to you that when a lover gives his mistress presents, he is somehow trying to give her representations of himself? Now, Helen, I have

more than a representation of myself to give to you . . .'
Was that too philosophical? Shouldn't it be more loving
than that? Then Robert tried again, and he went out of
his door, and he came in again, and this second time it
seemed to him that Helen was standing right in front of
him, and he felt sick with love for her. 'Helen,' he said,
'darling Helen, you have no idea of the effect you've had
on me, you don't know how awful this last year's been,
since the death of my father, because I never told you
that, did I, I never told you that my father died in a plane
crash, the Christmas before last, but you saved me, you
saved me, my darling Helen, you made me see that life
was worth living, you don't know how much good you've
done, I'm sure you've never realised it, but I want you
to know now. So, Helen, take this now, take this part
of me, which isn't a part, but is the whole of me . . .'
Did that seem a bit melodramatic? Yes, it probably was.
Yes, he must put a check on the melodrama. I mean, he
felt melodramatic, that wasn't surprising, considering the
circumstances.

A quarter to one. His stomach was imploding, a true
gastropod state. He couldn't decide whether time was
passing intolerably quickly or intolerably slowly. Perhaps
if he walked to Newnham at one mile an hour he would
get there exactly on the dot of 1.30. One thirty. The magic
1.30, nearly, nearly there. He quickly worked it out. Yes,
he could set off now.

It is extraordinarily difficult to walk at one mile an
hour, particularly if you are in a hurry. Whether he tried
small, faster footsteps, or larger, slower ones, the feat was
an impossibility. So he tried window shopping. He even
went so far as to try on a pair of trousers in Ryder and
Amies, but his terror at leaving his blood unguarded in

the changing room while he had a look at himself in the mirror was too great, so he told the assistant they didn't fit, and quickly slithered out of the shop. Then he had a brainwave. A cup of coffee. So he went into a café opposite King's and sat down. But it was lunchtime, and the waiter looked contemptuously at him and told him that either he had to have the full lunch or sorry but he had to go. So he said, straight off, 'Then I'll have the full lunch', but every knot in his stomach told him that he would be sick if he ate anything; 'Well, no, perhaps I'd better be going,' and he left, humiliated, as if he'd been caught out.

It was now nearly ten past one. Things were looking up. He decided that he could now walk at a reasonably normal pace. He carried the blood in his hand, camouflaged in brown paper so as not to look too odd, and even felt quite merry. He crossed the bridge in Silver Street, and noticed that the sun, which had been dithering all day, had at last decided to come out in full, and he felt the warmth of it on the crown of his head and his shoulders. It felt like a pat on the back, and he was all optimism. He wasn't thinking what he would say to her any more. He trusted that the words would come out, and that she would understand him.

He arrived. Newnham. One thirty. But what a different man he was from the one who had come here only twenty-four hours previously. How sane, how generous he felt now. He ran up the stairs like an enthusiastic boyfriend, like an ordinary person who was in love. How brilliant it was to be ordinary. He was aware of the spring in his step, and it wasn't controlled, and it wasn't wild, but it felt wholesome, without complications.

It is true there was a pause before the door. It is true that his stomach had the last word. Then he walked in, ready for her. Helen. Oh my God where was she? There was a chasm opening under him, but seconds before total engulfment he found a note on her desk. It read: 'I'm in the bath, but don't let that put you off. Go on down the corridor and it's the third door on your right. I'm in the middle one. Just knock and I'll let you in.'

On down the corridor he went, the blood still in its brown package, his hand wrapped tightly round it. He found the bathroom door; he knocked.

'Hello. Is that you, Robert? Perfectly on time as usual. What a man. Just a sec, I'm just stretching over to unlock the door. There, come in.' And she slid down the back of the bath to resume the luxury of it; and said to Robert, as he came in, 'Lock the door behind you, will you? And please sit down, don't mind the clothes. So what have you been doing since I saw you last? Any revision?'

'Well, yes, I have done a bit of revision, actually. I was in the Library yesterday, at any rate.'

'At last you're beginning to take it seriously, then.'

'Yes, I suppose I am.'

Robert had no clue what words were coming out of his mouth; he could have been talking Latin, for all he knew. He was transfixed by the sight of Helen lying outstretched in the bath, her perfect body in its white surround; beauty encapsulated, three inches below the surface of the water. Desire made him deaf.

'Well, are you going to tell me or not? Robert, are you there?'

'I'm sorry, I didn't hear you, what was that?'

'I asked you, what's in that mysterious brown package you've got clutched to your breast like that?'

'Ah, it's a present,' said Robert, 'it's a present for you.'

'I thought as much, dear Robert. For future reference, you've got it absolutely right, presents are definitely a way to my heart. So, are you going to give it to me?'

'Well, it might seem a little odd at first. I think I probably ought to explain the meaning of it before I give it to you,' said Robert, trying to remember the speeches he'd been practising, but unable to think of anything at all.

'The meaning of it? Goodness, does it have a meaning? My dear Robert, what a philosopher you are. Let me tell you, this will be the first present I have ever received that has any meaning in it whatsoever. You shall win me, you know, hand over fist.' And the lovely Helen smiled at him, and looked more radiant in the steam of her bath than he had ever known her, and his love for her, at that moment, was unbearable.

'You are miles away,' said Helen. 'Come back. I insist that you give me my present.'

'Oh Helen,' said Robert, 'every minute of the day I've been longing to give this to you, you don't know how much.'

'You're so melodramatic, Robert. Honestly.'

Melodramatic, thought Robert, no, I must not be melodramatic. 'Well, Helen, I'll give it to you.' But then there was a pause, and he continued to hold on to the parcel.

'Right,' said Helen, 'I'm going to close my eyes, and put out my hands, and if the present isn't there before I count to ten, I shall send you away, and I won't allow you to make love to me this afternoon.'

Well, Helen was asking for it, wasn't she? Robert opened the bag, took out the bottle, and poured his blood over those expectant hands. There was a second, yes, I think it might have been as long as a second, when Robert reached a height of ecstasy entirely unknown to the majority of men, when, as they say in Latin love poetry, he reached the very stars. He had given himself over; he had put his soul in a vessel and he had given it to the woman he loved.

You'll want to know, of course, what Helen said and did when she opened her eyes; you'll want to know how the blood fell through her fingers into the bath, and how the rivers of it turned the water a deep pink; how she jumped out in disgust and shouted at him and told him to get out, and never try and see her again, or she'd tell someone, she didn't know who, a policeman, a psychiatrist, anyone. Just get out. But I don't want to go into the details of this scene. Helen was appalled; this episode marked the end of their affair; and Robert did not see her again before she graduated and left Cambridge for good.

But Robert, do not be unduly worried for Robert. His mind was like a thermostat, and when it reached a certain temperature, it simply cut off. He cut off for his remaining two years as an undergraduate and absorbed himself in his work. But perhaps the true preserver of his sanity was his violin, which he played, quite regularly, until three in the morning, bewitching all those who listened to it through the walls; and once, when he played the night through, a small gathering collected in the corridor outside his rooms, unable to pull themselves away from the grace and depth of what they heard.

On that day an impulse had driven Robert back to North Wing 5, back to Isaac Rosenberg, back to page 63; but this time, it was the last verse he read:

I am the death
Whose monument is beauty,
    and forever,
Although I lie unshrouded
    in life's tomb,
She is my cenotaph.

PART

2

FOUR

In 1961 Robert had been a geologist for six years. He had graduated with a first, and, on the day he learnt that the oldest rock on earth was as much as a quarter of the age of the universe, and was therefore more relevant than he had dared to hope, he decided that geology was the course he wished to follow. He liked the idea of being able to touch something so old: it made him feel like a strange offshoot of nature, simply part of a larger pattern, which must have been an enormous relief at the time. It seemed to him that all the atoms in his body were tending towards the earth waiting to be reunited with it, and that their appearance in him, in Robert Standing, was momentary, a small jerk in a cardiograph a hundred miles long.

His research was on the eruptive mechanisms of volcanoes; he wrote an extraordinary PhD. thesis on the way in which magma broke out of a blocked vent, which earned him both enormous esteem from his colleagues and a fellowship at Trinity. In the last couple of years he had been studying new data from fieldwork in the Alps on the subject of orogenesis, and for several months had been feeling on the verge of a breakthrough, which might, so Robert thought, do for geology what the discovery of DNA had done for life sciences.

But these last few weeks of the summer had been bad; solutions seemed as far away as ever, various hypotheses had turned out to be false, even close colleagues were beginning to doubt the workings of his famous imagination. He began to feel isolated and restless. At the end of August he applied for a sabbatical year, to begin almost immediately and, despite the short notice, those in charge of such things recognised that he badly needed it. It was with this background that on 30 September 1961, Robert set off to spend a year in Europe.

But Europe, on this, his first cultural tour (he'd been on field trips to Italy, but had barely left the mountains in which he was working), did not inspire him at all. In fact, it bored him. You have to remember that he was a geologist, and that he now knew, almost as part of himself, every layer of rock that made up the earth's crust, the limestones and the mudstones, the granite and the basalt, the layer of molten magma beneath them, poised to erupt and join its ancestors; and he knew the olivine of the earth's mantle, two thousand miles deep, lying on the molten iron core; so that when he surveyed Europe's great cathedrals, he felt as much disappointment as a great French cook would feel watching his layer upon layer of exotic sponges and icings being decorated by spindly plastic models of the Eiffel Tower.

Robert himself was puzzled by his reaction to Europe. He gazed at the ceilings of Michelangelo, and felt, more than anything else, neckache. Occasionally, perhaps, he would feel a glimmer of what he was supposed to feel, but never more. But it was as a result of this failure to be moved that he devised his first premise of the Theory of the Beautiful (which he was to work on for almost twenty years), namely that there were three constituents of the aesthetic experience, the subject, the object, which might be more or less beautiful, and the filter through which the object was seen or heard. The problem with Europe was this third thing, the filter. In other words, other people. They talked. They were an obstruction. They altered the true function of everything around them simply by existing. Cathedrals were not art galleries. But art galleries failed too – paintings were not painted to be hung alongside a hundred others. What can one hope to *feel* in a room full of paintings? How can any feelings have the time and the privacy to be allowed to reach the correct depth? The appreciation of the beautiful demanded privacy, and in Europe there was none.

It is true there were occasions when he arrived alone at a ruin, when he lay face down on a marble floor, two thousand years old, and felt it with his cheek and tongue. There was beauty here, sure enough. It gave him pleasure to see these man-made buildings sink again to their source, stone to stone, the perfect reunion. But the rest of it left him cold, and he might well have gone back to Cambridge after a fortnight were it not for the women.

He had remained loyal to Helen's memory for two years, but when he resurfaced in 1954 as an outstanding scholar, he saw himself afresh. He was still, after all, exceptionally handsome, and he began to enjoy once again the ineluctable privilege of being looked at.

He liked to walk through the streets of Cambridge and determine, from quite a distance, exactly the type of woman who would be drawn to him; he would then pretend he was looking at something in an entirely different direction, so that she could admire him unabashed, thinking it safe to do so. Then, without warning, Robert used to turn on the unsuspecting admirer, catching her eye at full stare and, if she was sufficiently pretty, he would smile at her. The result of this was a weakening in the poor girl's knees, and the detection of it was, for Robert, a tonic. For women's love, at this stage of his life, was exactly that, a tonic, innocently taken.

I have spoken to nine women with whom he had affairs between 1953 and 1961, probably a small proportion of those who actually fell for him. I remember one, in particular, still unmarried. She was, perhaps, the most bitter of all those I interviewed. At twenty, she had come up to spend a few weeks with her grandfather, the Provost of King's. She was one of those whom Robert had smiled at in the street. He then told her she was as beautiful as a peach, and that was enough: she fell. When she heard him play the violin, she fell even further and persuaded her grandfather to allow Robert to play passages from the Bach *Mass in B Minor* in King's College Chapel ('One violin', he said to her, 'for the Bach *Mass in B Minor*?' 'Oh yes,' she said. 'You listen to him, you'll see.' And he did.) The lovesick girl had (this without permission) given two hundred candles to the audience, and gave instructions for them to be lit during the final chorale, with the result that Robert felt he was a god (with those two hundred candles held towards him) and that poor girl knew that he must be. But the peach was soon eaten, and the stone thrown away (along with the others) and Robert barely realised the havoc he had caused.

The peaches in Europe, then, kept him going for about twelve weeks. He consumed three Frenchwomen, two Spanish, two Portuguese and four Italian virgins (he decided he enjoyed virgins – he liked the challenge of behaving tenderly and brutally at the same time). He developed new, more imaginative methods of seduction. By the end of his stay there, they were becoming distinctly subtle. (It gratified him, that if he failed as a geologist, he was at least good at this.) He gave a pretty Venetian girl an egg in Paris, and told her, 'If this gets back to Venice in one piece, phone me and I'll be lying next to you within three hours'. He kissed her goodbye on the train in St Lazare (she was crying), and went back to his hotel bedroom in a dingy part of Montmartre. It was 11 December, he was feeling sick, as though he'd eaten a meal of sixteen courses. He lay on his bed, and opened up the copy of *The Times* he had bought at the station, pleased to enjoy it without some girl or other leaning over and creasing it. Within a few minutes he had decided to return to England. An advertisement had caught his eye. It read:

Due to maternity leave, physics teacher required for two terms at St Peter's, a girls' boarding school in Hampshire. Apply, Miss Hackshaw, headmistress etc. etc.

'A good clean start,' he thought.

For the next day and a half he wrote out his application, paid off outstanding bills, and packed his suitcases. Then, at the very moment he was saying goodbye to the female receptionist, he had a telephone call: 'It's me,' said the Italian accent, 'it's Maria. The egg is all together, Roberto, the egg is all together.' Well, he said to himself, let this be the *petits fours*, and he wrote at the end of his application, 'I have business in Italy, and will not be able to attend the interview'. Then he posted it first class and set off for Venice.

Sadly, Maria was not as pretty as he remembered her.

St Peter's was a girls' boarding school in a rural part of Hampshire. There were two hundred and sixty pupils, between twelve and eighteen and, as the prospectus made clear, they were concerned with turning out girls who were (what they considered) 'complete'. The school had never boasted an academic record – few of their pupils ever went to university – but old Petrovians could always play tennis, often the piano, and were considered respectful, gentle and well-adjusted. The school produced good wife-material, and this was exactly what the upper-middle-class parents paid for.

At the beginning of that academic year (1961) St Peter's had a new headmistress, Miss Hackshaw, who was quite unlike her predecessor. Unfortunately for Miss Hackshaw, this predecessor had been immensely popular. She had believed in standards. Standards of behaviour. Miss Hackshaw, on the other hand, was ambitious for her pupils' minds, and believed, as things stood, they were only half developed, like raw shellfish. She herself was a graduate of St Hilda's, Oxford, and she intended to provide every opportunity for Petrovians to follow her there. She wanted them to have a good grasp of science, to know about Greek Art, to enjoy writing poetry. Petrovians should be educated *and* complete.

Therefore, when Miss Hackshaw received Dr Standing's application for the post of physics teacher, she couldn't contain her delight. She walked up and down her head-mistress's study, her heart contracting with pleasure and anticipation – she was going to make her mark on this school, she was sure of it – one day it would be as famous as Cheltenham Ladies College. We are entering, she said to herself, a new decade. This school will never look back. The secret lay in good teachers, and here was a Cambridge don wanting to spend his sabbatical in *her* school. There were other applications, of course – a geography teacher, Miss Blunt, who thought she might be able to double up for physics. She barely registered the three or four other applications. Jeanne Hackshaw, tall, slim and bright-eyed, sat down at her headmistress's desk and wrote the following letter:

17 December 1961

Dear Dr Standing,

What a delight it was to receive your application this morning, which was far superior to any other we received. I am slightly anxious that you cannot attend the interviews next week, but obviously your business in Europe must come first. However, I feel certain that I shall be able to persuade the governors to appoint you on the evidence of your application and references alone (provided that the competition is as weak as it seems to be on first perusal). By the time you get this letter, I shall know exactly how the situation stands. Please telephone me as soon as you get back to England. I do sincerely hope that you will be starting at St Peter's on Thursday 8 January next year; count on me to be a good advocate.

Best wishes,

Jeanne Hackshaw
Headmistress

Her secretary, a Miss Plimsoll, who had been at the school for forty years and was an institution in herself, registered some alarm at the letter. 'This isn't the regular letter at all, Miss Hackshaw. Are you sure you wish to send it as it stands?' and then, after a meaningful pause, she added: 'After all, Dr Standing is a man. And we don't have men at St Peter's. We simply don't have them. They are simply not employed here.'

'But *you*, Miss Plimsoll, *are*,' said Miss Hackshaw, smiling, 'So could you be so kind as to type it for me?'

Miss Plimsoll retreated, and muttered to herself that if a man were ever allowed to teach at St Peter's the school would never be the same again. But she comforted herself by the thought that the governors would never allow such a thing to happen, and the look on her face as she typed that letter was one of smugness. Dr Standing's application would, of course, be rejected, and she was looking forward to the humiliation of this new-fangled headmistress.

As it was so close to Christmas, the private lives of the school governors were naturally very busy. A number of them were already off on a skiing holiday. So it was decided that they should meet only on the one day, 22 December, the very day of the interviews. Miss Plimsoll ushered the governors into the study, smiling ingratiatingly; Miss Hackshaw invited them to sit, and handed them the six applications, one to each of them, to be read in rotation. There was half an hour's silence while they did so. One by one they looked up as they finished the last: their faces had betrayed nothing.

'Well?' said Miss Hackshaw.

'It's just for two terms, isn't it?' asked the Chairman, Mr Harrod, the only man among them.

'Yes, yes,' said Miss Hackshaw. Then, when nothing more was forthcoming, she asked, 'Well? And does any application strike you as being better than any other?'

After a few minutes of irrelevant comments amongst themselves – 'I see here that Miss Blunt has taught at Queens'; 'Weren't we short of a gym mistress? Here's one that could do gym as well'; 'Here's one that's taught physics before'; 'Yes, but she hasn't a qualification in it' – Mr Harrod dared to bring up the subject of Robert's application: 'And we have an application from a man,' he said, 'with a good reference from a professor. What does everyone feel about this?' Again a pause, faces uncertain of which expression to adopt, looking at each other for guidance, but none forthcoming. Limbo.

'Miss Hackshaw,' said Mr Harrod (he liked her, he thought her chic, and had played a significant role in her appointment) 'are we to rule out a man?'

For these last few days Miss Hackshaw had been mentally preparing speeches in defence of Dr Standing's maleness, the very irrelevance of it, his outstanding credentials, his enthusiasm, for God's sake, for the subject – 'Who are we to turn down a teacher with a first in Natural Sciences from Cambridge, and an outstanding record of research, *because of his sex?*' But by this stage of the meeting she knew it was all going to be a pushover. She could afford to be gentle.

'The post is only for two terms,' she said, 'perhaps I should be anxious if it were a permanent post. And it is, after all, physics he will be teaching, hardly a popular subject – what is it, forty girls he'll come into contact with? And girls *who*, it has to be said, are among the most sensible of our pupils, or at least the most academic, and the least flighty. No, I don't think his sex would be a problem. Naturally I have given this careful consideration.'

'Of course, you have, Miss Hackshaw,' said Mr Harrod, 'but I am alarmed, as doubtless are my fellow governors (and here murmurs of agreement), that Dr Standing is unable to attend the interviews.'

'Well, of course,' said Miss Hackshaw, 'that is extremely unfortunate. As his letter says, he has pressing business in Europe, which surely cannot be held against him to the point that we rule him out'

'You're right,' said Mr Harrod, 'and we shouldn't rule him out.'

There was a momentary flicker of alarm among the women, and one of them, a Mrs Forbes, piped out in a high voice, 'I'm rather impressed by Miss Blunt's application. She seems a sensible, solid type. I rather incline towards Miss Blunt, and the advantage is, we shall actually meet her.'

Miss Hackshaw was not deterred. 'Indeed, we shall,' she said.

But that afternoon, the solid Miss Blunt was not feeling very solid at all. She was waiting in the great hall of St Peter's in an armchair which promised comfort but gave none, and when Miss Plimsoll came in to ask her to 'come through' she extracted herself out of it with some difficulty, and cursed the onset of her arthritis. The vast expanse of shiny parquet floor between herself and the interview chair seemed to her a veritable ocean, and all the time in mid-crossing she said to herself, 'I must not slip. I must not slip. Curse these shoes.'

Little did the poor Miss Blunt know that the safest part of her voyage was already behind her.

After some preliminary chat about how she had come to leave her last school (and this was embarrassing enough),

Mr Harrod moved headlong into the nitty gritty: 'And what makes you think you could teach physics?'

In her head and on her face she said, 'Well, perhaps I couldn't, but I need the job'; with her mouth she said, 'Physics is a subject which has always interested me.'

'Which aspects of physics do you find interesting?' asked Miss Hackshaw, gently.

'Mechanics,' she said. 'How things move. And I know a lot of experiments I could do with the children, which would bring it to life for them.'

Then there was a pause, during which the governors waited for her to continue, and she waited for further questions. The pause lapsed into a silence. And then the silence suddenly became intolerable to bear, and to stopgap it Miss Blunt said the first serious word that came into her head: 'Gravity.'

The word sank like lead. And the awful thing was, Miss Blunt couldn't think of anything else to add, she couldn't think of any experiments to prove gravity. She kept having images of apples falling off trees, and whenever she was about to open her mouth, apples kept on coming into her head like interference on TV.

'And how', said Mrs Forbes, 'would you set about teaching your pupils about gravity?' Seven faces waited for her reply.

'I would take them to an apple tree,' was what came into her head immediately. 'I might ask them to drop their pencils,' she said, 'I think experiments are extremely important. I think a child learns not from books, but from experience.'

'Quite right too,' said Mr Harrod, encouragingly. Another pause. 'Well, if anyone has any more questions?'

'No, no,' the women murmured.

'Thank you very much, Miss Blunt. We shall be making a decision at the end of the afternoon, and the letters will be in the post tonight. Thank you very much for your time.'

So Miss Blunt walked out, and she knew she had been a disaster. The four who followed her were no better: one by one they walked back through the great iron gate of St Peter's, and each knew she had failed. Of course, they all had.

Victory belonged solely to Miss Hackshaw, who felt a new thrill flush through her as each of these dreary women had left her study. A Cambridge don at her school. She longed for the governors to be gone so that she could contemplate the full excitement of it in privacy. She wouldn't be surprised, even, if there were a few girls who wanted to take up physics again. The word will spread round, of course it will: 'You will *learn* something from Dr Standing', that's what they'll be saying to each other. But Miss Hackshaw's professionalism was such that not a trace of such excitement revealed itself: 'Well', she said, 'disappointing'.

Mr Harrod was meanwhile in a state of renewed stupefaction at the poverty of female minds. Thank God, he thought, I was born the right sex and went to Radley. 'I suppose the standard simply won't be very high at this time of the school year. We can't expect much,' he said.

'Does that mean', said Miss Hackshaw, 'that I should write to Dr Standing and offer him the appointment?'

'Yes indeed,' said Mr Harrod, 'and you never know,' he went on, 'he might bring a little bit of muscle to our girls' minds, not a bad thing.'

'And, I suppose, it *is* only for two terms,' said Mrs Forbes, 'no one could cause too much of an upset in two terms.'

***

'No,' said the other women, 'we've been going a hundred and fifty years. No one could cause too much of an upset.'

Robert arrived at St Peter's School, Hampshire, three days before term began. He looked up at the ugly grey building, and thought, 'How much better this is than anything I saw in Europe. What a good decision it was to come here.' Miss Hackshaw, well – her last good night's sleep was behind her.

She saw him get out of the taxi. She'd only half been expecting him. Today or tomorrow, he'd said, and he hadn't rung to let her know. In an odd way, she realised, it hadn't occurred to her that he might have a body. He had always been simply a good idea. And now he was coming towards her, smiling, holding out a hand. She tried to smile back, do the correct thing, but for some reason she was feeling a little awkward.

'Dr Standing?' she said.

'Miss Hackshaw?' he replied.

And they shook hands.

'I can't tell you, Miss Hackshaw, how pleased I am to be here. What a fine school you have. It must have quite a history behind it.'

'Yes, I believe it does have a history,' but then she could think of nothing more to add.

'Well, thank you', he said to her, 'for recommending those lodgings to me. I have completely settled in. Mr and Mrs White are charming. Do you know them?'

'No, I can't say I do,' and her mind was vague.

'I thought I'd get myself a bicycle. The house is only three miles away, and it's extremely pretty countryside round here. I can't tell you how good it is to be back in England.'

'I hope your business in Europe was all right.'

'A bit disappointing at the last. In fact, I think I shall put a stop to my business interests in Europe. It's good to be out of there.'

'Don't you like Europe, then?' asked Miss Hackshaw, relieved that the conversation was beginning to flow a little more naturally.

'Well, the truth is that I don't much. I find there is an extraordinary lack of innocence in Europe. Everyone is so *knowing*, and everything is so *old*.'

They were talking only a few feet away from where Robert had been deposited by the taxi. Miss Hackshaw had simply forgotten, in the heat of the moment, to invite Dr Standing into her study. But now she said to him, 'Look, I hope I don't seem frightfully rude, but I'm supposed to be seeing someone now – it shouldn't take more than about twenty minutes. To be honest, I wasn't expecting you so soon. Perhaps you would like to look round our grounds, or Miss Plimsoll, my secretary, could make you a cup of tea.'

'I shall be absolutely fine, don't worry about the tea,' Robert said.

'Come to my study at four, then,' said Miss Hackshaw, sounding as much like a headmistress as she could manage.

She was seeing nobody. Miss Hackshaw had lied, a rare occurrence. She tried to work out why she had. Then she got it. Oh my God. Innocence. That was his word wasn't it? Does he want innocence? What will he do with innocence if he finds it? Why had she never considered his motives before? She immediately sat down at her desk and began searching for the other applications, but they offered no solace. 'I do not want Miss Blunt here. I will not have Miss Blunt here,' she said aloud, in anger. But it was the thought of Miss Blunt, no less, that gave her courage. After all, no mistakes had yet been made. The governors were behind her. Dr Standing himself might be innocent. On what grounds could she suspect him? For goodness sake, no sins had been committed yet. And he was teaching physics, not English; the laws of motion, not *Wuthering Heights*. There would be no direct contact with the most susceptible pupils. And the governors might never meet him. She was beginning to feel better.

Then Miss Plimsoll came in and there was malice in her face. 'A letter to sign,' she said.

Miss Hackshaw signed its impatiently.

'There's a man walking across the lacrosse pitches,' she went on.

'That will be Dr Standing,' said Miss Hackshaw, now in full control. 'He's coming to see me in ten minutes. Could you show him in when he gets back?'

'Of course, Miss Hackshaw,' and Miss Plimsoll left her, clipping the door efficiently behind her.

A final few moments of privacy. Instinctively, she took the combs out of her hair and forced it severely away from her face. She walked up and down her study, her last bastion of defence, dark and solid, serious and civilised, furbished to bring a quake to every erring girl and convince every would-be parent that the school prided itself on being an institution. A portrait of the founder hung over the mantelpiece, a peculiarly ugly man covered in warts, who must have been very devout indeed, or he would have asked his artist to be kinder. There were tall, mahogany bookcases, in which the books, mainly Classics, seemed untouched, none of St Peter's' sixteen previous headmistresses having been tempted to enjoy them (perhaps a rather ambitious present by the founder). French windows led directly on to the head-mistress's garden, a rather formal affair with angular hedges surrounding square plots in which over-pruned roses grew out of ugly, cloddy earth; and the garden had the bewitching effect of making anyone who walked in it feel anxious and faintly sick. Parents, who had perhaps been a little chatty during their initial interview, were soon silent here. It was now looking starker than ever.

Miss Hackshaw stood by the windows and tried to imbibe authority from the room. She felt her back becoming straighter, as she prepared herself for the knock on the door. It was now four o'clock.

She was looking out on to her garden, her ears pricked. But suddenly the waiting was over: there he was, hurrying across from the games pitches to the main school, and worse, he saw her standing there, and worse, much worse, he stopped in his tracks (which were towards the main entrance) and realigned them in her direction. Suddenly, she was totally unprepared. Her back became straighter still.

Robert wound himself round the angular hedges as though they were a child's maze, his step was light, his expression one of absolute friendliness; his black hair had been dishevelled and his cheeks reddened by the January wind. He looked angelic. 'Hello,' he said through the glass. 'Is it all right to take a short cut?'

'Of course,' said Miss Hackshaw, and smiled at him as she unlocked the door, 'just don't after term begins. You'll find there are a lot of rules here, Dr Standing, rules which you will probably think ridiculous, and some of them are. This garden is only used by the headmistress and her guests. But there's no reason why you should have known that.'

'I'm sorry,' said Robert, as he walked into the study, as happily as if he'd been walking into his own bedroom. 'You must give me a list of things I must remember. I don't want to break any rules. I am quite determined to make a success of it, you know, partly for your sake, as it was so good of you to persuade the governors I was appropriate without even an interview. I am incredibly grateful to you, and I won't let you down. Really, thank you.' And he took Miss Hackshaw's hand and held it tight for a moment, and looked at her directly as if to add some sort of solidity to his gratitude.

Miss Hackshaw felt she was going up and down in a lift at some speed: there were moments during Robert's speech in which she felt positively optimistic, and her spirits rose, but at others (and this was the moment in which she was currently situated, the having-been-looked-at-by-him moment) her spirits plunged, and she thought, 'Whom else will he look at like that? If he is capable at looking like that at *me*, a headmistress, what is going to happen at this school?' She pulled herself together. 'It was nothing,' she said, and smiled again.

Robert sat down in an armchair (or at least it wasn't, but he sat down as though it were) and continued enthusiastically: 'I'm so pleased I'm going to be teaching physics. As you know, I'm actually a geologist, but sometimes I wish I'd set out on a different path. They are making astonishing discoveries in physics all the time, and it won't be many years before physicists will be able to provide us with a complete history of the universe and I envy them. It's not even strictly in my field to give an account of the first second of the earth, though I think I probably could.' (There was a pause here during which this was what he was evidently attempting.) 'I could certainly give you, though,

---

an account of the first second of our continents – what is your geography department like? I could always help the staff out from time to time.'

'I'm sure that won't be necessary, thank you, Dr Standing, but I shall certainly introduce you to our geography mistress, Miss Hunn, who would know better than I.'

'Can you imagine a time,' continued Robert, barely registering the existence of Miss Hunn, 'when "terrestrial" takes on the meaning of "provincial"? That will be an exciting time, won't it?' And he looked at her straight, a long generous look.

Miss Hackshaw felt she was falling down a lift shaft. 'Let me tell you about the girls you'll be teaching,' she managed to squeeze out.

'Yes, of course,' said Robert, responsibly.

'I'm afraid we don't have any A–Level girls this year. Well, actually, we never have had any. Perhaps you'll be able to inspire a few into doing an A–Level?'

'Well, I shall certainly try my best to inspire them,' said Robert, glowing with the very idea of it.

Miss Hackshaw held on to her desk and continued: 'Now you'll be teaching three forms, the Lower, Middle and Upper Fifths, and there'll be about fourteen or fifteen girls in each. The Lower Fifths are thirteen to fourteen years old, and this will be the first serious science they've done. I have a list of their names here.'

Robert took the list and read the names. Marjorie Wallace. Jane Dunn. Catherine Henderson. Fiona Kirkpatrick. What was he supposed to say? But he was obviously expected to look at them, so he did.

'And here is the Middle Fifth.' Another list. More names. 'And finally the Upper Fifth. They'll of course be doing their O–Levels in the summer.' A third list in his hands. Davina Patterson. Felicity Streetly. Sophia Wykham. Josephine de Salis. Miranda Thompson.

And perhaps it was because he was given these names, names which as yet meant nothing to him, but which belonged to people who existed, the first tangible evidence of his appointment, and the realisation that he was to teach and they were to be taught, that he was the subject and they were his objects, and the objects were souls with names attached, virgin souls, ready for impressions, and he was the impressor, that he began to realise his motives for going there at all.

Beauty in Europe tended towards its own death. In retrospect, he had felt both a fear and a contempt of it. The fear, perhaps, was more a sense of compassion, fear for his own death. The contempt was because everyone kept trying to pretend that the decay wasn't happening, or if it was, that it was irrelevant, when of course it was the most relevant thing of all. They tried to pretend that the sculpture, the paintings, the churches were somehow timeless, that when the scaffolding went up it was a temporary embarrassment. But how long could all this stuff last? Could it even last a thousand years? Or two or three thousand? Even if you were generous and said that a church could stay standing for ten thousand years, for God's sake what was ten thousand years? A split second in a geologist's calendar. Or in any objective reckoning of time.

And then, exactly as Miss Hackshaw was giving an account of the school day, a church came into his head, and it kept falling apart, and hundreds of men kept rushing to rebuild it, as though all the church wished to do was fall, and all the men wished to do was prevent it from falling. He saw it as though it were in a film speeded up, and it seemed like hubris, like the prevention of destiny. Yes, he now understood what he had come to see. It was beauty tending towards its acme rather than towards its death. Youth was as far away from death as he could conceive. And he wanted to witness it.

'Dr Standing? Dr Standing?' said Miss Hackshaw. 'Does that seem all right?'

'Ah yes, of course,' said Robert, though he hadn't clue what she was talking about.

'I think you'll like the Upper Fifth. They're a bright lot.'

'I'm sure I'll like them. Do you have a copy of the syllabus? And could you tell me where the science library is? I should like to prepare some lessons as soon as possible.'

Robert, conscious that he had been caught drifting, became ultra-efficient.

'I believe your predecessor, Mrs Charlton, has written down everything you need to know in that direction. All the books you'll need are in the physics laboratory itself, and tomorrow I'll take you down there. In fact, we may as well do a tour of the school tomorrow – would you be able to come in after lunch – says about two? I would take you now, but I'm afraid I've a meeting with the housemistresses at five.'

'Two would be fine,' he said. 'I'll look forward to that. You know, Miss Hackshaw, I have a feeling I shall be extremely happy at your school. Can I take those lists of the girls I'll be teaching away with me?'

'Why, of course you can. Now I know that the syllabus you were asking for is in the laboratory, and if you . . .'

'Don't worry about that, Miss Hackshaw, I can wait for tomorrow,' Robert said, taking her by the hand again. 'Thank you for everything, Miss Hackshaw; you're a good woman.'

By some extraordinary feat of mind over matter, Miss Hackshaw had managed to remain a fairly normal colour throughout the interview: now she closed the study door behind him and felt her cheeks burn. There was no meeting with the housemistresses: another lie. She covered her face with her hands and considered how to prevent a catastrophe. 'It's all too late, much too late,' she said to herself, 'I'm powerless. And it's not a question of forty girls. It's anyone who happens to cross his path. It's the entire school.' And with this thought, she burrowed her head deeply into her hands.

In fact, however, Miss Hackshaw need not have worried as much as she did that evening. There was no catastrophe. The school survived its first week of Robert Standing remarkably well. His method was more one of a slow, steady biological warfare. It is also a matter of opinion how lethal his doses were and whether their effect was always for the bad. For there were even moments in those two terms (and yes, he did last them) when Miss Hackshaw experienced short flushes of happiness, because a few of the effects which she had hoped for (pre-arrival) were actually taking place: it was as though the whole school had been woken from a hundred-years' sleep. The girls' eyes took on a depth, previously lacking, their clumsy limbs became almost graceful, and though their concentration was slightly erratic, the work they produced lost its former, pedestrian quality. That term, the spring term of 1962, posters of Elvis Presley did not even bother to go up. Other previous shrines were severely neglected. And all in all, this can't have been much of a bad thing.

In a way, Robert and the St Peter's girls were the exact complement to each other: Robert desired to possess, and the girls desired to be possessed. It was not even a question of sex. There was not a squeak of lust on either side: the girls were Beauty Itself for Robert, and Robert was Beauty Itself for the girls – and idols don't have bodies you can actually touch.

But to say there was no thought of sex does not mean that the physical did not feature on the St Peter's landscape. Indeed, the sensitivity of the girls was so heightened that if a fly were to land on the elbow of any one of them, it would send an electric current right down to her toe. There cannot have been any girls who completely escaped him, who did not look in their mirrors for the first time and see 'female' rather than 'person'. If you were to have eavesdropped in the dormitories at this time, you might have heard, 'Catherine, can you feel your bosom developing? I think I can. I'm sure I can.' But almost all that frivolous talk of sex, and what it might be like, and who might have done it, and how it could conceivably be enjoyable, all that had more or less stopped. Instead one girl told another: 'Dr Standing told us how to make an atom bomb today.' 'Dr Standing says that one day he's going to find out what makes things beautiful. How in the *world* do you think he will set about doing that?' 'Can I tell you about light, Miranda?' 'You'll never *believe* what Dr Standing did today, Felicity. He was telling us about how sound waves travel, and my goodness, how slow they are, and then suddenly, right in the middle of the lesson, he got a violin out from under the sink and started playing it. You've never heard anything so wonderful. He's a genius, that man.'

There were more than eighty girls who asked to take up physics again. Queues waited outside Miss Hackshaw's study after lunch (the time set aside for these sorts of queries, but it had never previously been taken advantage of). One by one the girls told her how they felt they needed to improve their science. They all spoke so earnestly about their sudden interest in the subject, and were already so surprisingly knowledgeable about it, that Miss Hackshaw had no alternative but to ask Dr Standing to take on extra classes, which he was more than happy to do. And by the end of that first term, every mind, breast and heart was swollen with love for him.

Some people hold the opinion that a schoolgirl, simply on account of her age, should not consider herself properly in love. Rather, she has a 'crush' or some other such derogatory expression. But surely the love of the fifteen-year-old girl is as pure and definite as love can be: she becomes as vulnerable as a beetle on its back – what reasonable woman in her twenties or thirties could give as much as that? Where is the older woman who hasn't learnt to put herself first? Who doesn't offer morsels of herself to her lover, one at a time, cautiously, ready for their rejection? The fifteen year old has not yet learnt the skill of self-division: she gives everything. This is surely the love of the poets. Or perhaps poetical love itself is no more than a momentary obsession, a passing 'crush' dressed up to be something greater. Whichever, it seems to me that schoolgirl love is near enough identical to it.

But if the schoolgirls were straightforward in their adoration, their teachers barely recognised their own. That was because, I suppose, their symptoms were so very various. If Robert were to have taken any of them aside, and confessed to more than an interest in them, some of the curious consequences of their love might have receded, and wholesome, clearer images of wedding dresses and country cottages come into the foreground. As it was, every schoolmistress found her own special way of dealing with this new onslaught on her heart: some angrily stifled it and some let it breathe within them.

The biology mistress who overheard Robert playing the violin in the middle of his physics lesson, was of the stifling kind. She spent that half hour for ever on the point of interrupting him, and when she discovered that she hadn't the courage, she let out her anger by railing to her colleagues in the staffroom, that *the man had to go*. Some immediately agreed with her, but there were others who were silent. And these others were busy experiencing what can only be called a rebirth.

Miss Harper, the needlework mistress, put away her pastel cottons, and out came the deep blues and reds of Gauguin. The 'Simplicity' patterns for blouses and A–line skirts were put in a bottom drawer somewhere, and she tried her hand at fashion designing, encouraging her pupils to use silk and satin in luxurious quantities (about forty mothers wrote to Miss Hackshaw to complain about such extravagance, and refused to comply with Miss Harper's recommendations). Miss Stuart, the history teacher, began to get carried away in her descriptions of royal marriages, when she suddenly decided that it was love and desire that accounted for eighty per cent of everything that had ever happened, and that people only pretended it was politics to give history some sort of respectability. She even decided to spend a good deal of money having her own family tree traced, just in case she was a member of the royal family herself. Miss Jackson, the art teacher, put away the pottery jars and arrangements of dried flowers that had been used for ten years as subjects for still life, and recommended that the girls take their clothes off and admire the beauty of the human form before committing it to paper. Free expression, girls, was what she advocated now. The divinity teacher began to centre her attention on the Holy Spirit and the Song of Solomon; and for Miss Hughes, who taught mathematics, her subject took on a new beauty and profundity, and she began to dream of discovering the largest prime number in the universe.

In the opposite camp, who believed that the only good Robert Standing could do was to leave within the hour, the most vociferous was Mrs Bennett, who taught English. She had been thirty years at the school, and no pupil had left without being able to recognise metaphors, similes, alliterations and assonance: every Petrovian had spent a major part of her Middle Fifth year in counting examples of these in 'The Lady of Shalott'; and the numbers they arrived at at the end of this great work were, implied Mrs Bennett, perfect, so that if there had been even as much as an extra metaphor, the balance would have been lost. 'Behind every word there is a reason,' Mrs Bennett used to tell her pupils. 'We can only follow the geniuses.' With the effect that Petrovians barely dared to put pen to paper, or if they did, the 'balance' was never 'right', because it was mathematically extremely unlikely that it would match the 'perfection' of 'The Lady of Shalott'. But Dr Standing's presence in the school was, argued Mrs Bennett, encouraging an extremely perverted reading of English literature. She knew it was him: all she had to do was to look at the expressions on her girls' faces when they read *Jane Eyre* and she knew it was him. And when their eyes took on a wild brightness, she would say to the class, with a terrifying urgency: 'Class, show me a simile. Miranda, why is that simile effective? Josephine, why do you think there is greater use of alliteration in poetry than in prose?'and she went on asking questions until the shine had left every one of them. All in all, Dr Standing posed as major a threat to the methods of teaching English literature at St Peter's as when the structuralists arrived at Cambridge in the mid 1970s.

A second enemy was Miss Hunn, the geography mistress, who had been outraged by Dr Standing's suggestions for her geography lessons. He had talked to her with such totally misplaced enthusiasm about eruptions from magma chambers, that she had come away feeling, she wasn't sure why, a sense of utter disgust, and had been unable to consume anything liquid for almost twenty-four hours. 'But let me tell you what happens,' he had said to her, 'when you get a blocked vent.' 'I don't have a blocked vent, and I'm sure I don't want to know what one is,' she had immediately replied; and when she later discovered what he was talking about, her humiliation was such that she couldn't be within sight of him without a red rash rising up her neck.

But there was one woman who managed to stay on the cross benches, and was happily immune to Robert. She had married only that summer, a Parisian with whom she'd been in love for years, so her heart was in the right shape to remain unaffected by him, and had no dent into which he might seep. She was also, perhaps as a result of her having spent a good deal of her childhood in France, a little more worldly than other members of St Peter's staff.

One day, when afternoon lessons were over and the girls were having their tea, Robert spotted her through the window of the classroom door and thought her pretty enough to go inside and speak to her.

'Hello,' he said, 'I don't think we've met' and he held out his hand. 'Robert Standing. I'm here to teach physics for a couple of terms, and I only wish it were longer. It's a good place, isn't it?'

'I'm Polly Declerc. I'm pleased you've enjoyed your first three weeks. I've heard all about you. You've made quite an impression, you know. But I'm sure you do know.'

'Have I made an impression? Good or bad, do you think?' and he sat down on one of the desks and begged her to tell him.

'I think good for the present, but bad in the end.'

'How can you tell?' asked Robert, delighted by Mrs Declerc.

'I have the evidence right here in front of me.'

There was an enormous Grundig reel-to-reel tape-recorder on her desk.

'What evidence is that? Have I been taped? Have I been spied on?' Robert was charmed.

'No, no,' said Mrs Declerc, 'or you might prefer to imagine you had. Every sound you make, every cough, every time you even pluck your violin, immortalised by two hundred and sixty girls and a Grundig.'

Robert shivered with pleasure at the mere thought of it.

'You're a wicked man, Dr. Standing,' and she smiled. 'Well, would you like to hear the evidence?'

'Of course I would.'

'On second thoughts, I think you should hear a before and after.'

'Before and after what?'

'Before and after you,' and she went to the shelf to select another tape. 'I teach French,' she said, 'and I'm always encouraging these girls to speak it – for years it's been almost impossible. They answer any questions you ask them with one word, and that's if they can understand the question in the first place. Here's a tape we did at the end of last term, just to put you in the picture. Each of the girls was given a slot of five minutes, and they had to talk about, let me see, this one is '*Mes Parents*'. Now, would you like to know about these girls' parents?'

'Ah, yes, certainly I would like to know about their parents. I've been here three weeks and it still feels as though I know nothing about them at all.'

'Well, now you will,' said Mrs Declerc, and she slotted in the reel and switched on the machine.

'*Mon père*,' began the first young voice, promisingly, '*mon père est grand. Il a les yeux bleus et il est stockbroker dans Londres. Ma mère est moins grand*. No, sorry, *moins grande* . . .' Mrs Declerc fast-forwarded the tape: '*Ma mère aime beaucoup manger les gateaux* . . .' Fast forward: '*Mon père aime jouer le golf avec ses amis aux weekends*.' Fast forward: '*Ma mère jouer bridge*. . . . Fast forward: '*Ils ont beaucoup de partis de diner* . . . Then she clicked it off. 'Well, there's before.'

'Yes?' said Robert, 'and after?'

'Listen to this,' said Mrs Declerc, and she put the original reel back on to the machine. A young girl's voice began anxiously: '*Aujourd'hui, il y a la guerre*'; then there was a pause during which her breathing could be heard quite clearly on the tape. '*La guerre est dans mon coeur, je crie dans mon coeur, il pleut dans mon coeur. Il ne sait rien. Je ne sais rien.*'

'Oh, what a sweet girl,' said Robert. 'What an angel she must be.'

'Do you want me to go on?' asked Mrs Declerc.

'Oh yes,' said Robert.

The next girl was even more hesitant. There were false starts, you could hear her struggling to find the words she wanted, and then finally she let it all out in a gush: '*Aujourd'hui l'amour est arrivé comme un oiseau.*'

'What angels there are here,' Robert said, in seventh heaven.

'Well, I think you've heard enough,' said Mrs Declerc. 'You're enjoying it far too much,' and she switched off the recorder.

'Please, just one more, and I'll be off, I promise you. They've improved no end, haven't they?'

'Yes, their French has improved. Perhaps I should thank you for that.' She smiled at him. 'OK, this is the last one. I think I'm wicked myself to have played you these. But I wanted you to know, in a way, so that you would take good care of them. You will take care of them, won't you? I don't want to sound like a headmistress, but you are in an extremely responsible position, you know. Look at the power you have over these girls. You wouldn't abuse that, would you?'

'I promise you, I wouldn't dream of laying so much as a finger on any one of them,' and Robert meant it when he said it.

'Well, I believe you. Or I think I do. Here's your last one, then.' And again she switched on her Grundig.

There was a superb finale, no hesitancy now; the girl's voice rang out clear and true:

Un soldat jeune, bouche ouverte, tête nue
Et la nuque baignant dans le frais cresson bleu
Dort: il est étendu dans l'herbe, sous la nue,
Pale dans son lit vert où la lumière pleut.

The poem was so beautifully spoken that Robert asked her name.

'Sophia Wykham,' said Mrs Declerc.

'I know her. I teach her.' He could have said, 'Eureka.'

'I'm sure you do,' said Mrs Declerc. 'That must be all the evidence you need, then. You'll take care, won't you?'

'Yes, yes, of course I will, thank you, thank you for everything. And what subject did you say they were speaking on?'

'An event in the news,' said Mrs Declerc.

'And what an event, dear Polly.'

He kissed her on both cheeks and sped out of the door, happy as a sandboy.

FIVE

Robert headed directly for the photographs he had once noticed pinned to a notice-board in the entrance hall: there she was, Sophia Wykham, dressed as Viola, what a lovely girl. The School Production of *Twelfth Night*, December 1961: what he'd have given to have seen that. What was he doing on that night, he wondered. He suddenly remembered Maria crying on the train and felt a tinge of guilt, an awkward, sticky feeling; but it was momentary, a shrug and it was gone. He was in the right place now.

He looked again at Viola. She had a photograph to herself. It had been taken from the floor, so her chin was held high. She was wearing an Elizabethan cap with a feather in it, and her eyes were strong and proud. What a lovely girl. There was a little list attached to each photograph, orders for copies, and he wrote down his name beside Viola, just to the right of her haughty chin. What a lovely girl.

What a good place this was. What a fine combination

of purity and receptivity, like warm wax. It was half past four, the time the tea trolley was wheeled into the staffroom: just what he wanted, a cup of tea. He set off down the long wood-panelled corridor, where school photographs had hung since 1899, where notice-boards were crammed with news of lacrosse matches and netball teams, and where there was a list, changed weekly, of twelve young girls whose turn it was to have a 'general medical examination'. Robert stopped by the list, and read the names. He was looking, of course, for 'Sophia Wykham'. He wanted to imagine Sophia of the haughty chin, naked, shy under her dressing-gown, her newly grown body shown for the first time to an outsider. But Sophia's name was not among the twelve: she was not on the Minotaur's visiting list this week.

He walked on and into the staffroom. Half of the faces looked up, and the other half down. The perfect division of loyalty. But all Robert noticed were six bright faces looking up at him (for the others were too dark to be seen), and for a brief moment they reminded him of the candles held towards him in King's College Chapel, when he'd played the Bach *Mass*. How much happier, how much more *complete* he was now. Miss Harper, the needlework mistress, immediately invited him to have a cup of tea.

'That would be lovely, thank you,' said Robert.

'And a cake, have a cake,' effused Miss Jackson.

'They look delicious,' said Robert, and he helped himself to a cake and sat down in an armchair, positively effulging with contentment.

'No sugar, is that right?' said Miss Harper, as she bent over to hand him his tea.

'Miss Harper, that's exactly right. My goodness, what

a lovely shirt you have on.' Great folds of white silk were hovering in front of him like a sail.

'Thank you, Dr Standing,' quivered Miss Harper, and she always remembered that moment with pride.

For ten minutes, until the bell went for evening lessons, the women flitted about him like fireflies each eager to tell him how their new approaches to teaching were reaping extraordinary results, and Robert drank his tea. Then, when the staffroom was empty again (except for a few dark faces marking prep at the table), Robert lay back in his armchair and closed his eyes.

He thought about the research he'd been doing at Cambridge, about those last few months. He'd almost clinched it, how close he'd been. Yes, he'd almost understood how the continents moved. But then he'd seen it all slip away from him, like the hand of a drowning man. He felt his temples contract at the memory of it. Thank God he was out of there. He'd been needing a rest, he hadn't realised how much, and now he couldn't remember a time when he'd been so well.

So, then. Why am I happy? I'm happy because I'm loved, actively loved. What a totally enriching experience that is. Helen, if only you had *known*, I might have enriched *you*. That was the trouble, you didn't *know*, and I was too young to persuade you.

Some people might blame me for understanding so clearly how these girls love me. But how am I supposed to be unconscious of it? How am I supposed to remain ignorant, and in my ignorance miss the richness of it? It would have been to Helen's advantage to have understood me, and it is doubtless to my advantage to understand these girls. I'll go further, one is barely human in a state of ignorance. Sometimes I see people going for their country walks, and they remind me of dogs, wagging their tails. What a meaningless thing it would be, to walk on the land and be ignorant of the nature of what you were walking on. And anything, anything at all, is enriched by knowledge of it: eating if you know about food, drinking if you know about wine, watching football if you know the rules. And this was what distinguished human from animal pleasures, knowledge of whatever it was. And the most valuable knowledge of all was that of the source of your own happiness.

Now, where was he? His eyes were still closed; he was warm, deep in the armchair. He heard the scratching of a pen. Ah yes, a school for angels. Sophia Wykham, he remembered. Ah yes, Sophia of the haughty chin, naked under her dressing-gown. He suddenly felt an enormous yearning for her, not for her body, you understand, but for her soul. He wanted to understand her structure, was that the right word? He wanted to be able to predict her moods with meticulous precision. He had seen how people could desert their own private structures, and turn into types, and it alarmed him. Friends of his at Trinity had come up to visit him in subsequent years, and it was as though they'd arrived – somewhere else. But these girls were still on the edge, they hadn't *become* people yet, they could still go in this or in that direction, they hadn't made their minds up yet. They were all *potential*, and there is simply more *energy* in potentiality than in actuality. The energy has all but dried up in you by the time you're actual. He had discussed this with physicists – whether it was possible to know something when it was in the process of becoming. Virtual particles, they'd called them. Well, is it possible? Yes, what a good thing it was to be at that school. He'd know soon enough.

'Dr Standing. Dr Standing, Wake up.' The first rude voice of three weeks: Miss Hackshaw. 'I've put black ink right through your name. I cannot think what you had in your mind.'

Robert started up and felt fuzzy in the warmth: 'Miss Hackshaw? Have I done something to upset you?'

It was seven o'clock, the staffroom was empty, supper time. 'Miss Hackshaw,' said Robert, standing up and trying to look responsible, 'have I done anything wrong?'

'I see you ordered a photograph,' said Miss Hackshaw, coldly.

'Yes, I did,' said Robert. 'Was that wrong?'

'Try, Dr Standing, to imagine why it might be wrong.'

Dr Standing was obviously thinking very hard.

'Dr Standing, you ordered a photograph of a particular girl. What would the girl think if she saw you wanted a photograph of her? What, Dr Standing, would she think? And more to the point, what would her parents think if ever they were to hear of it? You cannot be at a girls' school and imagine you can take of it what you choose. You are a responsible member of staff. And I'm sorry, Dr Standing, to have to say this to you, but understand this: you will be leaving this school immediately if you do anything like this again.'

Miss Hackshaw had finished: she had turned quite pink and Robert pitied her.

'I'm so sorry, Miss Hackshaw, I really am, and I'm totally in the wrong. I won't let you down.'

Miss Hackshaw could tell that he meant it, and her voice relaxed: 'I'm sorry to be so tough on you. The trouble is, Dr Standing, there have been a number of complaints, and I want you to know that I am for ever defending you. But in this instance . . . You have to tread very carefully, here, Dr Standing.'

'I assure you, I'll tread very carefully.'

He spoke with such obvious sincerity that Miss Hackshaw was touched. 'Well,' she said, 'there's no harm done, your name's been scrubbed out by an indelible marker. I agree with you, it's a nice photograph.' She smiled at him, as though all was forgiven.

When she left, Robert considered his new position. He was determined not to put a foot wrong. He did not wish to be cast out of paradise. So he set to work on planning his latest venture – the secret acquisition of a soul in the very process of its becoming.

Sophia Wykham was near enough the only girl who hadn't written Robert little love poems. Every morning Robert would go to his pigeon-hole in the staffroom, and sift through six or seven 'psalms' as he called them, after one girl had clearly plagiarised the seventeenth. (Incidentally, the pink piece of paper, signed 'Yours, Jane Dunn' has survived. Her poem reads:

> Make me the apple of your eye,
> Hide me in the shadow of your wings,
> By still waters with me lie,
> And talk to me of interesting things.

Nor did Sophia keep her eyes fixed on him throughout the lesson, nor put her books away slowly at the end of it in the hope of having a brief snatch of conversation with him after the others had packed up and gone. In fact, it occurred to Robert, she was the only girl who began getting ready to leave the moment the bell went, while the others would linger for as much as ten minutes, solemnly closing and then reopening their books 'to check things', with the result that seventeen out of the eighteen pupils in the Upper Fifth would be late for their next lesson.

Once, Robert thought she'd been listening to him playing the violin when she ought to have been having her tea, but then, looking back, there had been no evidence. The following day he had tried to ask her about it, but he couldn't think how to approach her. Opening lines had never been his problem before. Perhaps souls in the process of becoming required different opening lines; perhaps, because such souls would for ever be flitting in and out of existence, it was more a question of good timing.

Sometimes, during the lessons, he used to try to imagine what she was thinking about. It was possible she was just thinking about physics. She was certainly good at it. And then he would despair, that he'd been at the school for twenty weeks, and he still didn't have much idea what *any* of the girls were thinking about. He felt like a codebreaker, with his first morning's work in front of him. The trouble was, he decided, he'd been behaving too well; he'd taken the warnings of Mrs Declerc and Miss Hackshaw too much to heart. He had a mission, and its secrecy was not to its advantage.

There were only three weeks to go. The Upper Fifths had just taken their Physics O-Level paper: they found it easy, and spirits were high. Even his dear Sophia was smiling readily at him. The end of exams meant that now Robert could teach anything he liked. And it was this freedom, coupled with the fact that time was running out and his investigation barely begun, that gave him the idea of how he should proceed.

One day he said to his class: 'Have any of you ever wondered how it came to be that I was teaching you? Have any of you ever thought it strange that a university don should go back a stage and see what life is like at a girls' school? What do you think my motives are?'

There was a quiver round the classroom. No one said a word. 'Well,' he continued, 'I came here because I wanted to find out how you function, the sort of things you think about and value. I've only a short time left at this school, and I'm afraid that I'm still rather in the dark. Now what I want to do is this.'

Even Sophia's eyes were fixed on him now. He paused a while to enjoy the sensation.

'Would any of you be willing to do an experiment with me? Would any of you feel able to talk about yourselves into a tape-recorder? On Thursday evenings the biology A–Level lab is empty,and I'm planning to borrow Mrs Declerc's Grundig and install it there. I want you to take it in turns to shut yourself up in there, cut yourself off completely from the world, forget where you are. Then when you feel that you can, I want you to switch on that tape-recorder and speak into it. Tell me what you're like, what your parents are like, what your aspirations are. I want to know about *you*'.

If he could have read girls' minds, he would have seen a thousand confessions.

'Would anyone be willing to go along with it?'

Not a hand went up.

'Josephine, Miranda, Patricia, Sophia, won't you let me in? Won't you tell me just a little about yourselves?'

Miranda giggled.

'Miranda, for that you will be the first.' And he smiled at her. Several of the girls looked jealously on.

'All right,' she said, noticing them with pleasure. 'When do I start?'

'On Thursday at five,' said Robert. 'And talk for as long as you have something to say.'

The experiment was soon running smoothly. With the French oral exams over, Mrs Declerc was happy to lend her Grundig ('Experiments in sounds' Robert had said to her, and she was happy to give him the benefit of the doubt), and for three weeks it stood on a corner table in the biology A–Level lab. The first Thursday evening, Robert took Miranda into the lab and sat with her, explaining how to switch the tape-recorder on and off. 'Remember, Miranda,' he said to her, 'no one else is ever going to hear these tapes, so feel free, say anything that comes into your head.' When she was finally alone, her heart was thumping so hard that she decided it must be audible and she didn't dare switch on the machine until it had quietened down. Then she switched it on and began to relax. The previous night she had made an important decision: she was going to tell Robert everything.

Later that night Robert played back his first tape, and was bitterly disappointed. Miranda spent the first ten minutes explaining how difficult it was feeling like a woman when people treated her as though she were a girl. 'I have all the emotions of a woman,' she said, meaningfully, 'even more,' and Robert, when he heard what she had to say, believed her, and considered that he had already missed the interesting, critical moment between girlhood and womanhood. 'I'm too late,' he cried out in despair, 'I'm already too late.' And after this abysmal realisation, he kept fast–forwarding the tape, as though nothing else could conceivably be of interest in the poor girl. Her sighs and her pauses reminded him, now she had told him what to look out for, of *women*, no less, and he felt uncomfortable, as though he hadn't cleaned his teeth for three days.

Miranda, on the other hand, was hopeful for her confessions, and the look on her face as she left the biology A–Level lab was what persuaded others to follow her. Soon it became apparent that Thursday evenings would not be sufficient for these recording sessions (there were only two Thursdays left), so that when Robert discovered that the science labs were empty on Tuesday afternoons, these too became incorporated into his scheme, and likewise became a day to long for and to dread.

Robert spent his evenings playing back the tapes. The girls were now queueing up to be heard, but, goodness, how little they had to say. Miranda, if anything, was the best of them. Sometimes they talked about their parents, but really only to say how much they hated being treated as children when, 'For goodness sake, I'm sixteen, and I'm as grown up as I'll ever be.' Josephine told him, in quite a lot of detail, about her first kiss during the previous holidays. It sounded quite hideous, although she had evidently enjoyed it. Then, after a good deal of sighing (Robert was now getting to recognise the signs of a long sighing session, and was able to fast-forward the tape with creditable accuracy), Josephine gushed out, 'I was thinking of you, Dr Standing' and then the poor girl obviously regretted her confession so much that she had tried to scrub it off, and there were clicks and blurred patches. (In fact there may well have been more which she *had* managed to remove.) But Robert was oblivious to all of it. He couldn't understand why Sophia had still not come forward, why she had been deaf to the encouragement of the others, why she was still, in effect, resisting him.

It was Tuesday, 11 July. The following Tuesday was the end of term. Saturday was 'Foundation Day', when the entire school, plus parents and a few grandparents, packed into Winchester Cathedral to thank God for helping Reverend Waddle found their school. The whole of Thursday was going to be taken up with a Foundation Day rehearsal, something which Robert had only recently learnt. So today was his last chance, and he was becoming reckless.

He waited outside the dining-room at twenty past one. He watched the girls through the glass swing door, piling up the leftover sponge and custard, and taking the dirty plates to trolleys which lined one wall. A few faces looked up and noticed him; nudges, giggles. Then he saw her. She looked sad. Not haughty now. A little salt had fallen on the shiny oak table, and she was running her finger through it, vacantly. Then another girl came and wiped the salt away. Robert felt angry on Sophia's behalf, being interrupted like that, but Sophia was passive and removed. There was a clattering of chairs as everyone stood up and silence when grace was said. They filed out.

Miss Hackshaw came first. She raised her eyebrows; Robert tactfully ignored her. She was powerless, anyway, surrounded by sixth-formers. The sixth-formers were equally powerless with Miss Hackshaw in their midst, although some still gave Robert long, meaningful looks which were lost on him. The other girls were unchaperoned, as members of staff ate in their own dining-room, and the prefects had already gone off with Miss Hackshaw. So when Sophia came out, the coast was clear, and he immediately went up to her. 'Sophia', he said.

'Dr Standing? Have I done something wrong?' said Sophia.

'No, no. Nothing wrong.'

Robert couldn't remember what he'd come to tell her. The juniors were squeezing through the double doors now eight abreast. Girlish giggling was becoming intolerable to him. 'Could we go somewhere more quiet?' he said.

'I don't understand what you want, Dr Standing.'

'I was wondering, Sophia, why you're the only member of the Upper Fifth who doesn't want to be taped. You've seen the others, you've seen how much they've enjoyed it, but you won't join in. And I simply wanted to say that I wish you would.'

'Haven't you got enough information for your project?' Sophia sounded more in control than she was.

'Sophia, it might seem strange, but I particularly wanted you . . . I particularly valued . . .'

'Dr Standing, do you honestly think I would be the last in the queue and pour myself out at you like every lovesick girl here? Do you think *that*'s the value I place on myself – Sophia Wykham, Number Eighteen? It makes me sick to imagine you listening to it. I wonder how much *she* loves me, you'd say to yourself.'

Her first communication to him: she was shaking.

Robert thought to himself 'I love this girl' and said: 'I'm sorry, Sophia, you're completely right. But I set up the entire thing for you, and that's the honest truth. I listen to them, but I think of you. I heard you say a poem, once, in French. Mrs Declerc played it to me.

Sophia, it was one of the most beautiful things I've ever heard, I don't know what else to say. Perhaps I wanted you to say something equivalent, so that I could keep it for ever, something to remember you by.'

Any curious eavesdroppers had been pushed on past by the herd behind them. Suddenly the dining-room was empty, and they were standing alone. Self-consciousness increases when you can hear what you're saying. Sophia wanted to say: 'Could you repeat what you've just said a hundred times, or stop only when I've had my fill of it?' But she hung her head and said nothing.

'Look, Sophia,' continued Robert, 'I don't want to tape your declarations of love, that's not what I'm interested in. Really, I want to know about *you*, and I know nothing. I want you to tell me about your life from as early as you can remember it, I want you to tell me about your parents, your brothers, sisters, even your dog. I want you to tell me what you think about all day, I want to know the position you lie in when you go to sleep. And I promise you, if it seems like I'm in the business of collecting souls just for the sake of it, that is not the way it is at all, it's *yours* I want.'

'Why does it have to go on tape?' said Sophia, 'Why can't I just tell you a bit, now?'

'If you spoke to me now, the words would disappear into the air as soon as you had spoken them. All I would have left was the memory of them, and eventually a mis-remembering of them. And I wouldn't know what to ask you, because I don't know where to begin. I could ask you how many brothers you have. Sophia, how many brothers do you have?'

'One,' said Sophia.

'My dear Sophia, just consider the irrelevance of what you've just told me. What do I know about you now? Sophia has one brother. Where does that lead me? In thirty years, what will that *do* for me? I met a girl once, she must now be about forty-six, her name is Sophia and she has one brother. What sort of memory is that? The sort of memory that might as well be forgotten. And if you told me other disjointed things, or not necessarily disjointed, but even if you told me about your family, each member of it in turn, how would I be expected to remember that in thirty years?'

'I don't understand what you're getting at,' said Sophia. 'Why would you *want* to remember it?'

'What I mean is, I'm not interested in knowing isolated facts about you, how could I prevent them from all slipping away? Sophia, I want your spine, the part in you that holds everything together, the part on which every other part of you depends. I think I know it already, I think I have an idea of what it is, but it just needs substantiation.'

And indeed that very part of Sophia leapt out to him. 'Have me all,' she might have said.

'OK, you can tape me,' and she smiled up at him. 'What is it again that you want me to say?'

'I want you to say anything that comes into your head.'

They walked down to the science labs.

The reification of the soul of Sophia Wykham took place on that very afternoon of Tuesday, 11 July.

'How long do you want me to speak for?' said Sophia. 'How long did the others speak for?' (A tinge of jealousy here. She could have been asking, 'and where did you take Miranda for dinner?')

'The others spoke for anything from five minutes to half an hour, but I'd like you to speak for the whole afternoon, if you can. In fact I'd better show you how to change the reels: I want more than one from you. You can say anything you like, Sophia, as much as possible. I want everything.'

That was exactly what she gave him. Two hours' worth. I've heard the tapes myself, twenty-eight years on, and in a way they are exactly what Robert had intended for them: a crystallisation of a sixteen-year-old girl. This is what she said:

'I don't have a dog. I don't have a dog because my father is a diplomat and I've lived in different countries all my life. Is that the sort of thing you want to know? Goodness knows how I'm going to keep this going, I don't know what I'm going to say at all. We're pretty rich, and certainly we've always had servants, but that's because of my father being who he is. He's Councillor in Saudi Arabia at the moment, and everyone expects him to be Ambassador any moment now. My mother acts as though she were Lady Wykham already, and I'm afraid I don't get on well with her at all. I like my father, but he's so massively busy that that's that, really. In fact, I'm afraid that I would have to say that my parents aren't important in my life at all. I've been at boarding schools since I was seven so that I'd learn how to be 'independent', and basically they've worked so well that I already am. I barely think about my parents at all. They might as well not exist, or at least that's what it *feels* like. When I go home for about three weeks at Easter – well, you can hardly call it "home", can you? – when I go and visit them we won't have a single *real* conversation. They'll talk about my school report for about five minutes and that'll be that. My father'll go back to work, and my mother'll say, "I see you've lost weight, dear", or, "I see you've gained weight, dear", as a sort of proof that she's noticed me.

'I sometimes wish my mother would have an affair or something. There is absolutely no *movement* in her, if you know what I mean. Her eyes look either dead or critical. I often wonder whether she ever loved my father; she certainly doesn't now. Or don't you think "love" implies some sort of activity, something actually *happening* between two people; I mean it's an active verb, isn't it, you're doing something to someone else, aren't you? But perhaps their marriage is no different from anyone else's in that respect, perhaps you only "discover" you loved them all along when they've gone off with someone else or they're dead. Even then, I'm sure it's just a question of missing what you're used to. The sort of love my mother has for my father is the same sensation as a man who likes biting his fingernails has for his fingernails. No, that's a complete exaggeration. If my father died, she'd feel as much grief as she would if she'd lost just one fingernail. But that would be enough for her to say "I must have loved him", and enough for her conscience, too.

'I often wonder if I love my parents. I try to imagine a situation in which they're dead. I'm in the front row at their funeral and everyone is watching me. I'm anxious in case I don't cry. That is, in fact, all I'm thinking about: they're all watching me to see if I love my parents or not. What sort of face should I put on? Am I doing all right? And the awful thing is, I don't do all right at all, they've both just died in a plane crash and really so what, my life will be just about the same, except no one

---

will tell me if I'm fatter or thinner and, whichever I am, suggest somehow, just with a look, that it was definitely the wrong thing to have become.

'So, I don't love my parents and my parents don't love each other. Well, how can I love them? I don't know them. How can you love people you don't know just because you happen to be related to them? Blood means nothing, that's what I've come to believe. Blood and duty. That's all blood means to me. It is weird, really weird, that I ever came out of her, or that there was ever some act of desire on his part that caused me. But perhaps my father never felt desire, perhaps that was duty too and he was thinking of someone else. I tell you, you have never seen so little love between two people in your life. They've spent their entire lives talking about arrangements. And they dare to preach to me about how organisation makes for a better life. Well, I've learnt from their example that that's not the case.

'But you might like my brother Oliver. There, did you notice that? I've changed my tone. I can hear myself sounding more relaxed, though perhaps I shouldn't. I love my brother. I've admired *him* all my life. He has always been generous and good to me, and when he was a boy, he was a genius. I remember a summer holidays when he was about twelve and I was eight. We were living in Dubai and on about our first day out there we went swimming with our nanny and I got terrible sunstroke. From that day on, I wasn't allowed even to set a foot outside. But Oliver, he even turned down scuba-diving expeditions to stay with me. And this is what I remember. He said, "Sophia, it's time you learnt Latin", and every day, for a couple of hours in the morning, and then again after tea in the evening, with huge patience and devotion, and with a love of the language that I've never seen in anyone else, and certainly not at this school, he would go through the declensions and the conjugations with me, till I knew them even better than my times tables, which I was supposed to be learning that holidays. And when I was already in bed, he would come into my room after supper, and sometimes he would even have to wake me up and turn on the light, but I never minded, and he would read Cicero or Horace to me. So, you can imagine how I loved him. Whenever he read a word that I recognised, I would start up from the pillows and shout out, "*rexit*", "*milites*", "*puellam*". And that was all the reward he wanted. He would be as excited as me. You can imagine what a dear boy he was, though my parents . . . here we go again, now you'll hear even worse things about them.

'When Oliver was thirteen, he became a King's scholar at Eton. Of course my parents were terribly proud. He was suddenly the apple of my mother's eye, and he certainly never got fatter or thinner. My father used to say to him: "Brasenose is the college for you." Well, even I wouldn't mind being told that. But I remember the night everything shifted. I could only have been about ten, but I remember thinking, "This isn't right. Father, stop it." It was embarrassing enough as it was when he used to read out Oliver's reports to anyone who'd happen to listen, and they were always brilliant, I mean, really brilliant. But this was the first night of the summer holidays. Oliver and I had been flying all day, and we didn't land in Jeddah till about midnight. I think it was Jeddah. The air was black and warm and we were so sleepy. I fell asleep in the back of the large diplomatic car that had come to fetch us.

'When we got home, my mother arrived at the door to greet us, in full evening regalia. "My darlings," she said – yes, there, Doctor Standing, did you see? I got the tone exactly right, "my darlings" – and she began kissing us rather effusively, quite unlike her. "Darlings, come through, come through . . ." They could have warned us. They were in the middle of some vast state occasion. Candles everywhere, how can candles be dazzling? These were. And there was my father presiding at the head of the table, and when my father presides, my God does he preside. "Oliver," he said, "my dear boy Oliver." I don't think he saw me. Then some dignitary to the right of him got the full force of my father's pride stuffed down his throat, how Oliver had never slipped from first place and all of that rubbish. "So, dear boy, how was last term? How did the exams go? No, don't say a word, go and fetch your school report, and I'll see for myself." "But it's right in the middle of my school trunk . . ." "No excuses, Oliver, go on, fetch it."

'The dignitary listened politely, and by that stage, so did everyone at my father's end of the table, while the report was read out. Oliver stood at my father's side, and I remember thinking how strange it was that each of them should go red in exactly the same way. There was a sort of tide-mark in a relatively straight line ending a clear inch below their eyes, and even their necks were red. Why did my father go on reading? Why did Oliver let him? "Wykham's concentration has been slipping this term . . . Wykham had not come up to scratch . . . Wykham's exam result was disappointing . . ." Neither seemed to notice everyone shuffling in their seats. It was as though the two of them were having a very private, intense conversation, the privacy of which was only magnified by its being public. When it was over Oliver asked if he could go to bed. My father just looked at him and said, "Remember, I'm expecting a scholarship. So sleep on that."

'But Oliver didn't sleep on that, or at least, he didn't sleep *well*. By the time he was doing his A–Levels he'd got himself into such a state that he practically failed them. They found notes he'd written to himself when he was taking his exams, well, not notes, they were longer than the papers, and they were mad. They said something like, "Dear Mr Oliver James Wykham. This is the most important day of your life. Your whole life hinges on this important day. Importance is the essence of life, and the distillation of living." It went on and on, something like that, pages of it. What happened was that the psychiatrist hinted to my parents that they might be partly to blame, this was a couple of years ago now, and the best thing to come of it all is that they now ignore me totally, and I can get away with anything. I can rest assured that they will never interfere. Oliver's now living in a private clinic off the King's Road. I've only visited him twice, both times with my mother. If I'd gone alone I would have read to him. He's so heavily drugged that all he can do is lie in bed. The last time I went there he'd grown a beard, and I thought, "How can this boy have grown a beard? Surely something's wrong."

'Perhaps Oliver's trouble was that he couldn't keep up with belonging to the world. But am I going to keep up any better? Will people get to know that I'm a fraud, will I slip up one day and they'll all point their finger at me and say: "No, she's done it now, she doesn't belong here" and then where will I go? Sometimes I feel that

I don't belong anywhere at all. Do people say "please" and "thank you" when they're married to each other? God, I hope not. I hope there'll be some place left where I can relax, where I don't have to keep the act up. How *do* people do it? I honestly don't know where one goes in order to be oneself. Perhaps that's why people go to the mountains. Perhaps that's why people become hermits – not for religious reasons at all, but because they simply cannot stand to say please and thank you all the time, they simply can't bring themselves to do all those things you have to do in order to "belong". Perhaps that's what I should do, perhaps I should become a hermit and escape from all this.

'Now I sound as if I hate being alive, whereas in fact I'm grateful for being alive every day. I'd like to be an actress, which is probably the least hermit-like thing you can think of. I'm a terribly good actress, Dr Standing. If only you had seen me in *Twelfth Night* at Christmas, you would have thought I was brilliant. God, I'm arrogant, aren't I, but it's the one thing I know I can do. In fact I'm now going to recite some lines for you, as you insist I talk on this tape-recorder all afternoon. OK? Which bit would you like best? As you know Viola's dressed up as a man, and she's been sent by her master, or should I say, he's been sent by his master, to persuade Olivia that he loves her.

'Are you ready? Here goes:

> Make me a willow cabin at your gate,
> And call upon my soul within the house;
> Write loyal cantons of contemned love,
> And sing them loud even in the dead of night;
> Holla your name to the reverberate hills,

And make the babbling gossip of the air
Cry out 'Olivia!' O! you should not rest
Between the elements of air and earth,
But you should pity me.

'There.

'Did you know that I can speak in Latin, completely fluent Latin?

'Ah yes, and I can do card tricks too. You would be amazed at the things I can do. In fact, I'm now going to talk to you in Latin.

Ille me par esse deo videtur; ille, si fas est,
superare divos; qui sedens adversus
identidem te; spectat et audit
dulce ridentem, misero quod omnes
eripit sensus mihi.

'I'm sorry, I've just told you a complete lie, though there are some people at school who think I *can* speak fluent Latin. I've just recited a bit of Catullus, in actual fact, a love poem; it's pretty hot stuff – did you like the way I pronounced *sensus*? I got quite a lot of oomph out of that last syllable, didn't I? The Latin teacher told me that "*sus*" ought to rhyme with "bus", but it was my brilliant idea that it should rhyme with "loose", so it's "*soose*", "*sensoose*', isn't that a brilliant word? Anyway, I've just won this Latin Reading Competition with that poem, so the judges must've liked the way I said it.

'I'm sure I'll end up singing to you on this tape. I can't think what else you want me to tell you. I can't think what idea you have of me so far. Am I any different from the others? I certainly *feel* different . . .'

Robert switched off the tape. It was nine o'clock on that same Tuesday evening, and he was sitting in the biology lab. The lights were off, and it was now dark. 'My dear Sophia,' he thought, 'I knew that you wouldn't let me down. This has lived up to everything I could have imagined, *this* is what it is like to be on the edge, an example of the final resistance before giving in to . . . what did she call it? Society? She knows what's going to happen to her, doesn't she? This time in ten years she'll be following every rule in the book, she'll be married with children, and teaching the little things how to say "please" and "thank you". I wonder how much she'll remember of what she is now?'

He got up and leant his forehead against the glass of the classroom window, trying to think of how to warn her: 'Watch out, Sophia. Don't grow up. Don't become, always be becoming. But you are becoming, Sophia, no wonder the adjective was made from the verb. There is no question that this sunset I am looking at is beautiful because it's becoming, because something is happening out there, but I'm not anxious about it, it will happen again tomorrow night, or if it's cloudy tomorrow, then that's fine, because I know it will happen again, but for you, Sophia, you are already in your sunset, this is the last time you'll be there, and then, what will you be? You'll be "set", that's what you'll be. And decay will follow. There is nothing that can be done to save you. If only there were. I would do it, Sophia.'

Sophia was watching the same sunset from her dormitory window. Her bed was next to it, so she knelt on it and pulled the curtains behind her, an island of privacy. If Robert felt as though he had received her soul, Sophia felt that she had given it, and having given it she wanted to belong to the person to whom she had given it, the one person in the world who now knew her, because she had let herself be known. She thought of him listening to her: 'What must he think of me? Did I stand out from the others? Does he love me? I thought he did after lunch – will he love me more now? Surely *yes*. What will he do about it? Will he ask to see me? Will he kiss me? Please God let him kiss me.'

On that night, after Sophia had watched the sun set from her dormitory window, and had even spotted, so she thought, Dr Standing walking up from the science labs at ten o'clock, she gave herself up to the glorious anticipation of what was to come. She missed not a minute of it, but lay awake for the whole night, rejoicing in a hundred imagined futures.

Think of her, then, on the Wednesday. She kept waiting for some message from him, but there was none. She thought he'd be waiting for her after lunch, but he wasn't. By teatime, she knew the truth – he hadn't liked her, he was disappointed in her, he thought she was no better than any other schoolgirl. He'd had faith in her, but she had let him down. The more she thought about the things she had told him, the more she blushed, the more ridiculous she felt. 'What could have got into me?' she said to herself all day. 'Of course, he'll be able to see right through me, and he'll have recognised that there's nothing in me worth knowing. *That*'s why I haven't heard from him.'

Another sleepless night on the Wednesday, but now for reasons of anxiety rather than longing, and another on the Thursday, as he seemed to have taken the day off while everyone else was rehearsing for Foundation Day. Then on the Friday morning, while Sophia was queueing up for her break in the dining-room, Robert walked up to her as though he were about to hug her. 'Sophia,' he said, 'it was wonderful, *you* are wonderful. I have never heard anything like it. I listened to you four times yesterday, eight hours' worth. I can't thank you enough for doing it for me.'

Sophia wanted to ask, 'And now what will you do with me? Don't you want to see me privately somewhere? Don't you want to tell me all of that again when we're alone?' But she said: 'I'm pleased you liked it. I really enjoyed doing it in the end. It was fun.'

'I told you you'd think it was fun. But thank you so much, Sophia, you've taught me a lot, you know, I'm sure far more than I've taught you.'

'You've taught me everything I know,' was what came into her head. But she said: 'I'm so pleased you enjoyed it, Dr Standing.'

'More than that, Sophia, I promise you. Perhaps I'll see you before you break up and we can talk about it? I'd really like that. But I've got to dash now. Look, Sophia, I'll be seeing you.' And he left her.

Robert's curiosity, satisfied, had left him complete. If love is an active verb, a wanting verb, he no longer loved her. He felt affection for her, he admired her, he thought she was truly lovely, but now he possessed her he no longer desired to possess her. There was no longer a gap between two electrodes across which electricity flashed: the circuit was now complete, and running smoothly, as far as he was concerned. Yes, he would like to talk to Sophia about what she told him, but it wasn't *necessary*.

For he already had what he needed. And the deepest feeling he felt for her was a sense of loss, the loss that was bound to be.

Sophia slept better on that Friday night, though her confidence had still not properly resurfaced. But her friends who'd been standing next to her in the queue all said to her, 'Gosh, he really *likes* you, Sophia.' What she was worrying about now was that time was running out: three days left, and she was flying back to Saudi Arabia on Wednesday morning, after spending a night in London with her grandmother. There was no doubt that he genuinely wanted to talk to her, but *when*? Why hadn't he left her a note with a rendezvous? It was easy enough, why hadn't he *thought* of it? What was going on in his head? Why was he waiting?

Foundation Day. No sign of him in the Cathedral. Lunch, buffet-style in the dining-room, three hundred hats, mayonnaise falling on to silk dresses, conspiratorial schoolgirls. No sign of him. The afternoon was dedicated to fund-raising for a swimming-pool: Sophia was in charge of the tombola, situated in the main hall. At half past three she took a bottle of wine from her stall and managed to kick it under the armchair to the left of her. She saw it as a sort of safety measure, she wasn't sure why, a last means to an opportunity. At half past four, with only two tins of asparagus left on her table, she saw him, and he came up to her, smiling.

'My dear Sophia, have you been enjoying yourself? You've been doing remarkably well, it seems to me.'

'Yes, it's been quite fun,' said Sophia.

'And have *you* had a go?'

'Yes, in fact I won a bottle of wine.' She looked meaningfully at him, but he didn't get the point.

'Well, you won't be able to take that back to Saudi Arabia with you.'

'I suppose I won't, I hadn't thought of that.'

'Perhaps you should bring it down to the science labs this evening, and we'll drink it then.'

Thank God for that, thank God for saying that.

'Yes,' she said. 'What time shall I come?'

'Oh, about six, six thirty, that sort of time.'

It was six fifteen on the dot. Sophia had changed into jeans and a black T-shirt, clothes normally allowed only Sunday afternoons. She had spent the previous hour looking in the mirror – she'd borrowed Josephine's lipstick, but had spent twenty minutes rubbing it off with soap. She'd washed her hair but then it looked so fine and static that she'd had to put vaseline in it. Then that looked so awful that she'd had to wash it again, and put it in a plait. She found a spot growing underneath her nose and rifled through everyone's top drawers looking for a compact. She couldn't find one but comforted herself that as Dr Standing was taller than she was he'd probably not notice, and she made a mental note to herself to hold her head at a particular angle. Then she set out, clutching the claret.

It was easy to avoid people: the whole school was engaged in a vast clearing-up session, or else the 'leavers' were sitting in little groups in the marquee (where 'speeches' had been held) talking about what they were going to be doing next and exchanging addresses. 'I have nothing in common with them,' thought Sophia, as she left the main school through a back door and made her way down to the science labs. She saw that the light was on: he must be there already.

I don't need to tell you the state of Sophia's mind

145

as she went down there, as she saw the light, as she anticipated the opening of the wine, the drinking of it, the mutual confessions and the kiss: imagine it. And now imagine this: thirty girls had arrived before her, and seven unopened bottles of wine were lined up on the bench. 'Now, who has a corkscrew?' Dr Standing was saying to them. 'How are we going to open these wretched bottles?' But Sophia only saw his back. She ran into the biology lab and shut the door.

If the Grundig had still been there, she would have told it a different story now, but everything had been returned to its proper place for Foundation Day, and it was back with Mrs Declerc. The room seemed to have registered nothing of the confessions of the last two weeks: it was as inanimate as ever. To Sophia, the room seemed squarer, the laboratory benches harder, the angles sharper, her prison of the evening, perhaps even of the night, yes, perhaps she would spend the night there, because she couldn't imagine leaving it, this, her refuge.

She put the bottle on a bench and sat down with it in front of her, trying to clear a path through the dizziness in her head. 'Has anyone got a corkscrew?' – was that what he was saying to them? I've got you all taped now, so let's get drunk, I don't need to listen to your little love fantasies any more, my sweet schoolgirls, so let's get drunk. We've nothing more to say to each other, have we? Is that what he's thinking now? Has he used us all up? Was there another girl, I wonder, who thought she was the only one tonight? Who'd saved her wine for him, who's gone through what I've gone through? Why is she still there, then, if that's the case? How could she smile with the others? I couldn't do it. Never.

So, then. A course of action. If she was to endure the night, she might as well drink the wine. There was nothing else in the room besides it and her: it was better than reading about the life of a fruitfly, and there was time to kill. My first night of melancholy drunkenness, remember it, Sophia, this is what it's like. She picked up the bottle and peeled off the lead cap, then she put it back on the bench in front of her. This is what it's like, Sophia. She read the label on the bottle. 'Claret. Bordeaux. *Appellation Bordeaux Controllée*. 1960. *Mis en Bouteille en France par les caves Saint Arnould.*' Well, Saint Arnould, what would you think if you saw your wine here with me now? Would you approve? Where, I wonder, are all your other bottles of the same batch? In better hands than mine? Who'll be drinking them now, some happy couple? Some fireside somewhere? There'll be a man, opening it now, all smoothly, with a corkscrew, smiling as he pours some into her fancy glass. You won't be thinking of me, like I am of you.

So, how shall I open you, Saint Arnould? Will you let me in? And she pushed her thumbs down on the cork with all her strength, but of course it didn't budge a bit. So she looked in the cupboards underneath the sink for some suitable implement to assist her: but most of the equipment was made of glass, beakers of various sizes, conical flasks, teat pipettes, Bunsen burners. There were some fine metal spoons with tiny heads, and dissecting knives with flimsy blades, but nothing short and stubby, nothing approaching what she was looking for. So she gave up that approach altogether, and in frustration began to look up and down the bookshelves for something to occupy her. *Reproductive Organs*. She remembered a time when she must have been about thirteen. She'd sneaked into this room one afternoon with Josephine, when the rest of the school were out on the lacrosse pitches for house games. They'd had badly chapped knees, and they'd got themselves off games at the surgery after lunch – a great victory, that had been. And they'd spent two hours giggling over the diagrams, and every wonderful reproductive word. For some reason 'gamete' had had them in hysterics, but she couldn't remember the joke now. The book seemed inordinately dull. She put it back and went back to the bench and the wine.

She heard laughing now. The clear path in her head fuzzed over. Have you noticed that I'm not there, Dr Standing? Are you wondering where I am? Of course you're not wondering. How egocentric of me, to have imagined that I in any way matter. How could I hope to matter? I wonder if there will ever be a moment in my life, a moment when I can stand back and say, 'I matter'. For right now, St Arnould, I would say that you and me matter about the same. Perhaps it would be fitting, then, for us to consume each other. Yes, one glorious act of mutual consumption.

Then she had an idea. There was a round enamel basin to her left. She put in the plug. Then she smashed the bottle against the side of it, and the wine was free. Drawing it from its new container was easy: she got herself a teat pipette from under the sink, and urgently began to suck up the wine, now a red sea among islands of green glass. When the pipette was full, she squeezed out the wine into a glass beaker, and when the beaker was full, she held it close to her and went back to her place at the bench, knowing all the satisfaction of a plunderer.

148

The melodrama of her act even gave her a little pleasure; it was a sort of revenge on the awfulness of her situation. And then she remembered, when she held up the beaker to drink from it, that she didn't even like wine much, but she began to drink it none the less, because the occasion demanded it. And when she began drinking the wine, things became clearer again. 'Yes,' she thought, 'I shall see him when the girls have gone, they'll all leave before him, of course, and then there'll be only me. All is not lost yet.' She drank the wine slowly, but consistently, and when the beaker was empty, she leaned over with the teat pipette, and drew some more from the basin. And while she was drinking, she remembered the life to which she'd be returning within the week, a life where the spirit simply has no place, she thought to herself, where everyone around me thinks they know more than me when in fact they know less. How can I bear it? How can I possibly pretend I don't exist for another eight-week stretch? You cannot even hide properly on a stretch of sand. There will be no retreat from it, no retreat from pleases and thank yous and pretending I'm one of them. We'll all sit together in the dining-room like a family, but that's all it will be, *like* a family, and the servants will treat us as though we mattered, when of course none of us matters, for if *I* don't, and I don't, then they matter even less than me. Daddy will be reading the Arabian newspapers, and I'll say to him, 'Any news, Dad?' and he'll say to me, without looking up, 'Nothing to interest you, darling'. Then Mummy will say to me, 'Good heavens, Sophia, where did you get that hideous cardigan? I'm sure I can't have bought it for you.' And I'll say, 'I borrowed it from Josephine', and she'll say to me, 'Oh, how I simply *loathe*

the way you borrow clothes from that school. Haven't you got enough clothes of your own?' And then she'll say to me, yes, I know she will, she'll say it again, 'I'm afraid you're turning into a frightfully spoilt young girl'. Spoilt. But how can I win? She gives me the things to make me spoilt, but I'd prefer to have nothing at all. Oh God, save me from that place. And Sophia sucked out a little more wine, with a little more difficulty now, as the dregs were fast approaching, and she was having to avoid the tiny splinters of glass that lay on the floor of the basin.

But then something happened to lift her from her despondency: the bell for supper. She immediately cheered up. I bet they hadn't considered that. They thought they'd be spending the whole evening with him, but I will be. And she almost skipped to the window to watch the girls leave, feeling a new surge of victory at the sight of every disappointed face. There they go. Goodbye Josephine, Felicity, Miranda, and then suddenly the fear set in, and she felt like an actress, on her first night, watching the last moments of the scene before her own entrance.

She was ready, now: she thought she knew her lines. 'Dr Standing,' called Sophia, from the door of the biology lab. He came out from the party room.

'Sophia,' he said. 'What a surprise. What on earth are you doing here? Why haven't you gone to supper with the others?'

'What have I got in common with the others?' she said. And when it was obvious that he hadn't understood her at all, she continued, 'You only heard half the story on that tape, Dr Standing, and I've come to fill you in'.

'You're drunk, aren't you, Sophia, you've been drinking, come here and let me smell your breath.'

Sophia walked over to him, her eyes like a cat's, and breathed over his face.

'*In vino veritas*, Dr Standing, there, you see, I told you I could speak fluent Latin.'

'Sophia, you must have some supper.'

'But bread alone will not feed the soul, Dr Standing.'

And Sophia gave him such a look at this stage, such a look of utter earnestness, as though, indeed, her soul were crying out for food, that he immediately gave in to her, and said, 'All right, Sophia, come in here, sit down, tell me what you want to tell me'.

When your soul has been full to bursting point for four days, and you are suddenly told, 'All right, let me have it', which part do you choose to translate into words first? Which part begs most attention? For the soul that grows in the place of the one that had been given away is altogether different: the first is made of chalk, one layer on top of another, but the second is singular, total, a block of granite all from one source, indivisible. There was no one part that came more readily to the surface – everything was equal. So she said, 'Marry me'.

'Oh, you dear girl,' said Robert, and her eyes said, 'Feed me'.

'You're a lovely girl, Sophia, you really are, and whoever marries you is a lucky man.'

'But *you* could be a lucky man. Why don't *you* be a lucky man?'

'How could I, dear Sophia, I'm almost twice your age, we have nothing in common, you know nothing about me.'

'But there is something we have in common, I know there is, I have more in common with you than anyone I have ever met. You don't *know* the sort of place I

151

have to go back to when term ends, you can't imagine how horrible it is, you've got to save me from it, you've got to, and I know I could be a really good wife to you, I know it sounds ridiculous, but I'd do anything you wanted me to, anything at all.'

'Sophia, I don't need a housekeeper, and I wouldn't dream of turning you into one.'

'But that's not what I mean at all. Look at me, I'm still all potential, can't you see that? Look at me. I'm ready to be made. I don't know what I'll be like when I'm properly grown up, but I feel inside me that I have the power to become anything, I could become anything at all. And all I know is that if ever I'm to have any say over what I'm going to turn out like, *now* is the time that I can make a choice, and *you*'re my choice, I've chosen *you*. Make me into the sort of person that you'd want as a wife, and of course I'm not that person yet, but I could be her, I know I could. You watch. Am I making myself clear, I'm sure I'm not, but it seems so clear in my head. What I'm saying, Dr Standing, is that I want you to create me. That makes sense. *Create* me.'

Sophia began shaking: she had given her gift, and the shell of her shook.

'Oh sweet Sophia,' said Robert, gently, 'I've never seen anything like this before. It's odd, Sophia, but you make me want to kiss you. What a lovely girl you are, Sophia, you truly are.' He let her bury her head on his chest, and he laid his hand on the back of it, stroking her hair; and then, after a while, he said to her, 'That's a large undertaking, to create you. What do you have in mind? How would you propose that I begin?'

'Kiss me,' she said, and she looked up at him, her brown eyes.

How could he not?

It was everything, more than, she could have wished for: it was her first kiss. She gave in to the wine in her; every nerve in her was occupied, and not a thought interfered. And then, after the kiss, she said, so sweetly, 'I love you'. And Robert said to her, because at that moment he knew it was true: 'I love you, too, Sophia'. For better or for worse, Sophia had hit a chord in him.

SIX

He married her; it was a lackadaisical move. This isn't to say that he didn't love her. There were moments when he certainly *did*; during Sophia's first violin lesson, he came up behind her and whispered in her ear: 'The secret's in the wrist, Sophia, the secret's in the wrist'. But he married more as something to *do*, as someone might approach a course of lectures, an interesting course, but a course none the less. He certainly felt no enthusiasm to return either to Cambridge or to geology, and Sophia, in comparison, was a piece of newly baked bread. 'There is no one in the whole of Cambridge like you, Sophia,' he used to say to her, in those early days.

It was oddly easy to marry her. Things proceeded in an uncannily efficient way. They both managed to carry on as normal until the end of term. On the Monday night Sophia telephoned her grandmother to say she was coming up to London with a friend, so there was no need to come and pick her up the next day. Robert collected her in a taxi, and removed at a stroke any good influence he might have had at that school by 'signing her out' at the staffroom, but by this stage good behaviour was no longer relevant. He heard mutterings of 'gross moral turpitude', but they fell off him as he made his final farewells. 'The lamps have gone out all over Europe,' he said wickedly, as he surveyed eight dark faces, and two smug ones (those of Miss Hunn and Mrs Bennett), 'Good-bye.'

They got on a train at Winchester. Sophia was glowing, and Robert told her she was looking beautiful.

'I hope you'll always wear that school uniform when we're married,' he said to her.

'I shall throw it in the dustbin as soon as we get to Cambridge. It's disgusting.'

'Sophia, I promise you, it suits you, and you must keep it on until your education is complete.'

Sophia was so happy that she said, 'Oh Dr Standing, I'd wear it in the bath if you wanted me to.'

'Oh Miss Wykham, and what can I do for you in return?'

'You can make me breakfast in bed, do I call you "Robert" now?'

'It's a charming custom that wives have of calling their husbands by their Christian names.'

'Robert, you must make me breakfast in bed. Twice a week.'

'And you must have a bath in your school uniform. Twice a week.'

'And you must paint my toenails. Twice a week.'

'And you must kiss my neck, twice an hour, Sophia. I won't be able to work unless you kiss my neck, right here, on the nape of it, you must come up behind me and give me your dues. Will you do that?'

'Robert, I would kiss your feet, your shins, your knees,

your thighs, your fingers, your elbows, and basically, every part of you.'

'Every part of me?'

'Yes, every part of you,' said Sophia, confidently.

'Very well. I'll look forward to that.'

'And will you take me out to dinner? Do you know, I have never, ever been taken out to dinner.'

'Twice a week,' said Robert.

'And what else twice a week?' asked Sophia, excited beyond measure for the pleasures in store.

'The cinema?' asked Robert.

'That'd be amazing,' said Sophia, 'I *love* going to the cinema and I haven't seen a film for ages. What else shall we do?'

'What else would you like to do?'

'We could go for walks in the countryside.'

'I'm afraid the countryside around Cambridge is very dull.'

'But no countryside is dull. There'll be a wood or something, won't there, a place where we can get lost. That's all you need, really, a place to get lost in.'

'Well, I suppose I do know a wood, Sophia, for us to get lost in.'

'There, you see, we shall go and have walks in the wood and collect mushrooms.'

'My sweet Sophia, what a lovely girl you are,' and he moved from the seat opposite her to the one beside her and kissed her cheek. Sophia had never known such happiness.

They crossed over London, and Sophia rang her grandmother again from a phone box in Liverpool Street station. She said: 'Granny, I'm completely happy and you mustn't do anything to ruin it. I can't talk now, or I'll miss my train. Granny, are you there? I'll ring again in a couple of hours.'

The train journey to Cambridge was equally delightful.

'What sort of house do you live in, Robert? Is it pretty?'

'Actually, I don't live in a house, I've rooms in college, which is a point, Sophia, because I might be able to smuggle you in for a night or two, but we can't *live* there.'

'I wouldn't mind if we lived in the park. We could snuggle up in some bushes, somewhere, couldn't we? It wouldn't bother me if we didn't have a house.'

'It would get awfully cold, Sophia.'

'How would it get cold? If we got blankets and wrapped ourselves round and round in them, I'd have all the warmth from your body and you'd have all the warmth from mine.'

'The perfect economy, that sounds to me, Sophia, and we'll show everyone in Cambridge how it's done.'

'Oh no, no one would see us, we'd have to wait until everyone in Cambridge had gone off to their houses, and then we'd wrap up very secretly somewhere until the dawn. Just imagine how beautiful that dawn would be, and then you'd kiss me. I can't think why anyone needs anything else. Everyone would be completely happy if they just knew how good it felt, in fact they'd never bother to live in a boring old house again.'

'My dear Sophia, what if everyone did as you suggest? What if tonight we went to Midsummer Common and saw a hundred little bundles in the way you describe, of dons wrapped up with their wives?'

'I would like to see a thousand, and not just dons, but solicitors and shopkeepers as well.'

'And then you'd get your own blanket and find us a little space amongst them all? It's the most horrible idea.'

'Perhaps it's lucky, then, that I'm the first to have thought of it.'

'No, Sophia, I think we'll rent some rooms instead.'

'If you insist, Robert, but you're being awfully boring.'

'I love you, Sophia, for thinking I'm boring. You shall make me a sane man.'

'But I don't want to make you sane at all. I hate sane people.'

'Are you marrying me because you think I'm mad?'

'Of course you're not mad. You just don't pretend to be sane, like everyone else.'

'And nor do you, my sweet, and if you marry me, I promise you, you never will.'

'Oh no, I shall never become like the rest, never till I die.'

'I shall hold you to that,' said Robert, and he kissed her on the forehead.

At the gates of Trinity, Sophia waited by her large school trunk and, it seemed, an enormous amount of other luggage that they had between them, while Robert went to speak to the porters. He told her (rather boringly) that it was probably best not to try to smuggle her in at all, because it would be almost impossible with that great trunk of hers. 'Don't worry,' he'd said to her, in the taxi a few moments earlier when he'd seen her face fall, 'we'll spend our first night together in the Blue Boar, where all the honeymooners go, and we'll set about finding some proper rooms tomorrow.'

'The Blue Boar,' thought Sophia, while Robert was talking to the porters, 'where all the honeymooners go.' She saw the hotel right there in front of her, and it seemed so *smart*, not the type of thing she had in mind at all, and she was worried because she didn't like to think of herself as a honeymooner one little bit. More as, well, more as an *eloper*. And what were elopers expected to do? 'I shall never do *that*,' she said to herself.

'Sophia, it's fixed. I've told them I'm getting married and they're longing to meet you, my darling. I'm afraid I was right though. They've been wanting to use my rooms all year, and there's no chance of keeping them. I shall have to make do with a small, dark tutorial room instead. But here's the key, and I have to show you what fine rooms they are before I lose them. My dear Sophia, don't look so sad. Come on in, the porters will cheer you up. I thought you didn't care about rooms, anyway, and I certainly don't.'

'Couldn't I change out of my school uniform first?' asked Sophia, looking more like a schoolgirl than Robert had ever seen her.

'Oh come on. The uniform looks fine, I promise you, it could even be the fashion, for all any of these porters knew.' But Sophia pleaded with him, so he said, 'Look, put my coat on you, if that'll make you feel better.'

They carried their luggage to a corner of the Porter's Lodge. Sophia instinctively hung her head so as not to be noticed, and pulled the large coat around her.

'Meet my wife-to-be, Miss Wykham,' said Robert to the porters.

'Come on, Miss Wykham, come and say hello.'

'Hello,' said Sophia, and she smiled sweetly at them.

'You're a lucky man, Dr Standing,' said one of them kindly.

Sophia cheered up slightly at this, and she smiled again.

'Right, Sophia, let's go. I'll show you where I live, where I *used* to live.'

They walked out into Great Court, and Sophia said,

'It's beautiful, Robert. I always knew you'd live some-where like this.'

'It isn't bad,' said Robert.

'Does the fountain actually work?'

'Sophia, of course it does.'

'Is Trinity very old?'

'Yes,' said Robert. 'Now, here we are, this is my staircase, N, and I'm N7, on the first floor. You come with me, my sweet.' He took her by the hand and they ran up the stairs, which were wooden and noisy, and then Robert unlocked a large oak door. 'Come inside,' he said, 'here is the only home I know.'

There were dust sheets all over the furniture, and there was a smell of disuse. 'You must have another home,' said Sophia, 'this isn't like a home at all.'

'Well, what did you expect? You see, you were expect-ing a pretty little house after all. Anyway, you have to have a little imagination.'

'Of course I can imagine what it's like without the dustsheets. Can we take them off?'

'There's no point. We're only going to be here for half an hour, this is just a sort of farewell. Look, cheer up, there should be some sherry in here. And take that coat off, you must be boiled. You look dressed for the Arctic, not July.'

'It's not very warm, for July,' said Sophia, defensively.

'Well, keep it on then. Here, have a glass of sherry. That's what dons do. They drink an awful lot of sherry.'

Sophia took the glass anxiously and sipped a little. 'It's quite nice,' she said, relieved.

'Goodness, Sophia, did I do the right thing to bring you here? Don't you think it was a little irresponsible of me?'

'Oh Robert, I've never been happier.' But she had been, about an hour ago on the train.

'Well, I hope that's the case. Perhaps you should ring your grandmother again and put her mind at rest. I should have a telephone somewhere under here, if you want to do that now.' He took the dustsheet from his desk, which was still covered with a few odds and ends to remind him of the previous September. There were a couple of Baedekers that he'd forgotten to take with him to Europe, and a few scrawled notes relating to his failed Theory. He felt a wave of nausea rise up in him at the memory of it, and a momentary dread of returning to it. There was a note with a number on it tucked underneath the receiver of the telephone. 'Ring me,' it said, scrawled across the page in pink ink, but Robert made no attempt to remember who it was, and he tore it up and put it in his pocket.

'Well, Sophia, they haven't taken the telephone away, there's a homely luxury for you,' and he gave it to her, while she was sitting on the dustsheet on the sofa trying to look comfortable.

She put her sherry glass down and rang her grandmother's number, but suddenly she couldn't think of what she was going to tell her. She could have talked for an hour at Liverpool Street Station, when all that noise was going on outside the booth, and with only her heart to dictate to her. But now Robert was there listening and her ideas were less settled. She began to see objections that might be raised and was uncertain how to answer them. 'Do you think you could speak to her, Robert? I'm sure she'll listen to you more than she'll listen to me.'

'Of course I will, if you want me to. Hand me over the phone and I'll speak to her now. Have you got a number for her? Sophia read out her grandmother's number from

161

a small, tatty address book with dogs on the front of it. 'Can you believe it, I've had this book since I was ten.'

Robert could well believe it. 'Is her name Mrs Wykham?'

'No, it's Mrs Floyd. She's my mother's mother.'

'Don't look so worried, Sophia. Ah, Mrs Floyd . . . Yes, that's right. So you've been in contact with the school? Yes, I'm so sorry, we really should have told you sooner what was going on, though quite honestly we only knew it ourselves very recently . . . I quite agree with you . . . You're absolutely right, of course she's young, I've considered that, but she won't be for much longer . . . We have a lot in common, you know, more than you'd believe . . . No, you're absolutely right about that . . . Yes I'm awfully sorry, I did go about it the wrong way, it was completely stupid of me . . . she's a lovely girl, your granddaughter . . . Yes absolutely . . . Yes, Yes. But you must come up and see us. What, your daughter's flying over as soon as she can? Well, you must both come up and we can all have tea. Of course I wouldn't dream of marrying Sophia if her family were against it . . . No, no, marriage, yes, that's right . . . I'm no seducer, I promise you, I love her and I wish to marry her . . . Yes, absolutely . . . I'm at Trinity, if you telephone them they'll leave me a message and I'll get back to you . . . Yes, I'm very much looking forward to meeting you too, and I can't tell you how sorry I am for the way this must seem . . . So you'll probably come up on Thursday? My room's N7, but the porters will tell you where that is, in fact I might be changing rooms so call in at the Porters' Lodge anyway . . . Teatime? Excellent. I'm looking forward to meeting you. Goodbye, Mrs Floyd.'

'Do you mean you won't marry me if my parents won't agree to it?' said Sophia, whose initial pride had turned to terror when Robert seemed to have handed over the final sanction to her dreadful family.

'Sometimes, Sophia, don't you think it seems like a game?'

'But it's not a game at all,' said Sophia.

'A thousand passwords against intruders, that's all you need to learn.'

'I don't understand at all.'

'And when the game is over, you can retreat back into yourself, where, thank God, you can be left in peace.'

Sophia, who was now feeling much happier – perhaps it was the sherry – said: 'You're right, Robert, you're right. You heard my tape, didn't you? Games have rules, don't they, and you, darling Robert, must teach me every rule you know.'

'The rules are less interesting, Sophia, than the retreat.'

'Oh yes, the retreat, tell me what I should think about when I'm retreating.'

'Well, perhaps the rules and the retreat should be taken together. Imagine you're a tortoise. Now, if I were a tortoise I would find getting food very boring indeed, and couldn't wait to get back into my shell. Home at last, I'd think. I'm sure I'd feel all the satisfaction of a very fat man after a very long walk who comes home and settles himself in front of the television, knowing that he doesn't have to budge for a few hours. What sort of tortoise would you be, Sophia?'

'I'm sure I'd be just the same as you, Robert.'

'Now, are you completely sure about that? You have to *think*, Sophia.'

'Well,' said Sophia, slightly less confident, 'I can't think what other sort of tortoise I'd be.'

'You might enjoy nothing better than wandering around for food. Think of the pleasure of finding it. You might bump into some other tortoises and pass the time of day with them, and you might even talk about the tortoise who spent all his spare time in his shell. 'Is he suffering', you might say, 'from some terrible introspective depression?'

'Oh no,' said Sophia, 'I'd be a tortoise like you.'

'Well, if you are, the first rule is, "pass the time of day with other tortoises to make sure they realise you're not introspective". Then you must learn how to appear like them, so they'll trust you. Then you can do what you like.'

'But surely it's better, Robert, just to be yourself.'

'Yourself? *When*, Sophia, are you ever yourself?'

'I feel myself with you, of course.'

'Do you?'

Sophia looked down and began fiddling with her empty glass.

'My dear Sophia, tell me something. Are you being more yourself when you look at me, or when you don't?'

'I honestly don't know what to say,' Sophia said, still playing with her glass.

'The answer,' said Robert, suddenly gentle, 'is when you look down.'

Sophia looked up and smiled gratefully at him.

'And you're yourself again,' Robert said as he kissed her.

'It's very confusing,' said Sophia.

'I'm obviously marrying you in the nick of time. Learn the rules as rules, and nothing more, never succumb to them, always remain on the outside.'

'You're brilliant, Robert, how do you know so much?'

'I know nothing at all. If only I did. I only know how to act, and I know how others act. And is it possible, I ask myself, to know more than that? That, my darling, is where the secret is, that is what we should aim for, the total communication of two insides of two people. But of course it will never happen.'

'But surely that's what love is,' said Sophia, enthusiastically.

'Ah, God knows what love is. You see, suddenly you find me without an answer. For all I know, *that* is what the tortoise is feeling after all, he's deeply in love, in fact, so deep, that he can think of nothing else for five months, till finally he can bear it no longer and he springs out of his shell and commits rape.' Robert looked at Sophia and she blushed. 'Love, Sophia, whatever it is, is something we do on our own. For two, my darling, we have sex.'

'Oh Robert,' said Sophia, pathetically.

'Sophia?'

'Oh Robert,' said Sophia again.

'Have I said something to upset you, my sweet?' Robert sat very close to Sophia on the sofa, and put his arm round her shoulders. 'You're so young,' he said, 'I keep forgetting what a girl you are.'

'Oh it's not *that*,' said Sophia, suddenly indignant and proud. 'I'm upset because you seem to despise acting so much. Do you think I should stop wanting to be an actress?'

'No,' said Robert, and he kissed her in Viola's memory. 'Acting is one of the few honest professions, because there is always the admission, at the end of anything you say or do, "I am acting". The trouble is, that in real life there is no such admission, and that is why it is all so utterly fake.'

'Good,' said Sophia, moderately relieved.

'Now I shall take you out to dinner. You must be starving, after all these lectures I've given you. I haven't forgotten, dinner twice a week, though you might have to settle for the Whim from time to time. But tonight, our honeymoon night, we shall go somewhere special.'

They went to a small Chinese restaurant in the Kite, and made jokes about the dull, polite people sitting at other tables. It was so enjoyable Sophia even forgot she was on honeymoon. 'No, the world won't suck *us* in,' she kept thinking, 'I'm in orbit with Robert, *we*'re among the stars.' And they talked about what would happen when Sophia's mother and grandmother came to visit, practising roles, and laughing so much that the people from the other tables stared at them with envy and contempt.

But those contemptuous, envious people all went home that night, after a nice meal out, and made love to their husbands and wives with ease and familiarity. The lights were off, the map was known, the rites completed. But Sophia, ten thirty at night, walking back to the Blue Boar, cast her mind back to ten thirty in the morning. What was she doing then? She was looking for her lacrosse boots, accusing Miranda of borrowing them and not giving them back. Why had she been bothered? She could not see, for the life of her, why she'd been bothered at all. That was ten thirty in the morning. She kept looking up at Robert. 'He's in such a good mood,' she thought, 'I wish he weren't.'

In the bedroom, small, comfortable, blue, with a double bed in it, Robert was easy, affectionate. There was still a chance, thought Sophia, that he might not try anything. Then she remembered, in dismay, that all their luggage was still in the Porter's Lodge, that she couldn't even hide herself in her nightdress, and remain, chastely, on her side of the bed, holding hands after lights-out and talking till they fell asleep. She either had to keep her clothes on or remove them. Or perhaps she could sleep in her underwear, or perhaps she could just take her tunic off and keep her shirt on. What was Robert *expecting* her to do? She decided to make no decisions until she knew.

'Would you like to use the bathroom first?' said Robert.

'Oh my God,' thought Sophia, 'do I re-emerge dressed or undressed?'

But luckily, the bathroom was down the corridor, so the decision could be delayed, she could stay fully clothed. Then, while Robert was in the bathroom, Sophia looked at some pamphlets on the desk about the history of the colleges, and she sat herself down, and pretended to be engrossed in it, an excuse for not having made further progress in her undressing. When Robert came back she said enthusiastically: 'Did you know that Peterhouse is the oldest college?'

'Yes,' said Robert, and he came and put his hands on her shoulders.

'Were you always at Trinity?' she said, without looking up.

'Yes,' said Robert. 'Are you still wearing my coat? I must say, you look awfully sweet in it. Are you cold?'

'No,' she said, because actually she was very hot.

He said to her: 'You're a lovely girl, Sophia, you truly are, with your pink cheeks in my great coat.'

'It's a nice coat,' she said.

'Well, you must have it,' he said.

'Can I really have it?' said Sophia, 'I shall wear it all the time.'

'If you do that I shall take it back,' said Robert, and he lifted her up from the chair and undid the buttons of it, which were done up right up to the neck.

'Gosh, you're hot,' said Robert.

'No, I'm not.'

'Have you still got that tie on?'

'Yes I suppose I have,' said Sophia.

'I thought you were going to throw your school uniform in the bin as soon as you got here.'

'You said you wanted me to wear it all the time.'

'So are you going to keep it on in bed?'

'I don't know.'

'You sweet girl,' said Robert, 'I should've booked two bedrooms, that's what I should've done.'

'Oh no. You shouldn't have done that at all,' said Sophia, 'I want to *sleep* with you.'

But Robert did not understand her schoolgirl emphasis, and thought permission had been granted. So he laid her on the bed, kissed her, and unzipped her tunic, at which action Sophia' s body immediately stiffened.

'Sophia,' he said to her, 'you mustn't think of this as though it were a medical examination.'

'No, no, I'm not, I'm not,' she said. But every muscle was tight. Then she said, when she was unable to make herself behave appropriately, 'Do you think we ought to wait until we're married?'

'You can break the rules with me, Sophia.'

'Oh I know I can,' said Sophia, with so much feeling that Robert kissed her again.

Then, when Robert began to untie her lace-up shoes, she said to him: 'Robert, would you mind if you waited outside while I got undressed and got into bed?'

'Of course, of course I will,' and he stood outside the door like a boy waiting for Christmas.

Sophia pulled off her grey socks and laid them neatly on the chair. Then she moved her shoes underneath the chair, and put them side by side. Then she took off her grey-worsted tunic, and said to herself, 'grey worsted'. She took her shirt off, white cotton, and her bra off, reinforced nylon (a battleship of a bra bought for her by her mother) and she took her pants off, school regulation white pants, which went as high as her waist. 'I'm pleased Robert didn't see all that,' she said to herself, as she laid them all neatly on the chair, her tunic on top to hide the rest of it. And she slipped quickly between the sheets, so that Robert wouldn't catch her naked. 'OK,' she called out.

Robert didn't notice the drawn forehead which greeted him from over the top of the sheets. He took his clothes off and left them in a heap on the floor. Then he got into the bed beside her, and was momentarily reminded of the pleasure that the four Italian virgins had given him. 'What a singular thing it is,' he thought, 'to feel so tender and yet so brutal.'

'Could you turn the light off?' said Sophia. She lay as though in a coffin, with arms by her sides and legs together.

'Yes, of course, my darling heart,' he said to her, and he turned out the light and leaned over towards her, and for the first time felt the young girl's body, with the love and dexterity of a cook handling choux pastry. But Sophia's arms remained at her side, and her legs remained closer together, and when Robert remarked on this fact she opened her legs about six inches and kept them there as though they were a carpenter's vice. Then Robert moved his hand on the inside of her thighs, and suddenly took her knees and held them apart, and Sophia didn't resist, not one little bit.

What a strange thing it is to be able to report the

exact words which were going through Sophia's head while this was going on, and even when the pain was at its worst, when she wished that the world would open up and engulf her in it so that she could be removed from all possible feeling, she kept these words going through her, measured, on and on, till it was all finished, till Robert was asleep, and till she could hide in a corner of the bed, with her legs tight together, and her knees folded up to her chest:

'*Amo, amas, amat, amamus, amatis, amant, amabo, amabis, amabit, amabimus, amabitis, amabunt, amabam, amabas, amabat, amabamus, amabatis, amabant, amavi, amavisti, amavit, amavimus, amavistis, amaverunt, amavero, amaveris, amaverit, amaverimus, amaveritis, amaverint, amaveram, amaveras, amaverat, amaveramus, amaveratis, amaverant, amor, amaris, amatur, amamur, amamini, amantur, amabor, amaberis, amabitur, amabimur, amabimini, amabuntur, amabar, amabaris, amabatur, amabamur, amabamini, amabantur, amatus sum, amatus es, amatus est, amati sumus, amati estis, amati sunt, amatus ero, amatus eris, amatus erit, amati erimus, amati eritis, amati erunt, amatus eram, amatus eras, amatus erat, amati eramus, amati eratis, amati erant.*'

And she only paused, when the deed was done, and when the rhythm and the habit of it made her continue the conjugation, and she saw, with a quiver, what she was saying, 'I will be loved. I will have been loved. I had been loved. Would that I had been loved.'

'*Vastata sum*', she thought, 'I have been laid waste. *That* is what it feels like. *Vastata sum.*' And, half an hour later, she fell asleep.

On the Wednesday morning they managed to rent some

large rooms in Bateman Street, on the second floor, with views over the Botanical Gardens. After lunch they bought some furniture in an auction of household goods, a bed, two chairs, two tables and a fridge. Sophia wanted to buy wallpaper, but Robert insisted that the walls should be painted white, as he found everything else a positive interruption. Sophia thought it would be stupid to ask, 'What would it be interrupting?' so she kept quiet, and concentrated on plates and knives and saucepans. At six in the evening, when Robert came back with all their luggage from the Porter's Lodge, Sophia considered she was the possessor of all she could ever desire, and she was even willing to endure what she had been through again and again, provided the rest of her life was as wonderful as this.

On the Thursday morning they made preparations for the arrival of Mrs Wykham and Mrs Floyd. They bought clothes for Sophia to make her seem serious and down-to-earth, a bottle-green jumper and a pleated skirt; they bought cakes from Fitzbillies and some Earl Grey tea; they removed the dustsheets from the furniture in Robert's rooms, because, as Robert said, 'What is important today is our *ordinariness*. I'm a don, Sophia, at Trinity, and you, my love, are a don's wife.'

At four o'clock exactly, the porters rang through to announce their visitors' arrival, and Robert and Sophia went down to meet them. Sophia (on Robert's previous suggestion) kissed her mother and grandmother and made all the necessary introductions. The party walked happily down the length of Great Court, Robert and Sophia on either side of the two women, who remarked on the prettiness of the fountain. Then up the wooden stairs they climbed to Robert's polished rooms, which invited further compliments. 'What a wonderful view,' said Mrs Floyd. 'How inspiring it must be to live here.'

'I assure you it is,' said Robert, 'I'm very fortunate.'

And then, while Robert was in the kitchen preparing a pot of Earl Grey tea, and laying out the Chelsea buns on a bone china plate with Latin painted in gold on the rim, Sophia talked to her mother, as she had never done before, about her father's work, about how long she imagined they would be living in Saudi Arabia, and how it compared with other countries where she had been a diplomat's wife. When Robert rejoined them, the conversation was running smoothly, and he smiled at Sophia in appreciation of how well she was doing. Then Sophia poured out the tea into delicate cups, and Robert offered the women milk and sugar. The sun shone through the windows and lit up the scene: they talked about Kensington (where Mrs Floyd had a house in Brunswick Gardens); about the intelligence of Siamese cats (because Mrs Floyd had a Siamese cat); and they talked about Oxford, because, as coincidence would have it, Mrs Wykham had also spent her childhood there. Then Sophia cleared up the tea while Robert took the two women round a tour of Trinity, and gave them a rather dull history of the college. In between, he again apologised for his alarming behaviour at the school. He insisted it was totally out of character and he'd been ashamed of it ever since, that the only way his conscience could be soothed was if they, Mrs Floyd and Mrs Wykham, were to forgive him for his caprice, but that they had to understand that he only realised that he loved Sophia when it was too late to give them fair warning. He was depending on their goodwill now: he knew Sophia was young, and he thought he could have waited to marry her if only she'd been living in England, where he could have visited her regularly, but as things were, he couldn't bear Sophia to become so inaccessible, and at any rate he wanted his love to have a normal, solid base, as he believed there was now. He didn't wish a distance between them to turn his love into an obsession, which he was sure it would become if they were forced apart against their wills.

The two women were genuinely astonished by him, Sophia's mother in particular, and the admission of love for her daughter genuinely moved her. She experienced an almost painful nostalgia for her own seventeen-year-old self that suspected such feelings as possible, but had never dared to demand them. She remembered the months before her own marriage, a society wedding in London, a nightmare of arrangements, and her anxieties, a week before it, that she didn't really love her husband-to-be and her occasional bouts of optimism that she would learn to. She was convinced that Jeremy had never loved her as Robert now loved her daughter, and the romance in her swam up. Her initial instinct of flirtation receded into a sense of appreciation, and she was determined that her own daughter would not have to fight for something she had never had. So when Robert left them for a while to find some book he had to give them on the history of Trinity, Mrs Wykham said to her mother, 'Do you know, I like him.' At which Mrs Floyd said to her daughter, 'I'm so pleased you said that', as though they'd both been witnesses of something magical. Their hearts were too full to ask the questions which were going through their heads, such as, 'What will happen to Sophia's education?', or 'Where is Sophia sleeping at the moment?' because they did not wish to hear the wrong answers and they weren't even sure what the wrong answer was.

Then, while the two women went home in the train that evening, and said to each other, 'And doesn't Sophia look *well*? Isn't she suddenly frightfully *adult*?', Sophia, her eyes tightly closed, held her breath and spread her legs, and Robert was congratulating her on her performance.

So permission was readily given for their marriage, to take place three weeks later, Saturday, 10 August at midday in the registry office in Castle Hill. This is what Robert said he'd prefer, and the women didn't complain. Robert also arranged a lunch to follow in the Fellows' Combination Room, and a blessing at three o'clock in Trinity Chapel.

They spent the next few days painting their rooms and listening to classical music on the radio, Robert never neglecting to tell Sophia what to look out for in a particular piece, and getting her to tell him whether she thought the music belonged to the baroque, classical or romantic period, having first explained the differences to her. When she got it right, he picked her up off the floor and kissed her, and Sophia, almost as though she were ashamed of feeling so much, and with the backs of her eyes pricking with inexplicable tears, would extract herself from Robert's arms and continue to whitewash the walls with renewed vigour, as though this was the only means of preventing her soul from floating off before its time.

When the painting was finished, and when Robert was conscious, to the slightest degree, of an air of 'What next?', he told Sophia that he thought it a good idea for her to spend a few days in London with her mother, because 'mothers expected to spend time with their daughters before they married'. But the truth was, he suddenly felt like some time off. He wanted to put his feet up and read a few books without interruption. It was also good to be able to resume an old habit of his without laborious explanation, for it was summer and Cambridge was full of young Italian girls on cultural tours. He certainly had no intention of seducing them – anyway, they were almost always chaperoned – he simply enjoyed looking at them, in the same way as one might enjoy looking at a Fragonard. He also needed the time to get his life into some sort of organisable shape, to find out what sort of work was going on in the geology department, something which he had been vigorously blanking out. In fact, he never made it, but it served as a good justification to be left in peace for a few days.

And it was peace. He gathered a small pile of substantial Russian novels from Trinity Library, and installed himself in his new tutorial room in Angel Court. The room was both darker and smaller than those on N staircase, but he immediately felt quite happy there. He found some coffee in the gyp room above, and made himself a large cupful. Then, back in his room, he put the books at the foot of the only armchair and sank into it. He had read the books before, as a child, but he remembered how he had loved them, and now it was a question of finding his favourite passages. For three or four hours he sat with the books on his knee, one after another, thumbing through dreams and awfulness and hope; his mother would be happy to see him, he thought, always so keen for him to read, and he, always so resistant. But then he remembered lying under the tree in his garden with some huge volume or other, and his mother was bringing him a glass of orange squash.

'Thank you, mother,' he said aloud, and he lay back in his chair with his eyes closed to enjoy in full this sudden surge of tenderness towards her. But a surge of guilt soon replaced it. He remembered the letter he had written her three or four days previously to tell her he was getting married on 10 August. He told her it was so soon (and this was partly true) because Sophia's parents lived abroad and it happened to be convenient. But why hadn't he told her anything more? The trouble is, he thought, that there comes a time when too much has happened in private, when even a week alone with his mother would be insufficient for confession, or even a month – and would he want to confess to her anyway? Yes, perhaps he would. Since his days as a teacher, he noticed that he was becoming rather articulate. And in this mood of generosity towards himself, Olga suddenly struck him as a woman both to admire and to trust. What would she think of him, if she knew him? Would she think him immoral? Was he immoral? 'I've done nothing wrong yet,' he decided, 'I've made Sophia happier than she ever thought possible, how can that be wrong?'

Meanwhile, Mrs Wykham was attending to the trousseau of her daughter, and Sophia truly delighted her mother by what she referred to as 'her new approach'. She did not say, as her heart said, 'Mother, I do not need so many nightdresses', or, 'I think that dress is perfectly disgusting', rather she said, 'Mother, you really are too generous', or 'Have you seen that dress in the yellow?' because the yellow was slightly less disgusting than the maroon. So the two of them got on famously, and Mrs Wykham somehow associated the change in her daughter with a sudden maturity inspired by love.

Later Robert was to tell Sophia that he thought the dress she wore on her wedding-day was extremely ugly (it was chosen by her mother during these few days together, and Sophia, in her new mode, hadn't resisted at all). But the significant thing was that she didn't know whether to feel hurt or flattered – for by this stage she was feeling so disembodied, so disconnected from her surroundings, and so convinced that she and Robert belonged to a world in which what one wore had no relevance whatsoever, that she took Robert's criticism, or at least she tried to, as though it had been a private joke against the embodied, one soul saying to another: 'the clothes they make you wear!'

Other aspects of 10 August were no more encouraging. It was a day that Sophia soon learnt to forget, not because anything *dreadful* happened, but because nothing much happened at all. Having discovered that marriage was a convention, she considered herself already married, and having laid aside a secret wish to wear a white wedding dress, she'd asked herself, 'well, *who* is this wedding for?' and decided, of course, that it was for everyone else.

But everyone else was equally far removed from the occasion. The Wykhams and Mrs Floyd were thinking of Oliver, Sophia's brother. They hadn't told Sophia this, but they'd hoped to surprise her and bring him along. They'd gone to the clinic early that morning to pick him up, but he'd locked himself up in his room and refused to see any of them. By the time they'd arrived in Cambridge, the Wykham contingent had relaxed a little, or at least enough to try to measure up the social standing of Olga in the registry office car park, but she offered no clues at all, and they concluded that she was an old, grey, rather anxious person and, to be perfectly frank, not worth knowing.

The spirits of Mrs Wykham and her mother were momentarily raised, however, to see Robert again. How accessible he was, how right they were to have trusted him. He overrode even the rather inhospitable air of the waiting-room (there was, for some reason, a pile of traffic bollards in the corner, and another waiting couple were having an argument) and shook the Wykhams warmly by the hand. Robert said how pleased he was to meet Sophia's father at last, and told the women how delighted he was to see them looking so well, and on such a happy occasion. Mr Wykham was actually quite impressed by his prospective son-in-law, and while Mrs Wykham and Mrs Floyd were fussing over Sophia's dress, they had a man-to-man talk about life as a fellow of Trinity and Robert's financial situation. 'I can always help you out, remember that, dear boy. A house? Do you have a house?' Part of his mood of goodwill was owing to his substantial relief on discovering he was such an ordinary, sensible man. When he had first been told that his daughter was going to marry her own schoolmaster, he had wanted to fly over to England immediately, but various problems in the Middle East had been so demanding of his attention that he had allowed his wife to fly over by herself and put 'this ridiculous matter' right. And now here he was, witnessing the consequence of his own neglect. Driving up in the car that morning he had blamed himself. And now he thanked God. He looked across the room at his daughter. His wife was putting lipstick on her. Was this his little Sophia? He hardly recognised her. Quite like a woman, he thought, in the pale green silk dress with matching silk belt, quite like a woman. 'You're a lucky man', he said to Robert.

Meanwhile, Olga couldn't get over the fact that her daughter-in-law could be no more than seventeen. Robert had told her nothing about her, apart from her name and a little about her parents. Olga and Sophia had introduced themselves to each other in the car park, while Robert was busy with the Wykhams. Sophia's reaction was mild surprise that Robert even had a mother: she had never asked him about her and had somehow imagined that he existed *in vacuo*; Olga, on the other hand, kept wanting to take the girl aside and ask her whether she knew what she was doing, whether she really knew the sort of man that Robert was, and shouldn't she wait a couple of years before taking such a permanent step as this. She couldn't understand why the girl's parents were so happily acquiescent: she even felt like taking *them* aside to point out what they were letting happen. But when the ceremony was over, and when she had signed herself as witness to it, the urgency of prevention left her. She felt resigned, and then, when she could conjure up no sympathy for any participant of the day, she felt as disconnected as the rest of them.

They all walked back from the registry office in Castle Hill towards Trinity. The weather was dull and humid, and Robert walked at the head of the group with his mother. She had gone grey since he saw her last, and he barely recognised her. 'She used to be a rather beautiful woman,' he thought, and he tried to tally the severe, drawn face with the rather flattering image he had recently formed of her. Before they met, he had decided to hug her and apologise for his cold letter, to spend some time with her and fill her in with what had been happening to him, suggest a date when they could visit her in Oxford, but now he remembered: there had been no semblance of intimacy between them for years, and how could he begin? 'Mother,' said Robert, 'I'm so pleased you could come. Is David still in Berlin, then?'

'Yes', said Olga, 'I'm afraid you didn't give him enough notice to get leave.'

'He should have said there'd been a death,' said Robert.

Olga raised her eyebrows and said, 'Tell me about your young bride. I know nothing about her.'

'Oh mother, did I tell you nothing about her at all? I'm terribly sorry. It was all so sudden. You should've rung.'

'I tried. But you must've moved. And I wrote.'

'God. Didn't I write back? I could've sworn I did. I am *so* sorry, mother. It's just that with all of this happening so fast, I haven't had a moment.'

'Tell me now, what does she do? Does she work?'

'She's still in the middle of her education, a good state to be in, don't you think? But she's rather keen to become an actress.'

'Where did you meet her?' asked Olga.

'At St Peter's. Did I ever tell you about St Peter's, the school I taught physics at for a couple of terms?'

'And Sophia was a pupil of yours?'

'Yes, she was, in fact.'

Olga turned round and saw Mr Wykham in animated conversation with his daughter. Mrs Wykham and an old lady dressed as though she were attending the Coronation were talking to two very respectable-looking young dons, whom they'd managed to corner just outside the Porter's Lodge.

'Well, you seem to have managed very well,' she said. 'I was wondering what you wanted for a wedding present. Do you need money? Money or china, Robert?'

180

'I'm sure you need the money more than I do, and that woman over there (looking at Mrs Floyd) has given us some dishes with cats on.'

'Who is that woman?'

'Sophia's grandmother.'

'They seem to like you, Robert.'

'I think they do,' said Robert, 'Mr Wykham has just offered to make a down-payment on a house.'

'And what did you say?'

'I said, absolutely not, but thank you.'

'You are proud, Robert.'

'It's not pride. I tell you, Mother, Sophia and I have this much in common, neither of us wants a house. What would we do with a house, anyway? What if Sophia suddenly wanted to start wallpapering all the rooms? God knows what she'd want to do with it. I love her for her simplicity and I want nothing to tempt her out of it.'

'Won't you let her have a modern kettle?'

'To do her credit, I don't think she'd want one.'

'I'll give you fifty pounds,' said Olga, 'buy what you like with it. It's no good saying buy what you *need*.'

This was the closest the two came to affection on that day. She smiled at him, and seemed to have melted a little (perhaps because William had never liked wallpaper either); but when the party arrived at Trinity, and the six of them sat down to lunch in the Senior Combination Room, conversation became diluted and stiff, Robert now thinking of his mother more than the Wykhams, and even the champagne seemed a little sour. There was a religious break in the chapel at three, and at four o'clock the happy couple were congratulated for a final time and everyone went home.

* * *

Robert had, in fact, offered to take Sophia on a honeymoon. 'Aren't I supposed to take you to Rome or something when we get married? Is that what you'd like, Sophia?'

But Sophia had been able to tell by the tone of his voice that it was the last thing he wanted, so she'd said, 'I'm quite happy staying here, I really am.'

'Well would you prefer our wedding night to be spent somewhere more special than Bateman Street? We could always go to a hotel in Norfolk, if you'd like.'

But hotels reminded Sophia of the Blue Boar, and she'd said, quickly, 'Oh no, there's no need to go somewhere special.'

'Won't your parents expect us to go away?'

'I'll just tell them we're postponing it a while. Anyway, it's not like we're having a grand wedding when a honeymoon would be *expected*.'

'I suppose you're right. That's OK, then,' and Robert hadn't given it another thought.

But now Sophia felt in desperate need of some sort of acknowledgement that something important had happened to them during the day, even though, theoretically, she knew that it hadn't. Robert lay on the bed reading a newspaper.

'Robert,' said Sophia.

'Mmmm,' said Robert.

'Guess what, Daddy gave me a cheque for a hundred pounds. We can get some more furniture. We can get some armchairs and a sofa, things like that.'

'That's an idea,' said Robert, still reading the paper.

Sophia shuffled around for about five minutes, before she said, 'Shall we go out to dinner tonight, Robert?'

'Is that what you'd like to do?' said Robert, still reading.

'Only if you want to,' said Sophia.

'That'd be fine,' said Robert, still reading.

After shuffling around some more, and tidying up the kitchen which didn't need tidying, Sophia asked, 'What are you reading about, Robert? Is it important?'

'No, not really. Nothing you'd be interested in.'

'Oh, I'm sure I would be.'

'Well Sophia, do you think Mr Kennedy should cut taxes?'

Sophia looked anxious. 'Well, it's pretty dull really,' but he went on reading. Then, when he'd got fed up with her sitting on the end of the bed like a puppy wanting to be taken out for a walk, he said, 'I'll tell you what, why not bike into town and buy us some champagne to celebrate?'

'Oh yes!' she said and she took the money Robert handed to her. 'Any sort in particular?'

'Just get whatever you fancy,' he said to her, and at last he put the newspaper down to smile at her.

'Oh, thank you Robert,' and the smile gave her the courage to kiss his cheek, something she'd been longing to do for at least twenty minutes.

'My dear Sophia,' he said to her, and stroked her hair, 'I want you to know how happy I am being married to you.' He said it in return for the twenty minutes' privacy that would now be his, little realising that the joy Sophia experienced on hearing this turned an eight-minute bike ride into a five-minute one, and she was back again in a frustratingly short time.

But her beaming face made him put down the newspaper once and for all. 'OK, Sophia, let's see what you've chosen. Moet et Chandon. Perfect.' And he jumped up off the bed and began to attend to her.

'So, a hundred pounds from your father? That's not

bad. What are you planning to spend it on?' he asked her, while removing the wire from the champagne cork, and peeling off the foil.

'I don't know,' said Sophia, 'what do you think we need?' And then, after a pause, she said, tentatively, 'Do you think it would be nice to have a sofa?'

'Well, a sofa's all right, but it's not terribly *exciting*, is it? I mean, how much do you think a sofa's going to improve the quality of life?'

'Well, it might, you know, those chairs we have are awfully hard.'

'OK Sophia, it's your money.'

'But what would *you* like to spend it on, Robert?'

'It's your money, you get us a sofa, if that's what you'd like.'

The champagne made its spurt, and Robert poured it into two mugs. 'You could always buy glasses,' he said, as he handed her a mug.

'I can tell you don't really *want* a sofa', said Sophia, bravely. And when Robert said nothing, she said, 'Come on, tell me, Robert, what should we buy? Pretend the money's yours.'

'I don't know why it is,' said Robert, 'but the truth is that I don't have much interest in interior decoration, once a minimal comfort has been achieved. And as far as I'm concerned, we're already there. But listen, you go out and buy what you like, and I'll give you the fifty my mother gave me. There, a hundred and fifty pounds. Quite a sum.'

'But I don't want to buy you things you don't like,' insisted Sophia.

'I promise you, Sophia, I neither like nor dislike the majority of things. They simply don't concern me. They are made, they decay, and they're gone. They might as well never have existed.' Sophia agreed with every word Robert said, but she still wanted a sofa.

'What does concern you, then?' asked Sophia.

A thousand things came into Robert's head. Process. Becoming. The possibility of a criterion of beauty. The best means of the communication of truth. Whether communication was possible in the first place. He said, 'Music'.

And when Sophia compared music to a sofa, she immediately understood how wrong she'd been.

'Well, of course,' she said. 'That's what you shall have.'

The next day they were in the hi-fi shop with a hundred and fifty pounds to spend, and they spent it all. They bought themselves a double-triode, cascode-connected Lowther LL15S stereo amplifier; a Goldring–Lenco GL70 transcription unit on a diecast turntable, which incorporated a special Swiss integral arm with nylon bearings; a Pickering 380A stereo cartridge, featuring an exclusive 'V–guard' push-in stylus; and finally two magnificent Quad Electrostatic speakers, looking like enormous fire-guards.

They were triumphant. They took it all home in a taxi, along with ten new LPs, and they barely left their rooms in Bateman Street for a month. And in that month, I would say, there was more unconditional happiness for each of them than at any other time in their lives. Robert's happiness lay in the music, the novelty of stereo, the beauty of its physics. Sophia's lay in Robert's happiness, in snuggling up to him in bed, in cooking him eggs, in watching him transported to somewhere she had never been.

Then, in the middle of September, each made a discovery, which, if not exactly ending, certainly altered the quality of their happiness. Robert discovered that a rival in the geology department had appropriated several of his ideas to develop a theory of Plate Tectonics, and that it was already enjoying world-wide acclaim; Sophia, meanwhile, discovered that she was pregnant.

SEVEN

I asked Robert, 'how did you feel when she told you she was pregnant?' He told me, 'To be honest, the first thing I thought was, How many other women have I made pregnant? Am I a father already? Is Helen suddenly going to present me with a ten-year old son? I'd never taken any precautions, and I don't think I can ever have properly understood the relationship between cause and effect – between the least innocent of activities and the most innocent of by-products. You have to agree they have little in common, adult passion on the one hand, and a delicate little baby on the other. Or at least, that's what I remember thinking at the time.'

The only way Sophia knew how to react was to look at Robert. He was obviously extremely surprised by the revelation. 'A baby,' he said. Sophia didn't know what happened on such occasions. She half expected to be sent out on her bicycle again for some more Moet et Chandon. Then, after about thirty seconds, he said, absent-mindedly, 'What a funny thing.' And then, when he didn't say anything else, Sophia said, 'Yes.' 'Well, there you go,' said Robert.

Sophia wanted to ask, 'Well, what do you think, are you pleased, do you want a baby?' but she didn't dare. She didn't dare to hear, 'Well, no, actually. A baby wasn't what I had in mind at all.' When she looked at his face she felt, somehow, that she had let him down, that she wasn't keeping to the plan he'd ordained for her.

'A mother,' he said.

'Yes,' said Sophia.

'Well, there you are.'

'Yes,' said Sophia.

Robert thought, 'If I smoked, I'd light a cigarette. What in the world does one do in situations like this if one doesn't?'

Sophia said, 'Shall I make you a cup of tea?'

'Thank you,' he said. 'A cup of tea.'

Neither spoke while the tea was being made. Neither spoke while the tea was being drunk. Sophia's thoughts remained in abeyance, waiting to understand the direction they should take. Robert burped, a rather low sort of burp, and her stomach sank. But when Robert saw that it was pointless to be discouraging when there was nothing to be done, he said (though his voice was low), 'Well, Sophia, I'm delighted you'll be having our baby. I think you'll make a lovely mother.' Sophia felt empty but said: 'Oh Robert, I'm so pleased, I so wanted you to be pleased.' And then, when Robert saw her face, he forgot about the baby, and only thought how much he loved her, so he got up and planted a kiss on the top of her head and Sophia's stomach rose up to meet it. 'We'll go out to supper, Sophia, to celebrate.'

'Oh yes,' said Sophia.

Very little reference was made to the pregnancy in the following months. There were two reasons: Robert was distracted beyond measure; and Sophia thought he was distracted because of the baby, so she thought it tactless to mention it. In fact, Robert was mainly thinking about his work, and the role he should now adopt within the geology department. Now that the problems of geology had all been solved (and this, he felt, was what the theory of Plate Tectonics had done) the subject began to bore him. It was like finding out how to win at solitaire: there was no point in playing it any more. One difficult thing for Robert was that no one realised that the theory had used two vital premises of his own and would have been impossible to devise without them. This meant he was given no credit whatsoever; they considered he'd taken a wrong tangent and that was that. Even worse, they all behaved in a way towards him which suggested at every look, at every gesture, at every new angle of the eyebrow, 'Bad luck, Robert, you didn't quite make it, did you, but I still like you none the less', which made Robert contemptuous of his colleagues, and he managed to make himself quite disliked: 'a bitter man,' they said.

You might wonder why Robert didn't try to show up his rival, why he didn't point out that the research he'd done had been plagiarised. To begin with, it might have been difficult to prove that it had been. Not that the evidence was slim, but it was, literally, difficult, and he would have to guide people through his complicated calculations to prove the point. It would have been a further humiliation to have them not understand, and therefore doubt, what he claimed. On top of which, he had to ask himself what benefit to mankind was it if he kicked up a fuss? And the answer was, of course, none.

The only benefit was to his ego, 'And I am surely above *that*', he said to himself. Thirdly, he had to give credit to the rival, who had, after all, carried the calculations to the right conclusion. Human knowledge versus human weakness. He certainly wasn't going to step in the way of the one to reveal the other. The important thing was that the world knew about continental plates. Robert Standing was nothing in the face of that. Yes, that was true, but it irked him to be treated as though it were.

He decided, therefore, to give up research and take on a greater teaching load. He approached the Head of Department and told him that he felt geological research was going to be at a standstill for a few years, and he rather liked the idea of doing something different. He'd been teaching during his sabbatical year and he'd developed quite a taste for it. Was the department in need of a lecturer, perhaps? The Head of Department, who considered that Robert had been something of a dead weight since his return to Cambridge, owing to the fact that he didn't seem to realise the importance of 'teamwork' (a favourite word of his which made Robert cringe), was delighted at his suggestion, and immediately arranged that he should be given time to prepare lectures for the following year, and from January 1963 he should begin supervising undergraduates.

Nevertheless Robert still felt at a loose end. A couple of years ago he'd been working fourteen hours a day, now it was more like four. He felt an obligation to turn up at the department because that was what he was being paid to do, but it was becoming obvious to him that his colleagues would prefer it if he didn't. The result was that he was spending more and more time with Sophia in the rooms in Bateman Street.

There is no question that Sophia rescued him from a severe depression. For she was still, essentially, *new* and she was unconditionally loving towards him. He used to come back from the department feeling lonely and gloomy and, yes, they were right, bitter. But Sophia would fling her arms round his neck the moment he was in the door, offer him tea, music, eggs (she was not a very progressive cook); and sometimes she would say to him, 'You must play me your violin. *That* is how I think of you. Do you know, I used to listen to you in the labs when you thought we were all at supper, and sometimes I watched you through the crack in the door. But all I could ever see was your back. Now I'm married to you I can see your face, Robert, I can see your face.'

Robert also attempted to teach Sophia to play the violin, but though she tried all she could and made a spurt of progress at the beginning, Sophia was not a natural violinist and grew despondent. Also, she began, in about November, to grow self-conscious of her stomach and once, when she was holding the violin against her, she noticed Robert looking at her in a way which suddenly lost all its gentleness, and it'd been a reflex to lay down the violin and say, 'No, I don't think I will ever learn the violin. You may as well give up on me.'

It was at about the same time that Robert stopped making love to her. 'Well, that's one good result of being pregnant,' she thought to herself, 'I can see what a relief it must have been to those Victorian women.' But at nights, when she could feel Robert considering whether he wanted her, and when he'd decided that he didn't and turned away, she wanted to ask him, 'Are you protecting the baby? Is that why you don't make love to me any more? Because you can still *hug* me, you know.'

But she never did. For what if he'd said to her: 'Oh no, it's not the baby, it's because you're so fat.' So she kept quiet, and every night there was a period of about half an hour, when Robert was asleep and she was awake, when she thought, 'It's got to be better than this when the baby's born. Things are *bound* to get better. It's just that we're both a bit worried at the moment because we don't know what having a baby is like.'

They spent Christmas with Olga in Oxford. Robert had imagined he would be doing his mother a favour by simply turning up there, and had told Sophia that she was a loving, generous woman, who would give them a huge welcome. But Olga was stiff and uncommunicative, and the house seemed colder than Robert remembered it, and badly in need of decoration. They arrived on Christmas Eve, there were four Christmas cards on the mantelpiece of an unlit fire, and the supper was tinned soup and cold ham. Nevertheless, Olga insisted on eating in the dining-room, for the rather negative reason, as her diary reports, of 'the kitchen being too cosy for my mood', and it being more appropriate that 'there should be spaces between us'.

They hadn't told her about the baby, but it was by now only too apparent, and despite Sophia trying to stand in ways in which it wouldn't show, Olga asked her, when the two of them were washing up in the kitchen that evening, whether she was expecting a child. 'Yes,' said Sophia, feeling as though she'd just been asked by the headmistress if she'd been cheating in exams.

'Dear girl,' said Olga, 'do you know what you're letting yourself in for? Do your parents know?'

'No, not yet,' said Sophia.

'Have you told anyone at all?'

'I've got a nice doctor, or at least, there are several actually, but it's a nice partnership.'

'And when is the baby due?'

'They think about the twentieth of April.'

'And have you got everything you need for it? Do you *know*, Sophia, what you need for a baby?'

'You mean nappies and things like that? I'm sure if I went into a baby shop they'd tell me soon enough.'

'Yes, I'm sure they would,' Olga said.

It didn't even cross Sophia's mind to ask Olga for any advice. She was determined to prove that she was quite capable of dealing with it all herself. 'If I ripped my dress on some barbed wire, I wouldn't go moaning to someone else, I'd buy a needle and cotton and sew it up.' Perhaps that was what it was, nothing more than a terrible accident, which she simply had to put right: but she felt capable, even strong. But there were also times when she hated herself: she had spent the day dancing on the moor in her party dress, and now she had to face the consequences of it.

It wasn't that Olga didn't like her daughter-in-law. She blamed Robert for the farce he had set up. She never, in all her life, forgave him for that flippant letter in which he had informed her of his pending marriage. 'Why is it that even now he has the power to hurt me?' she wrote in her diary. So, even *that* had been denied her, an introduction to her son's future wife. Well, let it be. And what sort of a woman was she, anyway, who had so little curiosity that she had not come to see the place her future husband had come from? Or meet the mother who had brought him up? And then, of course, she had found out: a schoolgirl. And

193

now the stupid girl was pregnant. How could she be expected to be sympathetic? Let her own parents pity her.

'I want to go home,' Sophia whispered to Robert on Christmas night, 'I'm afraid your mother doesn't like me.'

'I don't know what's got into her,' said Robert, 'she's not herself at all. Perhaps it's the menopause.'

'It must last an awfully long time. She's ancient,' said Sophia. 'I hope I'm not like that. Can we go home in the morning?'

'Of course, my sweet.'

On New Year's Eve, Robert asked Sophia whether there was anything she wanted to improve her life in the new year. Sophia effused, as usual, that her life was already perfect, and put the question to Robert.

'How about a change of diet?' he suggested. 'Meat, Sophia, do you think you could learn to make a stew?'

'I didn't think you liked food much. I'm sure I could *try* to make a stew. Following a recipe doesn't look that different from chemistry, really,' said Sophia.

'My dear Sophia, the chemist. You got a grade one for chemistry, didn't you? You know, you shouldn't be cooking at all, you should be going to university. Aren't you awfully bored hanging round these gloomy rooms all day?'

'I'm not bored at all.'

'How's your acting career coming along? Did you ever contact any of those groups we discovered?'

'No, not yet, perhaps after the baby.'

'Ah, yes,' said Robert.

'Robert,' said Sophia, 'do you think we ought to buy a cot?'

194

'Yes, you go and buy a cot,' said Robert.

'What about a pram?' asked Sophia.

'If I give you some money you can find out what's needed and get it. How about that?'

'Is that really all right?'

'Yes,' Robert said.

In January, Sophia bought the baby equipment. She bought a cot, a highchair, twelve bibs ('You can never have enough bibs,' the shop assistant had told her), twenty-four deluxe nappies ('terries', she'd kept calling them, and Sophia only understood what she was going on about when they were all piled up in front of her), a dozen large safety pins, zinc and castor oil, a plastic baby bath on a metal stand, three soft white baby towels, three vests, three nightdresses, a foldaway pushchair (Sophia decided she couldn't have a pram because of the stairs), six sheets, three blankets, and a yellow teddy on a piece of elastic. 'There,' said Sophia, as she introduced the equipment to Robert who'd just returned from a supervision, 'what d'you think?'

'Goodness. Isn't there rather a lot of it? Are you sure the shop didn't fob you off with a bit much?'

'Oh no, Robert, she was terribly nice. No, I completely trusted her. And they did a special delivery for me and helped me get it all up here.'

'Did they make the poor thing's bed as well?'

'Oh no, that was me. I was just trying to imagine what it'll all look like once the baby's here.'

'Well, it looks fine.'

'And look, do you like the pushchair? This was a *real* bargain, and look how easy it is to fold out.'

'It doesn't look that easy to me.'

'Oh, Robert, don't be so horrid, look, there, it's up.'

'Didn't they have it in other colours?'

'What in the world's wrong with green?'

'There's green and green, Sophia.'

'For God's sake, it's only a pushchair, you won't even see the colour when the baby's sitting in it.'

'You're in a bad mood today, Sophia.'

'I'm not in a bad mood.'

'Did you manage to buy anything to eat in your great shopping-spree today?'

Sophia had not. The evening passed badly. Hard-boiled eggs on yesterday's bread.

The following day Sophia wrote the following letter to her mother:

Dear Mummy,

It was lovely to get your last letter and I'm so pleased to hear you're both so well, and that Daddy's knee's all right again. You must tell him not to play so much tennis. I'm sorry not to have got round to writing before now but we've been awfully busy and have only just got back from spending Christmas with Robert's mother in Oxford. She lives in a huge, old house, and there is a big garden with an enormous cedar tree in it. On Christmas morning Robert climbed to the top and I was positive he was going to fall but of course he didn't.

I don't know what you're going to think about this, but whatever happens YOU MUSTN'T WORRY. I'm going to have a baby in the middle of April. I know that's sooner than you probably thought but the one advantage of having babies when you're young is that you're still really young when they're grown up, so I'm going to be living my life back to front. We've got all the stuff already so you needn't worry about that. The doctors in Cambridge are really terrific and don't think there's going to be any problems at all. I'm sorry if the news is a bit of a shock to you, but DON'T WORRY. We're both really excited about it and we're going to call him William after Robert's father.

Things are fine in Cambridge but as you've probably heard, the winter's been awful over here with snow non-stop, and the gas-fire in our flat doesn't work awfully well. But I can't tell you how beautiful Cambridge is looking at the moment. It makes up for everything.

I'm longing to see you. When are you coming over next? I'm afraid I can't come and see you next month like you suggested because I'm not supposed to fly. But please come if you can get away, it would be lovely to see you.

Lots of love,

Sophia XXXXX

It was the most affectionate letter that Sophia had ever written to her mother, and when, a fortnight later, Mrs Wykham received it, she immediately found her husband in his study and read it out to him. 'Sophia sounds frightfully happy, don't you think? I must say, though, that I don't think it's wise of her to start a family quite so soon. Though I suppose *I* was only a couple of years older, and it never did me any harm. That superb Nanny Wilkins we had, do you remember her, Jeremy?'

Mr Wykham was preoccupied with a war, and had barely looked up from his desk. 'Yes' he said, 'nice woman.'

'Well, what do you think about being a grandfather?'

———

'She's a bit young, isn't she?'

'But she's *mature*, a lot more so than I was at eighteen.'

'Well, I'm sure she'll manage fine, then.'

'Did you hear that? She can't come here next month so we'll have to go and visit her. But that'll be all right, won't it? I'd rather like to see where she lives.'

'I'm afraid I won't be able to get away,' said Mr Wykham. 'Why not let's wait until the baby's born? No point in making two journeys so close together.'

'You're right, I suppose, but it's a bit of a shame. My dear Sophia. Perhaps I'll go alone, or perhaps that's a bit extravagant. She'll be so disappointed.'

Sophia would have never imagined she'd be disappointed not to see her parents, but she was. It was already February when she got her mother's letter, and time was passing unbearably slowly. Now Robert was such an active supervisor he spent a lot of time out of the flat, and even when he was in it he would switch on the hi-fi and enter another world. It had once been a joy to watch his face contort like a shaman's, but now it seemed to her exclusive, and in some ways his mental removal from her was more painful to bear than when he was simply out. She decided he was like this because she was so fat. She thought her stomach was hideous, and was as careful to hide it as Robert was to avoid it. Everything would be normal again once the baby was born and she was her old, thin self.

There were times, however, when she felt more affection for what was going on inside her. Sometimes, when she knew that Robert would be out until the evening, she would lie on the bed and lift up her dress and examine herself. She'd prod her stomach so hard that red patches sprung up over it, and she'd say, 'Come on, William. Kick, you lazy thing', and when she was rewarded with a limb moving across her like a space probe, she'd say, 'Now, you hurry up and be born'.

One day Sophia said to Robert: 'Robert, don't you think it would be a lovely idea to call our baby after your father if it's a boy?' She'd been looking for an opportunity to ask him for two months.

'I think that would be a morbid thing to do,' said Robert.

'How is it morbid? Other people do it. I think it's a rather nice thing to do.'

'Do you, Sophia? You think remembering the dead is a nice thing to do?'

'Well, other people do it.'

'Anyone you enjoy remembering in particular? Do you know someone who's dead?' Robert asked her.

For some reason Sophia immediately thought of her brother. But then she said, 'No'.

'Well, then, you wait till someone dies before you tell me that it's a good thing to remember them.'

'Other people . . .' began Sophia, and then she was silent. She opened her eyes wide so that the film of water on them wouldn't collapse into tears. Then she gave her last show of strength: 'Nobody suggests it's enjoyable, but surely it's *good*.'

But Robert couldn't stop himself: 'It's a good thing, says Sophia, to remember the dead. Good for whom? Let's work this out, Sophia. Are you thinking of duty, perhaps? Is that why people go and see their dead relations in cemeteries? To whose advantage are the daffodils on the grave? What human pride might we find in a well-kept cemetery? Plant a few daffodils, feel a little virtue, spit on him when he's living, but feel a little virtue when he's dead. It disgusts me. Or has guilt nothing to do with it? What do you think, Sophia? Is it pleasure they're looking for? But I won't call it "pleasure" for you, I'll call it "inner peace". Do you approve, my dear moralist, of "inner peace"? The living remember the dead for reasons of "inner peace". What religious hokum I am talking. What has peace got to do with remembering that people you once loved are gone? Absolutely and categorically gone? Listen to me, there is no peace, there is no pleasure, there is no satisfaction or guilt. Listen to me, look at me. It's not a good thing to remember people who are dead. There isn't one ounce of good in it, have you got that, Sophia?'

Sophia sobbed. Deep, old sobbing, three months' worth. He hugged her, and told her that he loved her. Then they went to bed and he held her close to him, baby and all. 'I don't know what got into me,' he said.

The following day Robert went out and bought Sophia a sofa, and for the final weeks of her pregnancy he was utterly attentive to her. 'Don't even move an inch,' he would say to her, 'I'll bring you some tea.' On one occasion he'd even bought her a record she'd said she liked, 'With Love From Me to You' by the Beatles, and whenever Robert wasn't there she played it on the magnificent stereo system, and even managed to forget she was pregnant at all. And then, in the final week, when Sophia seemed downcast and bored, he said to her, 'My dearest Sophia, you have made me the happiest man alive. What can I do for you in return?' Sophia thought a while, and sat up on the sofa to look at him. 'Choose a name for the baby, Robert.'

'You dear girl. You must choose a name. After all, you'll be using it more than I will.'

'No, for good luck, you choose it.'

'I think he should be called Caesario, after you.'

'Robert, be serious.'

'I am being serious, Caesario for a boy, Viola for a girl.'

'Or Violetta,' laughed Sophia.

Or Violettinetta,' suggested Robert, in utter seriousness.

'My dear Robert,' laughed Sophia again, 'will you ever change? I hope not.'

Viola Standing was born by Caesarian section on Tuesday, 17 April.

'A shame it wasn't a boy,' said Robert, 'Caesario the Caesarian – he'd have had to live up to something there, wouldn't he?' and he kissed his anaesthetised wife. 'I'm sorry you had such a rough time. Have you just woken up? You look awful. Are you sure you're all right?'

'Yes,' said Sophia, but she looked close to tears.

'Are you in pain?' asked Robert, suddenly concerned.

'No,' said Sophia.

'I'm sorry it didn't all go according to plan. I hear you had a bad time. I'm sorry I missed it. Well, actually, I'm not sorry. I would have hated to see you in pain. They traced me in the library, can you believe it? A stranger came up to me, and said, "Dr Standing, you have a daughter", and I said, "That'll be Viola". My dear Sophia, don't look like that. Can you talk? Can you tell me what it was like?'

Sophia shook her head, and then she smiled, and then she cried.

'I've seen her, she's tiny, please don't cry, you sweet girl.'

'*I* haven't seen her, Robert, *I* haven't.'

The omission was soon rectified. There were apologies: a changeover of the staff.

'Ah, she's come round, now, has she? How are we feeling now, Mrs Standing? A bit sore, are we?' The nurse took her temperature, felt her pulse and filled in a chart at the end of her bed. 'So, you'll be wanting to meet her, then. Have you a name for her?'

'Her name's Viola. After her mother', said Robert.

Sophia kept thinking, 'You can't be serious, you can't call the baby Viola, that was a joke we had, you can't call a baby Viola.' But she had not a flicker of energy in her to object to the name, and by the time she had, she'd grown used to it. 'Well, I'll go and get you your little daughter, then,' said the nurse, and a minute later she brought back with her a tiny conical-headed daughter in a pink blanket. 'No, you can't hold her,' said the nurse, as Sophia outstretched her arms. 'No, you'll be much too sore to hold her just yet. Perhaps in a couple of days, but they're heavy, these babies, and I don't want you straining your stitches.'

Robert flinched. 'Will she always have that funny head?' he asked.

'Oh good heavens, no, that's just because the labour took such a long time. Don't you worry, tomorrow she'll look as right as rain.'

'Well, that's a relief,' said Robert.

'What do you think to her, then?' said the nurse to Sophia. She held out the baby to her for inspection, like a cook might present a leg of lamb to the Lord of the Manor at a banquet.

'Very nice,' said Sophia. 'When will she wake up?'

'I shouldn't think for a while, but she's a healthy little thing, she's already had her first feed, you know. But I'll tell you what, when she's awake again, and when she's hungry, I'll feed her in front of you, so you can see better what she's like. That reminds me, has anyone given you the pills to suppress your milk yet? Probably not, seeing as you've just woken up. OK then? Have you had a good look? I'd better get her back into the nursery, she's getting heavy. And while I'm getting those pills, do you want a painkiller? The anaesthetic will be wearing off soon.'

'OK,' said Sophia, 'Thank you. That would be nice. Thank you.'

Robert didn't stay for much longer. Sophia was attached to various drips which he hadn't noticed when he first came in, and the thought of all those liquids going in and out of her was repugnant.

'Have you telephoned my parents?' asked Sophia.

'No, that's something I must do. In fact, perhaps I should go and do that straight now. When are they coming over?'

'The twenty-first,' said Sophia.

'Well, I'm sure they'll be delighted to hear about Viola.'

'Please don't go so soon,' said Sophia, 'they can wait.'

'Well, the truth is, there are a few things I have to get done before tomorrow. But I'll be back first thing . . . when is visiting time? Three, is it? I think it is. I'll be back at three tomorrow. Goodbye, you sweet girl. You've done wondrously well. I'm sure you'll be feeling much better in the morning after a good night's sleep. At least they seem to be looking after you.'

———

'Yes,' said Sophia.

'Goodbye, then.'

Robert left the hospital and breathed in the air outside, as he used to after hour-long chapel services at
school. Then he went back to Bateman Street and listened
to Pergolesi's *Stabat Mater*. He was so moved by it,
and suddenly so struck by the memory of the pale face
of his little Sophia, his little *dolorosa*, that he almost went
back to see her. But he didn't, nor did he remember to
phone Sophia's parents, nor his own mother. At eleven
o'clock that night, he found himself a crusty bit of
cheddar cheese in the fridge, and went to bed.

Sophia's parents spent five days in the University Arms
Hotel, and visited their daughter every day.

'My poor darlings' said Mrs Wykham, when she came
to see her that first afternoon, 'I've heard what a terrible
time you had, how awful for you. And stuck in this ward
with all these dreadful people. I do think Robert could
have got a private room for you.' She whispered these
last observations affectionately to her daughter, whose
heart instinctively froze at her mother's snobbery, and
who thought, 'Have I not seen my mother for nine
months to be told *that*?'

But then there was the opening up of little parcels,
beautifully wrapped up by The White House of Bond
Street, seven little dresses, three cotton, four larger ones
made of wool for the winter, all hand-smocked; then
another parcel wrapped by Mrs Wykham herself, who
couldn't resist saying what it was before it was opened.
'A christening dress,' she said, '*your* christening dress,'
and Mrs Wykham looked so lovingly at her daughter that
Sophia suddenly felt like crying, and said, 'Oh thank you,
it's beautiful, did I really wear that?'

'And I wore it before you, and I think it was your grandfather who wore it before that. Now it's yours.'

'Mummy, it's amazing, it's beautiful, where's Viola?'

'Viola?'

'Yes, Viola, yes what do you think of the name Viola? It's Robert's idea, he says he wants to call the baby after me. That's quite romantic, don't you think? We must show Viola her christening dress.'

There was an urgency in Sophia's voice which was somehow off-key, but Mrs Wykham didn't notice it at all.

'Viola. Well, I think that's a pretty name, don't you Jeremy? I mean, I think it's nicer than Violet – well, where is she?'

'She'll be in the nursery, didn't you see it as you came in?'

'No, but I'll find it.'

'It's the first room on the right as you go down the corridor.'

'Jeremy, have you given Sophia her grapes?'

Mrs Wykham went to find the baby, and father and daughter were alone. The experience was such a rare one that both of them suddenly felt rather shy. The handing-over of the grapes provided a short, easy script, but then there was an uneasy gap before Mr Wykham thought of a suitable question: 'Well, how's it going, Sophia? What's it like being a mother?'

'Well, the truth is, that it doesn't feel very different. Sometimes, Daddy, it feels very strange that I have a baby at all, because they look after her so well here, and they tell me to rest all the time, they say, "You've had a major operation, Mrs Standing, you must take care of yourself". I won't *really* know what it's like being a mother till I get home.'

'Well, I'm sure they're right, you know. Do you know when you'll be going home?'

'About ten days from now, I should think.'

'What a lovely baby, you clever girl,' said Sophia's mother.

'Didn't you bring her in?'

'She was sleeping so soundly I didn't want to move her. Jeremy, you simply *must* have a look at your grand-daughter.'

The Wykhams' visit to England went very smoothly. It was a shame, they said, that they didn't manage to have a look *in* the house, but they went round and had a look at the Standing's marital home at 9 Bateman Street. 'Lovely *size*, and lovely looking right over those pretty gardens,' Mrs Wykham had said to her daughter on a subsequent visit, and Sophia had felt it would be unkind to disillusion her as to the fact that they only had the top floor. And thank God they hadn't managed to look inside, for even with the sofa installed it was a bare sort of a place, not at all the sort of place her mother would consider a *home*, at any rate, and goodness knows what she would have thought of the hi-fi system, which seemed to take up about a third of the entire flat. It was worth having a Caesarian to avoid *that* scenario, she'd thought to herself.

Robert had done well with the Wykhams too. They'd taken him out to dinner twice, and on both occasions he'd been charming. They flew back to Saudi Arabia, after a quick visit to Oliver in his clinic, which had caused less anguish than usual, and Mrs Wykham said to her husband, 'Isn't it good to leave England knowing that our children are being well taken care of? It does feel, at last, that things are settling down – I mean, compare now with a couple of years ago. I feel so *proud* of Sophia, don't you?'

Robert was being nice to Sophia. She and the baby had been home for a week, and it was the day of her seventeenth birthday, 8 May.

'We'll go out to dinner tonight,' he said to her, 'Where shall we go?'

'Robert, I don't think we can. What about the baby?'

'We can find a babysitter, Sophia, that'll be no problem. What about that woman from the downstairs flat? She was googling a bit this morning. Why don't you ask her?'

'Well, actually, Robert, I feel a bit tired tonight and the baby has to be fed at eight, and at midnight.'

'That's all right, feed the baby, Mrs Whatshername from downstairs can keep an eye on her for a couple of hours, and you can feed her when we get back.'

'All right, then, we'll go,' and Sophia flung her arms round her husband and told him how much she loved him.

But Mrs Whatshername from downstairs wasn't in, and when she found she wasn't in, she suddenly felt a lead weight descend on her again, and her former exhaustion rerooted itself. Robert suggested tracing one of the undergraduates he taught – 'Come on,' he said to her, 'there must be someone who can look after your baby, you need a break, don't give in.'

But it was too late, she already had.

'Are you still in pain?' he asked her.

'Oh no, no I'm not in pain at all. I suppose I just didn't realise that babies had to be fed all during the night as well. I just can't believe that all these women I see with babies all get up in the middle of the night to feed them. Why don't they complain or something? I mean, eight o'clock, midnight, four in the morning, how long does it go on for like that?'

'Well, you're managing awfully well, my sweet, and I'll get you a birthday present to reward you one of these days.'

In fact, he never did, but nor did Sophia particularly notice. It wasn't even that, at this stage, the baby was a particularly demanding one: she slept between feeds, and cried only when she was hungry. Robert's life was, therefore, barely interfered with, as they had a system whereby Sophia would sleep on a camp bed from the midnight feed onwards. When Robert was out, Sophia would listen to the Beatles and wait until the baby woke up again, when she would change it, feed it and lull it back to sleep. The fiercest grudge that Sophia held against the first month of motherhood was not that it was demanding, only that it was terrifically boring.

One of the most boring things she had to do was take the nappies to the launderette. It was her one expedition of the day. Sometimes it was too boring to contemplate, so she left it until the nappies stank so much that Robert complained, but the advantage of that system was that Robert was happy to babysit ('provided you're *sure* the baby won't wake up') while she dragged the sodden nappies in plastic bags for the four-hundred-yards' walk required. Another boring thing was that the baby was sick rather a lot, and got through the three nightdresses alarmingly quickly, so she had to be dressed in those pretty dresses given her by her grandmothers and be sick all over those as well. But there was little extra work: the sicky clothes just got put in the washing machine with the nappies, and that was fine.

When the baby was about three weeks old she got spots. By now her head was the right shape, but her skin had become distinctly blotchy. Coupled with this affliction was a little pink-eye, so that one eye in particular leaked a yellowy gunge. 'She's not a very pretty baby, is she, not that I know about such things,' said Robert.

Sophia, who was secretly in despair at her ugliness, said, 'I think it's just a phase she's going through.'

'Let's hope it is,' said Robert. 'What's her character like, then? Has she got one yet?'

'I don't think so,' said Sophia, 'but I don't really know what to look for. The trouble is her eyes aren't focusing yet, and her head's still totally floppy. And she doesn't have anything else with which to *express* a character.'

'I suppose these things take time. At least she eats and sleeps.'

'At least you eat and sleep,' she said to the little Viola while trying to prop her up on her knee, her head lolling on to one side. 'I must take you to the doctor about that eye of yours.' In fact, she never did, and three weeks later it had managed to clear by itself. But three weeks later there were other problems.

They call it three-month colic. One day the baby is sleeping and feeding, and the next it can do neither. It takes the teat hungrily in its mouth, sucks violently for ten seconds, and then cries for hours on end: no lull, no song, no rub will make it change its mind.

Day one of the new pattern Robert said to Sophia, 'For Christ's sake, can't you shut that baby up?'. Day two Robert spent all day in the Library. Day three was a Saturday. At lunchtime Robert said to Sophia, 'You're going to have to take that baby to a doctor.' In the afternoon Sophia took the baby for a walk in the pushchair to give Robert a rest from the wailing. In fact Viola cheered up a bit and Sophia could pause to cry a little herself on a bench in the Botanical Gardens.

Then she turned the pushchair towards her to examine the lop-sided head of her daughter. She was awake, though to judge by the glaze in her eyes she might as well not have been. She was pale, blotchier than ever, and to add to this she had by now become almost bald, with only a few wisps remaining of ill-looking, mouse-brown hair. 'That'll be gone in a couple of days,' thought Sophia, 'I wonder if I pulled at it whether it'd come out in my hand?'

Then the baby was sick and Sophia hadn't brought a handkerchief with her, so it was home again for a change of clothes. She might have left her with the sick all down her, but a couple came to sit on the bench next to her, and gave her such critical looks that Sophia had no choice but to move on.

'Back already, are you?' said Robert.

'Yes, I'm sorry, the baby's been sick again.'

'Well, there's no point in trying to listen to this,' and he switched off Mahler.

'Look, I'm sorry, I'll just change her clothes and I'll be off again.'

'Don't bother. It's not your fault. Stay. Let her cry.'

'She's not crying at the moment.'

'What time does her evening session begin?'

'I'm sorry, Robert, I don't know what to do about it, I really don't.'

'Is there any food in the house?'

'I'll have a look.'

'There isn't.'

'Well, why did you ask me, then?'

'What about the nappies?'

'What about them?'

'Do they need washing, Sophia? Perhaps you could pop out to the launderette.'

'You can't imagine what it's like. Look, I'll go out again, you're just being like this because I interrupted your stupid music.'

'I thought you liked Mahler.'

'I hate him.'

'Well, perhaps Viola does need a little more fresh air. And while you're out, you couldn't try to find us a bit of supper, could you? Here's a pound.'

So Sophia carried the bulky pushchair down the two flights of stairs yet again, and she half-wished that she might drop it, and very nearly did so, because it was growing dark and the tears came, yet again, to blear her eyes.

Robert's first reaction, on the restoration of his privacy, was to put the music on again. But after five minutes he found he couldn't concentrate, so he stopped it. What a stupid life I'm leading, he thought. Why bother to be alive at all if you don't live with conviction? How, when you are given a span of a mere seventy years, can you allow a pause of not living it to the full? It's like this, he decided, you are given ten minutes a month to see your lover in jail, behind a grille, a political prisoner. Three minutes into it, you say, 'Excuse me, I've got to go and have a pee.' He got up to make himself some coffee.

No milk. Oh, Sophia, there is no milk in the house. There was a tin of Cow and Gate by the stove, so he tried a spoon of that, but for some reason it didn't dissolve properly, but remained as globules on the surface. He tasted it and threw it down the sink.

He tried a bit of music again, Bach this time. He couldn't concentrate. He went out to find his wife.

He looked for half an hour; not a trace of her. The shops must have been shut for an hour, at least. He'd sent her out to buy supper and the shops weren't even open. What a waste of time, he thought, and went back to Bateman Street.

When he got back he heard baby and wife crying through the door. He decided to go out for a walk. He walked fast, down the Hills Road, then through Downing and Pembroke towards the backs, towards Trinity. He walked through New Court and sat down on the banks of the river, the great Wren Library looming up behind him. Another sunset, there's a comfort, he thought, and he lay down now, conscious of the cold earth underneath him and taking pleasure in it. How much better than lying dead in a cemetery. He pulled out some grass and sank his fingers deep into it. Ah, you'd know there was life in here, he thought, my dear Earth Mother. What a brilliant scheme it is that causes gravity to direct me to you, the great includer, of which I'm one living cell, who's come up for a brief intake of breath. Doesn't God raise Adam out of the earth? Yes, He knew what he was doing.

He closed his eyes and imagined that he had been buried deep in the earth for millions of years, and then, just at that moment, he had been plucked out of it. Here you are, here's air for you, here's light. What you do is you breathe it in, like this, do you feel it going through your nostrils, so cool? Are you feeling the air going inside you? Then make room for more.

The red sun had gone, and its last light was slipping beneath the horizon. But the light that was left filled Robert with joy, that it existed at all, and that he had ever seen it. 'I'm even less than a single cell,' he said to himself, 'I'm part of one.' Then he noticed, with gratification, that his hand was bleeding. He must have scratched it on some roots as he'd clawed into the ground. 'Part of one,' he said again, and rejoiced equally at the sight of the earth in his wound, and the thought of his blood in the earth.

On his way back to Bateman Street, Robert was calm. And all was still behind the door of his flat. Sophia was lying on the bed with her face down in the pillow, and Viola was sleeping next to her. He knelt by the bed and kissed the back of her hair, 'You mustn't be taken over by all of this, you know, you've got to resist it. Viola is going through a bad phase, that's all that's the matter, but we can endure that, can't we?' at which Sophia, unaccustomed to such patience, was so moved that she burst into tears and woke Viola up. If Sophia alone might have inspired pity, the pair of them together made Robert long to rejoin the air outside, and he immediately geared his mind into manoeuvring the situation so that he could.

'Sophia,' he said, above the din, 'we're going to have to think of a way of reorganising things.'

'I'm so sorry, Robert,' blubbed Sophia, but she didn't manage to say anything else, and as Robert looked from one blubbing face to the other, he found it difficult to determine who, at that particular moment, was the blotchier.

'Shall we go out and get some fish and chips?' he asked, and because he hit a slightly tender note in the word 'chips', Sophia cried all the more. But at last he was moved to hold her and the flow began to ebb.

'My darling Sophia,' he said to her, 'I love you, please don't ever forget that, and I'm sorry if I get angry. I promise you, it's more to do with my work than anything else. Everything feels so trivial sometimes, Sophia, that's what makes me in this mood, and I hate myself for taking it out on you, my sweet, when you, of all people, are so innocent. You're goodness itself, Sophia, you're a lovely girl, so let me buy you a large portion of fish and chips.'

Then he kissed her, the first proper kiss since Viola's existence had made itself felt, and Sophia felt herself come back to life, and Robert went out into the night air.

By Monday their heads were still sufficiently above water for them to make a policy decision: Viola would go to a doctor, and Robert would spend more time in the Library.

'I'd prefer to sit this out alone,' said Sophia, 'in a way I'd feel less bad about this if I knew you weren't affected by it too. At least then I wouldn't feel so guilty about it.'

It was also agreed that Robert should eat his supper in Trinity, because he understood that Sophia simply couldn't manage to shop efficiently while she was getting so little sleep.

The doctor couldn't offer any help at all: 'She won't be like this in a few weeks,' he assured Sophia, so Sophia prepared herself for a siege, and said to herself, 'I can endure anything, I know I can.'

'Things are better now,' Sophia convinced herself, 'now that I'm alone, I can mope about the house all day, without Robert implying with every look, "Where's the old Sophia? Where's the fire gone in you?" I don't want company.' And Sophia did mope. The lack of sleep made her mouth feel as though it were full of cotton wool, that it would require extreme effort on her part to open it at all, and the muscles in her jaw ached from the continual clench in which she held it. So when Olga wrote and asked her whether she'd got the flowers and the rattles, and apologised for not having visited her and suggested that one way of meeting her new granddaughter would be if she and Sophia were to come and visit her in Oxford while Robert was busy attending to the university term, Sophia wrote back and said, thank you, she wasn't feeling up to travelling at the moment, but as soon as she was she'd let her know.

Robert, meanwhile, was finding himself again. What pleasure there is in solitude, he thought. His tutorial room in Angel Court was a positive haven of quiet. After a three-course supper on Trinity High Table, he would retreat there for a while, perhaps for an hour, perhaps two, before making the reluctant walk back to Bateman Street. But he felt he owed it to Sophia to return, despite the fact that when he did, she was either doing something to the baby or sound asleep, so he often thought he might as well not have bothered.

Of course, the one thing that he did miss was his hi-fi system. For some reason, he didn't think of appropriating it straight away; perhaps silence was sufficient music after the noise of his daughter. But after a while, and after going to a few unsatisfactory concerts given by undergraduates, where the audience coughed and shuffled, and after reading a few unsatisfactory books on the subject, where he felt that a ludicrous selection of adjectives was used to describe some of the finest music ever written, he felt a craving for the Goldring-

Lenco turntable, the Loewther amplifier, and the Quad speakers. So one day, about three weeks into the new regime, he said to Sophia, 'I don't know what you'll think about this, but would it be possible, I mean would you mind terribly, if just for these few weeks while Viola isn't sleeping properly and making that frightful racket, I moved the hi-fi system to my room in Trinity? You can trust me that as soon as she's sleeping and things are a bit more orderly in the day, that I'll be moving it all straight back.'

Sophia said: 'Of course you must have it,' and that was the last that Bateman Street saw of any hi-fi system for about ten years.

EIGHT

I asked Robert when it was that music seriously began
to get a hold on him.

'No, no,' he said, 'it wasn't music; music was as relevant
as the pins which hold out the specimen on a dissecting
board.'

'You can't say that, Robert. You can't reduce music
to that.'

'Then perhaps it was the scalpel that reveals the gut
to the light for the very first time.'

'The gut?' I queried.

'The soul, Olivia, the soul. I wanted to make it real,
I thought I could somehow solidify it and make it won-
derfully, irrefutably accessible.'

'But for whom, Robert, did you want to make your
soul accessible?'

'I wasn't concerned with who such a person was,
I'm no snob. Obviously it would have been someone
musical . . .'

'But didn't you care who it was?'

'Olivia, you have to understand what I was doing. I'm not talking about some sort of muddy . . . what's that hideous word in vogue at the moment, 'relationship', I certainly didn't want one of *those*. I was looking, if you like, for the perfect and acknowledged communication of two souls. Isn't that what beauty is? The perfect, honest charting of a soul and its reception by another. If I'd been a genius I would've written the music in the first place; though even if I had I would've considered my work only half done till I had found the man who could truly receive it. If Mozart had still been alive, I would have gone to him, I would have hugged him, I would have *known* him. Or that's what it felt like at the time. Perhaps he would have disagreed with my analysis, my dear Olivia, of course he would have disagreed with it, but Olivia, understand how possible, how wonderful everything seemed to be then. For God's sake, that initial optimism drove me on for twenty years, that's all I wanted, it wasn't much, I wanted one man to pick up the scores and say, "*yes*".'

'But Robert,' I said to him, 'surely you could have found someone who shared your passion for music, you could have found someone to talk to about . . .'

'Talk?' said Robert, disparagingly. 'What use has "talk" ever been? You make arrangements with talk. You fill time with talk. You criticise with talk. The words I'd be looking for simply don't exist, "talk" hasn't needed them so it hasn't invented them. Olivia, what is the corresponding verb of "beauty"?'

'Beautify,' I said.

'Now, what sort of pathetic word is that? It reminds me of interior decoration and wallpaper. There's no enlightenment from "beautify". But it's typical, isn't it, for language to skirt round anything in the least bit difficult. Perhaps other languages are braver than ours, perhaps the fault lies with English. Perhaps somewhere there's a word or a sigh or a grunt that represents exactly that activity of making a beautiful thing, or the activity which precedes the making of it, which, if it is true, makes inevitable the beauty which is to become . . .' And then Robert suddenly hung his head and said, 'the nonsense I talk nowadays'.

'Robert,' I said to him, 'my dear Robert, it's not nonsense, it's not nonsense at all. But you have to tell me, what gave you the *idea* of your project in the first place?'

' "Project"? Is that what you call it?'

'No, of course it wasn't just a project.'

'For God's sake, Olivia.'

Eventually, however I got what I wanted. In late June 1963, Robert was skimming through a copy of the *TLS* in the Senior Common Room, when he came across a poem. Robert could remember neither the title nor the author (and it was with some difficulty that I managed to retrieve it from the University Library – it's by Stephen Romer and the title is 'Beneath the Tree') but its meaning (as far as I see it) was the one identifiable cause of how he was to conduct his life for many years. The lines which caught his attention were these:

> if we could hold music in the mind
>
> and receive, as something solid,
> the *Blessing of God in Solitude*
>
> or the *Fountains of the Villa d'Este*
> – but the trills and octaves stream away
>
> to leave us asking what it was, exactly,

which flashed through the cerebral tree

of nerve-cell and synapse, whatever they are,
imponderable matter

where all is registered.

I cannot be so sure, however, what gave him the idea of
the colours. The poem gave him his end, but it was his
means that were so ingenious. 'Did *I* think of it?' he said
to me. 'Are you sure there wasn't someone before me?
Some medieval monk somewhere? There must have been.
Or if he hasn't lived yet, he surely will, for it seems such
an obvious thing to work out. For language is so pathetic,
and so incapable of referring to the bulk of what it is to
be human, that *of course* there has to be a meta-language.
I think in the end I hit upon fifteen thousand shades of
colour, representing fifteen thousand shades of emotion,
though that's a paltry number compared to what there
actually is, it was just workable with. Even for that, I had
to limit the range of pieces of music that I analysed, just
so that the exercise could be possible, and not get out of
hand.'

   Robert laughed when I spoke to him about decon-
struction. 'Oh *that*,' he said, 'isn't that the philosophy
that suggests that nothing exists "*hors-texte*" or some
such expression? Forgive me, I don't know much about
it, but what would one of these deconstructors tell me if I
showed him one of my colour samples, say, of a thousand
shades of blue? Could they name fifteen of them, perhaps?
Then what happens to the others? Do they exist or not?
Or what would the intellectually honest deconstructionist
say to you, if you asked him, "How do you feel today,

Jacques?"'. They're all French, aren't they? So what would he say? "Like this pillar box, here, actually," or to be more precise, and I trust that the sense doesn't change in the translation, "*Enfin, comme cette boîte aux lettres*". But I've never met one, or at least I've never argued with one, so perhaps I'm being unkind. Perhaps they have some alternative, excellent grid on which they feel things. In fact, they might even give their feelings a solidity I might envy. I am only suggesting that in my experience there are a limited number of synapses, and an unlimited number of shades of feeling, and a deficiency in language has nothing to do with either. That there is no *hors-texte* seems to me a nonsense thing to say.'

I asked him, 'What colour did you *feel* when you read the poem?' and he made me feel like a journalist, he said: 'You don't have the idea at all, you cannot *say* what doesn't have a *name*, and anyway, I hadn't begun plotting the colours at that stage, and they have a dependency on each other which cannot be taken out of context. But I suppose, let me see, if I were to imagine myself hearing what I felt then in a piece of music, and remember that I am out of practice and haven't done this for a few years, I would imagine that what I felt were very clear, bright colours, perhaps an aquamarine at its most intellectual, warming to a sort of siennese magenta – listen, this exercise is useless, there are simply no words available, and it's wrong of you to try to corner me into them.'

So, Robert read the poem and within a few moments, remarkably enough, had devised his means of literally 'holding music in the mind', by analysing it into its emotional parts and then solidifying it into a code of colours which had no yardstick besides the *consistency* of their relationship to each other. There was never an outright tallying of single note to single colour: the colour conjured up in Robert's mind would depend on the note's relative position in the piece of music. When I first heard him talk about it, I thought of Wittgenstein saying that there was no such thing as a private language. I was excited and said, 'Robert, you've done it. Haven't you invented a language? And isn't it utterly self-contained?'

'No,' said Robert, 'it was never self-contained – it was the very opposite, it was a language which was without precedence in its precision . . . All I needed was someone to understand it, to recognise the colours as true, to be able to say, from the bottom of his heart, "I understand, I know them too" – what greater communication could exist than that?'

And this was the hope that fed him.

There used to be a small art shop in St Edward's passage, with a steady if not very large trade. Robert had always wanted an excuse to go inside it. It was there he went now. There was a man of about sixty in a white overall behind the wooden counter, and Robert said to him: 'A tube of paint in every colour, please.'

'Every colour, sir?'

'Yes, please, every colour.'

'But there are many types of paint, sir, and many makes of paint. Do you require water colours or oils?'

'The lot,' said Robert.

I'm only mentioning this episode because I managed to trace the man, a Ronald Pickering, now in his late eighties, who told me that when Robert insisted that he wanted a tube of every single paint that he had in his shop, though of course he felt this was a very odd request indeed, he felt his face breaking into an enormous smile.

'I remember', he told me, 'I'd never been in that situation before; it had always been a tube of this, or a tube of that, and suddenly this man comes in and says, "The lot, please". What's more, the way he said it made it seem as though it were an obvious thing to be asking for, "The lot". And when he left the shop, can you believe this, I had to sit down, and I always stand behind my counter, but I had to sit down on that occasion. And it wasn't just that I was feeling pleased with the size of the cheque he gave me, though of course that was very nice, particularly at that time of year when the students are down and the trade's not so good; no, it wasn't that, it was the *conviction* that got me. You don't see much of that nowadays, you don't see much of that at all. I kept thinking, I remember, what can the man be *painting* if he has a look like that. Tell me, what was it? What did he use those paints for?'

In fact, Robert didn't use the oils at all: he still has ninety unopened tubes, or at least, eighty-eight: he'd forgotten to buy turpentine (the truth was, he didn't realise you had to), and was trying to mix titanium white with lemon yellow, but it was taking so long, and he was so impatient to get on with the task ahead, that there came a moment when he put the caps back on and threw the tubes in a box which he promptly forgot about. I said to him, 'Couldn't you have taken them back to the shop and switched them, or got your money back or something?', but he looked at me, and said, 'You don't understand what it was like, at all, do you?'.

But he spent till three that morning mixing two shades of blue in the watercolour. He didn't leave his room: he forgot food and peed in the basin. He tried out every conceivable ratio of the one paint with the other, then would fill his brush with water and apply it to the blue at slightly varying pressures. Then when he finally went to bed, he could hardly sleep, because he remembered that he hadn't even *opened* a tube of white. 'What's going to happen when I start adding *white*?' He was back at his desk by 5 a.m. with a tube of cadmium white in his hand and a whole day in front of him.

Though he had been extremely tempted, not surprisingly, to listen to music while he was mixing, he knew that it was important to keep his mind entirely free from any associations: he thought, perhaps, that if he were mixing pinks while he was listening to a passage in Bach, then he might tend to think of pink if he heard anything that reminded him of it, however subconsciously. In fact, one of the hardest things to do, he found, was to find passages of music which were entirely association-free – the ten LPs that he had bought during his marriage were useless, quite apart from their range being too broad. It was important to find music that he didn't know too well, or preferably not at all, so that he could listen to it for the first time under controlled conditions. It was equally important, he found, to get to know the music well before actually analysing it, because though this was less apparent with nocturnes and lighter music, he increasingly discovered that the various movements of a symphony, for example, were interdependent, which made it important to know what happened later before it was possible to feel, with total exactness, what was happening in the introduction. He also determined to change nothing in the room for the length of the experiment, so every picture (at least, all two of them as donated by Trinity) had to remain in exactly the same position, as did every piece of furniture, so that what he saw while he listened remained absolutely constant. He also didn't allow himself to listen if he was feeling happier than normal, or sadder than normal, so that if the day was too beautiful, or if he'd had an argument with Sophia, he waited until he had returned again to the equilibrium. In fact, he managed to train himself to stay within the bounds of the equilibrium for large stretches at a time, only allowing himself to break away from it when he was with the music. This system, he found, increased his sensitivity to such an extent that he could isolate single notes and be as moved by them as most would be by an oratorio.

He spent about a month on a nocturne which he then scrapped, but it taught him how to go about things. To begin with, he discovered he wasn't being at all rational about the colours he was using. It was his inclination to be far too romantic about the whole thing, to sit with all the tubes in front of him and, when he recognised a chord which matched a colour exactly, he'd try to 'find' the colour: he'd stop the music and, keeping the particular chord in his head as clearly as he could, he'd frantically start mixing the paints until he had, almost by accident, come across the colour he was looking for. Then he'd listen to that particular passage in the music again and again, to make sure it was exactly right, and if it wasn't, he'd add a little white, or a little black, or he'd make the colour brighter by adding more paint to it, or more luminous by adding more water, or he'd try a different hue altogether. But this method was extremely slow, and it also didn't do much for his enjoyment of the music, because he kept having to stop it and start it, and after about a month he decided he needed a different approach altogether.

He knew what the problem was: he had to become a better expert with the colours, or at least, he had to cut down on the number of them or rationalise them somehow. So he devised himself a chart. I've seen it: it's three metres across by two metres deep. There's a band of white at the top, and a band of black at the bottom, with a total of 14,850 colours in between, each covering a space of four square centimetres. There's a middle band of hues (colours with no black or white added), a hundred and fifty of them, beginning with bright red and ending with almost bright red, or red with the tiniest, tiniest bit of blue in it. The reds move through orange to yellow: there are an enormous number of different hues here, almost twice as many as the purples – Robert tells me this is how the colours are by nature, as their wavelengths are longer, and therefore more distinguishable to the human eye; from yellow the hues proceeded to green, from green to blue (an extraordinarily beautiful bracket of colours here); then on through about thirty purples to red again. 'If you took it off the wall you'd have a cylinder,' Robert explained. 'Do you see how the colours on the right-hand side connect up with those on the left? What I did was to take each hue in turn, and using scales that I'd taken from the laboratory, I would add white, first at two per cent of its total weight, then four per cent, then six per cent and so on, until it was ninety-six and ninety-eight per cent and finally completely white – do you see my method? Then it was exactly the same with the black, with two per cent increments each time. I know sometimes I couldn't keep to the chart, sometimes an odd percentage of white was unavoidable – I'm thinking of that sonata of Beethoven's I analysed about eight years ago, *Opus 110 in A flat major*, about two thirds of the way through where it goes da da, da da (and he sang a few notes), I mean there's no question that the E flat there is neither thirty-six per cent nor thirty-eight per cent white. I got the hue right, no question about the hue, but it was the *shade* that was so difficult. I must have played it back a hundred times. In the end I gave up and settled for thirty-seven and a half per cent, somewhere around there, anyway.'

Once the chart was up on the wall the analysis became a lot easier. To begin with, he would decide in which section of it a particular passage of music was located. The music never went, for example, from an orange to a purple: though theoretically it could, he explained, it would be a hideous piece of music, barely deserving of the term; it could lead you to purple, there could be purple in a different movement, perhaps, but *never* adjacent – you cannot have mood-swings within split seconds, like that. 'It seems to me that there's always a node of colour from which an entire movement springs, which gives it its structure if you like, and makes it accessible by making it just so slightly predictable – do you see what I'm getting at? Can you begin to see, now, how the colours work?'

His aim (and he achieved it) was to be able to hold a paintbrush filled with a particular colour, and then, as he recognised the colour in the music, he would paint in above the score in a diagonal, occasionally marking down a simultaneous observation in pencil, perhaps one of those signs which mean 'more than' or 'less than', so that he could prepare himself for the next colours he'd be using. When the music wasn't harmonic, when there'd be two tunes playing simultaneously, for example, he'd have to content himself with placing one colour above and one below the score, though sometimes, he found, even if the colours were disconsonant, there was a unity of feeling which resulted from it, and even now you can see on the scores the greater flourish in those colours that he had to fight for than those he came to with ease.

At the beginning of September Robert set to work on Mozart's *Prague Symphony*. It was to take him two years. The score is now a work of art: over every part of it are diagonals of colour. I kept saying to him, 'Robert, what were you *feeling* at this bit?' pointing to a profusion of yellows, from the almost white to the almost orange, and when I did he got impatient, even angry. He'd say to me:

'What do you expect me to say? Do you want me to say that red is happy, or that yellow is pretty and optimistic – how many times do I have to repeat that we are dealing with almost fifteen thousand colours, Olivia, representing fifteen thousand moods – if the colours cannot be named, if the music cannot be named, how can you expect me to name what I'm feeling when I listen to it? I'll give you an example – blue. You might notice I have shades of blue where the music is slower, often in a minor key, and you'll say, "yes, I've got the secret, where the music is sad, he uses blue". But when music is sad, how sad do you actually feel? I doubt you'd feel sad at all – you're far more likely to think, "this is moving", or even "this is beautiful", and you'll get more pleasure than pain from it. But it's not exactly pleasure, either; there's something in the music that you crave, sometimes you're almost sick with the longing for it and it's always just out of reach – no, blue is never a resting place. It's like the lover on Keats's Grecian urn, always reaching out for his beloved, and always an inch or two away from her.'

'Oh yes,' I said, 'I know those lines:

> Bold Lover, never, never canst thou kiss,
> Though winning near the goal . . .'

'You're right,' said Robert, 'never couldst I kiss, you're right. And I want to show you this, Olivia, I want to show you a pitch of intensity rarely reached – see this, the perfect hue, the colour of bristol blue glass. And now, look below, on the score, what do you see? Nothing, not a note. What led to it was no more than an interval of a seventh between the C and the D. Look at it, Olivia, and remember that the purest experiences in music lie in the silences. How can I emphasise that? Would you understand what I meant by transcendental?'

Meanwhile, what of Sophia?

'You need to make more friends,' Robert had said to her ingeniously one day. 'You need to get out a little more . . . try reading a little poetry . . . did I ever show you where the Fitzwilliam is? Are you interested in art at all? Shame you never stuck at the violin, you showed promise you know. I can't remember why you gave it up. *Do* something Sophia, you must be getting awfully bored.'

He told Sophia only briefly about his project, not that she understood it. In a way, Sophia was thankful for his involvement in it, for he no longer taunted her with his expositions on the smelliness of nappies or the emptiness of fridges; his moods, as well, had stabilised to such an extent that when Viola cried, his eyebrows didn't betray even a flicker of annoyance, and he would say things like, 'Poor old you, never stops, does it?'

229

Robert used to leave the house at about a quarter past eight in the morning, earlier if Sophia had forgotten to buy breakfast, in which case, without a single word of reproach, he would leave at half past seven and have a cooked breakfast in Trinity. He would come back at about ten at night and, if Sophia was still awake, would kiss her cheek and say, 'Had a good day? How's the baby, then?' Sophia would say, 'Thank you, yes, fine'. Then they would go to bed, six inches lying between the parallel bodies, Sophia facing his back, biting her lip to prevent her arms from wrapping themselves around him, and if her breath so much as accidentally fell on his shoulder, she felt his body flinch away from her, even when he was asleep. Then sometimes she would cry into the night, though crying is perhaps the wrong word for the silent, steady stream that soaked her pillow – not a gasp came out of her, in case she woke him.

Sophia's days were less painful than the nights: by the middle of August the colic had subsided, Viola smiled and held up her head, her skin was more even-coloured, and her hair had grown, just a little, removing the skin-on-marrow look of her scalp; she held down farex better than she'd done her milk, and she could now sleep for a six-hour stretch of the night. But more sleep made Sophia more acutely aware of the state in which she now found herself.

Even when she'd been ill at the beginning of July, when she hadn't known whether Robert was in the bed with her or not, when she hadn't gone to the doctor because of the effort of getting there, when the nappies stank more than usual because it had been four days since she'd managed to get herself to the launderette, when Viola cried twice as hard because of nappy rash, when she had hidden herself tight in the bed with the blankets blocking out the noise and the light, even then she'd managed to comfort herself with vivid dreams – or were they memories? – of her bedroom in the embassy, the mosquito nets draping over the high bed, the embroidered silk coverlet, her mother coming in to see her and saying, 'Darling, aren't you feeling even a little better? Miriam, could you get that sponge again? Won't you try just a little soup? Toast, Sophia, wouldn't you like some toast? Miriam, you pull down the blind and we'll let the girl sleep.' And the wooden slats came ricocheting down, what a comfort that noise was, the cool dark that followed, the click of the door as they left her, looking up into the high ceiling, trying to count the revolutions of the fan, the smell of the flowers her mother left for her on her bedside table – that was good of her, surely, to have put flowers there – how come she noticed now, when she hadn't at the time? – greeny-white flower heads floating in a bowl of water, odd how they should be a comfort two years on.

Only in June she'd turned down an invitation from her parents to spend part of the summer with them. Still her automatic reaction: she'd rather do anything than go back *there*. 'You can't bring up your daughter like *that*' – she knew she'd have slipped up if she'd gone back, that she couldn't have acted the part of a mother well enough, and for so long a stretch, so she'd written: 'Robert has things to see to in Cambridge. There are a couple of College Feasts and he desperately wants me to go with him. Anyway, I think he's planning a holiday for us in Norfolk – can you imagine, Viola's first seaside holiday, she smiles now, you should see her, and I'm sorry you won't just yet, but thanks for the invitation anyway.'

By October she knew she'd have to pull herself out of it. She went to the Fitzwilliam but the pictures might as well have been wallpaper for all she looked at them. She kept smiling at the other people looking at the pictures but they looked at her as if to say, 'I've come here to be private, and you should learn, that's why people come to art galleries.' She had coffee in a café opposite, and overheard two bedders talking about 'undergraduates nowadays' and 'the price of a cup of tea'. Then the bedders went out and the table was taken up by six of the very same 'undergraduates nowadays', who had squeezed up together at a table for four, four men, two girls. Sophia was sitting alone at her table, she was going to suggest that they could sit with her, if they wanted, but they seemed so happy to have an excuse for being all squashed up, and anyway, she didn't know which word she should let out of her first because each one she tried out in her head sounded so gauche. She was quiet, but she eked out her coffee so she could watch them and listen to them, because, you never knew, there might be an appropriate point at which she could interrupt, if someone said, 'Does anyone know what exhibition's on at the Fitzwilliam at the moment', for example, and if no one knew, she could tell them, she could say, 'Actually, I've just been there myself', and they might say to her, 'Oh really, and was it good?' and she'd have them all listening to her, waiting to hear her verdict, and she practised saying to herself, 'Actually, I thought it was a bit disappointing, it didn't live up to my expectations at all' (because that's what she'd heard someone else saying in the gallery); yes, Sophia had the whole conversation mapped out. But they didn't talk about art at all, they talked about a concert they'd all been to the night before, Beethoven's *Eroica*. Hadn't Robert told her about the *Eroica* once? She kept trying to remember what was important about it, there's still a chance, she thought, there's still a chance I might be able to say something. She listened out for clues.

'For some reason', said one of the girls, 'I don't like the idea of Beethoven's face being riddled with smallpox scars. I'd always had this image of him, I'd always thought of him as a sort of Shelley figure, a wild man breaking out of his time, and yet he's too ugly for words. I've never minded him being *deaf*, I mean, that *adds* to it, doesn't it?'

Sophia kept thinking, 'Shall I say it? Shall I tell them that he never even heard a note of his *Ninth Symphony*?' but she didn't dare, but kept her eyebrows raised, as though she were on the point of saying something very important, in case they might notice her and invite her to speak: they didn't.

'The beginning's incredible, isn't it?' one of them said.

'Yes, it's brilliant', said another.

'What about the end, though, it's ridiculous, I always think, why don't they just *cut* this.'

'Well, we know why *you* weren't concentrating last night.'

'Oh my God, Patrick, how was it?'

'Have another doughnut and don't be so fucking nosy,' said Patrick.

'Mm, I'll have a doughnut with a hole in this time. There are some tasty-looking ones over there. Fancy one yourself?'

Yes, the Beginning of Romanticism, that was it.

'Excuse me,' said Sophia, but then there was chaos in her head and she hardly knew what she was saying or wanting to say, and suddenly the baby starting crying, and suddenly they were all looking at her like she was an alien, she thought, they're thinking I look too young to have a baby, they're thinking, 'Where the hell does she come from?'

'Can we help you?' said one of them.

'No, no,' she said, 'no, I was just thinking, I'm off now, so you might want to use my table as well, if you like.'

'Well, that's very kind of you,' said one of the girls.

She never did look to see whether they took advantage of her offer, she just walked straight out, pushing the door open with the pushchair, catching the wheel on a hinge as she did so. While she walked home she felt her cheeks burn, but in a way it was like the first conversation she'd had in months.

One day Robert said to her, 'Now term's started up again, why don't you go and visit St Peter's, say hello to your old friends? I'm sure they'd like to meet Viola, and it'd do you good to get out of Cambridge.'

So, on 29 October, a taxi took her from Winchester station to the Upper Sixth block, about half a mile away from the main school. She didn't know the mistress whose exclusive task was to tend to the welfare of these sixth-formers, and there was no danger of her meeting any former members of staff. It was an old stable block, recently converted, and a real incentive to 'stay on', as they called it. She saw Felicity first. She'd never been particularly friendly towards Felicity, but when she saw her now, through the window of the taxi, she suddenly felt warm towards her, and saw all the good in her that she'd missed. Hadn't she once sewn up an aertex shirt for her when she'd ripped it in the armpit while playing lacrosse? Felicity, who couldn't do maths for toffee, but who could sew like a dream and made all the costumes for the school play? Sophia thought, 'I'll thank her now, I'll tell her I remember it perfectly, as though it were yesterday,

---

and that I have a feeling I didn't thank her well enough at the time', so eagerly Sophia got herself and Viola out of the taxi, got the pushchair out of the boot, paid the driver, and went to find her. But she'd missed her: she was biking up to the main school. A few seconds lapsed while Sophia stared after her, and then she was gone.

Suddenly a window opened, and a head came out of it, with a large mouth and a long fringe of mousy-brown hair hanging lankly over the forehead: 'Christ, Sophia,' shouted the mouth, 'It's *you*, my God it's actually *you*.' Then the head disappeared, and re-emerged a minute later with eight others at the front door.

'Fucking hell,' said Miranda. 'Where've you been all this time, then?'

'Screwing Dr Standing, I shouldn't wonder,' said Josephine, 'that's yours, is it?'

'Yes,' said Sophia.

'Well, I can see you've been busy since you left us. Still with him, are you? I suppose it's a bit stupid to ask if he's the father of that babe there.'

'Of course he is,' said Sophia, 'I'm married.'

'Are you? You never said. I'm amazed you've condescended to visit us, being a proper married lady, and all that. Nice being married, is it?' asked Josephine.

'Can I come in?' asked Sophia.

'Well, it's a bit scruffy,' said Josephine, 'might not be what you're used to, what are you now? Mrs Standing? Come in if you dare.'

They took her into the sitting-room, which consisted of a bookshelf, four sofas and a TV. They told her to sit down and make herself comfortable while they made her a cup of coffee, and then all eight of them left her there so they could talk about her in the kitchen. They immediately decided to forgive her for her desertion, mainly because she wasn't nearly as pretty as she used to be, and when they re-entered they were all smiles and congratulations, a couple of them even looked into Viola's pushchair and said, 'how sweet' and, basically, they said sorry if they were a bit cold, it was just a shock to see her there.

'So,' said Josephine, 'tell us what it's like'.

'What would you like to know, in particular?'

'Well, first of all', said Miranda, 'tell us what *it*'s like – you know, *sex*,' said Josephine.

'Well, what do you want to know about it?' asked Sophia.

'Go on, what does it *feel* like, what do you have to do?'

'Come on, you know what you have to do, we've talked about it often enough.'

'Sophocles, you can't go off for a year and a half and have a baby and then not *tell* us anything. Go on, have you had an orgasm yet?'

'Of course I have,' said Sophia.

'Well, *there* you are,' said Josephine, 'Go on.'

'You tell me what's been going on around here,' said Sophia, but the tone of it fell flat, and eight pairs of eyes insisted, 'You first, Sophia, you first.'

'Well,' said Sophia, 'the first time you'll find it hurts quite a lot.'

'How much does it hurt?' asked one of them, 'I mean, did you get any pleasure at all from the first time? Or was it *all* pain?'

'What did you have to *do* exactly? Did Dr Standing show you what to do? How did you know if you were doing it right?' asked another.

'Come on,' said a third, 'we want a step by step account of what happened that night – was it the first night you left here?'

'Did you bleed?' asked a fourth.

'Didn't you feel incredibly embarrassed? Did he make you take your clothes off in front of him?'

'Did he feel you up first? Did he undress you?'

'Go on, Sophia, you've got to tell us, *everything*.'

'We were married,' began Sophia. 'We spent the first four nights of our marriage in Norfolk. He was very gentle with me, and very loving. He let me get undressed alone and I got into the bed in my nightdress. He knocked, and I told him he could come in. Then he did it.'

'You can't get away with *that*,' they all said to her; but in fact she did, because the baby started crying, the first time the crying came as a positive relief, and Sophia said, 'I'm sorry, I'm going to have to feed Viola now.'

'Viola?' said Josephine, 'Hell's teeth, what sort of a name is that?'

'Go on,' said Miranda, 'how far did you have to spread your legs?'

'Where's your kitchen? I need boiling water, a spoon and a saucer.'

When Viola was fed, Sophia said she was just passing through and had to be on her way. 'So, how's old Hackers?' she said, as she packed away the nappies and farex.

'Didn't you *hear*?'said Miranda. 'Hackers got the sack and she's been replaced by an absolute dragon, who's about eighty-five with a black moustache. And it's *you* who got her the sack, you and that Standing man, they never got over it.'

'But she had nothing to do with it', said Sophia. 'How can they blame her?'

'Old Plimsoll kept a copy of what she called "a most unprofessional letter" – God knows what was in it, but it was bad enough for the governors to sack her straight away to avoid a scandal, and didn't you know this, we all, or at least, all our parents, got sent these awfully apologetic letters, and there's an official policy, old Sophocles, and this is all your fault, of *no more men*.'

'Well, I'm awfully sorry to hear about Miss Hackshaw,' said Sophia. 'She was nice.'

'Well, it's all right for you to say that, you haven't had to put up with the replacement. You should hear her moan on about *manners*. It's a nightmare. Well, only one more year to go in this hell-hole.'

'I'll write to you,' said Sophia.

Of course, she never did.

The end of their marriage was very sudden. The new academic year meant that Robert had less time for his music, but he was unwilling to compromise. So he would listen to the music until one or two in the morning, until his mind had ceased to register what he was listening to, which was, of course, when he had fallen fast asleep. He found that life was infinitely easier when he had shed the last few conventions: sleeping in a bed, saying good night to his wife, removing his clothes before sleeping – why in the world did anyone bother to take off one's clothes at night, when (a) one wasn't aware of what one was wearing when one was sleeping, and (b) it was a positive delight to find oneself already dressed on waking – how much time it saved, how much sooner one could get on with the task in hand. A bath once a week was plenty. He smelt himself quite regularly to check that it was, and it was. He explained himself to Sophia on a Saturday morning at the beginning of November. She hadn't seen him for three days:

'Sophia, my love, I'm sorry, but I can see that in the term-times I'm going to have to spend most of the time in College. That project I told you about, it's going very well but I'm afraid it needs my absolute attention. You understand that, don't you?' And when Sophia looked as though she were going to burst into tears, and he couldn't have borne that, he went on, 'Sophia, you don't understand how important what I'm doing is, look at me, Sophia, you and me, we'll die, but this won't. Viola's great-great-great-grandchildren will die, but this won't. I'm creating a language, no that's the wrong word, I'm discovering it, because somewhere it was there all along, I'm only making plain what was known all along.'

But this speech of his didn't stop Sophia from crying, and no amount of putting his arm round her shoulder made her stop.

'What are we going to do about this, Sophia?' he said to her, but Sophia couldn't speak, and when she could, about half an hour later, she said that the only thing she wanted to do was die, because she wasn't worth a pillar of salt. Robert told her that a pillar of salt was quite an amazing thing, but Sophia wasn't convinced and cried all the more. Then at about lunchtime, Sophia started shouting at him, she said, 'Go back to your bloody music. *I* can't offer you anything, can I?'

So he did, though he didn't work, he was quite strict with himself on this, he obviously couldn't get down to business while he was in this mood. So he waited a couple of days in which he wandered fairly aimlessly around Cambridge, popping in to Trinity for his meals, and Bateman Street whenever he happened to be in that part of town, but Sophia was always the same, and so exhausted him that he thought, 'No, this can't go on', and he said to her, 'Look, why don't you and Viola go home to your parents for a while, or go and stay with my mother, didn't you say she'd invited you? Cambridge isn't doing you any good at all.' But at anything he said to her, she cried all the more, and he was quite worn out by it. In the end, he said to her, 'I'm sorry, but I think I shall live in Trinity for the rest of term. I don't have the time to enter into this, I'm sorry.'

Sophia's mother came to visit her about a fortnight later. She was only in the flat for ten minutes: it was more of a collection than a visit. The place stank of nappies, the sheets were grey and smeared, mould had grown on a pile of unwashed plates, the woollen dresses from The White House were all sicked-over and squashed up with other stuff in plastic bags, and Sophia herself was pale and thin with red, swollen eyes. The baby was all right, though, and even smiled at her grandmother. Within a week Sophia had been given a suite all of her own in the Embassy, and Viola had been given a nanny.

Robert received a letter from her even before he knew that his wife and daughter had gone. It read:

My Darling Robert,
I know that I shall never love anyone like I love you. I know I was a hopeless wife to you, I know I have nothing I can give you, I know that I'm ignorant and can't amuse you, I don't even know what you ever saw in me. It's fine here. My parents are the same as ever, I suppose. No, I shouldn't say that, they're really being quite nice to me, but they keep saying horrible things about you which I can't bear because I know they're simply not true. I was far more to blame than you were, I was hopeless, I know I was, so in the end I gave up and went home. It's lovely and warm here. My mother made me write you this letter.

She said, 'Get down and write him a letter, tell him you want a divorce'. When I put it in inverted commas it doesn't feel as bad as if I'd said it myself.

In fact, Robert cried, and as a result of crying he didn't let himself get back to work for a month, so he could well and truly flush out every reaction to it that he'd had. What were those reactions? They were those of a monk, who thinks he's doing the right thing in turning himself exclusively to God, but who suddenly gets a letter from his parents, and they say, 'We miss you . . . you have a new nephew . . . your friends ask after you . . . can we really not visit you for three years?' There's the smallest, most niggling of doubts that something must be askew, that surely two worlds, each of which contains so much good, should not have to exist in parallel. One life was all we have, and all possible good should be included in it. And Sophia was good, and when he read the letter he thought, 'I love this girl'; but then he realised that he was not even fit to use the word 'love'. He walked back to Bateman Street, but he'd lost the key, and he had to break down the door. It smelt as though someone had died in there, worse, died a few months back and had been decaying ever since. He went into the bedroom. Soon after they'd moved in there Sophia had covered her school trunk with a sheet and placed it at the end of the bed. There'd been a milk bottle of wild flowers on it then, flowers she'd picked on a walk with him. He instinctively removed the sheet and opened the trunk: those clothes she'd worn on that first day were on top, the tunic, the tie, the socks, even those lace-up shoes. He laid them all out on the bed, and then layer by layer he took out her other clothes, a neat pile of white cotton blouses, then another of aertex blouses, two grey cardigans, then there were a few of her school exercise books, a bible, a copy of the *Aeneid*, and here was her copy of *Twelfth Night* with every 'Viola' underlined. He sat on the end of the bed with the book in his hand. He sat a long time flicking through the pages and reading not a word of it, and sometimes he would say, 'my Viola of the haughty chin, what happened to you?' But he didn't take the book with him, he didn't take anything, he left it all just as it was, all piled up on the bed. Then, in the afternoon, he went to see the Bursar about having a bedroom in college, just a small room with a bed in it was what he requested. The Bursar offered him his old rooms back, he said surely he'd like some proper rooms now he was back with them again, but Robert said, 'No, I like the room in Angel Court, I want it just the way it is'. He heard no music for a month, he concentrated on his lectures and his supervisions – no student noticed any change in his behaviour at all. Then, in the Christmas vacation, he put the music back on and found, to his delight, that he was more sensitive than he'd ever been, and that the colours came more readily and were truer than he'd ever thought possible.

I visited Sophia in her large apartment in the rue de Seine. She wore lipstick and smelt of scent.

'How did you get my address?' she asked.

'Well, I knew your father used to work in the Foreign Office and I found out . . .'

'He didn't give it to you, did he? For Christ's sake.'

'He gave me your number, I rang . . .'

'And you asked the maid for this address?'

'Yes. I'm sorry, Sophia.'

' "Sophia" '? You seem to know me quite well already.'

'Shall I call you Madame Lacan?'

'Call me what you like,' she said. 'You're not staying long.'

'He loves you, Sophia.'

Perhaps I shouldn't have said it. I wanted her to warm up.

Just then her two sons came in to see her after school. She went up to them and began talking in rapid French. '*Mais Maman*,' they said to her, as she pushed them out of the door. '*Allez, allez*,' she said, as she shut it.

'It's no good,' she said to me, 'I don't think about it. I don't talk about it. You'd better go.'

In fact, I was at the end of the street before she called me back.

'Tell me one thing,' she said. 'Did he marry again?'

'Yes,' I told her.

Was she pleased or sad? I couldn't tell.

'I'll talk to you,' she said, 'but I mustn't see him. Remember, I must never see him.'

'Do you want me to give him a message?' I said to her.

'Tell him I'm well. And Viola is.'

And then she paused. 'And tell him one other thing. I'm happy.'

NINE

Five March 1983. Robert is in his room, New Court, Trinity. It is 6 a.m., still very dark, and Robert hasn't slept much. In fact he hasn't been sleeping for quite a while now, not for a week or two: he keeps having this dream, he's in a tunnel, and he's trying to get out to the light. The trouble is, there's no gravity in the dream, and he doesn't know whether he's burrowing deeper into the centre of the earth, or getting closer to the surface of it. He's feeling claustrophobic, and he badly needs the air. Then he has a hunch, and he changes direction. It's as though there's a magnet in him. He's swimming up the tunnel and he's clawing at the earth, great clods of it are floating by him as they come loose, but he knows that he's getting closer now, and that makes the work easier. 'Just a foot more,' he says to himself, and then he wakes up. He always wakes up. And at six that morning, 5 March 1983, that's what he'd just woken up from.

He's dressed, but cold. He turns on the gas fire and the purr of it soothes him. He is making his mind blank ready for the day's work – a Sunday, he can do a good, fifteen-hour stretch today, he thinks, make some headway into Bach's *Toccata and Fugue in D minor*. But he's tired, and no sooner has he planned it, he unplans it, he decides he might be getting 'flu, and he has never, these twenty years, listened to music when he thinks he might be getting 'flu. So he pulls his armchair closer to the fire and decides that today he will write his preface.

He goes over to his desk and finds a piece of paper, a pen and a book to lean on; then, back by the fire, the first words come easily: 'I do not know whom I'm writing this for. It is strange not to know the man who, if he understands this work, will know me better than any man living.'

Now he pauses. He has completed the analysis of almost twenty scores, and they sit on his bookshelf, one on top of the other, in the order that he did them. He walks over to the shelf and affectionately runs his fingers down the spines of them. Every one of them represents to him a passage of time: he's remained oblivious to everything outside it. If you were to say to him, 'What did the sixties mean to you?' he would tell you, 'Mozart *Sonata in C Minor*, Brahms *Violin Concerto in C Major*, Sibelius *Symphony No 2 in D* . . .' Not a mini-skirt distracted him. He's moving his fingers down to the symphony on the bottom of the pile, Mozart's *Prague*, and he's remembering the details of it and, for the first time in twenty years, he's curious to look.

He takes it down from the shelf and it's like he recognises something that he once loved, He leafs through it, and every pattern of colours makes his heart wrench up at the memory of it, those blues he used then. So many naked hues, that orange. Was the *Prague* as intense as that? Surely not. But of course it must have been.

Then he gets down the Beethoven and the Sibelius, he gets down the Schumann and the Brahms, he gets down more Mozart scores, Berlioz and Liszt; he gets them all down, and he lays them out on his desk. The sun is coming up now, good, he needs to see these colours in a natural light. He's not looking at the composers now: he's laid them all out chronologically, and he's doing it quickly, methodically, ignoring the fear that's already mounting up inside him, and he sits down.

To the untrained eye the difference is hard to detect, but Robert sees it all within seconds. It's as though the *Prague* were a supernova, and every subsequent work a billion light years further from it. Robert isn't even given whatever comfort there might have been in a gradual, consistent dimming of the colours: no, it must have been six years ago when an even greater shift began. He laughs bitterly; here is a difference not even between two works or two composers, it's between two halves of the same sonata. What the hell was he thinking of? He laughs at his idiocy. Then he's still, as he remembers. No, he thinks, a week off wasn't long enough, I underestimated. It should have been a month. Then it's as though David's right there in the room with him, he's there as clear as day, and he's saying, 'Our mother's dead, and look at you, for Christ's sake, will you ever learn how to *feel*? What are you thinking of with your blank eyes?' He hadn't gone to the funeral of course, well of course he couldn't have done that. He'd said to David, 'Would you like some toast while you're here?'. He smiles as he remembers David's face. Then he remembers his mother. Well, there you go, he loved her. Twenty years he devotes to the creation of an

---

249

absolute criterion of how music is affective, and all he is certain of now is that he loved his mother.

He feels an odd light-headedness, it suddenly occurs to him that nothing can be serious. He remembers his father telling him that there's no such thing as a free act, and he's trying to remember the arguments, he's trying to escape from the feeling that everything he does from that moment will have a free fall, will be random and floating; but it's no good: the momentum of his life, having been shown to be false, has left nothing to hold on to.

Then he goes over to the the Wren Library in search of the serious, something which might help him say, 'Good, we can start with this, this much we can be sure of'. It's a quarter past seven now, the place is empty, and the early light is streaming in through the windows, showing up the dust. He moves quickly down the high, deep room, past busts of famous men on pedestals, bays of books on either side of him. He begins taking leather books from the shelves, and decides to build a tower in the middle of the room.

He puts Argelander's *Observationes Astronomicae* on the marble floor; then a little geography and some history; and he gets more books from the shelves, Swift's *Polite Conversation*, a book on farming and three on medicine. 'More science', he says, and he seeks out three volumes of Newton's *Principia Mathematica*, but the tower's wobbling. They're too large to fit comfortably on the top, so he begins the tower again and puts them immediately on to Argelander, and a pretty book of maps catches his eye and he slips that in too. Then when the tower is built, he looks for something small to put on the top of it: *By the honourable Robert Boyle Esq. A discourse on the Imperfection of the Chymist's Doctrine of Qualities*.

'This'll do,' he thinks, and he takes it from the shelf and reads the preface: 'That this should be published is the ardent wish of the sincere Lovers of Real Knowledge.' Perhaps they wrote the preface to the Chemist's Doctrine too. And he's suddenly talking aloud and he's saying, '*This* is the only true preface. I *feel* that I know.'

Then the tower's finished, and he stands back to admire it. 'You're as tall as me,' he says, 'but more likely to fall. Your head has nothing in common with your feet, nor your neck with your calves. And I'll tell you something else, you're out of date, you're unread, and you thought you knew. Sir Robert Boyle, I feel you looking at me accusingly. Just then I felt my heart go out to you. You ask me, where are the sincere Lovers of Real Knowledge now? They're in the Reading Room next door, where the *modern* books are – but comfort yourself, the ceiling's lower, there are fewer busts, and in a hundred years they'll build on another, and the ceiling will be even lower, because at last they'll come to understand that nothing can be known, that nothing stays still. For the trouble is, Sir Robert, if you analyse, you falsify by exclusion, you pretend to see the whole but you cannot see the parts. What else is a map but the analysis of place? Falsity for the sake of clarity. If there's a map that's true, it exactly covers the area it's a map of. But where's the room for the man to stand back and look at it? He would sooner see the back of his own head. So analysis is false, synthesis is blind, and there is nothing valuable on this earth which can be shown to be true. And what does that make this library? No more than a monument to hope.'

Then he realises how hungry he is and has breakfast. He is sitting opposite the world authority on fruitflies and next to the world authority on Spenser. One says to the other: 'Wouldn't you say these sausages are off?' A point in common, Robert thinks, they are eating from the same batch of sausages. He says to the fruitfly man, 'Tell me, James, do you still love your wife? How's your marriage been recently?'

James shuffles and says, 'Of course I do, what sort of a question is that?'

'Well, I was wondering why you ate your breakfast in college – is she still in bed at this time, your wife?'

James says words to the effect that he should mind his own business. He says to the Spenser man that he thinks yes, the sausages are off and he talks fast about the best route to London at that time of day.

Robert goes back to his room, prepares his paints, and he puts on the *Prague Symphony*. The colours he uses are strong, and for a moment he is optimistic. But then he sees: where there were yellows in '63 there are now greens, where there were greens, there are now blues, everything is askew, worse than he could have imagined. Whether his mind was deranged then or is now he doesn't bother to consider, he lays down his brush and he knows it all, he cannot even communicate with the man he once was.

Robert wallowed in the depths of relativism for a week. If there was a scale of 0–17 which could measure precisely that feeling of feeling random, and if you imagine that the majority of us, on a particularly wretched day, might home in at about six, think of Robert hovering around the sixteen mark for the whole of that week. But it would be a mistake to equate such an FR scale with straightforward feelings of unhappiness: because it is possible, in general, to attach those feelings to causes, and these causes can often be tackled. But randomness, by its very nature, has nothing to connect to, it is freedom in its absolute form: the freedom to say, to act, to think, to kill or to die, the perfect anomie, a sort of dynamic boredom.

It was the last week of term: he didn't miss a lecture. 'Today', he said to his class, 'I am going to talk to you lying down, because I haven't been sleeping very well and frankly I'm tired. Can anyone here spot the connection between tiredness and lying down? Any connection at all? Now, odd as this may seem, I haven't been kissed for twenty years now. Would anyone suggest that the feeling of other lips is relevant? Would anyone here be able to tell me a little about other lips? Who can remember what it feels like to be kissed? Hey, what about tongues? Anyone here use tongues to kiss with? No?'

The class, they were loving it, and they let him go on.

'Anyone here spot the connection between magma and saliva? The question is, am I qualified to tell you about magma if there *is* a connection between magma and saliva and yet I haven't known other saliva for a while now? In fact, I think I could say that it's something I've forgotten. Perhaps if someone were to kiss me now, would someone volunteer? If someone were just to remind me, I could go on with the lecture. If I closed my eyes, I understand if the volunteer would prefer to remain anonymous, yes, I quite understand that this is an irregular request . . . but don't all be silent on me, I'm not asking for a fuck, you know, in fact I wouldn't want one of those at all, well, would anybody lie on me, then? What I would like is the full weight of another body on mine, that's not much to ask, is it? But I need the weight.'

There was a giggle.

'I am speaking now to the person who giggled, the girl who giggled, I think it was a girl – are you beautiful? No, the question is irrelevant, I couldn't care if you were beautiful or not, no, the important thing is that you have a body to weigh something – isn't it brilliant the way our bodies have sufficient weight that they should make an imprint on the earth?'

In between lectures he sabotaged art galleries and musical performances held in college chapels: he overheard a man pontificating to his wife about the golden mean and the position of the various colours in a particular picture (which was a very dull picture indeed) and he said to him, 'What do you feel about the spot in the middle of your wife's chin? Is it the uglier for its being symmetrically exact? If it were positioned a little to the right would it be an improvement, do you think?'

Then he gave a memorable speech at the end of a concert in King's. He began quite properly, he even thanked the performers, and the organisers imagined that perhaps one of the others had invited him to speak. But then he went on, he said: 'How many of you are there here, do you think? Two, perhaps three hundred? Did you enjoy what you heard? Did you presume, did you hope, that there was one single soul who heard it too? How well did you hear what your neighbour heard? The deaf, at least, in the knowledge that they are deaf, find other means of communication, but you don't bother, do you, you think that to hear is enough to belong; but let me assure you, and trust me that if I know anything it is this, that what you hear is stuck in your own head, and it has no means of escaping it, and the greater the beauty of what you hear, the more tragic it is that you hear it at all – what will make you remember what I tell you? It is like seeing an angel in a world of blind men.'

Then, on the following Sunday, when the energy of his revelation was beginning to subside, not because he had begun to doubt the truth of it but because he had simply not been sleeping, he saw, quite suddenly, in the window of a small, little-known art gallery in King Street, that very angel. At least, it wasn't an angel, it was a boy on a lion, but he might easily have been one, and in fact, as the caption said, it was St Mark.

Unfortunately, the painting no longer exists. It is easier to describe the effects than the subject of it. The boy is driving this lion over a hill; it is almost dark, and the last dregs of light shine up the boy's face, and his eyes know, but his mouth is shaped like a child's. And what Robert said to himself when he saw the painting was this: 'Whoever painted this exists. That is all I need to know.' And it didn't matter a toss if the whole world was blind, because the creator of it was living.

The gallery was closed, but he rang the bell, and sure enough the lady proprietor came downstairs and answered the door. The painter was a woman, she said, yes it was odd that she didn't sign her paintings, she couldn't talk now because she was off to church, please come back on a weekday, ten till six. 'Her name,' insisted Robert. 'Just tell me her name.' 'Ruth Mostyn' said the woman. 'Thank you,' said Robert.

Finding out her address was easy enough: a telephone directory. Eleven Selwyn Road, Newnham. It was a small house, no care had been taken over its upkeep, and paint was peeling off the door and the windows. He knocked and she was there.

'Ruth Mostyn?' he asked.

'Yes,' she said. 'Come in.'

She led him into a tiny room piled high with canvases and paints and asked him: 'What can I do for you?'

And Robert, well, he knew exactly what he wanted, what he had come for, and he said, 'I want you to lie on me.'

But for you to be able to understand why Ruth reacted as she did, I must first tell you what sort of woman she was.

TEN

I've wanted to remain objective in this book, and like the good historian who explains any bias he might have before he begins his treatise, I am now going to explain a bias of mine. Ruth alarms me.

I don't know how our first interview managed to get on to such a bad footing. I've always thought of myself as a good interviewer. I'm confident, I look people in the eye, but not so much that they feel on the defensive. Usually, I'm in control. I seem compassionate, and people like that, they confide in you. I'm a prison visitor and I know for a fact that the prisoners tell me a good lot more about themselves than they tell my colleagues. I've always prided myself on the fact that I can elicit confessions. But for some reason I was anxious before meeting Ruth. For the first time, I felt more of an intruder than a biographer. So perhaps, rather annoyingly, I came across as the intruder.

Perhaps it was a question of the difference in our size. I'm five foot four and thin. Ruth is almost six foot, and she's large, if not exactly fat. Some tall people learn how to make their height irrelevant, by keeping at a certain distance, so the eyes don't meet at too steep an angle, or by sitting down. But Ruth didn't like me. And we couldn't sit down anyway: the front room was small and stuffed with canvases; she obviously wasn't used to visitors. So we had our first conversation standing up. No cups of tea, nothing.

'You live with Robert, don't you?' she said.

'No, Robert lives with *us*, my family. How do you know?'

'And you're writing a book,' she laughed.

'I am.'

'Are you in love with him yet?'

'I think you can write a book about someone without being in love with them.'

'But can you write a book about someone without thinking them remarkable?'

'Yes,' I admitted, 'I think he is remarkable.'

Ruth looked at me about as coldly as a vegan watching someone eating steak. 'I imagine you've been to bed with him,' she said.

'Of course I haven't.'

'I'm not accusing you. In fact, I'd expect it of you, in the best possible sense. If I were reading the biography of the inventor of the traction engine, I would expect an account of how a traction engine operated. In the case of Robert, well, how can you rely on second-hand information in such a crucial area?'

'I have a husband,' I said, 'and three young children. You're mistaken about me. I'm happily married.' I looked at her straight.

'Ah, but you'll miss him when he's gone,' she said, and the awful truth was, my looking straight at her necessitated her looking down on me. Then she smiled, and there are few worse things than being smiled down on. I stood back to lessen the gradient between us.

'I've come here to ask you if I might interview you,' I said, with legs straight and shoulders back.

'Actually, I don't think you're Robert's type. You're too proper, and your shoes are too delicate.'

'I'd be grateful if you'd consent to be interviewed.'

Ruth laughed: a horrible, contemptuous laugh. 'I can imagine you interviewing a woman who's been repeatedly raped during her marriage. You'd be sitting there with a little pad, drinking tea. Tell me, you'd say, if you'd be so kind, how's it been over the last few years? Would you say it had put you off sex at all? Please take your time about it, don't hurry . . . what nice tea this is, Earl Grey, is it?'

'Did he rape you?'

'If it had been rape I would have found you a chair. I could have made a statement. I could have said, "It happened like this. There you are, now write that down for your paper." '

Suddenly I wished Robert had raped her and I could've scuttled away with my story. I want to put an end to this, I thought. 'Perhaps I could see you again at some more convenient . . .'

'Why are you writing this biography? God, I can't bear the idea of how smug you'd have made him.'

'I tell you this, he's not smug.'

' "I tell you this, he's not smug, have confidence in me, he's not smug, I know all about him, more about him than you, in fact." I must remember, I'm speaking to the expert.'

'I want to be objective in this book. If you tell me he has a tendency to be smug, that's relevant.'

'Why, why are you writing it? I can't stand the idea of him having that privilege. God, how reassuring it must be to have one's life researched. Every action relevant, every action vindicated, meaning emerging from a hideous morass. We don't need therapists, we need biographers. Analysis first, followed by glorification. We should all have books written about us.'

'I want to be fair,' I said, 'I want to write about you, too.'

'Leave me out of it. For God's sake, do me the favour of leaving me out.'

'Well, thank you anyway,' I said to her. I was grateful when she opened the door for me.

I went back a couple of days later. 'You've changed your shoes,' she said. 'Was that for Robert or for me?'

'I was wondering if I could just ask you a couple of questions.'

'No, don't ask me questions,' she said, nonchalantly, and was about to shut the door on me.

'Then I'll tell you something. Robert loves you.'

It had worked so well with Sophia, I had to say it. Anyway, it was in her own best interests. I had to make her speak to me, I had to know her side of the story. But I hadn't bargained for the fact that Robert had been living with this woman a mere two months previously, and that Ruth was neither gentle nor passive.

'Love,' she said simply. Then she hit me.

I was pleased. Shocked first – I've never been slapped across the face like that. But then I thought, now I really *belong* to this book I'm writing, I'm part of the story. I held my head up and said, 'I want to interview you'.

Then she hit me again, harder this time, and I remember wanting to fall.

'Come in,' she said, suddenly polite. 'I think today we could have some tea.'

Victory. Even though my head ached and my cheeks burned, I thought, 'Here's my story. I'll have my story.'

It took her eight hours. There were no pauses. Each memory gave way to another more vivid. Quite often she seemed to be talking to herself, but then, when a revelation had been particularly painful to her, she knelt by me on the floor and cried, 'Now do you see? Now do you see?'. By the time she finished it was already midnight. I was cold and shivering – I didn't want to distract her by fetching my jumper, it seemed ungrateful somehow – and anyway, I felt I deserved to be shivering. I had invaded her, and it made things more equal.

I wouldn't have got in contact with her again. I would have felt ashamed to have called her now and said, 'There's something I need to be a little clearer on . . .' Anyway, she had already told me everything I needed to know. And I must confess, there's another reason why I was reluctant to get in touch with her. When she said goodbye to me she hugged me hard, for quite a long time. Perhaps telling me these things had been a huge relief to her, I know she meant it. But as for me, I felt awkward. I was unable, if you like, to *receive* that hug. My body was stiff however much I tried to relax. Ruth didn't notice, at least I hope she didn't, but once out of her arms and free and walking down the street, I decided I didn't want to go back there.

When I was home I saw that I was shaking. I knew I wouldn't be able to sleep. I laid out the children's clothes for school the following morning, I cleaned out the fridge and polished my husband's shoes. But the energy wouldn't wear itself down; it was as though something urgent still had to be done. I went down to the basement bedroom where Robert was sleeping. I wanted him to wake up. I wanted to kiss him too, I wanted to get into his bed because I was cold and shaking. I took my clothes off and got in beside him. This was the only sex I ever had with him.

I don't think I would have got in touch with Ruth again. I felt ashamed when a month later she wrote me a letter and said that she wanted to see me. I couldn't exactly say no, so I rang her up to arrange a time.

'Was there anything particularly you wanted . . .?' I began.

'Yes,' she said, 'there's something I didn't tell you.'

So there I was, on Ruth's doorstep for a third time, and actually invited to be there. Yet it was the only time that I felt I *ought not* to be there. I tried to ebb my curiosity – if curiosity is the desire to know, I didn't have the right to that desire. This was Ruth's story. At that moment I didn't want it.

When Ruth opened the door she was friendly, if rather business like. She made tea and we sat at the kitchen table. Then she said suddenly, 'I didn't tell you about the wine, did I?'

'No,' I said, 'I don't think you did.'

'In fact it's only occurred to me these last few days that the wine is significant. I was thinking about it during Mass last Sunday, and I thought, yes, that's the clue, the missing link, if you like.'

'But you've already told me so much . . .'

'I thought after that night you were here, "But where's the order in all this? Where's the logic?" '

'Perhaps there I can help you,' I said. 'Perhaps when you see what I've written . . .'

'Don't you want to hear what I have to say?'

'Of course I do, and I'm grateful, I promise you, for your time . . .'

'For my "time"?'

'No, of course not just for your time. Ruth, I am very, very grateful for everything, and I want to hear your story.'

'Good,' said Ruth. 'Then listen. I'm a Catholic, you know that already. Have you ever been to a convent?'

I shook my head.

'I pity you. There's nothing better than a convent. Even the things which are bad about it have their own happy logic. I remember, I even used to praise God for the nun who hit the back of my calves with a ruler during ballet. Quite right, I thought. I had bosoms and hips, and was a foot taller than anyone else. I was continually offending her sense of propriety; yes it surely was an offence, and I understood its nature exactly. The fact that I could do nothing about it was irrelevant. I was happy to take on the sin of my body and the sins of my forefathers, and quite honestly, any sin that needed atoning for. I found submission relaxing. Belonging to something bigger than oneself is so reassuring. Being contained so that one is able to feel the full expanse of one's smallness. Do you know what I mean?'

'Yes, I think so,' I said, though it all sounded fairly masochistic to me.

'Can I tell you the worst thing about living in the time we do? All you hear nowadays: should shops be allowed to open on Sundays? The debate should be, should churches be allowed to close when it's not? There should always be a church – somewhere open, quiet, receptive – for anyone who needs solitude and prayer. Deny a person that and may God help him. But at our convent we had a true luxury – we had a chapel that was never locked.

'I used to think it smelt of lingering incense but in retrospect it was polish. There was a plaster cast of the Virgin Mary painted in pastel colours, and when I was alone there I used to kneel at her feet with my head bent so low that the muscles in my neck hurt. This was where I said my prayers. She was like a mother to me – no, I don't think I was ever looking for human qualities in a mother, I wanted unquestioning love and wisdom, and this Virgin Mary had it.

'Quite often when I couldn't sleep – did I tell you I boarded there? – I'd suddenly decide that I needed to pray. I'd put on my dressing-gown and head off down the corridors for the chapel. There were always candles burning, that was all the light there was, and when they were stubs I would pray for them to go out, so that I could lie prostrate in front of my beloved Mother, but they never did. A nun would appear from nowhere and light new ones. I knew she'd notice me, so I'd look as devout as I could. Sometimes I'd catch her eye and she'd nod at me. Ah yes, we need nods like that. The absolute approval.

'So the chapel was unlocked, but so, unfortunately, was the vestry. The vestry was where the wine was kept, and as soon as Catholic girls are seventeen their main preoccupation is how they can get hold of it. I, of course, thought I was above all that, I wanted nothing to do with it. But one Saturday night towards the end of the Christmas term, when would this have been, 1961, I think, a girl called Alison with an ugly mouth suggested we all needed a few swigs of wine, and that we should pull straws to see which one of us should fetch a bottle from the vestry. The short one fell to me – it was bound to. But there was no use arguing with them; I hated them all and wanted to get out of there anyway, so I put on my dressing-gown and went to the chapel.

'As soon as I got there I knew what I was going to do. I would pray for a couple of hours, and by that time they'd all be asleep. In the morning I would tell them a story of how I'd been caught. I felt comforted by the plan, and knelt down in a pew near the front, so that I could watch the candles.

'He wasn't exactly a priest. He was from a seminary in the town, and we called him Brother Anthony. He used to help officiate at early morning Mass on Sundays. We watched him moving to and from the altar in his robes, and we watched the nape of his neck when he hung his head. There was nothing remarkable about him to look at, it was more a question of being bidden to what is hidden, particularly when it is forbidden. Those who were especially bidden fell in love with him. An entire week's worth of happiness depended on the look he gave you when you drank the wine from the chalice. The game was, to try and look him in the eye. God knows what he must have thought of us, all thinking fleshly thoughts and desperately trying to attract his attention. The fact that we were simultaneously drinking Jesus' blood only added to our pleasure: far from feeling anxious at the dilution of our spiritual thoughts, we revelled in the new depth admitted to our bodily ones. As for me, yes, he did look at me. Which was why, perhaps, I knew immediately that it was him.

'I was praying quite happily when I felt a large, warm hand on my head. I didn't even look up, I just wanted to ingest the warmth of it. There's no doubt that being blessed feels holier than taking communion. I can never decide, even now, whether to take the cup or sip from it, whether to chew the bread or wait for it to melt. It's all too conscious. But when you have a priest's hand on your head, you don't have to think about anything at all, you just feel it warm on you, and it's odd, but it really feels as though there's something coming down into you, there's a sort of certainty in the pressure of the hand that sends its warmth deep down. There was certainty then, and I didn't want to miss an iota of it by seeing his face, so I kept my head down.

He said to me, "Are you praying, Ruth?".

' "Yes," I said, but he wasn't satisfied.

' "Have you come for the wine?"

'I felt my cheeks burn.

'Then he said, "Come with me".

'He took me into the vestry. "We're six bottles down on what there should be," he said, but he didn't follow it with, "Did you take them?". I was waiting for it, I thought, he's going to tell the priest.

'But he said, "Do you want a bottle, then? You're a woman, Ruth. I'd quite understand if you wanted some wine. You don't belong here."

'I must have looked at him as if he was mad, because he went on, "Do you have no idea, my dearest Ruth?". I think it was "dearest" he called me. I thought he was going to kiss me, God knows what I'd have done if he'd tried, but his voice suddenly changed, the softness went, and he said: "You look at me as though I've touched you. Do I repulse you so much?"

'I was standing there watching him count out communion wafers for the morning mass, wondering what I ought to do next. He didn't look at me.

' "What have they told you at your convent, that it's a sin to love?"

' "Of course they haven't," I said. "Love is the greatest human gift."

' "Then what sin am I committing now, dear God above us? Here, Ruth, take your bottle of wine, go back to bed."

'I was about to say, no, I couldn't possibly take it, I'd come there to pray, why did he think I'd come for the wine? But anything I said I knew would sound like a lie, and I wanted to tell him the truth. What was the truth? I considered saying, "I love you, Brother Anthony, don't worry, I love you too". But when I heard those words in my head, there was too much pity and too little passion in them.

'He was handing me the bottle, but I didn't take it. He looked at me and again he offered it. "That's not what I want," I said.

' "What do you want, Ruth?"

'I saw his hand around the bottle, so large that the bottle seemed small, and I remembered how warm it had felt on my head. I suddenly said to him, "Bless it, Brother Anthony, bless it."

'And that's exactly what he did. He was so serious about it, he dedicated it to the Virgin Mary. When he gave it to me it felt like something holy. It was still warm from him, and I held it close to me underneath my dressing-gown. Only Alison was awake when I got back, and I said to her, "Brother Anthony caught me, the man who helps the priest", and because I must have sounded upset, she let it go. I lay in my bed in my dressing-gown until I was asleep, and then I hid it. I wrapped it up in a jersey in my bottom drawer and slipped it into my trunk a few days later. For years I kept it. I used to think, "On what occasion could this possibly be drunk?" so that I went on moving the damn bottle from flat to flat, always terrified that I'd break it and be cursed. Finally it ended up in this very house. I've already told you the good use to which it was put, the inevitable celebration of it, but I've never told you how it came to be mine. Do you know the strange thing about history? You never know the story it's going to tell. And you never know the relevant parts of your own history until you've reached the end of it – you don't know the love which was *the* love, which was the mere education, and which the reality. I drank the wine knowing the reason why I had ever owned it. And the pleasure of it all, in retrospect, is that Robert had nothing to do with the cycle. He never contaminated it.'

'You survived it all, Ruth,' I said to her.

'At least I understand it. This week, even, I've come to understand how it is. Olivia, I don't know how involved you are with Robert. You say you've not slept with him and I believe you. But you know, you will love him. You're going to say to yourself, "Who is this man who makes me feel not just good, or sexy, or loved or any of those, but who makes me feel so *human*?" – that's it, isn't it, he makes one appreciate and even love one's own vulnerability; he lets one strip off layer upon layer of civilised, learnt behaviour – till what have you left? I'll tell you: the fear that you're nothing.'

Then suddenly Ruth lost her energy and neither of us could think what to say next. She began washing up the cups and I suggested I left.

'I'll walk with you,' she said, 'I'm going to evening Mass.' So we walked together the Church of Our Lady on Lensfield Road, and I felt ashamed and awkward. It even crossed my mind to jettison the book. It was raining hard and cold, and we huddled in our coats, heads bent down.

But I hated the silence. I hated the cold wind blowing against us, I couldn't be quiet.

'Have you got a good priest?' I asked her.

'Functional,' she said.

And then, when we were standing outside the church, she suddenly laughed. 'Do you know,' she said, 'I once thought Robert was a priest. Do you think he would have made a good one?'

Then the bell went for Mass. I was grateful that the noise drowned out some stupid reply. I kissed Ruth goodbye and went home.

ELEVEN

When Robert knocked at Ruth's door and asked her to lie on him, she smiled and said, 'I'm heavy.'

'Brilliant to have weight,' he said. There was blood on his chin – he had evidently cut himself shaving – and his hair was unkempt and half-grey. But there was no wildness in his eyes, perhaps a singularity of purpose, but no wildness, no lack of coherence.

'He's a priest,' thought Ruth, 'who's been demoted for some carnal sin, but who's been more religious, in his time, than any of them.' Which was why she invited him in.

'Would you like a cup of tea first?'

'No,' said Robert.

But there was no patch of floor sufficiently large to accommodate the lying-on, and they had to go up to the bedroom.

Robert had lived as a ghost for twenty years: his body had died, while his mind and heart were full. Women's flesh had become as irrelevant as his own, not a pair of legs distracted him. Then, with the failure of his life's work, and with the consequent reinstatement of the subjective, bodies suddenly became the only reliable criterion. It wasn't a question of female parts but female total. He walked into a stranger's house and the desire for the whole of her made him say, 'lie on me', and she gave him her whole weight. 'Now I owe you everything,' he said, as he kissed her, and put his hands underneath her shirt.

Robert, what does a ghost feel who stretches out his ethereal fingers and arrives at something solid? Isn't it infinitely easier for us to imagine a spiritual existence than for a spirit to imagine a corporeal one? I can imagine the spirits debating the existence of physical bodies. 'Mummy,' says one of them, 'what does "touch" mean?' 'It's a myth, my dear,' says the mother spirit, 'some say there are tiny particles in space, some say they've had a personal experience with them. But they can't prove it, and they can't begin to describe it. Take my advice, darling, the modern way of looking at it is simply to suggest that the inexplicable doesn't exist.' Well, the son spirit grows up and lo and behold, as he's floating over a sunny part of the ethers, he suddenly experiences the warmth of the sun, but he can't talk about it to his friends – they consider such words as 'warmth' to be mere metaphor. The son spirit says, 'No, no, I promise you, this happened to me'. But the experience is so other-worldly as to be unimaginable, and they say to him, 'Are you sure you felt something more than an ordinary feeling of love or wonder or goodness?' 'It was better than any of those,' says the son spirit, 'but I shall never convince you. You will only know the truth of what I'm telling you when you feel the warmth for yourselves.'

'How is it,' said Robert, 'that I know you by feel?'

'You don't even know my name,' said Ruth.

'Ruth Mostyn,' said Robert, 'and I saw your painting of the boy on the lion.'

'I hope you bought it.'

'I wanted to know the artist first.'

'And do you know me now?' asked Ruth, and she wanted him to say yes.

'I know you better than I've known anything for a long time.'

'And do you want me for more than my body?'

'If there were more than your body to want you for, I'd want you for it.'

'And why do you place so much emphasis on the physical?'

'Because,' said Robert, as he pressed a finger deep into her thigh, 'only the physical leaves an impression.'

'And look, the impression has gone,' said Ruth.

'Are you suggesting there is something else which lasts longer?'

'I'm sure I can persuade you.'

'Persuade me, then.'

'But I don't know your name.'

'Is it more important to you that you know my name or to persuade me?'

'I don't know who you are.'

'Ruth, if I tell you that no one knows me better than you, will you persuade me to value your body less than I do?'

'So are you ready for me, whoever you are?'

'The tragedy is, my dear Ruth, I'm less ready for your defence of the spirit, because I'm assuming that's what you're going to give me, than I've ever been.'

'Your spirit is so large, whoever you are, that you can't see it.'

'My spirit is inexpressible, and therefore, rather sadly, dumb.'

'Your spirit is seamlessly sewn to your body, and your body's been making confessions all afternoon.'

'Spirit and body are equally dumb.'

'Each needs the other to speak.'

'Ah, my dear Ruth, and my dear neglected body, has it been making confessions? What did it tell you? Lie on me again, Ruth.'

So she did, and felt utterly contained by the spirit which she saw and which he denied. 'Why do I trust you?' she whispered to him. Then, while Robert was stroking her back and her hair, and while she was floating off to sleep, she answered her own question, 'You do as you will. Compromise, calculation, manipulation, all these are unknown to you. There's no part of you which drives itself away, to consider and consider, in isolation from the object of its consideration, which means there's no part of you to distrust. You're either a child or a god. With you, it's going to have to be a question of faith. And I don't even know your name.' And Ruth was smiling when she fell asleep.

But when she woke up, she was shy. She found herself naked, lying on top of a man she didn't know the name of. She must have slept for hours, it was already after midnight, and she felt disorientated. She put on a dressing-gown and asked Robert if he'd like some tea, or supper, goodness, she hadn't offered him any supper, what must he think of her. She went downstairs to have a look in the fridge, but it was empty. The only alcohol in the house was the bottle of Communion wine from the convent. It crossed her mind to give it to him. 'Is this the cause for celebration?' she thought to herself, and she blushed, remembering her first sex in seven years. 'Was there more to it than that? What was I saying to him? Was I mad? Was he?' She didn't want to go back upstairs to find out. The kettle boiled and she tried to find clean mugs. She couldn't, and she began to clean dirty ones with cold water, but the greasy rims wouldn't wash away. Robert came into the kitchen. 'Don't bother,' he said. 'I'd better get going. I've got to give a lecture first thing in the morning.' He looked at her as if he didn't know her, and he let himself out of the door.

Robert went to his bedroom, because the room with the music made him nauseous, and he lay under a cold sheet. He tried to remember what she looked like, whether she was pretty or not; he tried to gauge her features, the length of her nose, the thickness of her hair, the exact colour of her eyes. He tried to make them solid in his mind, to separate her from the boy in her painting. Sometimes he thought she was disappearing, and he heard himself cry out for her. 'This is ridiculous,' he said, sitting upright in his cold bed, 'I'm going back for her.'

'Lie on me again, Ruth,' he said to the sob in the dark, and that's exactly what she did. And when he should have been giving his lecture the following morning, he bought the painting of St Mark on the lion, and hung it above the bed. 'Now, how can I ever leave you again? Ruth, I love you.'

This was how their affair began. Robert barely left her house for the whole of the spring holiday. Nor, for those few weeks, did they refer much more to the existence of the spirit, being too involved in their bodies. What they said to each other was basically meaningless, grunts and murmurs which implied that what was happening to them was some strange mutual absorption. They had one relatively sensible conversation on whether what was happening to them was pre or meta language, Robert going for pre and Ruth for meta. Then suddenly it was the beginning of the summer term: Ruth returned to teaching art at the Cambridge College of Further Education, and Robert had to go back to Trinity.

Robert's loathing of anything cerebral dramatically increased. Having relegated the acquisition of knowledge to a positive backwater, and holding it to be a rather pathetic psychological necessity of man to look for structure when there was only flux, it goes without saying that he believed not a jot in the supervisions he was obliged to give, and his once celebrated lectures were beginning to pall. This, coupled with reports of his rather eccentric behaviour at the end of the previous term, caused the Master of Trinity to summon him to his study and suggest that he wasn't well, that he was tired, and that he needed a rest. There was no beating about the bush: he was offering a sabbatical year on half pay, officially beginning from the October of the following year, but of course, there'd be no need of him as soon as exams began, so he could count himself free from that point. There was another thing: was he still living in his rooms? He'd been trying to contact him for a while by telephone – 'I have to be frank with you,' he said, 'is there a woman? It's been suggested to me that there might be a woman.'

'There is.'

The Master waited for some further explanation, some excuse, some apology, but Robert gave none. It irritated him. 'Well, I think that's it, then.'

'Yes, it probably is,' said Robert.

Robert didn't mention the episode when he got back to Selwyn Road. In fact, he didn't mention any of these dull, irrelevant occurrences, nor anything which was extraneous to his life with Ruth, nor anything which could conceivably contaminate its purity. All he wanted was to lie tight in a blanket next to her and be still. On one occasion he attempted to explain to Ruth how conversation was artificial, and how there was an integrity in silence which could never be surpassed by all the vagaries of speech, but Ruth had put up her arms and said, 'Do you expect me not to speak to you? Don't be absurd, Robert. It is a hundred times better to talk imperfectly than to live in perfect silence. What kind of a life do you want for us?'

Because the truth was, Ruth liked to talk. She liked to tell him about her childhood in Yorkshire, about the convent, about when she was an artist in Montmartre. And she liked to talk about her work. One afternoon she came home and she was full of it. 'Today,' she said, 'I lied to my class, and it had a most curious effect. I was showing the first years a series of rather dull paintings which happened to be good examples of a particular method of brushwork. They all looked so bored, and I felt sorry for them. We were looking at a picture of a mother and child, the child was bringing his mother some nuts, seventeenth century, a little sentimental, well-executed though. Then one of the girls, who's noticeably more pregnant than she was last term, and God only knows who the father is, sighed and said, "I wonder what happened to her". "We know," I said suddenly. "Her name was Mrs Galloway, the child was called Robert." I named him after you, Robert. "It was painted a month before the outbreak of the Civil War. The child's father was a Cavalier and was

276

shot soon afterwards. Why we know so much is because their house is still standing, in a village near Stratford, and some sort of story emerged from letters found in the attic. You mustn't ask me for details, but soon after her husband was shot Mrs Galloway herself was arrested. Apparently she saw soldiers coming towards the house, hugged her son goodbye, and hid him in some chest or other. She was released only a short while later, but when she got back to the house the child had gone. She never even found his body. The letters were mainly from friends and relatives in neighbouring villages expressing regret that they hadn't seen him. But, you might say, at least she had this picture of him to remember him by."

'I could see they were all terribly moved. I felt a bit guilty about it. Some of the students came up to have a closer look at the painting. They suddenly decided it was infinitely better than it in fact was. "Why didn't you tell us about it before? How could you have considered not telling us about it?" "Always be suspicious of narrative," I said to them. "You have to learn to look at the qualities of a painting, at the stillness of it, and unfortunately this painting isn't a particularly good one, and perhaps I shouldn't have shown it to you at all." But Julia, who's pregnant, wouldn't let me off the hook at all. "I think you've betrayed this woman," she said, and the way she said it made me feel as though I had. "This is the most beautiful painting I've ever seen."

'Robert, what would you have said, and why did I make up the story at all?'

'I don't know, Ruth,' said Robert, who was only half-listening, 'are you trying to prove something?'

'Do you think I am?' Ruth immediately decided he was right.

277

Ruth couldn't sleep that night with the excitement of trying to understand what she had been trying to prove. Robert was irritated with her. 'Be still,' he said.

Before setting off for the college, Ruth said, 'You're right, Robert, I think I know what I was getting at.'

'Tell me this evening,' said Robert, reluctantly.

When they had eaten supper and drunk wine, during which time Ruth had been patiently waiting for her cue to begin her revelations, and when Robert had given her none, Ruth said, 'Well, I think I've discovered what you were getting at. You're so right to have made me think about it. The answer is, Robert, that paintings are not ends in themselves, they are not goals. Rather they are bridges.' Ruth waited for some spark of recognition of her genius, but there was none, so she went on, 'You see, Robert, a thousand paintings are like a thousand different pairs of spectacles, each with a different thickness of lens. I used to imagine there was a perfect thickness of lens, and people were simply blind who couldn't see through it, when of course different people see better through different lenses. But the important thing is this, Robert, that the very thing we are all seeing through these different lenses, the very thing that lies across those bridges, is God, Truth, Beauty, call it what you will, it's the one criterion of all human communication, it's the only thing which joins us all up.'

'I'm impressed, Ruth,' said Robert, but really what he was impressed by was the beauty of Ruth's eyes when they were lit up like that. 'So why did you tell your students the lie?'

'The painting wasn't art. It wasn't a true bridge. By itself, it led nowhere, and I was frustrated by it. I was frustrated by the bored faces of the class. Sympathy is on the way to empathy. Sympathy is personal, empathy is universal, but you cannot feel the second without learning to feel the first. I got the class on the right track, that was all.'

'I'm alarmed,' said Robert, 'at the status you give suffering. It doesn't deserve it.'

'Suffering deserves all it can get,' said Ruth. 'At my convent, I alone stood in defence of it. The nuns tried to pretend it didn't exist, or at least, where it did, it was somehow deserved. A world without suffering would be a place for children, everyone would have what they wanted, everyone would be loved. But how could we prove ourselves worthy of such a place *in* such a place? Where is there room for morality? What happens when one of these heaven-dwellers says to his neighbour, "Let me buy you a new coat", when the friend either doesn't need a new coat or has enough money to get himself one if he did? He might as well ask him if he'd like butter on his potatoes. Robert, we *need* this world first, we *need* to suffer.'

Robert said nothing. Ruth looked up at him, and though his face was expressionless, he suddenly made her feel ashamed. 'That's a disgusting thing to say,' she said, 'I obviously haven't suffered, or I couldn't say it.

'But Robert, can't you see how right you are? Words are nothing, words say nothing: the greatest form of human communication – no, even that word is mean, it's a sinewy word, it suggests telephone lines and efficiency – the greatest form of human communion, Robert, is to sympathise with someone who is suffering, and for the suffering man to experience that sympathy.'

'Do you know, Robert, a curious thing, that when I say something I think is important, I find myself shaking.

Look at my hands now, shaking away. Please hold me, Robert.'

So Robert held her close to him. Ruth reminded him of himself as a young man, and he felt old. He remembered with nostalgia the time when he had the energy to think. But thinking had never succeeded in altering the condition or direction of his life in any satisfactory way, thinking was a fruitless course. And so would it be for anyone who built up for himself a system of beliefs which were away from the crowd, for who would listen to him? And how can he go on, hammering away in his heart and mind, when the world is deaf to him? No, the only power one has in a deaf world is to remain silent.

'Darling Ruth,' said Robert, 'I want you to know how completely sympathetic I am,' and it was true, he wanted to save her from the despair he foresaw for her.

'I know, I know,' said Ruth, content that she had finally been understood.

And the pair of them wrapped themselves up in bed and spent the weekend there, body to body, with barely a word to come between them.

But on the Monday evening, Ruth found herself, yet again, wanting to have a conversation.

'Robert, I still haven't fully understood what you do. Can't you tell me about it? I know a little about science. I should love to know what it's like in a volcano.'

'You already know as much as anyone, Ruth. You would have to experience it to know more.'

'Well, what do you talk about in your lectures? Can I come and watch you?'

'Ruth, you must never watch me, never put yourself on the one side, and leave me alone on the other. But you can come and stand beside me on the podium, if you like.

You get a good view from there. There's a large chestnut tree immediately outside to the right, and every lecture the tree is fuller and greener.'

'Robert, I love you, and what shall I do while I'm standing next to you on the podium? How shall I prevent myself from looking ridiculous?'

Robert thought and suddenly hit upon it, 'You should be yourself. Pretend nothing. You should paint.'

'Do you expect me to come with you with my easel and oils and paint the view from the podium?'

'Paint the chestnut tree. It's a beautiful thing, come with me tomorrow see for yourself.'

'And what would you be lecturing on while I was painting?'

'You and I, Ruth, would be doing the same thing. Rationalising nature. Finding order in the chaos. Demonstrating it to our audience.'

'And if our audience laughed?'

'Let them laugh. If they laughed from delight, how could we deny them that? Or they might laugh because they didn't understand. In which case I would explain it to them. I would say, "Nature has more depth than surface. Ruth here is demonstrating the proposition. She's giving depth and clarity to the green of the chestnut tree. And I'm going to attempt to do the same, though I regret I'm not as talented as Ruth, to the green of the olivine of the earth's mantle." '

'What if my painting were a terrible failure?'

'Dear Ruth, I have complete faith in you. Never doubt it. You are a limitless receptacle for life, and you have no ghastly ego which meddles with it. Look at your painting of St Mark, look at this light on the boy's face. No one fails to understand that.'

'You admire that painting too much. The legs on the lion are too short. I'm as liable to fail as anyone else.'

'If you believe that, then you will. But that wasn't what you thought when you painted it.'

'No, you're right, but it's not a feeling you can beckon.'

'So you're not going to come and join me on my podium?'

'No, I don't think so,' said Ruth, but there was disappointment in her voice, because she admired the part in her which for a moment had entertained the possibility.

It frustrated Ruth that Robert didn't talk to her about his previous life, nor, when she talked about her own, did he show much curiosity to know more. She once tried to talk to him about her father. And because she was beginning to feel embarrassed that she seemed to be the one that was always doing the talking, she began, 'Tell me about your father, Robert'.

'Why should you want to know more about my father than my mother?'

'I don't know anything about either of them. Are they alive?'

'No, dead.'

'I'm sorry. Was that a long time ago?'

'A while back, I suppose.'

'Were you close to them?'

'I discovered that I was, quite recently, and quite unfortunately.'

'Why was that unfortunate?'

'My mother unwittingly interfered with a project. She was dead at the time. I wanted to tell her, and of course she was dead.'

Ruth laughed, more from anxiety than pleasure, and said, 'Well, you could hardly blame her.'

'I didn't want to blame her, Ruth, I wanted to tell her that I loved her, and had loved her all along, because she was the sort of woman who would have wanted to know.'

'My dearest Robert, of course your mother knew that you loved her.'

Then Ruth hugged him and felt ashamed at being witness to an emotion that didn't involve her, and simultaneously admiring of the heart from which it sprang. And because it was unlike him to make such admissions, she reckoned it must have cost him a good deal to have said it, and felt flattered.

Robert, on the other hand, was rather alarmed at the exaggerated reaction his statement received, and didn't understand it. There followed an embarrassingly one-sided embrace, during which Ruth told Robert that she understood, and Robert told Ruth that he didn't. 'I loved my mother,' Robert said to her. 'Surely that's a common reaction.'

'Your love wasn't common,' Ruth whispered to him. 'It wasn't common at all.'

A couple of days later, Ruth tried again. 'What was your father like?' she said. Robert, bristling at the memory of that other evening of cross-communication, said, 'These conversations aren't necessary, you know. They add nothing.'

'Don't you want to hear about my father, then?'

'All right. Tell me about him.'

'I hated him. I hate him.'

'Then I can't see why you want to talk about him so much.'

'Why don't you want to know?'

'Tell me about him, then.'

'It's no good. You don't sound enthusiastic enough. Say, "Ruth, what a curious thing it is to hate one's father. Why do you hate him?" '

'OK then, so why do you?'

'I hate his voice.'

'I can understand that.'

'You should have heard him when he said Grace. I used to think, "You're even sucking up to God now". If you could have heard his smarmy monotone . . .'

'I'm pleased I haven't.'

'My mother, on the other hand, might have been quite grateful if he'd used that voice with her – she got worse, far worse.'

'I can't see how,' said Robert.

'It was the same monotone, but it was violent.'

'A violet monotone. I understand exactly. Well put.'

'Violent, Robert, violent. Aren't you listening to me?'

'I'm sorry. I misheard.'

'I can't understand why you're not the slightest bit interested in my past.'

'You don't have to know the ingredients of a cake, Ruth, to enjoy eating the cake. In fact, thinking about flour while eating cake might actually put you off it.'

'Robert, I am not a cake.'

'No, you're not a cake,' said Robert, with the amazement and delight of a child who suddenly finds his favourite toy come to life.

'Oh Robert, Robert . . .' said Ruth.

'I love you, Ruth, for everything you are now, today, I love you utterly and completely, I don't love you for what you have been.'

And Ruth sighed. 'Oh Robert,' she said.

A few days later Ruth was lying alone on her bed. It was six in the evening and she was waiting for Robert to come back from a supervision. The sun was streaming through the window, showing up the dust. 'I haven't cleaned this room since Robert came,' she thought. 'It's so small and ugly. And I hate that cupboard.' The cupboard she was looking at stood at the end of the bed, one huge, dark, monotone, thirties cupboard, that would have looked out of place in a room six times the size. It contained the junk of twenty years, or 'junk' she decided when she opened it, though only a couple of months previously it contained items that were precious to her. 'I'm going to chuck it all out,' she said, and she went downstairs to the kitchen to get dustbin liners.

While she was vigorously throwing the contents on to the bed, squashed black velvet hats she had worn in the sixties, programmes of concerts, magazines she had edited as an undergraduate, an optic-art mini-skirt that had done little for her thighs, a plastic cherub that an old boyfriend had made for her to sit on her shoulder ('was this another reference to my bloody thighs?' she thought) notepads of drawings she had done in Montmartre, hundreds of Indian silk scarves, she kept thinking to herself, 'Is Robert right? What sort of a man is it who wants to know about his predecessors? Why should he want to know about these episodes of my past, simply on account of their having happened to me? I don't believe that the people I've known have made me essentially different from the person I might have been otherwise. I am, as Robert insists, me.'

Ruth went on taking the things out of her cupboard. When the bed was too full, she began to throw things in the bags. Then she got down to her old clothes and set them aside to take to Oxfam. She went on thinking, 'And what about Robert's past? If I decide that Robert is rather noble to consider my own past doesn't matter, then isn't it rather squalid of me to guess at Robert's?' And suddenly it felt squalid because she thought of previous girlfriends. Of course, he would have had them. He was no virgin. And knowing Robert as she did, he would have loved them too. Perhaps there was a girl whom he had loved utterly, as he did everything utterly. Perhaps she'd left him. Perhaps that was why he avoided talking about his own past, or prevented her from talking about her own. It was fear of bringing the whole subject up. Sometimes, now she came to think of it, he seemed deeply, privately sad, and lost to her.

'You look sad,' said Robert, as he came into the bedroom and kissed her cheek. 'No,' said Ruth, 'I'm just sorting out all this old stuff. I should have done it years ago. It's rather depressing, really, remembering what one was like, what one wore, how one thought. I don't like it.'

'There's even wine in here,' said Robert, taking it from its home among the jumpers, 'We should drink it.'

'I'm pleased you found that. I was wondering where it had got to. No, we won't drink it. I want to keep that. Give it to me and I'll put it somewhere.'

'Or it could be vinegar. What have you done with the label?'

'There was no label. It's Communion wine.' Ruth smiled. Her first secret. His first curiosity. 'I got it from the convent. Do you remember I told you I went to a convent?'

'So, it's the real thing,' said Robert, 'once bound for a couple of hundred convent girls, and now in your cupboard. I wonder whether their gut would have digested it as blood or wine. The gut couldn't be deceived, could it? But it never got there. Ruth, you robbed them of it.'

'Not at all,' said Ruth, and she smiled again. 'It was given to me.'

'I can see it all. The nuns gave it to you as their parting gift. "Ruth Mostyn, take this wine," they said, "but beware, you must only take three sips of it, each on an occasion of the direst need, and it will save you from all manner of catastrophe." I envy you for it. It could've saved me on a number of occasions.'

'So when would you have drunk it?' laughed Ruth.

'A few months ago. I could've done with a bottle of the stuff.'

'That's more than three sips, remember, you'd have burnt up or something.'

'No,' said Robert, 'I couldn't have stopped at three sips. Sooner burn.'

'So tell me the occasion,' said Ruth, still smiling, 'on which you would sooner burn.' But then she saw that his face was now serious, and the tone of her voice no longer matched it. But she went on, anyway, forcing lightness: 'It's never even crossed my mind to take the cork out to smell it.'

The mood shift had gone too far. The ten-second silence seemed to repeat the question.

'Something was stolen,' said Robert.

The relief was enormous. Something was stolen, nothing more, and the 'more' sank back, unexamined.

'What was it? Was it valuable?'

'Only of sentimental value.'

'What was it?'

'I couldn't hold it, Ruth. It slipped through my fingers like a fine powder. Or was it blown away?'

'I thought you said it was stolen.'

'Stolen or lost, the end's the same.'

'Oh God,' thought Ruth. She said, 'You must've loved her'.

There was a pause. Then Robert said suddenly, 'How finely does glass have to be ground to be sure of its not cutting you?'

'Oh God,' thought Ruth again, 'this was bad.' But she tried to sound relaxed. 'You must've loved the woman who gave it to you.'

'Love?' said Robert, and his eyes were blank; but Ruth, owing to the fact she was looking extremely hard, saw depths in them beyond measure, and decided she really didn't have the stomach for all of this, she didn't need a confession, so she said lightly, 'Anyway, it wasn't the nuns who gave it to me at all'. And when Robert didn't question her further, she jumped off the bed, in as sprightly a way as possible, and said, 'Well, I'm going to make us both a strong cup of tea'.

They barely spoke to each other for the rest of the week, which Robert found quite a relief, though Ruth managed to make herself quite anxious over the missing confession. And then, quite suddenly, Robert found himself called up again by the Master of Trinity.

'The quality of your lectures,' he said, 'has once again been called to my attention. I didn't appreciate having to sign for one of your exhibits.'

'Oh,' said Robert, 'which one?'

'There's a ton of granite outside the Porter's Lodge.'

'Then there's been a mistake. I ordered half a ton.'

'For God's sake, Dr Standing, a ton or half a ton, is that relevant? The bloody thing was freighted from Wales.'

'Isn't it a shame,' Robert sighed.

'A shame?' said the Master.

'That there's no granite in Cambridgeshire.'

'Dr Standing, get rid of the granite. You have two lectures left. Forget them, they're neither here nor there. I don't know what's going on in your life and I won't pry. Over the years you've been a good, reliable teacher and I don't want to lose you. Come back, Dr Standing, in fifteen months. Let's forget these weeks ever happened.'

Robert pushed the granite along the roads on a large porter's trolley. There was a headline in the *Cambridge Evening News*: 'Off his Rocker,' it said. Just outside Whittlesford he rolled the rock into a chalk pit, where it remains to this day, confusing all naturalists who question it.

When Robert got home he looked at Ruth and said, 'Why not let's go and find ourselves an island in the Outer Hebrides to live on? We'll find an island with a croft on it, and you could bring a few canvases along with you, what do you think?'

'My dear Robert,' said Ruth, 'look at you, where have you been? Look at your bleeding hands, what have you been doing?'

'It's true,' said Robert, 'all day I've been feeling like Sisyphus, and I'm not getting anywhere. It's no good, Ruth, Cambridge isn't the place for us. Everything will become clear in a different air. You'll see, I know it will.'

Ruth thought to herself, 'How self-indulgent I am. All I've been doing these last few days is imagining and suspecting, while Robert is genuinely suffering. What could have driven him to do that to himself?'

So this is what they did. Ruth selected some paints and wrote a note to the college to say she wouldn't be returning there. Then they packed a suitcase of clothes between them, and they were on the sleeper train from Peterborough to Scotland that very same night.

'Robert,' said Ruth, happily, 'for the last four hours, while we've been packing up, it's felt as though all my life I've been waiting for someone to say to me, "Why not let's live in the Outer Hebrides?" Now you have, and it's like a dream. It seems such an obvious thing to be doing, and yet I don't even know why we're doing it. Why are we going to live on an island in the Minches? Tell me, Robert, please, why we're sitting on this train, heading north?'

'We need some weather,' said Robert, 'we're both badly in need of some weather.'

So that, on the first night of their arrival in Eilean Tighe, deserted except for a single croft and six hundred sheep, Robert had laid himself out on the grass for an hour and a half in the rain, and Ruth had watched him through the window of the croft, and had seen him smiling with the water pouring down the sides of his face, and she'd wanted to join him there, but she felt shy: she thought it would be like interrupting someone else's prayer.

TWELVE

It was as easy as Robert promised it would be to find their island. They met the shepherd and the fisherman at the Star Hotel in Tarbert. Ruth kept saying, 'But what extraordinary *luck*', but Robert shrugged his shoulders, as though he expected no less, and he said to the barman over the formica counter, 'Two whiskies here for the Macleods', and he said to the Macleods, 'Now, tell us a bit more about this island where you're taking us – the landlord lives in New Zealand, you say, and there's a single croft on it, which is only used when the sheep have to be seen to. Otherwise, there's no one on the island at all – is that right?'

'Not a soul. But there used to be,' said Hugh, the elder of the brothers, and the fisherman, 'there were seven families who lived there, but only one left by 1923. That's right, isn't it, John?'

'Aye,' said John, the shepherd.

'But that family, there were eleven of them, but they were a wee bit self-sufficient, kind of close-knit. Aye, there were three daughters in that family, and they were all pregnant when they were lifted off, and there were two wee ones besides. The father had his way with his elder daughter, so they say, she's dead now, but the daughter that came out of it, she lives in Glasgow, I think. There was a man in Harris who met her, that was a while ago, I think she worked in a shoe factory, never married, said her mother painted a picture of Eilean Tighe as a real paradise, and it is an' all. The odd thing is, or that's what the woman said, that her mother was never lost for company, she thought her life was full and holy and complete. The other daughters were all pregnant by their brothers, but when they got to the mainland they all married in the normal way and started their own families and lost contact with each other, which was probably for the best, all things considered.'

'And are we to live in *their* house?' asked Ruth.

'No, their house is just a ruin now, we built the croft in front of it, and that's where you'll be staying. It's pretty basic, but there's a good fire, and there's a spring only a hundred yards away. There're a couple of easy chairs there too, which we took from the lighthouse when it closed down, and two pairs of bunks in the other room, you see, the height of comfort, two rooms, one for sleeping, one for eating. You won't be put out, will you, when the shepherds join you? When'll you be going out next, John? I must tell you, I've never been there in the winter, the Minches are rough in the winter, and there's only two hours' light in the day, but you want to stay over the winter too?'

'That's right,' said Robert. 'We'd like to live there, for a year at least, and if it's good, we'll stay on, if the owner doesn't object, or if the shepherds don't mind sharing with us when they come over – John, are you sure we won't be in your way?'

'Not at all,' said John, 'I'd like to see how you get on, and I'll look forward to visiting you there. The present owner has never even seen Eilean Tighe, so he won't mind.'

'And you say that you can deliver food to us once a month, potatoes, carrots perhaps, tins, we won't need much.'

'No, no problem at all, John'll bring over the supplies, won't you John? They'll be a wee bit irregular, but don't worry, you won't starve, and you've paid us well, Robert. Your wife's looking scared, don't you worry, I'll make it as close to every four weeks as I can.'

'So you can see nothing to stop this happening, then?' said Robert.

'Nothing at all.'

'And when can you take us?'

'Tomorrow at eight. Be on the jetty at eight and I'll take you then.'

Ruth was sick in the hold during the crossing. She had volunteered to make the tea, but the hot water had spilt over her hand and by the end of the three-hour journey blisters had come up. In the end she'd left her canvases behind: they were too bulky, and didn't justify taking up half their luggage space. Instead she'd taken a box of pastels and a stack of paper carried in a plastic bag, but as she walked over the deck to the wheelhouse with two cups of tea for the men, the boat slid down the back of a large swell and a sheet of water slewed across the deck, filling up the plastic bag as though it were an udder, and the paper flowed out with it.

'Well,' she thought, 'there's a lesson. What Eilean Tighe holds cannot be kept, there'll be no record of it.'

The cups of tea had been reduced to half, and the men laughed at her through the window of the wheelhouse; then Robert came out and said, 'Well, what about this then? It's not bad, is it?'

'Take your tea,' said Ruth, and she went back down into the hold. But Robert made a face to Hugh to suggest that it was now predominantly sea-water, and he left the cups on the deck. Then he stood up by the mast and held on to it, feeling like Canute with his sceptre, the wind blowing his hair away from his face as though to say, 'you won't hide anything from me', and he watched the dark shapes of the island become paler. And he thought, 'there can only be one thing better than this, and that is not to see those shapes for the first time, but to recognise them and to know them, and to be able to say at this moment, "I'm going back to what I know". It occurs to me, do we ever envy people who are dead? Is it possible, I wonder, to envy the life of a popular king, if he's now dead, or the man who had the money to build a city to his own design, when the city lives, but the man himself is dead? Because I think I envy the people who lived here, even in their deadness.'

When they landed (by means of a dinghy which they kept with them) Robert was like a gourmet hunting out promising restaurants in a foreign city famous for its cooking.

'Jurassic mudstone,' he said to Ruth. 'Look at this, this is all Jurassic mudstone, a hundred and fifty million years old, quite something to be a fossil in that. Perhaps Ruth, if we die here, we might be human fossils, and in another hundred million years there'll be geologists chipping away at us. I think we should arrange to die exactly one on top of the other, so that when we're chipped at they'll say,

"A new species". You know that myth of Plato, where he says that man and woman were originally one, and spend their whole lives searching for their other half and feeling *eros*? "Well, imagine," they'll say, when they find us, "the myth is not a myth at all, we have the living proof of it." '

The Jurassic mudstone was only the beginning. When Robert saw the columnar basalt at the north face of the island, five hundred feet steep out of the water, every ledge occupied by puffins, razor-bills, shags and guillemots, he was so moved that he made Ruth put down the luggage which she was carrying to the croft and walk with him for about a mile over grassy headland to reach it, and then he insisted that she sit next to him, legs dangling over the edge, and then, no, that wasn't good enough, he made her lie so that her head was dangling over the top of it, for otherwise her knees would get in the way of the full view. 'Now,' he said, 'see how *black* that basalt is, can you see it? And feel it too. Are you feeling it, Ruth?'

Ruth felt it, extremely self-consciously, and aware more of the rocks five hundred feet below her than those in front of her nose. Her arms, as Robert spoke to her, had been by her sides, somehow making sure that the bulk of her weight remained firmly on the land, but then she'd made an effort to join Robert, she thought it appropriate that on this the first day of their stay on Eilean Tighe, she should show as much abandon and spirit as the man she loved, and reluctantly her arms let go of their sure place on the grass beside her and hopelessly began searching for a solid piece of cliff to hold on to. But she knocked some stones off a small ledge, and immediately sat up with a start imagining for a moment that the crag on which they were lying was going to break off. To make matters worse, the birds considered this to be a direct attack on their eggs, and they started flying at Ruth, so that she let out a cry; but Robert hadn't noticed a thing, he was still lying on his stomach, head down, and the cry was drowned in the general cacophony.

After about ten minutes he sat up and said: 'Well, Ruth, this is it, and the odd thing is, that if you'd been here any time during the last fifty million years, everything would have been much the same. Even those birds there, the shags, with the bright green eyes and the oily black backs, they'd have been here too – but sixty million years ago, things were happening then – can you imagine, molten lava would have squeezed in between the faults of the mudstone, can you see what a sight that would be, red molten columns squeezing out and up, wouldn't you give anything to have been there? And the ancestors of those very shags would have seen it all, and we're here now, and the shags have eggs, my God, Ruth, I love you.'

Then he laid Ruth down in the flowery grass and kissed her, and said he'd like to have a baby with her, that the only thing he could be sure of was that he'd like to have a baby with her, and when Ruth realised what he was saying it seemed that the whole of her life had been lived in order to arrive at that moment – this idea of Fate, you see, this search for structure that consumes us all.

They fell asleep and the rain woke them up. 'The luggage,' said Ruth, 'My God, we never got the luggage in'. But by the time they got back to the croft, everything was sodden, including themselves. So they took off their clothes and spread them out on every available surface, and wrapped themselves in the hard grey woollen blankets that they found on the bunks, and they tried to light a fire but the driftwood piled up outside against one wall was itself too drenched to catch fire. Ruth shivered and found another blanket. Robert said, 'The rain's surprisingly warm' and left his in the croft. He went outside and felt it on his face and shoulders, then the wind blew the rain at an angle against his body. The croft looked directly on to the sea, and it crossed his mind to swim, but the tide was out and he kept slipping on the rocks, sliding on the bladderwrack and the oarweed, so that he fell and cut his knees against the mudstone. He stayed a while, leaning against a rock, his feet lodged in a warm pool of water. It was about half past nine at night, breaks were forming in the clouds, the sun had not yet set and the moon was up. The sun's rays were stronger on the horizon, but the moon had the upper hand in the sky, and the rivals sent out two paths of light across the water, the one narrow and bright, the other full and generous. But then the clouds moved across the moon, and the sun was winning. It somehow offended him that the sun was winning, that they were no longer equals, so he got up and began to climb back over the rocks to the croft, but the clouds were moving faster now, and by the time he had reached the door even the sun was blocked out and it was dark, about as dark as four o'clock on an English winter afternoon, for during summer in the Outer Hebrides even at midnight the sky is never black.

The rain began again in earnest; it was heavier and colder than before, but he felt it washing off the debris from the seaweed, and he liked to feel so warm right there in the middle of him where his gut was, and so cold where his skin was. So he lay down on the grass and the water streamed off him, and it was then that Ruth saw his face through the window of the croft and felt jealous of the rain, for how could she ever match it?

Ruth caught a cold but Robert didn't. She never complained and Robert didn't notice it. Slowly their clothes dried out, and slowly some sort of routine established itself. They slept together in a two-foot-six bunk. The only way that they could fit was if each slept on their side, Ruth's back against Robert's chest. They woke up when they woke up: by the end of the first week both their watches had broken and neither of them minded one jot.

Breakfast took about two hours. First of all, they had to make the fire. Then they had to set off with buckets to the spring to replenish their water, but if they extracted it too quickly mud would come up to the surface and the water would be unusable for anything but washing-up. Then they put the water on the fire to boil, some in a kettle for the tea, and some in a pan for the porridge. Sometimes, when the supplies were fresh, their breakfast was correspondingly large. Their first week there saw breakfasts as good as Trinity. There were eggs, bacon, sausages, even tomatoes for two or three days. But by day five the sausages were finished, day seven the bacon, and within a fortnight the eggs had gone.

'Perhaps we should have hens here,' said Ruth.

'The sheep would eat them,' said Robert.

'No they wouldn't,' Ruth said.

'It's too windy for hens. They'd be blown off.'

That was the biggest attempt at self-sufficiency they made, and when the eggs ran out, it was simply a question of their bowls of porridge being proportionally larger.

After breakfast what they did next depended on the weather. About three times a week it was possible to go out for a row in the dinghy, otherwise the sea was simply too rough for it to be safe. When they were in the boat they spent a lot of time singing to the seals, who quite regularly popped their heads out of the water to listen to them. Singing in a boat in a sea twenty miles from the mainland was something they both did with utter joy. At the beginning, they sang songs they already knew, Scottish ballads and civilised things like that. But when they grew more confident and more abandoned (Robert after about two days, Ruth after three weeks), they began to make up their songs as they went along, words and tune and everything, a sort of Dada of choral music. They made up a very good song about Loch Lomond, in which there was a rival loch called Loch Himond, and Robert would sing in a low voice about Lo-Lo-Lo-mond, and Ruth would sing in a high voice about Hi-Hi-Hi-mond. You get the gist of it.

They spent as long in the boat as the weather permitted. Sometimes they rowed into caves, and the swell carried them fast under the island. There was one in particular which was covered in pink sea lichen, and one day they took a torch so they could explore it. The water breathed them in; they turned a corner and the cave darkened around them. The mouth of the cave and the open sea had disappeared from view. They were deep in a watery underground.

'I don't understand' said Ruth, 'who this is pink for. Why does it bother to be so beautiful when it will never see the light of day?'

They rowed on, or at least, pushed themselves off the rocks with the oars, as the passage had narrowed. The swell sucked and pulled around them, lurching at the cavities in the rock. A shag appeared just behind them on the dark, unreflective water, eyed them for a moment and then plunged beneath, leaving a frothy puddle on the surface. As Ruth looked over the side of the boat she saw the bird beneath her, its dark and oily shape flitting out away from them towards the mouth of the cave.

'Do you want to go on?' said Ruth.

'Don't you?'

And they went on another thirty or forty feet.

'OK,' said Robert, 'I'm going to turn the torch off now, are you ready? Put your oar in the boat and come and sit next to me.'

So in the black of the pink cave, Robert kissed her neck and untucked her shirt and felt her body warm underneath it, and said to her, 'Are you conscious, Ruth, that you have a womb? What I mean is, can you feel it inside you, do you know instinctively where it is?'

'I should imagine,' said Ruth, 'that just like you're only conscious of your bladder when it's full, you only become conscious of your womb when that's full.'

'Well, when your womb's full you must give me a day by day account of it, because I'll want to know.'

'Robert, there'll be nothing I leave out.'

So it became quite a habit, making love under Eilean Tighe.

When it was too rough for the dinghy trips they went for walks. They took a picnic of potato crisps and a tin of ham, and a flask full of spring water. For the first couple of weeks they went together, but then Robert suggested that perhaps walks were better by oneself. Sometimes Robert would disappear for what must have been about ten hours, quite a feat on an island only four miles by two: 'Where do you go?' Ruth asked him. 'There are no trees and yet I never see you, where do you go?' And then one day she found him.

It was a day on which they might normally have chosen to go in their dinghy: a hot, calm August day, two months after their arrival, and two days after the shepherd John Macleod and his fifteen-year-old son had left them again in peace. In addition to being happily restored to their single bunk, the store-cupboard was now filled with apples, oranges, sausages, eggs, and the most exciting item of all, fresh bread.

'We should make a proper expedition today, right over to the other side of the island, climb a few cliffs, take a proper picnic, what do you think, Ruth?'

Ruth had made egg mayonnaise sandwiches with tomato and they were all set. 'Apples,' she said, 'let's take the apples too.' But after they had walked perhaps two hundred yards, Robert suddenly turned to her and said, 'Look, I'm awfully sorry Ruth, I want to be alone today.'

How could she argue with him? 'No, I'm sure that you *really* want me to go with you, you're mistaken.' So she said, 'All right, then, here's your half of the picnic', and tried to sound bright about it, but those words of his suddenly made her lose all the energy she'd felt at breakfast, with the eggs and bacon on the fire and the sunlight pouring in. She watched Robert walk off, watched him climb a steep hill the other side of the beach with the ease and agility of a twelve-year-old boy, and meandered back to the croft.

She tried to make a plan and lift herself out of her present disconsolation. The same sun streamed into the croft, but now it seemed like effrontery. She did a huge pile of washing up, which would normally have been done after breakfast but which had been left in their enthusiasm 'to get on with the day'. She longed for a book to read, something to take her out of her mood, but they'd brought none with them. A walk would have been a shadow of a walk. The thought of washing the clothes made her feel tired. She went back to bed but she couldn't sleep. She went outside but with the sea so calm and the birds gone since July the quiet stifled her. She sang but her voice grated inappropriately, a tuneless sabotage of a church choir. She wanted to cry but the drama of crying required energy she did not have. Then she lay on the grass and thought about Robert.

It occurred to her that he seemed more mysterious to her now than even on their first day together. Then what he required seemed so obvious: he was like a man finding ingredients for a recipe he knew, and to be found by him was the inevitable consequence of his looking. Once he'd said to her, 'You ask me questions as though there was a self, a shiny red billiard-ball of a self to be held and turned round in your hand as though that were a way of understanding me, but I promise you, all a history of me would give you is a distortion of who I am, for it seems to me that I am entirely disconnected to it, and the man I am now has nothing to do with my past at all, and who I might be in five years has nothing to do with me now, and the most honest and the most accurate picture I can give you is what you already have, this body, a hundred and seventy pounds of it, so take it, and if you see more, take that as well. I shall never hide anything from you, Ruth, you have me all.'

She'd been persuaded by him at the time, but then again, why did he never seem to have an opinion about anything? The world outside might as well not have existed, for the interest he took in politics, and when she'd suggested that they should go and see an exhibition at the Fitzwilliam, he'd said, enigmatically, 'Why should I go in search of something which I already have?'; and then he'd said, and she'd been touched by it, 'Your painting above our bed is more beautiful by far than a hundred others hung up in a row: they are mere imitations of yours, dear Ruth.' And the curious thing was, that though it was true that Ruth was the one who was always talking, always, as she imagined, revealing herself, it sometimes seemed as though Robert was the honest, generous one, while she was the one who was holding herself back. Sometimes, even, she felt as if she were deceiving him. Hadn't she just now, after all? Her fake, bright voice as she handed Robert his sandwiches.

She cringed at the memory of it and jumped up to try to shove it off her, and thought she might wash her face in the sea. But while she was climbing over the rocks to get to the beach, the sun disorientated her. The rocks had moving red edges. The horizon wobbled. She slipped and cut her knees.

'Bloody rocks,' she said.

But she got herself to the beach and washed her knees in the water. She looked at the blood mixing with the sea. Robert would have enjoyed seeing that. Robert would have thought that terribly poetic, no doubt. Perhaps I should mention it to him. Perhaps we could talk about that, my blood and the sea. I can't think of anything else to interest him.

'Oh Robert, where do you go for your private celebration of nature? For God's sake, how can one feel jealous of a place? Dear Deirdre, my fiancé would love me more if I were a cliff of columnar basalt. What can I do? It is one thing to want to be alone, but Robert isn't wanting that at all, he's wanting to be *with*, and he's out there now being *with*, without me. But I can't accuse him, I can't say, look, you ought to be different, because surely there's a way in which he's right in the way he is, more right than I shall ever be, and I envy him for it. It's as though he's taught himself to feel fluently, without self-consciousness, without thought popping up every thirty seconds to suggest alternatives. I envy him for it.'

The afternoon was better. She washed the clothes and hung them outside to dry. The sandwich was delicious. She decided to go for a walk.

Of course, she hadn't been expecting to find him. It was one of the few occasions when she hadn't been half-looking for him, half-hoping to be able to shout 'Robert' and run over to join him. She'd been walking an hour when she saw his head.

A hundred yards away, Christ, was his head, as though it were growing out of the earth. For fifty yards she decided that a rabid sheep had decapitated him and gone off with his body. But then she saw that the head was quite happy, that a pile of clothes lay beside it, and that Robert had buried himself in the ground. She came up to him and she laughed. It was a laugh of relief more than anything else, God knows why we laugh.

But the laugh must have sounded nervous, there was something askew with it, even Ruth heard it and blushed at the noise of it. Perhaps if the laugh had been at a different pitch, was lighter, was less light, had an ease about it which was lacking, it would've all been fine. It might even have been funny. But the laugh that happened irritated Robert to the core.

It as the hottest afternoon of that year. Ruth realised she was sweating and began to undo the buttons of her shirt. 'For God's sake, don't join me,' said Robert.

'I wasn't going to,' said Ruth.

Neither spoke.

'Anything I can do for you?' said Robert, and he began burrowing himself out. 'What is it, something need mending, wood needs chopping?'

'Please don't let me interrupt you,' said Ruth, 'don't get out for me. I must get going. I'm sorry.'

She left him there and walked back. Crying didn't seem such an effort now.

The week that followed was bad. They didn't go out in the boat. Robert went off by himself more than ever; Ruth hung around the croft; the fresh supplies ran out; they were back on porridge and tinned ham.

Then, one evening, the candles were lit, they were drinking soup, and Robert said, 'It was peat, you know'.

'Pete?'

'An amazing thing peat, Ruth. Have you seen it up there? Galileo would have sold his soul for a pot of peat. You can take it in your hand, you can hold it like this, I'll take you there tomorrow, you must feel it, Ruth, to know what I mean. A paradox is a quirk of logic, a game in abstraction – didn't you notice how black it was when you saw me there? Didn't you see it? Black, dense, rich stuff – but you know what it is? It's decay, decay as the end in itself, not as an accident but as a perfection. The trouble is, Ruth, that beauty is something you cannot hold, it always shifts, I hate it shifting, but the stuff up there between the rocks, you can dig yourself down into it, it's the point where a mere word and actuality meet, you can say it, Ruth, you can say it while you're touching

it, you can say, "This stuff here is decay, this is what it is."
It's like harnessing a beam of light midway on its journey
between sun and mirror – for the beam of light is both
a process and yet remains itself, you see you have it all,
you win on all fronts, the perfect integrity.

'But tell me Ruth, you're a Catholic, or you know
about these things, wouldn't this be the sort of thing
your God would do? Wouldn't He say, "Peat, you who
know no deception, you who have never tried to be more
than you are, who have never decked yourself in precious
stones, I have chosen you to be the source of all life, and I
decree that all those who scorn you, because you are not
of pretty colours, will not be fed by you, and when they
die their bodies will sink into the earth, into well-drained
earth, so that they become nothing." There Ruth, what
do you think? Have you noticed something like that in
the Old Testament?'

'I do not think,' said Ruth, slowly, shyly, 'that I have
ever met a more religious man than you,' and unable to
think of anything else to say, she lit more candles, and
began to clear away the plates.

The shepherds visited them again in the summer, and
were surprised to find them happier than ever, and
more friendly and open with them than before. On
this occasion, when the sheep were less demanding of
attention, there was time to show them round, point out
the various ruins and suggest where the families might
have ploughed their fields. They told them what the
houses would have looked like, how they wouldn't have
had windows, and that the floors would have been made
of mud.

'But why did they all leave?' asked Ruth.

'You wait till you try a winter, and then you'll know all about it.'

'Did they have enough to eat?'

'Usually they did, because they would always have had the sheep.'

'Where did they all go to, then? Winters on the mainland would have been just as bad, wouldn't they?'

'They were poorer here than on the mainland. There might've been eleven in the one room, in a room which wouldn't have been fit for a cow on the mainland. And they wouldn't have used candles, to save money, so fancy that, if you will, eleven bodies stuck up in these blackhouses, that's what they were called, blackhouses, and there's no wonder they were. They'd be there, perhaps four months of the year, late November to late March, and all they could do in the darkness would be to eat, sleep and wait for spring. You cannae blame them, can you, for anything else they did. Rules won't work in conditions like that, do you not think?'

'I don't think', said Robert, 'that it sounds a bad life at all; I quite like the idea of being buried for the winter with my wife and children, all secret like that, nothing public, feeling in the dark. And I imagine that they wouldn't be bothered as we are, with night and day and going to bed and getting up: there wouldn't have been the space for it. They would have slept when they fell asleep, and woken up to the wind and the consciousness of a warm body next to them; and that body they would have needed for fuel, not for company, not for chat, not amusement, all those demands that we have of each other now: they would have needed each other like they needed food, the warmth of other bodies would have been a necessity, not a luxury, not a bonus, but part of the way they lived. I don't think I should have minded that at all. And where did they go to, did you say?'

'Australia. They thought they'd be better off in Australia.'

'Well, I wonder whether they were,' said Robert.

The autumn consisted of waiting for winter. When the winds began, when the nights became darker, it was all with a view to the winter beginning in earnest. But anticipation adds to the present, and perhaps it is true that more harmony existed between them during those two months than at any previous time. In September Robert found Ruth's pastels in a plastic bag at the back of the store cupboard; 'no paper' Robert described as being irrelevant, the tertiary mudstone directly in front of the croft was made for drawing in pastels – hadn't she said she used to draw on pavements? So Ruth flourished, at home at last, drawing the landscapes of dark skies and the sea, lit up by a light that seemed to come from nowhere, and yet was always present. Robert used to watch her, and the pleasure he got from watching her was equalled only by his pleasure in watching the drawings being washed off by the rain, the colours streaming down the sides of the rock, pausing momentarily in florid puddles beside it before draining down into the earth.

But by the beginning of December the pastels were finished and so was the light. It was also the end of the fresh supplies: the shepherds came in the middle of November with three more sacks of potatoes, and tins and tins of beans and soup and ham, and said, 'Good luck, we'll be thinking of you – you've got the flares, haven't you, in case there's an accident – but I'm afraid you're going to be stuck out here for a while, we can't guarantee we'll be back before February, or maybe the beginning of March; but you've got loads of food here, enough to last you ages. And look, my wife's put in a tin of turkey spam for Christmas, and a pudding, so you'll be all right.'

When Ruth wore away the last colours of the last pastels against the rock, she was aware of being about to enter what seemed to her a final phase. She put the empty box away in the cupboard and stoked up the fire. The three hours of light were over for the day; four or five hours of an indeterminate grey were to follow. Robert was collecting driftwood from the beach. She lit some candles and began peeling potatoes. She peeled them slowly: from now on her days would be measured by actions such as these; she felt herself learning to be satisfied by them.

Then Robert came in and warmed his hands on the fire. 'Why is it', he said to her, 'that today is the first day of winter, today of all days?'

They decided that winter deserved to be treated some-how, more reverently than the other seasons: this was the fast after the feast. They hadn't been out in the boat for more than a month, but it was only now that they brought it well up on to the beach, turning it over and fastening it securely to rocks, and covering it up with a tarpaulin weighed down by heavy stones. They decided, also, to sleep in the room with the fire, and to try, as far as possible, to keep the fire constantly burning. It was also pointless to pretend there was a day and a night: they should behave entirely according to their moods and eat and sleep whenever they felt like it. In this way, suggested Robert, they might be totally awake for midnight, when no sky could be blacker on the earth than theirs; or they could take a walk out in the grey, have a picnic in the grey and watch the light come up; and the light itself was so precious that they should never miss a moment of it, and, once any necessary work was done, such as the washing of the clothes or the collecting and chopping up of driftwood, they should spend their time in the positive consumption of what was remaining, and let no flush, no glow, no shaft of light escape them.

So they moved all the blankets from the bunks and took them into the room with the fire, and perhaps sixteen or seventeen hours of every day were spent huddled up under them, and when they heard the rain clattering down on the corrugated iron roof above them, they lay together as closely as was physically possible, and Robert was as rapt as if he had been listening to a symphony, and Ruth rejoiced, because the weather couldn't touch them. At last, they were fellow-conspirators against it.

One day they argued about the date. They argued about whether it was 22 or 23 December; but even in the middle of their argument about it they realised that the date had simply been lost, for even if one of them had been right, they had no way of proving it one way or the other.

'We won't know when to eat our turkey spam,' said Ruth.

On what might have been Christmas Eve Robert woke up in the night. 'Ruth,' he whispered in her ear, 'shall we go for a walk?' So Ruth, sleepy as she was, stoked up the fire, boiled some water, and made a thermos of tea. And they walked, each of them with two blankets around their shoulders. The night was uncannily still; the moon was almost full: the light from it was more beautiful than either had ever known it; the air was so clear that they saw a hundred galaxies, and they sat on the beach and watched the water and drank their tea.

'Here's your absolute for you,' said Ruth, 'here's beauty you can hold.'

'Please, Ruth, I'm trying to hear the sea, I want to know the noise of a calm sea.'

'There is no noise. Tonight, I'm afraid, your pleasure will be exclusively visual.'

'There's no such thing as pleasure which is exclusively visual. Be quiet, Ruth.'

Ruth was quiet for a while. For a minute or so she pricked her ears, and then she said, 'I can hear you breathing.'

But Robert said nothing, and Ruth held the blankets tighter around her.

'I suppose you think,' said Ruth, 'that human beings have a psychological susceptibility to beauty and there's an end to it.'

'Shh, Ruth, did you hear something then, something deep? Was it the sea or the wind? Listen, Ruth, listen.'

But Ruth didn't have the patience to listen that night. She was still tired, and she'd scalded her hand when pouring the boiling water into the thermos. She thought, 'Why don't you listen to *me* for a change?'.

'Why don't you listen to *me*?' she said.

'Don't I listen to you? I'm sorry. It's true, and I'm sorry. What did you want to say?'

'I once told you that I could persuade you that the spirit . . .' But suddenly Ruth wasn't in the mood to tell Robert about the spirit and she stopped. Then she said, 'Robert, look at me, why do you never look at me when I talk to you?'

'It's dark, Ruth, I wouldn't see much of you.'

'But you never look at me.'

'Look at the sky, Ruth, have you ever seen so many constellations of stars?'

'I've looked at the sky. And I know, it's very beautiful. For God's sake Robert, I know it's beautiful.'

'And does it matter to you, that the dawn will come?'

'I hate the dawn.'

And then Robert did look at Ruth. 'You hate the dawn?'

'No, of course I don't, but I hate you when you're so removed like this. Sometimes I think you'd love me more if I was a piece of Jurassic mudstone.'

'I don't know what's got into you tonight,' said Robert, 'you're not yourself at all.'

'No,' said Ruth, guiltily. And she thought, 'Well actually, this is me. If I'm not allowed to write or read, I may as well think. For God's sake, there's nothing wrong with *thinking*.'

And because she developed this sudden desire to think, the following week was a torture to her. She found herself out of rhythm with the place: suddenly the chores were chores, and the long, dark hours were long, dark and empty. She longed to read a book. Why had Robert insisted they take no books with them? What a waste to be stuck there for so many months, without so much as a bible. 'Or I could have taught myself Italian,' she thought, 'or Russian. Or we could have read poetry together – how can we be in a place as remote and beautiful as this, without a poetry book between us? What I would give now for Robbie Burns. And Plato, for God's sake, all those dialogues I've never read because I've never had the *time*, and here I have nothing but time. What the hell are we doing in this place?'

And this was what was brewing inside her one morning, while Robert was scrubbing out the porridge pan. 'Look at you,' said Robert, 'your limbs are all stiff, and your face

312

is so set, and these last few nights you've been fidgeting and sighing. What's the matter with you, Ruth?'

'The truth is I'm bored, I'm terribly bored, and I would give anything for a good book.'

'A good book?' said Robert, incredulous, as though the two words were utterly self-contradictory.

'Yes,' said Ruth, 'more than anything I'd like a good book.'

'What would this book be about?'

'I'm afraid I'm not fussy. I wouldn't mind what rubbish it was.'

'But I don't understand *why*, Ruth? Don't you like it here?'

'Sometimes I look at the hours, the interminable days we have here, and what am I doing with them? I feel guilty, lazy, ignorant. It's all right for you. The reason you're so pro-ignorance is because you're not.'

'I don't understand what you're getting at.'

'For God's sake, Robert, you bury yourself in peat, and it's quite an experience for you. But don't you understand why it's more of an experience for you than it would have been for me? It's because you knew exactly what the peat was made of. "Decay" you called it, poetically. And you know the names of all the flowers, and the breeding habits of all the birds, you know it all. The first afternoon we were here, and you told me that shags hadn't evolved for sixty million years – the fact, Robert, that very fact, plain, dry and learnable, moves us. And the truth is, I don't know as many of those facts as you, and I want to learn some, rather than be for ever questioning you, because I know how little you like the sound of my voice; it would have been a good idea if we'd brought a few books with us, don't you think?'

313

'How can you say I don't like the sound of your voice? I love the sound of it – it's gentle, even musical, you speak with a real rhythm.'

'Why do you pretend, sometimes, to be such an idiot? You listen, Robert, to the sounds I make, and not to the words I say. What has ever happened in your life to make you so suspicious of *words*, for Christ's sake? I can't bear it.'

'I'm not suspicious, Ruth, I'm sad for them. The dictionary is the most optimistic book ever written, a desperate attempt by men who fear . . . well I sympathise with them, I understand what they were trying to do. They needed objectivity, and went to all those lengths to provide it for us.'

'And wouldn't you say they had succeeded, just a little? Or to what do you owe your enviable education?'

'Ruth, if only you knew the extent to which words castrate our world, and give us an arrogance we don't deserve. They make edges where there are none, when everything is part of the whole. Words prevent fluency, by dividing up, by categorising – and don't you see what happens when you get categories? Bitter, sweet? Black, white? The choices they involve? Pretty, ugly? I've no time for any of that at all, the whole system we've inherited appals me. Imagine, Ruth, if I started saying to you, "No, you're not looking as pretty as you were yesterday", or worse, if I started judging you against other people, started isolating facets of your personality and comparing them with other women – not as bad-tempered as Sarah, a better painter than Miranda – for that's what language, by its very nature, makes us do, it makes us judge and criticise, compare and categorise: vicious, divisive activities. But Ruth, I shall never judge you, never; I shall go on loving you for ever for everything you are, in exactly the same way as I shall love Eilean Tighe for everything it is.'

'For one so dismissive of speech, you're quite an orator. But I'm learning fast how not to be convinced by you. I listen to you every day, showing off, reciting the names of the different kinds of rock, or flowers – why do you do it, if knowing them is so irrelevant? What sort of a hypocrite are you?'

'You're right Ruth, it's a childish thing, and an old habit of mine. But I hope I distinguish and name more in a mood of wonder than of ranking – it's this ranking I can't bear, Ruth, yes, no, yes, no, all this stuff about values, how I distrust it, the cause of as much damage as it's allegedly prevented, I've no time for it. But can't you see how the very breathing in and out of air is a more valuable "yes" than any recommendation of a way of behaving? We don't need noes to live. My dear Ruth, you come here and let me kiss you, let me show you how I love you.'

'How can you show me when you know nothing of love? We might lie on top of each other for the rest of our lives, but what sort of love is that? It's a hopeless, shallow love, it's a meaningless love.'

'It's the only love, Ruth, it's love with no edges, no conditions.'

'And what if I want edges and conditions? What if I'm fed up with being loved like . . . Well, how do you love me? You love me like you might love the sea, the edgeless sea. Well, I don't want that sort of love, I don't value it, I don't like being the rival to a lump of rock. Oh yes, Eilean Tighe will age better than I will, and it doesn't bother with language at all. It has remarkable integrity, don't you think? This stalwart place, that behaves entirely according to its nature. But tell me this, Robert, you've a hard choice here – a life without Eilean Tighe, or without me? Because you've never got sentimental over the word "human" have you?'

'Ruth, I love you.'

'No, you can't speak to me, you're compromising yourself even to speak to me.'

So they were silent.

And suddenly Robert said, 'Shh, Ruth, can you hear that wind? Listen to the sea, there's a gale coming up . . .'

'Shut up shut up shut up shut up, how does that sound? How's the rhythm? Shut up. I hate you, and I hate what you're doing to me.'

Then Ruth gathered up a bundle of blankets and went out into the weather. There were two sheep nuzzling up together in the shelter of the croft, and she shouted back towards the door, 'Those sheep know how to love better than you do.'

Then she clambered up to the top of the hill, with the blankets flying behind her. There were less than two hours of light that day, and she walked for both of them, perhaps as much as six miles. She watched the clouds moving fast across the sky; she watched them darken; she felt the first drops of cold rain on her face; and she thought, 'This is all for the good, everything is in sympathy with me, let it rain'.

But when the light was nearly gone for the day, and the rain began to fall more heavily, she hid herself between three rocks, and pulled the blankets over her, and knelt on the cold, soft, muddy ground. She was already cold, and tried to reorganise things; she tried putting three of the blankets underneath her, and held the others tightly around her; she could feel the force of the rain on her back, but not yet the wetness of it. 'A question of waiting?' she asked herself. 'Is it a question of waiting for it?'

Her knees and her shins and her feet were already wet, and she cursed herself for having allowed them to become so. Then she felt the deep cold of the earth beneath her, and a numbness came on her like a shadow, and her last thought, before she slept, was, 'Ironic, wouldn't it be, if my rivals saw me die'.

Robert had seen her with her blanket-cloak and he'd shouted, but she'd gone on ahead oblivious of him. Then by the time he'd got to the top of the hill, she was out of sight. But he went on calling for her: 'I love you,' he shouted out, 'Ruth, I love you,' but rain and sea drowned his voice – 'Do you love us?' they seemed to say, 'or do you love her? For we won't let her hear you, shout all you like.'

Then when the grey came, he lay down on the ground and sunk his hands deep into the cold mud, and let the rain wash over him. 'Dear God,' he shouted out into the racing sky, 'what more can I do? What more do you expect me to do?'

He had no torch with him, and while he wandered over the island he kept imagining that the dark shapes of rocks were moving; he would see one, perhaps fifty yards away, and run up to it, with the joy of a thirsty man finding water; and in the same way as joy turns to despair when the water is found to be no more than a projection of hope, so Robert despaired, when he found, again and again, that his dear Ruth was no more than a heap of stone.

He barely knew that he was cold; his body seemed to have lost all feeling. He was only aware of the yearning in him: he might be dead already, for all he knew. He was blind, and he was looking for a fire on a moor. But he found her. He touched her body crouched under blankets between the three rocks, and she moved. He felt it was he who had been brought back to life. 'Dear God,' he said.

They lay under the blankets together, and they shook. Neither saw the grey turn to black, neither was aware that the rain stopped, or that the moon was shining on them. Their bodies were numb, but their hearts and their tongues were warm, and it was as though tongues weren't made for speech at all, but as evidence for life.

They were there until the dawn of the following day, which might have been at eleven in the morning, and they both knew that if they did not move then they would die. It took all of the light to get them back to the croft: they had to jettison the wet blankets, and their very bodies seemed like extraneous items not entirely necessary for their journey. If anything, it was a rational rather than an emotional decision that got them back at all.

They changed their clothes only because they knew what was best for them; then they made a fire. They knelt by it and held their hands as close to it as they could without burning them. Slowly they felt sensation prickle back: the inanimate giving life to the animate.

For the next few days they felt too full to pay attention to anything but the particular. The stirring of the soup on the fire, the finding, washing and drying of the blankets, the collection of driftwood, the recognition of constellations: all was done with the enthusiasm and easy honesty of children.

And then, after a week, when the winds died down and the sun was up for a full afternoon, Ruth insisted that they launch the boat and go back to visit the pink cave. So they rowed deep into the middle of Eilean Tighe, and she said, 'Robert, I have a womb, too'.

THIRTEEN

'I'm afraid,' said Ruth, 'that this'll mean going back to Cambridge.'

'But we can't do that, we don't want to leave here, we could have the baby here, of course we could.'

'Of course we can't have the baby here. I'd die in childbirth.'

'Of course you wouldn't die in childbirth, what with your hips, it'll be a piece of cake.'

'Don't be ridiculous, Robert.'

'I'm not being ridiculous at all. Those shepherds would help, I'm sure they would, all that lambing they do, it can't be that different. Or if you'd prefer, I'll see how they do it in the spring – perhaps this would be the best thing of all – they'd know all about it, and they could teach me what to do; they could even get any equipment we needed from the mainland, they could even bring sutures over in case I have to give you a Caesarian, I know all about Caesarians, I know exactly where to cut. But with your hips I'm sure you won't need a Caesarian at all, and frankly even the idea of it is a bit on the pessimistic side. Just imagine, Ruth, the three of us on Eilean Tighe, imagine being born in this place, imagine the sort of soul you'd have if you were born here.'

'I'm afraid its soul would have left this earth long before we had a chance to find out.'

'It's all a question of rhythm, Ruth, go with the rhythm.'

'I'm thirty-seven, Robert, it's really dangerous to have a first baby at thirty-seven.'

'Of course it's not dangerous.'

'I'm even supposed to have an amniocentesis test, to check the baby's all right.'

'Have you been watching "Healthcheck" on TV or something?'

'What if I'm diabetic? What if I had high blood pressure or got eclampsia?'

'I can't decide whether you have too much imagination or too little.'

'I'm sorry, Robert, but I really want this baby, and I'm afraid we're going to have to go back.'

It was February. The days were rapidly becoming longer, and it was a question of waiting for the shepherds to come and pick them up. Ruth spent the time being sick and watching out for the fishing boat from in front of the croft. It had become almost as though her baby wouldn't properly exist until the hospital scan had shown it up on their screen, until her course of antenatal classes was well and truly under way.

Robert spent those last few days by himself: every daylight hour was spent walking or with his legs dangling over the edge of a basalt cliff looking out into the sea. That sea, he thought, at least I have that sea stored in my head, at least I know what it's like. So many people can't even know that, and the tragedy is that they bothered to be born at all.

When the shepherds came, on the first of March, the first thing restored to them was the date.

'So how have you been?' John asked. 'We've been putting bets on, over in Tarbert. There's not a soul over there who thinks you'll last another month here, even with the winter not being so bad this year – but I've told them, those Standings, they're different, they're stuck to the place, they'll last it out. So tell me, what are you doing? Are you coming back with us or what?'

So there was a feeling, as they got back on to the boat, two days later, that they had failed. Ruth, of course, spent the entire journey being sick over the side, and Robert felt rather envious of her having such a vivid means of expression. The Macleods, however, thought they were being entirely sensible to go back to England 'for the sake of the baby' and congratulated them, asked to be sent photographs, suggested that perhaps when the wee lad was older (there was an assumption that the baby would be a boy) the three should come back and spend a few months there again, 'you give the lad a love of Eilean Tighe, you can't go wrong with that', they said.

They barely spoke on the train as they went back to Cambridge. Ruth's guilt at being the cause of their return was easily outweighed by the joy of the knowledge of what was happening inside her: but she knew perfectly well that it would have been inappropriate to have in any way expressed it, so she kept it in her like a secret, in the way that a woman feigns boredom in her marriage to prevent her husband from suspecting an affair, while all the while she can barely think for the fire in her. After about four hours of mutual glumness Robert said to her: 'You would have stayed, I know, if you'd waited only two weeks, for the birds come back in March to breed.'

'Those birds frightened the life out of me,' said Ruth.

When they arrived back in 11 Selwyn Road, the house felt pitifully small, almost as though it were physically hemming them in. Ruth decided to move all her paints and canvases from what had once been a sitting-room into a shed at the end of the garden, to reveal the solitary piece of furniture: an ugly 1930s sideboard.

'I'll buy us a sofa,' said Ruth.

'It's damp,' said Robert.

'Only because it hasn't been lived in for a while, you'll see, it'll be fine in a couple of weeks.'

But even when there was a sofa in the house, and even when the smell of the damp had gone, Robert spent his time being away, away from Newnham, away from Trinity, away from libraries, away from the geology department, away from everything which reminded him of his former life in Cambridge: for not only had all these places failed him, he decided that the very reason that they *had* failed him was that they were not in fact places at all, they were no more than stage props, and in his case, at least, the props seemed to have sunk into the sand; and he began to suffer from what he described to Ruth as 'placelessness'. There was a term in physics for it, he said, all things tend towards it, so why shouldn't he?

'For how, Ruth, is one expected to understand a place when even the number of hours of light in a day becomes irrelevant, where the people seem to spend their entire life smoothing over the differences in the seasons, their houses all at constant temperatures, light-bulbs mimicking the day?'

'But a place,' said Ruth, 'consists in what is in the place, in the buildings, in the churches, in the pavements, in the shops, what is actually solidly there, not in the weather or the time of year.'

'So your idea of a place must necessarily change more than mine: for you seem to believe that what makes a place a place are the temporary features of it, and I believe in those which are constant.'

And this time it was Robert talking to Ruth, and Ruth resisting: 'I'm not in the mood for this, Robert,' she would say, and tell him news of the progress of the baby, to cheer him up; and when even this did not lift him from his gloom (he wouldn't even go to the hospital with her to see the scan), she would say to him, 'Why don't you go back there if you miss it so much?' And Robert used to say, 'I will, Ruth, when I have occasion to; I'm sure that I will.'

That occasion was sooner and sadder than Ruth could ever have have dreamt of.

It was one of the most beautiful days of spring, blossom everywhere, and Ruth was five months' pregnant. She'd been spending the morning painting a portrait of a seven-year-old boy in the small second bedroom of her house, which she used as a studio. She'd recently been painting quite a number of portraits: it was an easy way of making money, and what's more, she thought, she could go on doing it once the baby was born. And that morning she'd just resolved a practical problem about where the baby was going to sleep: of course, why hadn't she considered it before? The baby was going to share her studio with her, the baby would never be left alone in his private bedroom to play with his fingers for hours on end: his first memory would be of his mother painting. And she'd also resolved upon this: to paint angels over every wall, and the very idea of it filled her with love for the child who would one day witness them.

It was all going so well, that day. She'd made some sandwiches for herself and a thermos of tea, and she'd sat on the banks of the Cam in Grantchester Meadows. She'd found herself smiling in a motherly way at the undergraduates who punted past her, and they'd smiled back at her. It was just going so well. For the first time since her stay on Eilean Tighe she was aware of what was growing around her, and took pleasure in recognising the spring flowers; she found one that Robert had taught her the name of, and picked it to show him. Perhaps Robert would come back early this afternoon and they could go for a walk somewhere; dear, restless Robert, probably out on the fen, but she knew it would be all right, for she knew him well enough to know that he would love his son as much as she would – she had full confidence in that – and there'd be a time, how sure she was, when what those shepherds had suggested would come true: the three of them would spend a summer, or even every summer, up there on Eilean Tighe. But right then, right in the middle of a smile to a passing boat, came the first contraction.

It often crossed her mind why she didn't make more effort to get herself to a hospital. She even considered blaming the weather for it: it was a day which said, 'don't resist what you feel', and the truth was, that she didn't feel like going to a hospital. She wanted to understand what was happening in private, to be alone with her womb, and the hospital suddenly seemed alien. But more than that, she instinctively knew that there was nothing that the hospital could do for her. It was too late.

She walked back to her house and she went on smiling at the passers-by: such was her decoy, till privacy was hers. She passed a telephone box on her way and stopped momentarily beside it, but it was occupied and she went on. Outside her door she felt a further contraction. She checked that she was alone and allowed her face to crumple up. Then she went into her house and looked for something to drink.

There was a quarter of a bottle of sherry which had been there over a year. She drank it. She was light-headed now, feeling easier. Almost careless. She looked for more. Nothing. A momentary irritation. And then she remembered the Communion wine. So *here* was the occasion. How odd that *this* should be it.

There was a certain ceremony with which she selected the finest wine glass in her cupboard, out of about a dozen which she had picked up over the years from charity shops, and washed out the dust in it. She found a corkscrew in the drawer, and she said to herself, 'Well, Brother Anthony, wherever you are, would you approve if you could see me now?'

She went upstairs and placed the glass and the cork-screw on her bedside table; then she went to the cupboard and unfolded the same old jumper she'd worn as a schoolgirl, and the bottle slipped down into her hand. 'What a relief to get rid of these last vestiges of my past,' she thought.

The light of the day flooded in through the window, and it made the room seem squalid. She suddenly noticed tea-stains on the duvet cover, and the carpet round two edges of the bed, which was too narrow for a hoover to enter, had a layer of dust so thick on it Ruth wondered whether she might be able to pick it up as though it were a fine blanket. She propped up the pillows against the wall and immediately felt a further contraction, causing her to bend double with the pain of it. 'I must thoroughly clean out this room,' she thought.

Then there was another consideration: she had to drink the wine before the baby came out, for there would never be another occasion like this for drinking Communion wine; she mustn't waste it, heavens, it might be another twenty years before she had such an opportunity as this. So she opened the bottle up, and she began to drink it; it was heavy, sweet stuff, and it reminded her of the Chapel in her convent, the one refuge in that place, the one permanence.

'So,' she thought, 'what happens first? What part of you will come out of me first? What are the rules on occasions like these? Will there be a limb? Will there be a little foot, or perhaps your whole head, or just an eye – or perhaps there'll be nothing recognisable at all, perhaps you'll come out as a mass of blood and formless flesh?'

She settled back into the bed to wait, and she went on drinking the wine, and she asked herself, 'What sort of picture would I make hanging in a London gallery? Would I be impressive? Imagine them looking at me at a private viewing – Henry, come and have a look at this one, here's a good one, "Woman waiting for dead baby". No, better, "Woman waiting for dead baby drinking blood of dying man" – that would get them flocking to me, wouldn't it; "There's art for you," they'd say, if I were decently painted, if they caught my face just right, if it wasn't too sentimental, if the light showed up the flaws in my skin, no, we wouldn't want it like a Renoir;

it would have to be pretty raw to work, I mean, they'd have to get the tea-stains in or is that going too far the other way? Please, not too awful, it might just go over the top, you see, frankly, it might be a bit *tasteless* to have a filthy bedroom, laying it on a bit thick; it all depends on how much you show and how much you leave out: for remember, what you need is proportion, clarity and integrity. Fuck your proportion and your clarity, for what happens when they're at odds with the third – for how can a painting be beautiful if it is also a lie? For God's sake, paint me as I am, and leave nothing out.'

It was fitting that the wine was finished at the exact moment of the birth. I say 'birth' because not only was the baby whole, not only was the baby perfectly made, with a brow and heavy-lidded eyes and lashes that seemed not dead but merely dreaming, but the boy gave out one breath of life, and tried for more; so that when Ruth held it in her mother's hands it fluttered like a dying bird, and she felt it warm, and then grow cold. 'Or how about this?' she said to herself, 'a study of a mother cradling her dead foetus.'

This was how Robert found her an hour later, sitting in a pool of blood, and he wrapped both the mother and the baby in blankets, and he told them to stay where they were; then he ran out on to the Barton Road and hailed every car he saw, till at last a car stopped and he said to the driver of it, 'I'm sorry, my wife's just had a baby, we need to get the pair of them to the hospital', and the driver drove into Selwyn Road, and he said, 'that's a quiet baby you have there'. Then Ruth was being seen to in the ward, while Robert held on to the baby in the blanket, till at last a doctor came up to him and said, 'Let's dispose of that for you, shall we?'

But Robert didn't talk to that doctor. He said to Ruth, 'Ruth, don't worry about a thing, babies are always floating in and out of existence, you just happen to have caught him at the wrong time. Don't you worry about anything, I know what he would have wanted. I'm taking him up to Eilean Tighe to be buried.'

So Robert and the baby made their way up to Eilean Tighe, by train and by boat, the baby still wrapped in a blanket in his father's arms, and no passenger who saw them would have forgotten the sight of it. For a night they shared a bed in the Star Hotel, and the Macleods took them across in the morning. 'You pick me up in a few hours,' he said to them.

Then he carried the baby to the grassy uplands, and he said to it, 'You see, my love, this is the spring here, and if you can't see it for yourself, I should tell you, that of all the times to be buried, this is the finest of the year. You should see these flowers. You should see these marsh violets here, and the thrift and the purple orchids. And all the birds are laying their eggs; what a good time to be buried in.'

And then he took his son to the very peat in which he himself had once lain for a day, and unwrapped him. 'If anything will make you grow, this is the stuff,' he said. 'You don't know how good this is for growing. And do you know, you have the shape of something that *will* grow, like a broad bean, with that great head of yours and your knees tucked in like that. All is not lost here, you know, all things are put right in the end.'

He dug a small hole in the peat with his hands, and laid the baby inside it. Then he covered his tomb with a scattering of sweet vernal grass, and as he did so a sudden joy swept up through him like a wind.

'Birth, death, they're all the same,' he said, 'but a marriage such as this to Eilean Tighe, generations will envy you for it.'

FOURTEEN

It was the shared memory of that year which kept them together for the next five, though the accounts each of them gave me of it were so different as to make me wonder exactly how much of it *was* shared. Robert insisted that they had both loved Eilean Tighe, and that Ruth was mis-remembering if she suggested anything different. 'I can see her face now,' he said to me, 'painting the rocks with her pastels . . . and *what* did she tell you she felt?'

Even now I'm not entirely clear of the exact mechanism which kept them together. Perhaps it is simply the case that unquestioned mechanisms survive longer, and that Ruth was left, in the spring of 1983, without the energy to question anything, and with too much grief to criticise. She didn't even have the energy to question her own marriage in 1985. For Robert, meanwhile, Ruth (as the mother of his buried son) seems to have become the proxy of Eilean Tighe, a living version of the basalt. He never demanded anything more from her than her physical existence: from morning until night perhaps two hundred words passed between them. He would come back from a day on the fen, or a day teaching, and he would slip into her bed at nine or ten o'clock and hug her hard and tell her that he loved her.

In fact Robert's memories of his time with Ruth are exclusively good ones. Of course, he told me, things weren't too good when they originally returned to Cambridge. It had taken a little time to readjust. But in the end, yes, when he came back that second time, after he'd buried the baby, things were fine. When I asked him whether Ruth's depression ever got him down, he said, 'Was she depressed? No, surely you're mistaken. A little sad, occasionally, but not *depressed*.'

His colleagues, too, noticed the change in him: he seemed happy to be back at Trinity that October, and within a month was renowned once more for the vigour of his supervisions. The Master of the College was gratified to see that the sabbatical year had obviously been a restful one; people remarked about 'the air of certainty' about him, and the following year he re-began his popular series of introductory lectures to first-year undergraduates.

Robert even managed to feel comfortable in his old rooms. When he saw the colour chart hanging up in exactly the position that he'd left it, he smiled, almost patronisingly, at the follies of his youth, forgetting, perhaps, that such follies had been committed only eighteen months previously. It didn't even move him sufficiently to bother to take it down, though when he considered listening to the *Prague Symphony* he realised he had reached the limit of his new easiness, and he put the record back into its sleeve.

Every summer for those five years they went back to Eilean Tighe. In the summer of 1983, they built a cairn for the baby, on top of that same cliff of columnar basalt they had been to on their first day there. An interesting symmetry occurred on these expeditions: Ruth's soul drained as fast as Robert's filled, for Ruth remained sane by forgetting, and Robert by remembering. She never, however, objected to going with him: for the muscle in her, namely all that she had ever believed in, had been weakened, and it was Robert who became her solitary axis.

But I don't want to suggest that no progress was made during this time. For example, in the fifth year Ruth began painting other subjects besides portraits: bowls of fruit and flowers, gentle landscapes – there's a pretty one of the market square that she did at this time. But of course there was nothing in any way approaching the painting which still hung above the bed, of the boy on the lion, and which even then caused Robert to say to her, 'Ruth, there is something in you which is more special than I shall ever know', but the words fell dead on her, for the final flicker of her self-knowledge at least told her this: that there was nothing special in her at all.

Who knows what might have become of such a marriage if subsequent events had not intervened in the smooth running of it? For their roles, now clearly defined, left no room for anxious reappraisals or accusations. No friction, however, is no movement: a slippery pole is unscalable. And the marriage was cut short.

The first of these events happened on 14 January 1989. Robert was preparing a totally new course of lectures on earthquakes, something he hadn't done for years. Indeed it was a mark of how 'well' people thought he was that he'd been asked to prepare them at all. But the periodical he needed had gone missing from the geology department, so one afternoon he decided to go back to the University Library and see if he could get hold of it from the West Room. There was a rather large woman in front of him, who was taking an irritatingly long time filling in the required form at the periodicals desk; as far as Robert could hear she was insisting that a particular review was published monthly, and the librarian was saying, no, she knew for certain that the review in question was published quarterly, and the woman kept saying: 'For God's sake, I teach the bloody subject, I think I should know, don't you?' So then the librarian was silent, and shrugged her shoulders, as if to say, 'well, we'll get you what's available, that's the most we can do'.

Robert might have gone to the side of her, given the librarian a sympathetic look, and managed to gain her attention; but he suddenly became fascinated by this unhappy hulk in the shapeless brown overcoat and old-fashioned boots with fur, which elderly women use to keep out the cold. He was beginning to feel sympathetic when she snapped again: 'How long is this going to take? I haven't got all day, you know.' He watched the veins in the woman's hands moving while she wrote out, *New Forum Musical Review*, and a defiant, 'November '88', and then her name: 'Helen Wakehurst.'

He never saw her face. He forgot about the periodical he'd come for. He walked as fast as he could back to Trinity and he locked himself in a bathroom. 'A bathroom,' he thought, 'there's the subconscious working for you. I see Helen and I'm suddenly in a bathroom.' But he smiled. This wasn't his problem at all. He'd come into the bathroom to look at himself in the mirror, not to imagine Helen, past and present, having a bath. In fact, he spent most of the following week in front of it.

It gratified him that eyes didn't age, and he tried to imagine what his eyes were like when he wasn't looking at himself. He couldn't rid them, however, of their curious, analytical quality, even when he tried to catch himself unawares, by treating the mirror as though he were the wolf in a game of 'grandmother's footsteps'. The rest of him, he decided, seemed to have nothing to do with him at all. His hair, for example, didn't *feel* grey, which it was; he tried various expressions with his mouth, but again, he found it difficult to remember the one that he normally had on his face. He tried hundreds, ranging from what he thought was total relaxation, to the face he thought he had on the moment before he began a lecture, that expression in which he was often conscious that his eyebrows were slightly raised, but then, exactly how raised were they? So he tried raising his eyebrows to about five different levels, and tried to determine which height was objectively the most attractive. Too high was absurd, so he slipped them down a notch or two, but suddenly he seemed far too critical, or worse, positively short-sighted. And finally he decided to grow his hair and cover his eyebrows altogether.

He was quite pleased, in fact, with his wrinkles. They seemed to him a proof that his face had been making the correct expressions over a number of years, for there was not a trace of bitterness in them; they showed him to be both alert and receptive: the alertness won out as he looked at himself, but he imagined that in a normal situation his expression would be one of receptivity, and he was pleased that that was the case. But then he suddenly became anxious that receptivity was also passivity – did anybody ever notice him? he wondered. Had he inadvertently become so much a part of things that he was no longer a feature of them? The question obsessed him for a week, and the mirror took the place of the fen.

The twenty-second of January was the day of gratification. An undergraduate whom he supervised but had barely noticed (which was odd as she had a mass of red hair down her back, and painted red lips), took her clothes off right in the middle of a supervision on seismographs. How could he resist her? It was short and to the point, but it was very sexy. And when he got home that evening, he said, 'Ruth, do you know what happened to me this afternoon?' as if he wanted to share a secret with a good friend.

When Ruth had properly understood what Robert was saying to her, she watched his mouth for a while without hearing him, watched his eyes, watched his face; it all had the expression of a boy describing a conker fight. She wanted to cut it with a knife to try and rearrange the lines on it, to get the smugness out of it. 'And her body was beautiful, was it?' she said to him.

'Her body, Ruth, you should have seen it, my God, she had a good body on her, a waist as thin as that, and hips like so, and bosoms full but without an ounce of droop in them . . .'

'And her face?'

'Have I mentioned her hair to you?'

'Beautiful hair, was it?'

'So beautiful, red, you know.'

Ruth went into the kitchen and she got a knife from the drawer; Robert went on talking to her from the other room: 'Are you making tea?' he said to her.

She put the knife in her pocket and she said, 'Yes, I'll make tea and we'll go upstairs'.

335

'Let me help you,' said Robert, and he came into the kitchen.

'Thank you,' said Ruth.

Robert carried the tea up and he put it on the bedside table. 'I didn't realise,' he said, 'how much this place could do with a bit of paint.'

'Yes,' said Ruth.

What was impressive was the care with which she did it. She took the knife and she slashed the painting above the bed; she cut through the boy and the lion first: she stabbed at the boy's face until no feature was left in it, and then she took broad sweeps across the hills and the sky, and while she did it she said, 'I loathe all beautiful things, I loathe and distrust anything you consider beautiful, and it's you, it's you, Robert, who have taught me how to loathe it, who have provided me with my education. And I think it's a good example of how complete it's been, the fact that I can destroy this and feel nothing at all.'

But Robert was calm. 'My dearest Ruth,' he said, 'it's a canvas with paint on it, but don't we still have what made it more than that? See, how you have educated *me*; you're destroying a bridge, but haven't we already got to the other side? You created a balustrade, Ruth, on to which others might hold while they find the place you have already been to, and I pray to God that I managed to follow you there. Did I follow you? You are the only person living who has the power to tell me, have I failed?'

'Where is this place to which you so poetically allude? I can't remember going there.'

'You live there, Ruth.'

'For Christ's sake, Robert, do you know the woman you're married to?'

'I know her and I love her.'

'If you knew her and you loved her, where is there room for your fucking, beautiful redhead, with a waist like so?'

'How can you blame me for the girl's proportions? Can you say to me: because it is in the nature of an orange to grow mouldy, that I should never enjoy a fresh one? That's all it meant to me: if there had been more to it, would I have been so happy to tell you about it? Have I deceived you in any way? Ruth, the girl hadn't lived, there was no *substance* in her.'

'Robert, I hate you. Go off and see to your fen. Go and check out the winter flowers. And take your redhead with you. Educate her. For imagine this, if you managed to introduce internal beauty to the external, what a feat that would be: doesn't that capture your imagination? You just get out of here, Robert, and see to it.'

'I'm not leaving you, never think that,' and Robert came up to her and kissed her, but Ruth pushed him away.

'Do you know the one thing which makes me wish for eternal life? The one thing? I'd like to see women like that redhead and others I can think of, I'd like to see them wrinkle up. I want to see them arthritic. I want to see them with no teeth. I want to see their sagging bodies. How often it occurs to me, and how true it is, that if you value your physical beauty above all things, the pain of watching yourself lose it must be akin to an artist watching his paintings burn: but as I never had it, I think, I won't have *that* pain, I shall only know the joy of everything becoming equal in old age . . .'

'Ruth, listen to me. I met an old girlfriend of mine in the Library the other day – don't look like that, she'll be sixty by now, and if ever there was equality in age you found it there. No, she wasn't like you, Ruth, she wasn't good

---

337

like you. In fact, I've never seen such a bad-tempered old cow. She was neither gentle nor earnest – do you mind if I call you earnest? – think of this, Ruth, the most beautiful undergraduate in 1952, is, in 1989, a bad-tempered old cow. Does that satisfy you?'

'I am nothing,' said Ruth, 'I don't even have enough spirit in me to be bad-tempered.'

Then Ruth began to cry, and she said things like how she hated herself, and how her life wasn't worth living, and how she'd often wished she were dead, and how she was only a shell of a human being, for she was sterile, and what was the point in living if you could neither paint nor write nor have children, for when you were dead it would be as though you had never lived, and after perhaps a generation or two, would there be one person left who would even remember your name?

Then Robert told her that that wasn't the way she should look at things at all: if old age was an equaliser in terms of physical beauty, there was one greater equaliser in all things, namely time: for even those with children, who had children to go and visit them in their graves, even they would be forgotten within a thousand years. So in the end, said Robert, it's nothing but vanity to make sure one's children and grandchildren are provided for, or to have one's art exhibited, or to write novels which are published. In the end, the only thing which we shall be sure of is this: 'humanity is like itself'; it is mere vanity to believe oneself a feature of it. We are as much a feature of it as a chance spike in a bowl of cream while it is being stirred, only to disappear again on the next revolution of the spoon. We are all nothing but parts of the same, and the only thing that can make that clear is time, and to fight against it is vanity, in all senses of the word.

Ruth said, 'I can't hear you, I can only see your mouth move'. Then she said, 'I'm going for a walk', and she went out.

He shouted her name, but he didn't follow her, because he wanted to look at the face of the young St Mark. 'Ruth, what have you done?' he whispered 'Did you do it for me?'

Then he stood on the bed so that his eyes were level with what used to be the eyes of the young St Mark, and he put his hands through the slashes of his face, half hoping that there might be something behind it, but his fingers met with the cold wall. 'You can destroy the window, but you cannot destroy the light,' he called out, and he sunk his fingers into the bright parts of the sky, but all he felt was the cold wall. 'Dear God, I can't see the light, restore the light to me,' and he lay down on the bed and sobbed.

But when he thought of his son, and of Ruth, and of Eilean Tighe, the three inextricably woven in his mind, he was soothed, and happily remembered that they were all still with him, and where's Ruth, he thought, Ruth has just gone out for a walk, but she'll be back, and then I can tell her how much I love her. And then he thought of the time when Ruth had laughed at him buried in the peat; he remembered it with surprise, as though there could ever have been a time when Ruth was sufficiently separate from him to laugh as she did, or for him not to say to her, 'Join me here, Ruth, take your clothes off and join me in the peat'.

'We'll do that in the summer', he thought.

But as the minutes went relentlessly on, he began to get anxious. He picked up the knife and pushed back the cuticles of his fingernails, and in a clumsy gesture knocked off a cup of tea from the bedside table and watched the liquid rest momentarily on the dust of the carpet before sinking into it.

It was the first time, it occurred to him, that he'd had this thought: 'Ruth is not here and I wish she was.' It was strange to have her gone; it was as though she'd flown out of orbit. He tried to remember whether she said she was going for ever or just going for a walk. He tried to remember whether he was expecting her back. Every ten minutes or so he went out of the front door to check if he could see her coming. It was already past six in the evening, and the night was dark and cold, no moon in sight, not walking weather at all. Perhaps he'd go to the end of the road and give her a shout. But when he got to the end of the road and shouted, it was as though the cold had set out to muffle it, and he might have been shouting in a solitary house a hundred miles away, for all the confidence he had that Ruth could hear him.

Occasionally he was sure: 'She said "walk", I know she said, "walk" '; and then he'd go into the kitchen, put the water on to boil and warm up the teapot; and he'd practise saying, 'Look, Ruth, I'm sorry, I didn't mean to upset you, it was an accident, a moment of vanity; I'm really not like that at all.'

During other moments of confidence he began cleaning up the kitchen and the sitting-room, wiping down the shelves of the cupboards, or scraping out the years-old grease from the gas oven with a broad-bladed knife; 'this'll please her', he said to himself; but whenever he completed a project he would sit down in renewed despair, or else go out again into the cold to look for her, shout out some more. Then he'd go back to the house and he'd shiver a while; then he'd say to himself, 'But there's nowhere else she can go to, she doesn't *know* anyone else, or no one that she could trust with this', and he decided to make up a fire, for he thought, 'she'll be cold when she gets back'.

He made himself a cup of tea and he sat by the fire. It was half past seven. Then he thought if he poured out the other cup he'd somehow inspire the Fates to return her to him. So he poured out the other cup, and promptly looked outside the door again and thought he saw her, but he didn't. So he decided he would change the sheets on the bed. He looked in the linen cupboard and there were about eight crumpled-up sheets. He took them all out and spread them flat on the bed to see if he could find a clean one: they all looked about the same, they were either all clean or all dirty, he wasn't sure which. He was trying to judge whether a particular stain was a new stain or a washed stain when Ruth came into the room with her cup of tea.

'I'm freezing,' she said.

'I'm warm,' said Robert, 'you come here.'

She was shivering and he hugged her, and with the thaw came new tears, and she said, 'I'm a ridiculous woman, I hate myself, I hate myself for being jealous. You're an amazing man, Robert, I know you are, and I can't think how you can go on loving me, and I'm so sorry, I'm so really, really sorry.'

'Do you know what I'd like to do to you, Ruth?' said Robert, 'I'd like to wrap you up completely close to me, so that there's not even a square gap of air between us, so that we're like one body. Would you like to be like one body, Ruth? Lie on me again, Ruth, lie on me on the bed.'

So Ruth lay on him, and she was still crying while she did so; again and again she told him how she loved him, and Robert took the corner of a sheet in his mouth and rolled over with her to the other side of the bed, wrapping themselves up in it. 'I love you, Ruth,' he said.

But after a moment this wasn't enough, and he wanted more. 'We shouldn't be able to move,' he said, 'we have to get tighter, and why, for heaven's sake, have we still got our clothes on? We've got to do this properly, Ruth, we need a strategy. We're going to have to start again.'

So they unravelled themselves, and Ruth stood shyly at the end of the bed, while Robert laid the sheets out, exactly so. She didn't try to help him: it would have been like helping someone to wrap up your own birthday present. For it has to be said that she understood the idea of it perfectly, and she wanted it to happen, she wanted to be held in place like that, with the idea and the feel of nakedness but not with the sight of it, and with the freedom of not being free, like that of a baby in the womb, that freedom of no decision in a safe place. So that when she watched Robert carefully preparing and folding the sheets on the bed, it was as though he were rigging a sailing boat for her, making preparations for the open sea.

'OK,' said Robert, 'take your clothes off, Ruth, the sheets are ready,' and he began to take off his own.

Ruth switched off the main light in the room and turned on the lamp on the bedside table. She noticed the mug on the carpet and felt the tea damp under her feet, and she filled up with love for him, as if she'd been suddenly let in on a secret mood of his, and that he was as fallible as she was.

Ruth took off her clothes and lay face down on the bed. Robert lay down on her back and kissed the nape of her neck.

———

'The good thing is', said Robert, 'that when we're wrapped up we can stay completely close without one of us exerting any weight on to the other. Now, Ruth, you're going to have to decide where you want your arms to be – at your side, around me, or behind you.'

'Around you, of course,' said Ruth.

Then Robert sat up and folded the top two sheets over their feet, 'I have it all worked out; now', he said proudly, 'we'll be one body, Ruth. Now, put your arms around me.' And he took the corners of the first two sheets in his mouth, and with his arms around Ruth, managed to pull the sheets around them.

Then Robert took the corner of the third sheet in his mouth, and already they were the shape of a baluster, so they rolled more easily now, and the fourth was easier still, because they got the rhythm of it, they got to know how to move their bodies so that the sheets came around them ever more tightly, and a sag in the one was made up for by a tautness in the next; so that, finally, if anyone had looked through the window of 11 Selwyn Road at about ten o'clock on the night of 22 January 1989, they would have met with a very strange sight indeed.

'Well,' said Robert, 'how are you enjoying it in here? Are you warmer now?'

'I am,' said Ruth.

'It's rather like being on Eilean Tighe, isn't it?'

'You could say that, I suppose,' said Ruth, and she kissed his ear, because their bodies were so tightly together that their heads had to be side to side, ear to ear, faces and bodies out of sight. She couldn't see the connection at all, but she knew it meant he loved her.

'You see, said Robert, 'I feel like I'm buried in your body. Can you feel where your body ends and mine begins?

343

Can you feel the edge of you? Can you detect the point where your stomach ends and mine begins? And if you can't, don't you then feel like a continuation of me?'

'It's true, I don't know where my body ends at all, or at least, I feel the parts of me that can still move, like fingers and toes. But as for the rest of me I'm only aware of being warm and held in, and I might as well be you as me – it's quite good that, in fact, it feels quite good.'

They were quiet for about twenty minutes. Then Ruth said, 'I'm sorry about slashing up the painting. But I might do another one. I really feel I could do another one.'

'I should love you to do that,' said Robert, and he kissed her ear, and pushed his hands into the flesh of her bottom.

'We should do this more often,' said Ruth. 'It'd make quite a good marital therapy, I should think.'

'I'm sure people are doing it all the time,' said Robert, 'those people next door might be doing it at this very moment.'

Ruth laughed and she bit his ear. 'I could stay like this all night,' she said.

'Perhaps we will.'

Then they were quiet again.

'My dear Ruth,' whispered Robert in her ear, but she was asleep. Robert didn't sleep: he was facing the light, but he didn't mind. He was thinking about being buried in the peat with Ruth in the summer. And then he had an idea that the fen might be just as good, and perhaps in the spring they should go up to Wicken Fen; when there was a full moon they could spend the night in the open air, and then they could bury themselves in at dawn. Well, perhaps it would be a bit cold at that time of the day. But they'd have each other. And then, can you imagine, they'd be buried in the peat, their two heads bobbing on the surface of it, and a very respectable family of National Trust members would come along and say, 'Gracious, darling, what are those people *doing*? James, Sarah, come this way . . . are they dead?' And then he'd shout out, 'No, we're just practising, be prepared for every catastrophe, that's what I say . . .' 'They're mad, they're mad, come away from them James and Sarah,' and he'd say, 'If the end of the world came now, who'd be madder? Or at least, we'd be the happier, for surely it's the sane and the happy who live according to how things are . . .'

This was what he was thinking of when Ruth woke up.

'Oh Robert,' she said, 'you'll never believe this. I need to go to the loo.'

'That's all right,' he said.

'No, but I need to go now, this minute, we're going to have to get out of this.'

'On no,' said Robert, 'you're not going to leave me for anything, anything at all. I love you.'

'I love you, too, Robert.'

There was a pause when neither of them said anything.

'I'm not joking Robert, I need to go to the loo.'

'Go to the loo? Surely that's something one does at dinner parties, go to the loo. What one says at Trinity Feasts is "Excuse me", and you get up, and you nod, and everyone knows exactly what you're going to do, and where, but you wouldn't even say the name of the room. I remember once, there was a guest with us, and I think it was "WC" he said, I can't remember, but people would have noticed him less if he'd said "Fuck".'

'Robert, I'm sorry, but we're going to have to unwrap ourselves.'

'Imagine, Ruth, we're in a Chinese torture chamber. We love each other but we haven't seen each other for a year, and they don't know we've even met before. They tie us up in bandages hoping to humiliate us. One of them says to us, "You stay here wrapped up three days, we come see you then. Not before." There's bound to be a bit of embarrassment the *first* time, perhaps you'd want to say, "Excuse me" – what do you think, Ruth?'

'I hate these jokes, they're stupid, let me out of here.'

'Why don't you relax? Surely I have greater reason to mind than you have, and I don't.'

'I can't talk to you without looking at your face. I want you to see how serious I am.'

'Ruth, I want you to know what we're talking about: ninety-five per cent water, a bit of salt, urea, that's what our protein decays into, and even that's been turned into some sort of pill for people to take who suffer from night sweats – you see there's nothing in the world that is disgusting, but thinking makes it so – and anyway, the truth of the matter is, I want to know what it feels like, I want to know what it's like to be warm and wet from something inside you, something manufactured in your gut, for though our skins might be touching, our guts can never touch, our spleens, our pancreases, our kidneys, our intestines: you see, we can put our arms around each other, but think how much more exciting it would be if our intestines were wound round each other? I mean, doesn't that make sex seem totally pathetic and trivial, just so *provincial*, don't you think?'

'Just let me go.'

'I can't' said Robert, 'I want it to happen too much.'

'I won't let it happen,' said Ruth. 'I have a will.'

'So do I,' said Robert.

Ten minutes went by.

'Aren't you hot?' said Ruth.

'No,' said Robert.

Another ten minutes.

'I'm not joking,' said Ruth.

'Joking about what?' said Robert.

'Please let me out,' she whispered.

'Relax,' he said.

Another ten minutes.

'I'm going to go to sleep now,' said Robert, 'I remember when I was a boy I used to have wet dreams occasionally, they were really nice, I remember, a sort of ecstasy in a way . . .'

'You're ridiculous,' said Ruth. 'You know I hate you for this.'

'But you don't understand,' said Robert.

'What is there to understand?'

'Imagine we're buried in this peat, because I've been thinking, that we should definitely start burying ourselves up together . . .'

'There's something wrong with you in the head, Robert.'

'What about in the summer on Eilean Tighe?'

'What, in the same peat that you dug yourself into on that day, the same peat you buried our baby in? What if we suddenly arrived at the baby when we were digging? I'm not like you, Robert, I don't have this obsession with earth and peat and rock, I have no interest in them at all, they're brown and dark and ugly.'

'I don't understand you. Why are you so keen, sometimes, to forget the poetry in you?'

'Now you bring the subject up, I loathe poetry, I loathe everything to do with it, and I loathe the grand gestures associated with it.'

'What grand gestures?'

And then the floodgates opened:

'Oh like leaving me in the hospital for you to complete your own grand gesture – you took the baby before I could even argue with you not to, you just took it, you hardly looked at me, you thought: "I can bury my son on Eilean Tighe." Eilean Fucking Tighe it should be called. I hate the place. I never want to go back there. Do you know what, it's *boring*? Well you go up there and it's springtime, I can imagine you as poetic as hell, and what was I doing meanwhile in the hospital? Well, let me tell you, I was filling up with milk, I was wanting a baby to feed, but *you* had him, you had him up there with you, and I was alone with the milk, you can't think what it was like, because, for all your imagination, Robert, you have never for a moment imagined what it is like to be someone else, and I despise you for it. And all these years, my God, how these things dawn on one all of a sudden . . . you see, Robert, you've got this air about you, you've got this air that you *know*, so that that when I suggest getting a stereo, you say, "Oh no, you wouldn't want a stereo", as though music would somehow be a danger to my moral welfare, as though listening to Mozart would prevent me from noticing the exact tenor of the wind – well it's all a load of *crap*, Robert, and it's suddenly too late, you've done it now with your poetic gestures, I couldn't care less any more whether you let me out or not, because it's all a matter of time, I feel I've been blind for five years – why did I ever trust you? For God's sake why did I? And what freedom there will be for me when you go, because you will go, you know, whether now, or in the morning, or even in three days so we can fulfil your little Chinese torture fantasy – Oh I'm sure you'll be able to justify it, you'll tell me, "love through suffering" – I don't know, nor do I care, but my God when you go, let me tell you what I'll do. I'm going to get a telephone. I'm going to buy a television and a compact disc player. I'm going to get myself a plastic jug kettle. I'm going to wallpaper the bedroom, buy new carpets, get rid of all this ugly furniture which came with the house. And do you know what? I'm going to go out and make some real friends, who'll say to me, "How are you this morning, Ruth? Are you feeling better?" Not, "what a beautiful day, I'm going for a walk". And the thing is, Robert, I always thought that you were right. God only knows I did. I always used to think, it's *me* who's the depressed one round here, everything's my fault, I'm so flat and boring, when you, the Poetical Robert, well how could you be wrong? For there's no doubt about it, you're good at the Big, at the Universal, but haven't you heard it said that goodness comes in minute particulars? For shall I tell you what I consider a perfect marriage to be like? I see these perfect marriages sometimes in cafés. The man and wife are in their seventies, and one says to the other, "have some more cake, dear", and the other says "thank you, I think I might" – you see, they have something that you don't even know the meaning of, courtesy. What an underrated virtue that is. I mean, I cook supper for you – my God, this was only last night, how could I have been so blind to the absurdity of it – you never said, "thank you for cooking for me", that would have been a very dull, husbandly thing to have said, wouldn't it have been; instead, what do you do, you start making these grand observations on mushrooms, but I listen to you, of course I do, and worse, I'm *persuaded* by you, but no more – you think of courtesy as a sort of dishonesty, don't you? But

I cannot live like that, you see, more than anything else I want to be loved in an ordinary way, and you wouldn't know how to provide ordinary love, you don't know the meaning of it – what friend of yours has ever come into this house? Because you'd think of it as some sort of a compromise, wouldn't you, to have *ordinary* friends, people that you might have to consider the rather banal feelings of, and be polite to; and the awful thing is, that you've infected me with your attitude, so that when the mothers of the children whom I paint say, "Ruth, you must come round and have some supper with us one evening", because they *like* me you know, they *like* me; I think to myself, "no, these people don't understand, they have nothing to do with me, they don't know what things are like here"; and sometimes they say, "you must bring your husband too"; and I think, "What the hell will Robert do if I take him to supper *there*?" So I say, "The thing is, that we don't really go out much", and they get the message and they don't ask again. Well, what would you do, Robert? They'd put some music on after supper, we're eating chocolates and drinking coffee, what would you *do*? Make a little speech about honesty and fraudulence, about living through mediums apart from ourselves and what is true, my God, I can hear it now, "Why do you pretend that this is what your souls are craving for?" or some other crap. For do you know what you make me long for of all things? Civilisation: what an excellent thing it is. When you leave me, I'm going to art galleries, I'm going to concerts, I'm going to go round Europe and paint all the great cathedrals, I'll get a publisher and make a book of it; I'll start going to church again, I'll stop thinking and I'll start believing; I'll go to this self-help group I've seen a poster for to help women get over losing their babies –

what a brilliant system it all is, and how I could ever think for a moment that I should trust *you*, even to the extent of forgiving you for what you did this afternoon to that girl, I must have been mad for letting myself forgive you for that, it must've been the cold getting to my head, for I shall never forgive you for anything. It's proved to be the worse day of my life when you knocked on my door that day, I only wish you'd left me alone, I was quite happy before, I was painting then, wasn't I? But now you've sucked me dry.'

Then the energy left her, and she was quiet. They were both sweating: their bodies and faces were wet. Cheek to cheek, their tears mixed silently.

For five minutes neither spoke. Then Ruth said, 'I understand why you're doing this. You thought, "What an interesting, curious, poetic predicament it would be to be peed on by my wife wrapped up in sheets. The final lack of privacy, the final honesty." Well, it's lost all interest for me, I'm suddenly not bothered at all, I'll do it for you if you like. Are you ready?'

She did it. There was a momentary flood of warmth, and then they lay, this cold, wet, sticky bundle on the bed. Then they began to roll, once again, to and fro across the mattress, and one by one removed the sheets from their bodies, each wetter and stickier than the one before it.

'You use the bath first,' said Ruth, 'while I pack for you.'

'I will,' said Robert.

It was two in the morning and the water was cold. Robert lay still in the bath and wondered whether if he lay there long enough the cold would reach his bones. The bathroom door was ajar; he heard drawers opening, a plastic suitcase being unzipped. He began to wash himself with the soap. Water is hard in Cambridge: he barely coaxed a bubble out of it, but ran the soap along his body in strips, as though he were mowing a lawn.

'The edge of this body,' he thought, 'is destined for ever to be an edge, and everything beyond it is necessarily alien to it. Until I die, at least. How I envy the dead, how I long to sink deep down into the earth, and join them. How reassuring to know that I shall soon have more in common with my ancestors than with any man living.'

He left Selwyn Road at two thirty in the morning, wearing a large coat, and carrying a bulky plastic suitcase and a small box of books. He kissed Ruth goodbye and was civil to her, as she was to him. She never let him back in that house again.

When Robert got back to his room in Trinity he switched on all the lights and lit the gas fire with a match. He found a safety pin on the mantelpiece next to the matchbox and instinctively pierced the thick skin on the index finger of his left hand. 'I am the blood,' he remembered, 'I think I change, but I don't.' And, then, looking for something else to hurt himself with, he took the *Prague Symphony* from its sleeve and played it; he put the volume up as loud as he could without distorting the sound of it, and remembering how to listen hard to every note, the tears came streaming down his face, and it was suddenly as though Sophia was in the room with him, and he was saying to her, 'Dear Sophia, I didn't mean to forget you at all, and is our daughter well? How's little Viola? Is she growing now?' And then there was a knock on the door, and he said, 'That'll be her'.

'For Christ's sake, do you know the fucking time?' said the undergraduate.

'I'm sorry,' said Robert, and he turned the music off.

Then he switched off the lights and sat down in the armchair, still in his coat, and tried to sleep. Then suddenly he was six and he was hugging his mother in the bed, and then he was arguing with her in the Whim; then he was flying with his father in the night, and it was as though the noise of the engine was right there in the room, and he was trying to hear what his father was telling him above the din of it. Then he felt a cold wind on his face, which was so real that he thought it was his father's ghost, and he started up from the chair, and said to himself, 'It's true, then, that you see your life pass before you first'.

It was typical of him that he attached no drama to his decision to die. Indeed, the very word 'decision' suggests that it happened at a particular moment, which it didn't. It seemed that having spent his life removing artificial edges, he'd even succeeded in removing that between life and death. 'What do you think?' he laughed, in retrospect, 'a two per cent increment of white to that colour of bristol blue glass?' I remember it. We were drinking brandy by the fire. He looked at me hard. 'Well, Olivia, you choose. Which is the naked hue to be? Life? Or death?'

But he didn't die. It was very odd what happened: some might think it an incongruity, others might consider it the inevitable progression of the kind of man he was. He couldn't sleep, so he thought he'd go for a walk instead. He let himself out of the gates of Trinity with his key, and made for Midsummer Common. It was cold, and he kept his coat tight around him. Everywhere the sodium lights let off an ugly glow, and the wind was blowing rubbish up the streets, but he knew where he was heading and was oblivious of it all.

The grass crunched underneath his feet as he crossed over the Common. He was humming passages of the

Stabat Mater to himself, and he was going to the river to die. He was quite happy, yes, you should know that he was quite happy. But just then he saw a bundle of blankets underneath some bushes and they reminded him of something; and he had to clear up what it was before he went on. He thought they were lovers and he had something important to tell them, he couldn't remember what it was but he thought that if he could only say hello, it'd all come back.

So he went over to the bushes, and he said, 'Excuse me'. And when there was no answer, he put his hand over the bundle and stroked it, and he said, 'Excuse me, I'm so sorry to wake you up'.

An old man sat up and looked at him blankly. 'I'm not moving on,' he said, 'I'm staying put.'

His hair and his beard were white and long, his eyes simultaneously anxious and defiant, like a child's.

'I'm sorry,' said Robert. 'You're not what I was expecting at all. Is there no one there with you?'

'No, there isn't,' said the old man, holding the blankets closer to him.

'And don't you wish there were?' asked Robert.

The old man shrugged his shoulders, and shivered.

'Aren't you cold?'

'I wasn't till you woke me.'

'What's your name?'

'Never you mind.'

'You're shivering.'

'It's a cold night,' said the old man.

'Here,' said Robert, 'have my coat, I won't be needing it, and it's a nice one.'

'I don't want charity,' said the man, 'I've never wanted charity.'

'Charity?' said Robert. 'There's never been a charitable thought in my head, I can promise you that.'

They were quiet for a while and then Robert said, 'Now, tell me, would you consider it a charitable act if I hugged you? What I mean is, I've just been sitting by a fire, and I'm perfectly warm, and though my cheeks are cold I could hug you, and it seems a waste, don't you think, not to use up the warmth I've got?'

'You're a strange man, Mister,' he said, and he went on shivering, more violently this time, and Robert sat down next to him, and put his arm round him, and said, 'This is ridiculous, you're freezing, see how cold your hands are, you've hardly suitable clothes on at all. You're having my coat, I swear you are; perhaps if you thought of me as a brother you wouldn't mind so much, your younger brother Robert.'

Robert took off his coat and wrapped it around the old man's shoulders, and then he said, 'Wait a minute, I haven't emptied out the pockets.'

There was a wallet, a key, and an address book.

'Here,' he said, 'you have the wallet, forty pounds, that'll come in handy, and look, here, have a look at this, a University Library card, you could use this, we don't look that different, same colour hair, just cut it a bit. I think you'd quite enjoy the Library. There's a good poetry section, I remember, North Wing something or other. Now, this key here, on a cold night like this you can use it to stay the night with me in Trinity, I've got a spare room, or at least I've got two rooms and you can always sleep in one of them, no problem. Of course, I know it's good out here, you've got the stars and all that, but if ever you want to come in for a cup of tea or a bite to eat, don't hesitate, will you? I'll tell you what, there's

355

a Feast coming up, and you could be my guest. In fact, if you *don't* cut your hair, you'll pass as some extremely distinguished academic, because I've often noticed this about dons in general, that their hair is quite a feature, and they'd like yours.'

Then Robert took the old man by the hands and said, 'You know, I want you to come. They need a breath of fresh air in Trinity. They could learn something from you – it's no ordinary man that could sleep out here night after night, hand in hand with the weather. In fact I shall introduce you as Sir . . . you never told me your name . . . because they like a Sir, and you would have been a Sir had things turned out a little differently, I can tell that about you, you're no ordinary man. So please, do me that privilege, promise me you'll come and see me, won't you? I'll be looking out for you.'

Then Robert, who now felt cold, kissed the man goodbye, and the old man hugged him and said, 'You're a good man, a rare one'. Then Robert took his address book, and started looking through it for a place to spend the rest of the night. He found our house at about five in the morning. He'd only met my husband once: it was on a walk a few months back in Waterbury Fen. I know that Robert impressed him; he's a publisher and suggested to Robert that he write a synopsis for a possible book on fenland flowers, but he never did. Our address was in his book, though, and that's how he found us. Or perhaps I should say 'me', because Rupert was at a book fair in America and I was sleeping alone. The lights were still on in the kitchen; there were children's toys all over the floor, half-eaten supper on the table. And when I felt him in my bed I knew, instinctively, that I could trust him. He put his arms around me like a child seeking comfort

– no, rather, I was the child, and he was the comforter. For there is something about hugging a man you do not know, when you have never heard his voice, when you do not know his values and his virtues, when you cannot even see his face, which makes it seem as though he is not a man you or I might know, in the sense of having a name and a history, but is rather the sum of all of them.

A Selected List of Fiction Available from Mandarin

☐ 7493 0780 3	**The Hanging Tree**	Allan Massie	£5.99
☐ 7493 1224 6	**How I Met My Wife**	Nicholas Coleridge	£5.99
☐ 7493 1064 2	**Of Love and Asthma**	Ferdinand Mount	£5.99
☐ 7493 1368 4	**Persistent Rumours**	Lee Langley	£4.99
☐ 7493 1068 5	**Goodness**	Tim Parks	£4.99
☐ 7493 1492 3	**Making the Angels Weep**	Helen Flint	£5.99
☐ 7493 1364 1	**High on the Hog**	Fraser Harrison	£4.99
☐ 7493 1394 3	**What's Eating Gilbert Grape**	Peter Hedges	£5.99
☐ 7493 1216 5	**The Fringe Orphan**	Rachel Morris	£4.99
☐ 7493 1510 5	**Evenings at Mongini's**	Rusell Lucas	£5.99
☐ 7493 1509 1	**Fair Sex**	Sarah Foot	£5.99